Jerusha's Tricks

Jerusha's Tricks

best wishes,
Pat.

Pat Mosel

authorHOUSE®

AuthorHouse™ UK Ltd.
1663 Liberty Drive
Bloomington, IN 47403 USA
www.authorhouse.co.uk
Phone: 0800.197.4150

Published by AuthorHouse 10/28/2013

ISBN: 978-1-4918-0086-7 (sc)
ISBN: 978-1-4918-0087-4 (e)

Copyright: Pat Mosel
Cover picture: Jessica Ruth Bailey

*This novel is dedicated to my beloved daughters who have **both** contributed so much to my happiness and well-being—and to my adopted country of Scotland. Although I 'come from' Africa, the book is set entirely in the Scottish Borders. All the characters are purely fictional and resemble no one I know, alive or dead.*

APRIL FOOLS' DAY 2010

Prologue

DIGGING THE HOLE

'. . . but you must. You know the rules,' said Jerusha. She lounged back on the *chaise longue*, sloping so that her feet lightly touched the floor. Voluptuous curves outlined her figure.

By contrast, Oswald sat on the edge of a chair, openly irritated. What she was asking them to do was absurd, meaningless and he was still put out by the breakfast thing . . . what he thought of as a silly little drama designed to amuse only Jerusha.

'Darling. You're still miffed about breakfast. Dear Ossie. Don't take it to heart. It was just a joke.' Jerusha played with her hair, bound with an elastic band on the top of her head and looking like the blades of a helicopter. Her round face habitually wore an expression of optimism. 'We can't *not* celebrate April Fools' Day. Where's your sense of fun, my precious?' She flicked her hair as if it would take off and fly. She wriggled around on the *chaise longue* to consolidate her position. She was wearing a purple tunic over a polo neck sweater, darker purple trousers and pink shoes.

Oswald was in his usual attire—a grey tracksuit. He would jog along the country roads at any time of day, obsessed with hanging on to his youth, which he felt was every minute passing by. He scraped back his hair over his bald patch in an effort to hide the years. 'James always takes so long getting dressed. You'd think he'd be down by now,' he said.

James had had breakfast in his red, silk dressing gown. They, all three inhabitants of a large country house in the Scottish Borders, Kirkfield House, had risen as usual, without alarm clocks. Jerusha had woken in her spacious bedroom filled with cushions, drapes and soft armchairs. She rolled out of the double bed in her ballooning nightgown, put on a pink, fluffy dressing gown and padded in slippers to the room next to her bedroom that was her workroom. She always did this to decide what she would sew each day and what she would wear each night. This room was a cave of shawls and prints, bolts of fabric, swatches and drapes, mirrors and chunky jewellery (her expensive jewellery was in the bank). She would walk slowly around and finger the fabric and garments.

Scattered around the room, which had one window overlooking the side garden, were three dressmaker's dummies, one bare, the others clothed. The one that stood by the window was dressed in the upper garment of a sari in apricot threaded with silver, soft fabric draped around its stiff shoulders. Jerusha always dressed for dinner and often the dress was ethnic. That day she couldn't decide between the sari and the red and gold Chinese tunic that was adorning the third dressmaker's dummy. She had to put a few finishing touches to the trousers to go with the tunic. These trousers were laid out on her worktop and her Bernina machine stood elegantly in one corner of the room. By the time she had finished making a reverent perusal of this hallowed space she had decided on the Chinese outfit for her evening wear. She would finish hemming the trousers while Oswald and James were in the garden. Meanwhile, she had promised them a cooked breakfast.

The kitchen was a large room. All the rooms at Kirkfield House were spacious, and the ceilings were high. It had been built of stone, centuries ago, and had turreted corners. One of these towers constituted the breakfast area of the kitchen but today she decided they would eat their morning meal in the dining room. She clattered away, singing loudly. "If I were a carpenter and you were a lady, would you marry me anyway . . . ?" The third time around she had married her favourite husband, Hamish Burnett, a gentleman of good breeding who had owned Kirkfield and several fields surrounding it. Just when Jerusha thought she had reached the pinnacle of happiness he died of cancer. He left the property to her. Friends, of whom she had many, suggested she move away from all the memories—the family portraits, the silver, the antique furniture, even the Aga on which she was now frying bacon and black pudding—but she refused to move. She couldn't put into words why she would not go. She clung to Kirkfield, never wanting to forget her husband. And she filled the gaps with James and Oswald. James was Hamish's half—brother.

Now he sauntered into the kitchen in his red and green, silk gown, a red sash tied around his slender waist. His sandy, curly hair was tousled. Oswald had woken him up as usual with a cup of tea at his bedside, their bed, and a whisper in his ear. 'Good morning'. Even now, talking to Jerusha in the kitchen, James was still half asleep. He slept so deeply. Yet Jerusha had an infectious way of stirring people into life and living.

'How are you this morning, my dear James?' She projected her voice like an actress. 'This fine April morning, the first day of a brand new month. Just look at the way the sunshine is streaming through the windows.' She didn't seem to expect any answers. 'Warm, bright sunshine.' She gestured towards the curved windows with an egg slice, her cloth apron clinging to the mound beneath her breasts.

James blinked. 'Did you get the cheque?' he asked in his melodic voice. Jerusha always said he had the voice of a poet. 'I left the rent on your desk last night.'

'Dear James. You are so responsible. There is no need, you know.' She dropped some halved tomatoes into the frying pan where they spat and turned brown.

'My brother's money won't last forever, Jerusha. Especially with the upkeep of this place.'

'I've done my sums. I can manage. Now, darling, let's not worry about money.' She seldom wanted to contemplate the subject. Some might say she didn't know how much money she had. 'I've got some bubbly we can open to celebrate. Be an angel and take it through to the dining room. I'll bring the food through. You and Oswald just take a pew. Oh, and here are the glasses.'

James took the bottle and glasses across the passage and through, into the dining room where Oswald was seated, looking hungry. He was re-aligning his place setting. 'It's a bit early for champagne, isn't it?' he asked.

'The boss says we're to celebrate.'

'Jerusha would celebrate the blossoming of a single daffodil if she could.'

'That's not such a bad thing.'

'Don't get me wrong. I love Jerusha as much as you do. No more than I love you, of course. It's just that she sometimes goes over the top. You know what I mean?'

Just then, the woman in question came through from the kitchen bearing a silver platter topped by a rounded silver cover. She held this high as a waiter would, a white linen napkin folded over her free arm, almost dancing into the room. Yet, try as she might to look professional, Jerusha couldn't act out of existence the motherly nature of her action. She was warm after the cooking, flushed with anticipation, with a slight smile on her lips. For a woman who had had no children, she could not help diverting her instincts and mothering James and Oswald. Even as the child in her was surfacing the mother was also present. She placed the platter, still covered, in the middle of the long, dark-wood table that was large enough to seat sixteen people. She had laid their places at one end. Now she stood behind her chair at the head of the table and, placing the napkin on the back of the chair, she reached out for the bottle of bubbly and popped the cork. 'To love and laughter,' she said as a toast.

'To levity,' said James, raising his glass.

'Come on Oswald. Your toast has got to being with an "l",' said Jerusha.

'Say, to luck, Oswald,' James chipped in.

'I'm hungry.' Oswald ignored the game.

'To life and living,' said Jerusha, sipping her champagne. 'To the best of surprises. Now take off the cover, Oswald.'

He did this eagerly, expecting bacon, eggs, potato cakes, black pudding but all he saw was a mud-caked, brown old boot, its laces curled around its sides.

There was a pause as each of the men registered the leather offering for the first time and Jerusha scanned their faces, not caring to hide a wicked grin. Then silence reigned for seconds until James picked up his knife and fork and pretended to saw away at the old leather boot. He began laughing, an open genuine kind of 'ha ha ha'. He was amused.

'April fools,' teased Jerusha and she too laughed, a high-pitched, trilling laugher which was reaching a crescendo when Oswald scraped back his chair and stood up.

'It's all very well for you. You've never been hungry. You've never known what it's like to long for seconds and there aren't any. You've never known what it's like to see your brother get a bigger helping than you, to see your whole family crying out in hunger, to envy people with plenty to eat.' He was pacing the floor. 'You think it's funny to serve up an old boot instead of breakfast. But it's not a joke. It's a manipulative trick. You, Jerusha, have a childish, misguided sense of humour. And you, James, should not encourage her.'

'You're taking this far too seriously, Ossie,' said James. He got up, went around the table and put a hand on Oswald's shoulder. 'Come. Sip some champagne. Breakfast will be here in no time.' He raised his brow and tilted his head in Jerusha's direction. She took the hint; slapped the napkin onto her forearm and theatrically lifted the offending dish. She was not put out by Oswald's outburst and merely thought, like James, that he was taking the joke too much to heart. More than that, she thought he was being melodramatic about his childhood poverty. He was a grown-man and those years of hardship were many years away. Jerusha wondered how Oswald would have survived her own childhood with her brother, Saul, playing tricks on her all the time. Saul would come up behind her and kick the backs of her knees so that her legs crumpled; he would mimic her when she was on the 'phone; he would flick her with elastic bands. He once cut her doll's hair and had strewn the hair over her bed sheet. Oh yes, Jerusha was used to malicious tricks, only she considered her tricks to be nice tricks, full of fun and laughter and signifying a heightened sense of humour. The boot trick had enlivened breakfast. James had laughed. What they didn't guess was that she, Jerusha, had a more complicated, more challenging trick in store for them. She smiled at the thought. Yet, as she was about to take up the china platter from the warming tray, she looked briefly behind her to see if someone were about to launch an attack on her knees. It would have been impossible that Saul was there because he was still in South Africa, as far as she knew. She dismissed the complications of Saul and carried the food to her current brood.

'Whose boot was it anyway?' asked Oswald who had taken a huge helping and whose mouth was full of food. It was a conciliatory question. While she had been in the kitchen, Oswald had been sitting swigging champagne, which seemed to comfort him.

'It belongs to my dear departed Hamish.'

'Oh, husband number three,' said Oswald, showing that he had not fully recovered his humour.

'Oswald, you are well aware that I make no secret of having had three husbands. To each, I gave what I could and from each, I learned a great deal. In my marriage to Hamish I reached the pinnacle of my achievements as a wife. I lived up to my name, Jerusha, which means 'the perfect wife'. Not forgetting that he was James' half-brother.' She turned to James. 'He was a wonderful man, your brother. Yet, God saw fit to take him away from us.'

'He's been dead for five years and you still haven't cleaned the mud off his boots,' said Oswald.

'He was the one who collected the mud. There are all sorts of reminders of him in this house.'

'Then, how come you're thinking of selling some fields?'

'Overheads are high. In order to maintain the house in accordance with his memory, I need an injection of capital.' Her suppressed worry about money surfaced, although she would not have admitted her confusion on this subject.

'You see what I mean. Wasn't I saying you can't afford to be generous with the rent,' said James.

'Why don't you go out to work, Jerusha? You could do some more teaching. That was how you started off, wasn't it?' asked Oswald.

'Now, we *are* getting serious. I fancy doing some acting.'

'You're good at that,' said James in a neutral way. 'I'm certain you should accept my rent.'

She ignored this. Her generosity towards dear James and Oswald wouldn't be hampered by accounts. 'Oswald, help yourself to seconds. There is plenty . . . film, I think . . . it's entirely possible that someone would need a forty plus, charming, dynamic woman for their script. I mean, look at the actors who get into TV. If they can do it, so can I.'

'You'd need to get some training and find an agent,' said James.

Oswald was too busy concentrating on eating to pursue a conversation about an acting career they all knew that Jerusha would never take up. When he had polished off the last of the breakfast, his thoughts turned logically to the washing up. 'When is the S.S. coming?' he asked. The S.S. was Sarah Sharp, a young tyrant who cleaned the house on a weekday basis, wearing a pink overall and a hairnet. She would arrive in her ancient, green Morris Minor and the two men would peer out of the downstairs sitting room window, whispering, 'the S.S. is coming', with sibilance and warning looks. There was some respite because Sarah would always start with the kitchen. Thereafter, they would dodge her vacuum cleaner from room to room until finally it was safe to say that the sitting room had been perfected. Jerusha, on the other hand, was not daunted by the military-bearing and obsessive cleanliness of Sarah. She would chat to her about her family and pets, and her grandmother who was very frail at the age of ninety plus years. Jerusha, by charm and persistence, had got behind the façade of their young home help. 'I've given her the day off,' said Jerusha. 'Her granny is in hospital.'

'Well, that's a relief,' said Oswald.

'I'll do the washing-up. It won't take a tick,' said Jerusha. 'But first, let's take the rest of the champers and have it in the sitting room.'

James went upstairs to get dressed. He went to the bedroom window that looked out over the vegetable garden at the side of the house, looking to the outdoors to solve the puzzle of what to wear. He never went by what

Jerusha and Ossie were wearing because, unlike them, he was a cold-blooded creature who easily caught a chill. Today, he chose unfashionable green corduroys, checked shirt and a brown sweater.

Downstairs, Jerusha was trying to win over Oswald. She needed him compliant if she were to carry out her plan. She filled up his glass to the brim with champagne and poured only a little into her own glass. He seemed not to notice.

'You're looking very fit nowadays, my young man.' Jerusha tried flattery as she settled into the *chaise longue*, holding up her long-stemmed glass as if to toast his health. She knew that Oswald struggled with two aspects of himself—the health-conscious person and the decadent boozer. She also realized that he wasn't young any more. He had celebrated his fiftieth birthday the year before. They'd had an eventful weekend in Paris to mark the occasion. Jerusha didn't have the self-effacing quality that would make her feel she was playing gooseberry. Generally, she was very much at ease with Oswald's and James' relationship. Jerusha loved the idea of love. She had had more than three intense relationships in her life so far and she was anticipating that another would come along eventually. In the meantime, while she was still mourning Hamish, these two men filled a gap. They were her friends, a reminder of partnership and a buffer for the loneliness she would never confess.

'The treadmill's fine for the winter,' Oswald was saying, 'But what I need is a bicycle. To get out in the fresh air.'

'I'll buy you a bicycle. In fact, I'll buy you each a bicycle. Or, one of those tandem things so you can ride together. If you'll do me a little favour.'

'That's very generous of you, Jerusha, but you have been telling us you're not a bottomless pit.'

'That's just what I want you to do, dig a pit next to the vegetable garden.'

'Is this for your potatoes, or what?'

'That's a secret. All I want is for you to dig a hole. I'll do the rest.'

'Doesn't sound like the way I want to spend my day.'

'Oh, but you must. You know the rules.'

He edged forward in his chair.

James came in, oblivious to what they had been saying, his green cords scraping as he walked. 'When does Sonia get back?' Sonia was Jerusha's niece, one of Saul's children, who had come across from South Africa on a working holiday six months previously. To Jerusha's chagrin, she seemed to want to patch things up between her father and Jerusha.

'She'll be away for a while,' Jerusha said vaguely and then changed the subject back to the pit and the bicycles. James poured himself the rest of the champagne and listened to Jerusha's proposition. The men began grumbling to each other about 'slave labour'. James was anxious because he did not want to get his clothes dirty. Oswald wasn't worried about his tracksuit.

'I can buy the bicycles, myself, Jerusha,' said James.

'Well then my friends, we have to think of the rules,' she answered with a little of the teacher in her voice.

'It has been so long since you've invoked them I can't remember what they are,' said James.

'I remember them,' said Oswald grudgingly.

'Let's say them together,' prompted Jerusha.

'Tolerance of Jerusha's eccentricities. Respect for Jerusha's wishes and being wise enough not to dig a hole,' said Oswald.

When she heard this, Jerusha's face crumpled and she burst into timely tears. This had both Oswald and James rushing to her side, James holding her hand. Her chest heaved and she hid her face with her free hand. 'I am not so bad,' she sobbed. These rules are meant to be good, meant for all of us.'

'All right. We'll dig your pit,' James capitulated. Okay, Oswald?'

'Okay.'

'Tolerance is the word. Respect everyone is our motto. And it is wise to keep the peace,' said James.

'How big do you want it?' asked Oswald.

'Six foot by three foot and two feet deep,' pleaded Jerusha.

' Can't you do metric?' asked Oswald.

'No,' she wailed.

'This a deep hole, big enough for a body. Where do you want it?' Oswald didn't believe she would possibly want to bury a body. So he turned to practicalities.

'I'll show you. James, you need to change your clothes.' She brought a tissue out from her trouser pocket and started dabbing her eyes with dainty, manicured hands.

The gardener, Luke Junior, could have dug the hole but he was off work with a sore back. That he called himself Luke Junior was misleading. He was a man reaching his seventies and his father, Luke Senior, had died many years before. His father had also worked as a gardener at Kirkfield and the two of them, in their own ways, clung to the property as if it were part of their own family. They took pride in perfectly mown lawns and trim flowerbeds and vegetables, fresh for the table. Jerusha knew that Luke Junior, with his wizened face and bulbous eyes, should retire but she also knew that retirement would kill him. Jerusha had a soft spot for him and a compassion that rivalled her eccentricities. She had lived in all sorts of strata of society during her forty-two years. She had landed up well off but she wasn't about to forget the underdog or the disabled. She wasn't about to drop her act as a rich widow either.

'At least, tell us what you plan to put in the hole,' Oswald said as they walked to the utility room at the back of the house.

'That's my secret,' she said softly, almost coyly, smiling to herself.

The utility room was where Sarah did the washing. It was well equipped with an expensive washing machine and tumble dryer. A basket of clean washing stood on the worktop above the machines and an ironing board stood ready and waiting on the concrete floor. It was a well-lit room with windows lined up on one side overlooking the garden. It was a peaceful room when the machines weren't going. On the far side, opposite the windows, were a series of shelves holding light tools and equipment and, beneath them, a closed cupboard housing more useful equipment. Jerusha picked up a metal, retractable tape measure and a ball of string. These were to mark out the measurements of the hole. Then she and Oswald went out to the garden shed to find stakes and the spades.

Outside it was sunny without being hot; the air was fresh without being dry. It had rained in the night and the soil was soft for digging. 'Perfect conditions,' thought Jerusha as she marched with Oswald through the vegetable garden and to the shed, her weight colluding with her motion in a surprisingly deft way. Her tears, which were genuine, had relieved the slight tension that she felt about carrying out her plan. She had emerged from them and into a positive mood. What she felt matched the spirit of the April day—bright, if chilly, and still at its centre. She heard the birds communicating their happiness. As she walked she took in the expanse of lawn and the incipient burst of colour in the scalloped flowerbeds. 'Always look on the bright side of life,' she sang.

'When you are finished warbling in my ear, tell me why you're not digging with us?'

'Because, my darling, there are only two spades.'

'I give up. Where's my spade, *darling*?' He emphasised the last word.

'In here.'

They entered the shed, which had an adjacent small garage where the motorized lawn mower was kept. In the shed was an array of tools that it had taken years to collect, covered with dry smudges of soil and those at the back laced with cobwebs. Leaning against one wall were two, well-used garden spades. They took these out and Jerusha, letting Oswald carry the spades, led the way to the grassy spot between the vegetable garden and the house where she wanted the hole dug. They began measuring out the dimensions. By this time, James had joined them, looking rather pale and naked in his light tracksuit. James always looked as if he had never seen the sun and his gestures were pale, too. This was possibly why he was attracted to the rugged, muscular Oswald with his history of hard work and hardship. Oswald had even lived with a wife and family at one time, before he came out as being gay. He and James had met in a pub in Edinburgh, Oswald an unwilling participant in a group of heavy drinkers. James had come on his own. Lonely and shy, he had been festering in a flat in the West End, after two years still mourning the loss of his parents.

'You want some company?' Oswald had asked, leaving his group and going over to the bar.

'That's very nice of you,' said James, always polite.

'I'm a very nice guy,' said Oswald without knowing that he was soon going to discover what a very nice guy James was.

Having measured the size of the hole-to-be, Oswald cut the turf and placed rectangles of grass and soil to one side, next to the wall of the house. He was careful not to disturb the vegetable garden that was on the other side. Jerusha and James hovered while this was being done. It was as if by concentrating they were helping progress the work in hand. When at last this had been done, Oswald threw a spade to James and the digging began.

'How deep did you say, again?' Oswald paused.

'Two foot,' said Jerusha.

'About sixty centimetres. That's easy.'

Having got this started, Jerusha went into the house.

James began by picking up pebbles, one by one, then superficially scooping the spade into the soil. There were no trees nearby so that roots were minimal, incidental, easy to discard. Nonetheless, James picked them up and brushed them off as if he had found treasure.

'You're dipping, not digging, my friend. Do it like this. Push the spade into the soil, push it in deeper with your foot and toss the earth onto your pile. We'll see who finishes up with the larger pile.'

With that in mind, James began to dig in earnest, working muscles he hadn't used for a while, his skin pale against the deep and rich, dark soil.

'You know, sometimes I think Jerusha is mad.' Oswald kept digging.

'Eccentric, yes. Mad, no.' James stopped to think. 'Anyway, mad as a description of mental illness is out-dated. In America the word means angry. Someone's mad at someone else. Strange that.' He resumed digging.

'Remember that time . . .' said Oswald and then was distracted. 'Ooh, that was a big stone. Look at the creepy crawlies coming out from under it.' He had moved a stone, which was getting in the way of his pile of earth and the sun shone onto the infested place where it had been. 'I'll not forget that fiasco before Christmas when she dressed us up as chickens, orange stockings and all . . .'

'And she was a shepherdess in blue and pink.'

'With a curly, blonde wig. And she took us to a party that turned out to be a staid dinner party, not a fancy dress party in that sense.'

'It was a posh party. All the men were in dinner jackets,' said James.

'Would you believe it? We had to have our meal standing up with the plates on the sideboard.

'I was so embarrassed, taking off my chicken's head to eat so that everyone knew who we were.

'People still joke about it,' said Oswald.

'And Jerusha acted as if nothing were wrong. She didn't even have the grace to blush,' said James.

'Comes of having had three husbands,' said Oswald.

'What's that got to do with it?'

'Well, you know. She's a woman of the world. All those divorces.'

'You're saying that divorce is the ultimate *faux pas*. But the last one wasn't a divorce. My brother died, God rest his soul. And what about you? Your divorce?'

'The thing is she wears her marriages like a badge . . .'

'I love Jerusha,' said James.

'I love her too, as a friend, but . . .' Oswald was going to continue when his spade hit a blockage and he stopped digging. It turned out to be James' foot and the latter sprang out of the deepening hole. James didn't swear but cried out, exaggerating the pain, and hobbled over to the deck chairs that Jerusha had put out for them.

'Hey, you can't leave me in this hole,' Oswald objected.

'Come out and take a break,' called James, patting the cushion on one of the chairs.

As if by instinct, Jerusha arrived with some freshly baked scones and tea. 'Jerusha, you are a darling,' said James guiltily, although she couldn't have heard what they'd been saying. So, the three of them sat with their backs to the hole which was still just a dent in the ground and Oswald's pile of earth was bigger than James' pile. They ate scones and drank tea and also thirstily drank glasses of water. Jerusha had provided a large glass jug of iced water.

The grass sloped gently down to the flowerbeds and beyond that a wooden fence. They could see over the hedge to the fields beyond and, in the distance, the river. The nearest field, which could be reached through a gate in the corner of the garden, held the secret to the name of the house, Kirkfield. At one end, among gravestones, stood a disused, ageing church. It could also be reached by a small road running along the other side of the house behind a mature beech hedge. The church was unlocked and Jerusha liked to go there to retreat and pray. She believed in God and believed that, through the cross, her sins were forgiven but she didn't trust other churchgoers to think the same way about her. She was far too full-blown a character to fit into a church community, and she knew it. However, this church gave her respite from her own strength of character.

On the other side of the field with the church in it, between the house and the village, were the other four fields that Jerusha now owned, as part of her inheritance from her late husband. They had lain fallow for many years, certainly for the nearly eleven years she had been resident. Now there was a controversy surrounding the land. Len Robson, a successful property developer, had offered her a large sum of money for these fields. That was in August the year before. Somehow the village had got wind of this impending deal and had protested through the press and the local council. It was highly charged opposition—the villagers did not want twenty or more new houses appearing on their doorstep. They were making a loud noise, even before the deal had been clinched, and before planning permission had been applied for. They had sent a community councillor to liase with Jerusha.

'What's happening about the fields, Jerusha?' asked James.

'I don't know yet. I'm seeing Len and the community councillor this week.'

'You're keeping the villagers hanging on,' said Oswald.

'It's a serious decision. A serious subject and I don't want to think about it today.' Jerusha ate another scone, lavishly praising their digging and privately wondering how long it would take them to dig to a depth of two foot. What she really thought was that Oswald was doing all right but James was lagging behind. She would give them homemade burgers and chips for lunch rather than the smoked salmon sandwiches she had thought of at first. After all, they were manual labourers for the day and she needed to stoke their energy. Some beers would help keep them sweet and keep the impending secret.

What started off as one or two beers turned out to be more, until they were wildly inebriated. Jerusha went away, refusing to serve any more after they started flinging dirt at each other and rolling about, laughing. They were smudged with dirt. Earth was in their hair and in their tracksuit bottoms. They fell about and grovelled until Oswald got up and looked at their handiwork. 'Some hole, this,' he spluttered.

'Wholesome,' replied James, endeavouring to keep his balance.

'Holy smoke. Holy hole,' said Oswald.

'Sum of the whole,' contributed James, looking proud of himself.

'Wanker. Holed in.'

'Holed out. In. Out. Turn around. Do the hokey cokey. That's what it's about.'

They were dancing. Then they seemed to lose enthusiasm and Oswald said, 'Let's get this damned thing finished.'

Jerusha was in her sewing room and didn't see them continue to fool around. She wanted to get the Chinese trousers finished for that evening. But she came down when she heard a clod of earth hit the window of her workroom.

'We're finished,' announced Oswald.

'In more ways than one,' added James.

'Just look at you!' she laughed. 'You should see yourselves in a mirror. You look like a couple of kids who have been making mud pies.'

'We have,' said Oswald.

'But you're fifty, Oswald and you are forty eight, James.'

'Two geriatric gardeners,' said James. 'At least we haven't reached the great age of Luke Junior.'

'We've dug your pit. Now tell us what you're going to put in it.' Oswald challenged her.

'I'll bury you in it if you don't go and have a shower. You're more dirt than man at the moment.'

'I'm beat,' said James. 'Jerusha can do what she likes. Bury a body, for all I care. I'm going to have a bath.'

'The wholesome hole is dug. Now let's away, partner.' Oswald struggled to keep his balance.

'Two foot you said and two foot it is. Mind the snails when you fill it in. They're slimy creatures but they deserve to live,' said James

'And you two mind what you say about this. I don't want anyone hearing about it. Loyalty is the fourth rule of this house.'

'My guess is you're burying treasure. Don't you trust the banks any more, Jerusha? I don't blame you,' said Oswald.

'I'm not saying. Now, go on and clean up for dinner.'

'We could just fill it in again,' said Oswald.

'You won't,' said Jerusha.

'What makes you so sure.'

'Because you've had enough manual labour to last a lifetime and because I'm asking you not to. Loyalty again.'

'Come on James, we'll leave the lady to do what she must. Let's away.'

'Take your shoes off at the back door,' called Jerusha. Hands on hips, she surveyed their handiwork, thinking it was a bit untidy but, nonetheless, what she wanted. She looked up at their bedroom window. They were not there yet. They would be preoccupied with the chocolate cake and fruit juice she had left in their room. She was excited that her plan was more than half done. She bent and picked out a leaf that had settled in Oswald's pile of earth. Then, after a suitable pause, she went indoors. Creeping up the stairs she went into her sewing room and across to the naked dressmaker's dummy. She picked this up, one arm around the torso and one holding on to the stand. She placed it gently sideways on the worktable. Then she selected a long piece of yellow, patterned fabric. Unwinding this, she proceeded to wrap it around the dummy, fixing it with safety pins. When the dummy was duly swaddled with swathes of fabric, she lifted it and, hugging it to her, went quietly downstairs. At the back door she rested it against the wall while she exchanged pink shoes for gardening boots.

Jerusha went outside. It was latish but still light. The dummy was not a heavy load but awkward, stiff as though rigor mortis had set in. She now took it to its resting place in the pit, to its grave. She anticipated, with glee, that Oswald and James would be watching her through their bedroom window and she imagined what they would be saying. She was not far wrong.

'Cor. She really is burying a body,' said Oswald.

'I can't see because you're misting up the window, breathing on it like that,' said James.

Oswald moved back slightly. Through the glass, and given their various eyesight, the two men could see only the outline of what Jerusha was doing. The dummy really did look like a corpse wrapped in yellow cloth.

'Maybe it's Sonia. She did disappear in a hurry. We ought to call the police,' said James.

'James, you know quite well that we're drunk. We can't see straight. We're making things up. It's treasure that she's burying. The police would just laugh at us.'

'Now she's shovelling in the soil. Stop her, Oswald.'

'I can't go outside like this, not in my underwear. No, what we saw was a package, covered with cloth. Maybe it was a dog?'

'Jerusha hasn't got a dog,' said James.

'Maybe it was a cat then? A neighbour's cat.'

'A dead cat. That's it.' James seemed satisfied.

'Really?' Oswald was not convinced.

'She's always helping out the neighbours.'

'We love Jerusha.' These three words surfaced through the drink. 'I hope she's not going to be too late with dinner,' Oswald added.

'My muscles are aching.'

'What muscles?' But James had flopped on the bed with his eyes closed. Oswald went over to him and stroked his hair, running a hand with dirt-caked fingernails over the outlines of his face. 'We'll sleep well tonight.'

It took Jerusha some time to shovel in the soil and when she had finished she jumped on it, to flatten it. Then she carefully put back the turf so that there were criss-cross lines where it had been cut. It would grow over so that one day the grass would appear undisturbed and her trick might be everlasting. She had no doubt that Oswald and James would think she had been burying Sonia, no doubt that they were too loyal or too drunk to go to the police. She was triumphant. She stood on the wounded turf, looking up at their window. She raised her arms as if acknowledging her audience and she projected her voice, as all good actors should. She shouted to the winds and high windowpane. 'April Fools,' she cried and then doubled up with laughter, her body quivering and shaking with mirth.

GOING BACK
TO SEPTEMBER 2009

1

A MATTER OF DROWNING

They spent the last week in September anticipating Sonia's arrival.

'Here we go again. Will she be down on our relationship?' Oswald asked no one in particular, deep-felt anger surfacing at the thought that some people pilloried James and him for being gay.

'What if she's teetotal or sleep walks?' muttered James.

'She's only coming for a month,' said Jerusha, without any great conviction.

They were walking along the path beside the river. The water ran in exuberant waves, heading ever onwards towards the sea in a rough and tumble that could have gone unnoticed in this quiet place. Trees lined the banks, some of them leaning in a debauched way over the water. The path circumnavigated the trees but not their roots, and pebbles were scattered beneath the threesome's feet. Jerusha and Oswald carried picnic hampers and James was left in the rear with his hands free but still he stumbled over the uneven ground.

'Ow. Wait,' cried James, leaning down and taking off a shoe.

Jerusha and Oswald halted and turned around to see what was the matter with the generally beleaguered James.

'Well, you will wear moccasins. Of course you're going to get a stone in your shoe. You should have worn Wellington boots like me or, at the very least, trainers,' said Jerusha.

James sat down on the ground and lifted the offending shoe, turning it upside down, high in the air. 'Ow,' he said again.

'What now, Jamie?' Oswald only used this nickname when he was concerned.

'The ground is hard and I'll get prickles.'

'Of course the ground is hard. That's how God made it,' Jerusha said under her breath.

Oswald stepped past her and extended a hand to James, helping him up.

'Now can we get on?' asked Jerusha. 'We've got to find Luke Junior. He said he'd be in his house.'

They found Luke Junior, not in his house but in the back garden, turning the soil, getting it ready for winter, shrubs carefully pruned and leaves captured not long after their fall. He was bending over with a large fork and humming while he worked. "Gin a body meet a body Comin' thro' the rye . . ."

"Gin a body kiss a body Need a body cry? . . ." Jerusha picked up the words of the Burns song.

'Oh, it's you Mrs Burnett. About the boat, do you want me to take you out in it or will you row it yourselves?'

'We can do it. It'll be fine. Oswald here has got strong muscles.'

'That's all right then.' Luke Junior was always very careful to speak the way Jerusha spoke when in her presence, although he had lapses into a Scottish dialect. He was a little gnome of a man who could have been a fixture in any garden. He wore glasses with thick lenses and even these didn't help him see very well. His remaining grey hair was pulled back in a pigtail. He lived with his bird-like wife, Zilla, in the house backing on to the river. It had a wood-frame picture window looking over the water and pebbledash exterior walls. Somebody had seen fit to replace tumbledown stone cottages with city-type terraced housing. Having suffered this, Luke Junior and Zilla never complained for it was not their way. They were not exactly subservient but they knew where they stood, traditionally, in the pecking order and never thought to step outside long-established boundaries.

Luke Junior took the threesome to the edge of the water, his back unfurling a little as he walked. The jetty could hardly be called such. It was half a dozen wooden planks on a dwindling structure and beside it a blue rowing boat was moored. Luke Junior went to get the oars out of a dilapidated wooden shed. Jerusha, clinging to her hamper, launched herself into the boat causing it to rock and tip hazardously. The other two picnickers waited until it had stabilized before themselves stepping in. They lined the hampers up in the middle of the boat beneath a wooden seat. Once he had passed the oars to Oswald, Luke Junior untied the boat and gave it a push. The boat drifted with the current as Oswald grappled with the oars. It was no more than a couple of hundred yards to the opposite bank. James was in the prow and Jerusha was sitting in the middle of the boat. However, she wasn't just sitting. She was swaying and clapping, singing: "Morning has broken like the first morning. Blackbird has spoken like the first bird . . ." She was victoriously caught up with praising the day, oblivious to the fact that her jubilant movements were affecting the balance of the boat.

'Jerusha, stop rocking the boat,' said Oswald who had by now got the hang of rowing.

'Rocking the boat! I always rock the boat. I'm proud of challenging the sanctimonious. And you are being sanctimonious, Oswald. Can't a girl celebrate a joy of living? He who is tired of life deserves to be censored.' For a moment, while she was saying this, she was still and they moved smoothly through the water but then she continued throwing her wool-clad body from side to side.

'Jerusha, you'll overturn the boat and I can't swim,' protested James.

"Mine is the sunlight! Mine is the morning . . ." she sang. Jerusha had quite a good singing voice but this wasn't the point at the time. The point was the stability of the boat and the safety of the sailors. Not to mention the confidence of the threesome.

Sailing with Jerusha's exuberance, they rocked their way to the other bank where Oswald tied the boat to a wooden post, there for that purpose.

'Now, it's time to get your socks and shoes off. And roll up your trousers,' said Oswald. 'Jerusha and I will carry the hampers.'

They were to wade through reeds to the grassy bank to picnic on the mown lawn on the fringes of an elegant country estate. The stately home could be seen quite clearly from the river and had a plethora of windows through which the inhabitants could see who was coming and going on their property. There was a tradition and an understanding that picnickers could lay down their rugs and tablecloths beside the river although there was a sign reminding them to use very appropriately-placed litterbins.

Jerusha negotiated the reeds quite happily with her wellies on, a hamper in one hand and the all-white tablecloth in the other. However, she did stop singing in order to carry out her exit from the boat. James had more difficulty. He dipped one bare foot in the water and found that it was cold. He swiftly put the foot back in the boat, examining his pink toes. He saw the others starting to set up the picnic and seemed to be torn between the boat that had now become a source of comfort, the slimy, wet, cold reeds and the prospect of spicy wraps and wine. He tensed, locked in these possibilities when Oswald came to realize his impasse. He came to James' rescue, standing firmly on the grassy bank and reaching out a hand. James hesitated a little longer then took Oswald's hand, scurrying over the reeds as if he had to do this project quickly or abandon it altogether. He complained loudly and nearly got his little toe caught in reeds but soon he was on the bank and glad to be there, not at this point thinking what would happen when they returned to the boat. Mission accomplished, the two men joined Jerusha on the rug and she handed around glasses of wine.

'To us,' she said.

'To us,' they rejoined.

There was an autumn chill but they were warmly dressed. The cold was a part of the thrill of the picnic; eating al fresco in low temperatures was a dare. In winter Jerusha would have them eat out in the snow; perhaps not cross a freezing river, but walk to a place where the snow was thickest and burrow a space for the ubiquitous rug. They'd be dressed up in sweaters, coats, hats and scarves, with Fagan gloves on so that they could hold the icy wine glasses. Whatever the weather, alcohol flowed in the vein of the lives of these three.

Now they drank the first of the day and relaxed into the open air and natural surroundings; their relationships soothed and eased, being alone, and together, outdoors. 'Do you think they'll invite us to tea?' Jerusha had seen a car draw up to the front door of the stately home and a figure get out of the back. The figure walked up the front steps and went inside as the car, obviously driven by a chauffeur, drove away.

'Don't be daft, Jerusha,' said Oswald.

'It was just an idea. It would be fun. James put your socks and shoes back on. Here.' She threw him a communal towel, being careful not to spill her wine as she did so. Then she stretched back to lean on one elbow, showing those famous, voluptuous curves.

The towel landed on James' knees and he clutched it up with one hand. He tried vainly to dab at his feet with the wine swilling and spilling from his glass.

'Use two hands,' Oswald said, starting to get ready to help James.

'Where do I put my glass? It won't balance on the grass.'

'You've just made a rhyme,' said Jerusha, not moving. She found James' predicament slightly amusing.

Oswald got up and went over to James, taking his glass so that he was standing with two in his hands. James rubbed his feet and dabbed between his toes. Then he looked up at Oswald, who was handicapped by two glasses of wine, and said shamefacedly, 'But my socks are wet.'

'I don't know how to help you this time, Jamie,' said Oswald.

'How did you get your socks wet, you idiot,' exclaimed Jerusha.

'I dunked them in the water when I was getting out of the boat.'

'Well, I hope you didn't wet your shoes as well,' said Jerusha.

'Nope. They're all right.'

'Just put them on and leave the socks out to dry.'

'Go on, just put them on,' said Oswald and James did as he was told, taking his glass back from Oswald and swigging back some wine.

'Now that drama is over, is there anything else? asked Jerusha.

Oswald was still standing. He towered above Jerusha and glowered. 'I want to know what's in this picnic that you've prepared, Jerusha. I haven't forgotten the time you put an

10

overdose of chilli in our food, just for fun. One of your tricks. Are there any surprises in this picnic? If so, tell us now.'

'I did think of putting in some arsenic but there wasn't any in the house.'

'That's just it, Jerusha. One of your jokes could go wrong.'

'You don't really think I mean any harm? Genuinely?'

'I don't think so,' chipped in James.

'Falafel wraps, green salad, couscous with lamb. You name it. Anything but sandwiches. I've been inventive. Creative.'

'Nuts and bolts, peppercorns, mouldy cheese . . . I suspect.'

'Come on, Ossie. I've been very good since . . .'

'Since you pulled James' chair away when he was about to sit down and he fell, breaking his wrist.'

'That wasn't Jerusha's fault. That was an accident,' said James.

'Oswald, when you get like this I think you are having a joke of your own. Making fun of me,' said Jerusha.

'I wish that was true,' said Oswald. 'The fact is that I'm suspicious, based on past experience. My point is that you're a health hazard.'

'Come on, Os. She's great fun to be with,' protested James.

'Yes, Os. I am a hoot. See the funny side. And you like the way I make life at Kirkfield . . . intriguing. It would be very dull if I didn't think up adventures. This is one of them. A simple thing like rowing a boat in order to eat well-thought-out recipes on a glorious Autumn day in the manicured grounds of a stately home. What more would you have? Murder? Death by couscous. Now eat up. I'm starving.'

They ate the picnic with no immediate mishap. They were hungry. And afterwards, when they had put the picnic things away, Jerusha ferreted around in her large bag and brought out a book. 'Cuddle up children. I'm going to read to you. Your favourites. Shakespeare's sonnets.'

The men lay on the rug, sprawled out, looking at the sky. It was blue and cloudy in patches and the air was crisp. The river tumbled and rippled and the sound of it acted as background to Jerusha's voice; that and the birdsong coming from crooked trees further down the riverbank. 'No one would dare to write a word if they truly revered Shakespeare. But then, none of the three of us write, so . . .'

'You write a journal,' said James. 'You've told me that you do.'

'I don't write for an audience. I write for myself. Now, listen. This is my favourite.'

"Some glory in their birth, some in their skill,

Some in their wealth, some in their body's force;

Some in their garments, though new-fangled ill;

Some in their hawks and hounds, some in their horse;

And every humour hath his adjunct pleasure,

Wherein finds joy above the rest;

But these particulars are not my measure,

All these I better in one general best.

Thy love is better than high birth to me,

Richer than wealth, prouder than garments' cot,

Of more delight than hawks and horses being

And, having thee, of all men's pride I boast.

Wretched in this alone, that thou mayst take

All this away, and me most wretched make."

Jerusha did not read for comments on the details of the sonnets from the other two. She read with heart and soul, expecting to affect their emotions. She went on to read the sonnet beginning, "Shall I compare three to a summer's day?" and several others as James soaked in the words and Oswald relished James' pleasure. He had, as a child, loved being read to but, after his father left, his mother preferred the comfort of the bottle to reading aloud to her children. Now, when Jerusha read to them, which she did quite often, he focussed on James and his obvious enjoyment rather than opening up old needs. In any case, Shakespeare was a bit too highbrow for him.

When Jerusha decided to stop, she lay back with her hands behind her head and said, 'Love writ large,' in an elevated, dramatic way.

'Unrequited love. What I want to know about is unconditional love,' said James.

'It was only with Hamish that I found unconditional love. The first two marriages were complex. The very first marriage was to Arthur. We loved each other in the beginning but he wanted children and I couldn't give them to him. Conditional love number two was with Bert.'

'You've told us you were unfaithful to him. That's what your brother, Saul, and you fell out about,' said James.

'My falling out with Saul, as you call it, was his fault and probably inevitable. Complex.'

'Everything you can't explain is complex, Jerusha,' said Oswald. 'And just because you've had three marriages doesn't mean you understand about love.'

'Don't be so hard on Jerusha,' said James. 'Experience counts for a lot.'

'Yes, you keep on criticising me, Oswald, as if you don't like me.'

'You do, Oswald,' said James.

'I'm sorry, Jerusha. No need for tears. It's just my manner. In truth, I love you like a real friend. Is that better?'

She nodded, her eyes watering.

'But we were talking about unconditional love,' said Oswald, 'and I don't think there is any such thing. People say that a dog gives unconditional love but if a dog is badly treated it will fight back. It will bite. It's the same with people.'

'If an owner loves his or her dog and treats it well, then that owner can expect love in return. It's a two way process,' said Jerusha.

'Shakespeare managed to love without anything in return,' said James.

'We cannot make sense of it,' said Jerusha, waving her hand loftily. 'I sometimes think that love can be a kind of madness. I am telling you that when I fell in love I was without my proper reason. It's only after living with someone that you see them as they really are.'

'I'm surprised you had time. You were wed and divorced so speedily,' said Oswald.

'Now, now,' said James.

15

'No, he's right. First it was five years, next it was three years and last it was seven years of living together,' said Jerusha. 'If you think about it, that's a total of fifteen years of marriage.'

'Before you say anything, Oswald, let's change the subject,' said James.

∞ɯɯᎧ

Oswald had started to chuckle at Jerusha's assumptions and Jerusha misinterpreted this as a sign that he was ready for fun. She decided that now was a good time to pull the plastic ducks out of her bag. She had planned a duck race. She asked the two men what colour they wanted—red, blue or yellow—assuming they would be up for the game. They usually followed her lead in these things. James chose a yellow duck and squeezed it with his fingers.

'Blue,' said Oswald. 'But before we put them into the torrents, let me go back to an earlier conversation. What if Sonia is homophobic?'

'It's obviously an issue for you,' said Jerusha. 'It isn't for me.'

'That's very nice of you but you mustn't forget people can be very aggressive about James and me being together, particularly religious people. Somebody like that could change the whole atmosphere at Kirkfield.'

'To be quite honest with you, I don't know very much about Sonia. Her father has made himself my archenemy but it's she who has decided to come and see me,' said Jerusha. 'I don't even have an inkling of her attitude towards me, let alone whether she is religious or not. I might add that not everyone who is religious is anti-gays.'

'So we're just going to let this person into our midst without knowing a thing about her,' said Oswald.

'She might know something about me but she doesn't know anything about you.'

'That's the problem.' Oswald took his duck from Jerusha.

'Sonia is family, Oswald. She's part of Jerusha's family. I think that's what she wants to explain to you,' said James.

'The daughter of someone you call your archenemy is family. Is that what you think?'

'Yes. James is right. That says it all. I'm not going to turn away a family member who has asked to stay,' said Jerusha.

'Come on. Let's race the ducks.' James got up and pulled Oswald after him, eager, like an excited child, the yellow duck clutched in one hand.

There followed a long and complicated conversation at the waterside about how to give the three ducks a fair and even chance, seeing that no starting line could be pegged into the water. Someone suggested that someone else strip and wade into the water to arrange the ducks in a line.

Then there was the question of how to give the signal to start. But, that someone was interrupted and a communal decision was made that no one would wade into the water. Instead, Oswald would lean out from the water's edge and float the ducks in a line, anchored by Jerusha and James who would each take hold of one leg, stabilising Oswald and keeping him dry. This depended upon Oswald being trusted not to give the blue duck, his one, an unfair advantage. It would work, they happily agreed. That still left the question of how to signal the start and it turned out that James had a surprising and appropriate gift. He could whistle with two fingers in his mouth. They gave some consideration to the problem of how he was to use one hand for whistling and the other for holding Oswald's leg. Did he have the strength for a one-handed hold? The last thing Oswald wanted was to be dunked in the water. They thought about all this and decided that Jerusha would be a strong enough anchor, and James would immediately replace his hand once he had whistled, by which time Oswald would be ready to step back to safety.

Following this prescription, the duck race began, Oswald staying almost dry and the ducks bobbing cheerily in the water until, one after the other, they were taken by the current. The three owners ran down the grassy bank, cheering the ducks, calling encouragement to their oblivious toys. From the beginning James' yellow duck had an edge on the others, especially when Jerusha's red duck did a flip, threatening to overturn. It righted itself and sailed on, neck and neck with Oswald's blue duck, which seemed to stare out of its plastic face on the lookout for the competition. As no one had thought to delineate a finishing point—which might have been the sea, the way they were going—but for what happened next they might have been breathlessly running for days.

The bank was manicured but the gardener of the stately home had skirted around occasional clumps of trees reaching over the river, surrounded by rings of nettles. James' yellow duck, winning by far, sailed unwittingly into one of these clumps of trees. It lodged in the cleft of some branches hanging low over the water and stayed there while the other two ducks sailed on. James was deeply disappointed. He had been a winner and now he had lost. The others had the grace to stop and commiserate.

'You can get it out and still join the race,' urged Jerusha.

'What about the nettles?' If his behaviour were predictable, he was hoping that Oswald would get the duck for him. He was out of luck this time. Oswald was egging him on to go and free the duck. So, hoping his trousers and moccasins would protect him from nettle stings, he waded through the malicious plants and made it to the tree at the edge of the river.

'Oh, my God!' His exclamation was completely spontaneous.

'Go on, James. You're just about there. Grab the wretched thing. We want to catch up with our ducks.'

'No. You don't understand,' said James.

'Get a move on, laddie,' called Oswald.

'You've got to come and see this.'

'See what? We don't like the nettles either.'

'You can do what I did. You've got to see this.'

'So you said. See what?'

'There's a body in the water.'

'Ow! I hope you're serious,' said Jerusha as she tackled the nettles.

James was dead serious. The body lay half-submerged, face down, caught by the tree. Its hair below a bald patch floated in the water. A speckled, long coat fanned out, stretching to the corpse's shod feet. The coat covered the body's sex but the bald pate suggested it was a man. This was not just any man, this was . . .

'It's Jocky, the homeless guy who sells his magazines outside the supermarket in Galashiels,' said Jerusha. 'I'd know that coat anywhere.'

'What's he doing here?' asked James.

'Well, there's that whisky bottle in his pocket.'

'I'll get it,' said James.

'No. Don't touch anything. We'll have to call the police. Has anyone brought their mobile?' Jerusha looked behind to Oswald, who wasn't there. While she was pre-occupied

James swiftly dislodged his duck. It wasn't that he didn't care about Jocky. It was just that he didn't want the duck involved in some crime. Oswald, meanwhile, had remembered seeing an abandoned canvas bag while they were racing after the ducks and he had gone to find it. There it was lying pitifully on the grass. He felt inside. A few magazines and some pound coins. Also a small, full bottle of whisky. Nothing else.

'Leave that there. You must not touch anything.' Jerusha came up to him. She was on a search for a mobile phone. Oswald had one back at the picnic site and they called the police who said someone would be on their way as soon as possible.

Meanwhile, James joined them, reluctant to be on his own with the poor, departed Jocky. 'Are you sure he is dead?' he asked.

'Of course, he's dead,' said Jerusha. 'It's my guess that he's been there quite some time.'

'We could try and give him mouth to mouth,' answered James.

'You do it, then,' was her curt reply.

'In this instance, I think Jerusha is right. And, as she says, we must not touch anything,' said Oswald.

In the event, they decided not to try and resuscitate Jocky and they were proved right when the police informed them later that the body had been in the water for at least eighteen hours. Yet, they didn't know that at the time. They had made a decision based on Jerusha's leadership and instinct and their disgust at the thought of putting their mouths to the mouth of a cold and decaying body. The police, when they arrived, were led by Detective Inspector Fergus Drew who had made acquaintance with Jerusha on an occasion when she thought she had been robbed and then discovered she hadn't. He knew Jerusha from this experience and by repute. He didn't judge her harshly but thought her eccentric. This time, however, she had discovered a dead body but it was unlikely that she had opened up a murder case. Jocky was also familiar to him. The empty whisky bottle in his pocket said it all. Too fond of alcohol, Jocky must have drunk too much, missed his footing and fallen into the river. The Detective Inspector was a clear-headed fellow and a campaigner against alcohol abuse. He was aware of the dangers of excessive drinking. He was called out to many an alcohol-related crime. Now, this case must surely be one of death by misadventure.

Even although he had privately drawn quick conclusions in the case of Jocky, surname unknown as yet, Detective Inspector Drew was a fair and open-minded man. He did have his limitations on account of having been born in the town he still inhabited and where he worked. However, he had seen a fair slice of life in a small arena. He was a man of about forty with sand-coloured hair, straight, thick and sleek; his fringe tended to fall over his eyes. It was his nose that was distinctive. Long, pinched and pointed, it gave him the appearance of looking down on people when he was doing no such thing. Jerusha, mindful of the phantom robbery, was taken in by the nose and expected some lofty criticism. However Detective Inspector Drew shook the hands of all three of them warmly. 'You did well to discover and report this. Jocky could have been lying in the water, unnoticed, for a long time.'

'We didn't know what to do about the body. Whether or not to try and revive him,' said Jerusha.

'He's very clearly dead. You didn't touch anything, I hope,' said the Inspector.

'Nothing, except for the bag we found up river,' said Oswald.

'Where is that now?'

'We put it back where we found it. With everything in it,' Oswald assured him.

'I'll get my men to go and have a look once they've finished fishing Jocky out of the water. By the way, what are you three doing here?'

There followed a long and garbled explanation from James who felt he had to make some sort of contribution. About the boat ride, the picnic, the sonnets, the duck race. 'We had no idea we were having fun while someone was dying. I mean, dead.'

'That's a story of my life, James,' said the Inspector. 'Now, what time exactly did you find the old man's body?'

'We lost track of time,' said James.

'It must have been about quarter to three,' said Oswald.

'Did you see or hear anyone else in the vicinity? There is no sign that the body has been dragged here from somewhere else.'

'No. There was no one else here,' said Jerusha.

'It's my guess that he fell into the water upstream and the current carried him here where the tree blocked his passage. Aah, here we have it. Yes, it's undoubtedly the homeless Jocky.'

The police officers had dragged the body out of the water. They established that there was definitely no pulse and one of them closed Jocky's glassy, staring eyes. He now lay face-up and the speckled, definitive coat humanized him. Although it took a great deal of strength to lift the heavy man (heavy in life and heavier in death) they had lifted him as far as the grass beyond the nettles. This could have been either a sensitive or a practical touch, the latter because examiners would not want to risk the stings. The pathologist would be there shortly, the Inspector told them. He was clearly going to explore all avenues and not going to draw prejudiced conclusions. The Scene of Crime Officers began to dig in stakes, around which they tied police tape to mark off the crime scene.

'And, just what do you think you're doing?' A stranger was walking down the lawn towards them.

'Standard procedure, Madam,' said the Inspector, without knowing to whom he was talking.

'You'll want to know who I am, of course. I'm Hazel Gifford, Sir Iain's housekeeper. This is my employer's land and the way you are treating it is dubious.'

'Madam. As you see, we have a dead man here. We're bound to investigate and go through standard police procedure.' He gestured towards the corpse with one hand, palm upwards.

They all stared at the departed Jocky. James thought he was going to be sick and, sensing this, Oswald put an arm around him. Fleetingly, Jerusha was lost in a memory, a memory of her dead husband, Hamish. She could still hear the groans, as he lay upstairs, dying, at Kirkfield. The groans became softer as he lost strength. And, finally, she understood that he was dead. He stopped breathing and his eyes took on a stare, akin to Jockey's stare before the police had closed his eyes.

'I know this man,' Hazel was saying. 'He sometimes came to the house. I would get cook to give him a meal, provided he had not been drinking. He accepted that condition.'

'I think we are all agreed that this er . . . was . . . Jocky, of no known surname. The pathologist, when she arrives, will tell us more about the cause of death,' said the Inspector. 'Are you sure he didn't come to the house last night, Ms Gifford?'

'Absolutely,' she said, scraping away a wisp of hair that was undermining her immaculate image. 'I was on duty all of last night and cook would never have fed him without consulting me. He was a pitiful man. He had been horribly abused during his childhood. While one must maintain standards, I am aware of people who have not been as lucky as I have been. There's a limit of course. I would not tolerate him staggering into the kitchen the worse for wear. In that state he couldn't even appreciate the food we offered him. He tried it once and we chucked him out I'm afraid.'

'Which does and doesn't explain what he was doing down here by the river,' said the Inspector. 'And it doesn't explain what his bag was doing on the bank. Had he deliberately put it down so that he could enter the water?'

'If he had put it down so that he could enter the water why didn't he take his coat off?' asked Jerusha, now caught up in the puzzle of this death. 'Or, was there someone with him who pushed him into the river and then left? You'd think they'd have taken the money, even although it was a small amount.'

'Mmm. Yes. I don't want you to worry about these details. They're a matter for further investigation,' replied the Inspector. 'Aah, here's the pathologist.'

The pathologist examined the body in a clinical way, which offended Jerusha because she couldn't help thinking of Jocky as a living person, a character, an outspoken man who was given to whistling, and jangling coins, who always said thank you, as if he were grateful, when he made a sale.

Eventually the pathologist, a woman in her late thirties, all in white with black, wiry hair, spoke to Inspector Drew. 'There don't appear to be any injuries consistent with a struggle. There are a few bruises, which could have been caused when the deceased hit rocks whilst being carried downstream. My first guess is that this is a man who fell in the river whilst under the influence of drink and was not sober enough to save himself. Further tests will show the level of alcohol in his blood. The empty whisky bottle suggests it will be high.'

'Yet, why would he leave a full bottle in his bag on the bank?' asked the Inspector.

'Could have been satiated?' suggested the pathologist. 'Could, plain, have not known what he was doing. Whatever the case, this is definitely death by drowning.'

At this point, Ms Gifford, apologising, interrupted to say that she had work to do and would like to go back to the house, if the Inspector did not mind. He replied that everyone but the police was free to go, and asked if Sir Iain would give permission for them to use the driveway in order to carry the body away.

'I'm sure that will be in order,' Ms Gifford said, hurrying away up the lawn.

'Let's go, Jerusha,' said James, tugging at her arm.

Although she was still caught up with trying to solve the mystery, she went with Oswald and James back to the picnic place. 'Seems all too simple to me,' she said.

'Motive, Jerusha. Motive. That's the thing that is missing here,' said Oswald.

'Who knows what enemies he has made during his life,' she said.

'Well, it wasn't robbery,' Oswald pointed out.

'There's nothing to say he wasn't with somebody when he went down to the river. And why come to the estate if he knew he wouldn't be fed because of the whisky?'

'Maybe he was sober when he arrived?' suggested James.

'Do you think she was telling the truth, that housekeeper?' asked Oswald.

'What motive would she have for lying?' asked Jerusha.

'There. We get back to motive. In this case, I can't think of one,' said Oswald.

'I think we should drink a toast to Jocky,' said Jerusha, pulling an unopened bottle of wine from the hamper, opening it and pouring it into their waiting glasses. 'May he rest in peace. He had a hard life. Now, it is time for him to be still.'

'To Jocky,' they chorused.

Jerusha sat down and leaned back on the rug, took a pack of cards from her bag and began to shuffle it. What was it to be? Rummy. She knew Rummy was James' favourite and he was the one who seemed to need cheering up the most. He always won at Rummy. He had the knack. The two men sat down but they refused to be drawn into a game. So Jerusha started playing Patience. A silence settled on the group like the darkness that would come in a couple of hours. Yet the silence was not to be expected like the fading light. It was rare and infused with the morbid experience of the afternoon. In it, they could hear the sip and slide of the wine. The silence made Jerusha uncomfortable and restless. She made a great drama out of re-filling their glasses. However, for a while she refrained from talking. The game of Patience was boring her yet she kept slapping the cards one on top of the other. They could hear birdsong but could not decipher it. Nothing moved up at the house. No cars. No people treading on the gravel. The police had taken Jocky away. The river ran in small eddies, tumbling in the seaward current, its sound the most intrusive. No sheep. No cows nor horses. The landscape reigned. James and Oswald stared into the country scene, keeping their thoughts to themselves for some time. It was James who finally spoke. 'I can't think of anything worse than death by drowning,' he said.

'I can think of a hundred worse deaths,' retorted Jerusha.

'You know what I mean. That poor chap,' said James.

'He would have been anaesthetised by the whisky,' she said.

'The water covering your face, your nose, so that you can't breathe. And then it getting into your lungs.' James shivered.

'You'd be best not to think about it,' Oswald said.

'What is this thing you've got about water, anyway?' asked Jerusha. 'You look at it like it's a deadly enemy. When, in fact, it's cool, soothing and can be quite beautiful. Millions of artists have captured reflections.'

'I've always been afraid of water and my mother decided that I was so frightened that I didn't need to learn to swim.'

'Hamish could swim,' Jerusha remarked.

'Hamish was only my half-brother, remember. And much older than me,' said James.

'Jerusha. If he can't swim, he can't swim,' said Oswald.

'He raised the subject' said Jerusha

'I was talking about Jocky,' said James. 'I hope he didn't realize what was happening to him.'

'Best way to go. In an alcoholic haze,' blurted out Jerusha.

'But if he hadn't been under the influence, he might have been able to save himself,' said James.

'I firmly believe that when your time's up, that's it,' said Oswald.

'We agree on that,' said Jerusha, finishing her game. 'Now can we talk about something else. You're getting maudlin, James.'

'We all need to digest experience in our own way, Jerusha,' said Oswald. 'I think we should go.'

'That's the last of the wine, so why not?' said Jerusha.

'I'm not looking forward to the crossing,' said James.

'We won't be on the water for very long. I'll hold your hand.' Jerusha was coming around to accepting that James was frightened of water the way she was afraid of snakes. Fear of water or snakes, or spiders were phobias. They could only be conquered by confronting them. Jerusha had made a grand decision to help James face his fear.

She was given to sudden rushes of generosity and once on the path of care she was fiercely loyal. Lorna, Hamish's sister was one example. Jerusha, ever since she had known Lorna, had stood by her during the highs and lows of bipolar disorder. She had visited her in hospital and cared for her at home. She had even become her financial guardian, concealing her credit cards when she was on an erratic, big-spending high. Now she had decided that James was her next charge. It flashed through her mind that she might teach him to swim. Not now, but some time in the future. For the present, her aim was to get him across the water when the sight of the drowned man had clearly unnerved him. She pushed past Oswald and put an arm around James' shoulders. 'What you've got to remember, James, is that drowning is usually a result of accident and it's rare. We came across the water safely, didn't we? We'll get back just as easily. Now, I want you to come with me to the water's edge.' James complied while Oswald tidied up the picnic and stowed the hampers in the boat. 'Oswald is going to row us swiftly across, so quickly you'll hardly know you're on the water.'

Jerusha got James to take off his shoes at the water's edge and then, little by little, persuaded him to dip in a foot. 'Cool, isn't it?'

'Cold. And I can feel a current.' James withdrew his foot, wiping it on the grass. 'I prefer terra firma. I understand what you're trying to do, Jerusha, but it's not working.'

'Let's get you into the boat then.' After some time and some pushing from Jerusha, James struggled through the water and practically fell into the boat.

'All right, mate?' asked Oswald.

'Let's just get this over with,' said James, sitting in the middle of the boat, clinging on to the seat as if that would steady the vessel.

'That's right. You be the ballast. You stay there and you'll keep the boat steady. But mind the tidal wave that's coming,' said Oswald.

Jerusha was getting in and the boat tilted sharply with her weight. Without realizing the effect she was having on the boat, she panted, 'It's all right, James, I'm coming. I'll sit beside you.' She clambered over to him.

He moved aside, thinking Jerusha would be best in the middle of the boat, would make better ballast than he would. Oswald untied the rope that tied the boat to the post and began rowing. James felt breathless when he saw the riverbank receding. Yet, when he turned and saw how close the home bank was he was filled with bravado. He drew great gulps of air. 'I can do this. I'm a grown man. Sing, Jerusha. Sing.' He himself began to sing. 'Danny Boy'.

Jerusha joined in, flushed with success that her charge had begun to relax and enjoy himself. She put this down to the wine and her careful coaxing. What she didn't expect was for him to get up and start swaying, still singing lustily. And she certainly didn't expect him to fall over the side of the boat and into the water . . . but this is what he did. Jerusha and Oswald were on full alert but frozen in a moment before emergency action. James' head bobbed up out of the water and he could stand but, instead, he was thrashing around in state of panic. He was gulping down water. He kept going under and coming up, his face contorted with fear.

'Here, hold these oars, Jerusha,' called Oswald but he was too late.

The boat gave a furious heave as Jerusha slid over the side. Chest-high in water she was wading across to the frantic James. Bare-foot, the stones on the river floor pierced and cut her feet. She felt the surge of the current as the water pushed against her body. She was single-minded in her haste to reach James who was still flailing and thrashing. When she got to him, he grabbed her and clutched at her without any apparent knowledge of who she was. He was so desperate for help that he might have pulled them under had she not managed to get behind him and clamp his arms to his body. This might have been abortive, because he was probably as strong as her, if he hadn't suddenly calmed at her touch and the protective hold she now had over him. She was in two minds about what her next move should be. Walk him to the other bank or get him back in the boat? Oswald solved this problem for her by bringing the boat close up to them. With James now co-operating she pushed him over the side and into the bottom of the boat where he lay like a stranded fish, coughing and spluttering. When she saw he was safe, Jerusha, exhausted, turned and waded to the bank where Luke Junior was waiting with towels. He and Zilla had seen the whole incident through their picture window.

James made a remarkable recovery, considering the ordeal he had been through. Sitting huddled in a blanket in Zilla's front room, he was now more embarrassed than anything and wanted to play down the fact that the whole incident had been of his own making. He was unwittingly aided and abetted in this by Zilla who insisted on treating her visitors as special. She was very conscious that the lady of the big 'hoose' had entered her humble home. She produced her best china tea set and, as if she had been expecting them, she offered homemade flapjacks that Jerusha and Oswald, in particular, took a liking to. The lady of the big 'hoose', Jerusha, enjoyed the attention and was rapidly forgetting the tussle with the panicking James. She slung the blanket Zilla gave her around her shoulders as if it were a shawl and dropped crumbs on it, in her haste to take another flapjack. Zilla hovered with the plate, having given them tea. It seemed clear that the food and drink were for the visitors only and not for Luke Junior and herself. This was a code of conduct, ages old, that nobody then questioned. If they had, Zilla would have been stubborn in her refusal to break it. Such a tiny, light woman would stand up for what she thought was right. At the same time as seeing to her guests, she had one eye on her husband of fifty years. Luke Junior, in his old age, was inclined to drool and Zilla had an endless supply of big, white handkerchiefs to help him disguise the habit. They showed a little more familiarity, not much, when the topic got around to the body in the water.

'Aye. I ken Jocky,' said Luke Junior. 'Buy his magazines and give him the odd tip.'

'Past tense, Luke. They're telling us the poor soul is deid,' said Zilla.

Whereupon Jerusha saw fit to describe what was now a tale, starting with the duck race and ending with the pathologist's analysis. She added graphics and hyperbole so that what emerged was almost a case of cold-blooded murder. Her hints were so broad and her suppositions so large that she had her audience enthralled and, this time, Oswald and James kept quiet. James was glad of the diversion away from his own ignominy.

On this note, they left Zilla and Luke Junior with enough gossip to last weeks. They also left wet patches on Zilla's best furniture. Weary, they took the path home, beneath the trees, over the rocks and roots. James took care not to look to his left, at the menacing river.

'I could do with a hot bath,' said Oswald.

'I never want to see water again,' replied James.

'We're not going to let you be a stinky pooh,' retorted Jerusha.

They all needed hot baths, or a shower at least. They were wet, tired, dirty and dishevelled as they came around the corner of the house to confront a young girl with a backpack, sporting a tracksuit.

'Goodness,' said the girl, looking at the three. 'What has happened?' And when she got no reply, she continued, 'I got an earlier train. I hope you don't mind.'

Sonia had arrived.

2

COMING OR GOING?

Jerusha watched her niece unfasten the straps and slither out of her rucksack. Sonia then kicked it into place against one wall of the hall. It was the kicking of the bag that surprised and interested Jerusha. Scant regard for her possessions? Firmness in her character? Judgemental, even? That would be just like her father, Saul. Aware that she was being observed, Sonia rubbed her hands together as if to say, 'What next?'

'Come into the kitchen and I'll give you a cup of tea or coffee and, after that, I'll show you to your room. The S.S., our home help, has been so it's ready for you. Then, I really must change out of these wet things,' said Jerusha.

Sonia might have taken pity on her aunt by suggesting that she change first but she was too uncertain of her position in this establishment and, besides, didn't have an overview of life's little events. She followed Jerusha down the hall and into the kitchen. 'It's very good of you to have me, Auntie Mary.'

Jerusha put the kettle on and then slowly turned to her niece, hands on hips, using her full size, curving through her wet clothes. 'It's not very good of me. You are family. However, if you're going to get along here you will call me by my correct name. Yes, I used to be called Mary but I changed my name when I divorced my second husband. I am Jerusha, which means, if you're interested, the 'perfect wife'. I answer to Jerusha. I don't answer to Mary. And you can drop the Auntie.'

'It's a lovely name, Jerusha,' said Sonia, trying to appease her aunt who was clearly passionate about the subject of her name. She determined to use the name as often as possible although, in the early days of her stay, she had the occasional slip-up. Partly to do with the fact that her father doggedly stuck to Jerusha's birth name when he mentioned her at all . . .

They drank coffee and Jerusha told her about the rescue of James and tried to probe, to get Sonia to reveal exactly why she was visiting. She had little luck with this as Sonia seemed to think her presence was a natural addition to the household and that, as they had agreed, family was important. For the moment, Jerusha was far too wet and uncomfortable to pursue the matter. In time, she would find out. Soon, she suggested she show Sonia her room and they went up the steep, sweeping flight of stairs. As they passed the different bedrooms, she pointed them out to Sonia before taking her into the small, immaculately clean bedroom that was to be hers. It took Jerusha a while to realize something was wrong because she hadn't been expecting any strong reaction, despite Oswald's cautionary words.

'They share the same bedroom? James and Oswald?' asked Sonia.

'Yes.'

'You mean, they're in a relationship under your roof?'

By this time, Jerusha was well aware of the girl's feelings. 'I don't know how things are in South Africa, but most young people in Britain today take homosexuality in their stride.'

'But the Bible tells us it is wrong. You must know that Auntie M . . . . I mean, Jerusha.'

'It's my experience that the Bible tells people what they want it to say. It also says we are to love our neighbours and your neighbours in this house are Oswald and James.'

'You must forgive me for having reservations. Dad did warn me.'

'What? What did your father warn you?'

'Only, that you were . . . you were unconventional.'

'I may be unconventional, as you put it. I'm also uncomfortable in these wet clothes. We'll talk about this later, just you and I. Won't be long. Just make yourself at home. Dinner will be a little late tonight.'

When she emerged from bathing and changing, Jerusha half expected to find Sonia gone but, no, she was to learn that her niece was made of sterner stuff than that. However, the next blow to the newcomer's happiness was to find out how much they drank. She drank only on anniversaries and at celebrations. She was to learn that in this household everything was a cause for celebration. At least they did love life, she told herself. That night the celebration was obvious. Sonia's arrival and James' survival. There were several toasts to the heroine of the hour who had plucked James from the water, risking her own safety. Jerusha basked in the glow of their congratulations. She was proud of what she'd done and proud of being herself.

The glow adorned her still the next day when she was clearing up after breakfast. The door chimes sounded and Sonia, being the closest, answered the door. A bouquet of twenty-four red roses all but eclipsed the boy who was delivering them. Sonia took the flowers and shut the door, wondering who they could be for. For Jerusha, of course. The card read: 'For a woman I hold in great esteem. Jerusha, from Len.'

Jerusha had come wading through autumn sunlight that filtered through the house. However, the flowers weren't a surprise to her. 'They'll be from Len Robson, the property developer who is trying to buy my fields. He won't give up.'

'Don't you want to sell the fields?' asked Sonia.

'I haven't made up my mind yet. Mmm, smell these. God they're beautiful.' She breathed in deeply the heady perfume of the roses. 'And I imagine they cost a bob or two.'

'Maybe he fancies you?' Sonia suggested.

'That's highly unlikely. He fancies the millions he could make by building houses on the land.'

'He's putting you in a difficult position.'

'And inviting controversy. Half the village has approached me to stop the sale. Sheena McPherson is around here every day, always with a different excuse, working on me to plant trees and bluebells. I quite like that idea.'

'So, will you accept his roses?'

'Of course, if he wants to waste his money on me. He's taking me out to dinner on Wednesday. That will give me a chance to thank him without revealing whose side I'm on. I quite like this game. Be a dear and put these in a vase for me. The vases are under the kitchen sink. They'd look nice below the mirror in the hall here.'

She swanned back to the kitchen to talk to the S.S. whom she introduced to Sonia as 'The godsend'. 'If ever a home needed help it's this one.' Sonia started to clumsily arrange the roses in a wide, scrolled vase, amateurishly cutting the fine long stems. When she accidentally cut her thumb on one of the vicious thorns she hastened to the kitchen to run it under the tap. But Jerusha had other ideas. 'Wait.

41

Don't move.' She rushed to a cupboard and brought out a box carefully labelled: 'Second Aid'. Aid began first with tender loving care, she thought, and delved into its contents for elastoplasts and cotton wool. Sonia, under protest, found herself hampered by a bulging bandage on her thumb. She thought of abandoning the plaster but decided that would offend Jerusha. Having been away from her arrangement for five minutes, she stood back and looked at it with new eyes. The tallest rose in the triangular shape she was trying to achieve was off-centre. She didn't consider that the vase Jerusha had given her was the wrong shape for the lavish bunch of flowers. She took out the blooms and started again. The truth was that domestic tasks such as baking and flower arranging were not her forte. She was happier tinkering with plumbing or working with wood. When she was very young she had enjoyed playing with toy guns with her younger brothers, climbing trees or spying on the grown-ups. She had dolls, yes, but they were mainly neglected or even abandoned. And so the grown-ups labelled her a tomboy and laughed behind her back until her stepmother started trying to reform the girl. She painstakingly attempted to teach Sonia to bake fairy cakes, to mend pyjamas, to touch type, to arrange flowers. Underneath, she now railed against this capture of her character.

After a few hours with Jerusha, Sonia had decided that this just might be a free spirit who would let her be herself. That was why she had not left after finding out that Oswald and James were in a gay relationship. The prospect of finding a mentor in her aunt was too tempting. However, she knew it was going to be a rocky ride because while she had attempted to escape her parents' strictures she never would betray the religion she treasured. She never would abandon her basic beliefs but, reflecting that all people are sinners, she would stay and find out what these sinners were all about. The overriding truth that she was a little homesick and wanted this to be a household where she could nestle in. Jerusha giving her a task that was unsuited to her was just an aberration. Next time, she would explain to Aunt Jerusha just how she felt. Not this time.

Jerusha swept through from the kitchen, 'How are you getting on? Oh, you've started all over again. The scissors are not sharp enough.' Jerusha fetched her a sharper pair of scissors although Sonia thought the other pair had been quite adequate.

When Jerusha had gone away again, Sonia gathered strength and plunged the still robust roses into the wire mesh, making a firm triangle, cutting stems to nothing so that the blooms would cover the wire, grabbing the petals and pushing them into place. She cut herself twice more but simply sucked the blood away, avoiding any fuss. It was while she was clearing up that the door chimes went again. Sonia listened to hear whether someone would answer the door but as no one came, she answered it. She found herself facing a policeman in uniform, behind him in the driveway a white police car with yellow and blue stripes.

෴

Sonia's mind was in a flurry. What were the police doing here? What had Jerusha done? Or, perhaps it was Oswald and James this policeman was after? In South Africa the police were relatively powerless but, nonetheless, she had been brought up to respect the long arm of the law. She breathed in deeply.

'I'm Constable George Rutherford. I'm here to see Mrs Burnett.'

'Mrs Burnett. Oh.' Sonia gaped.

'Tell them I'm coming,' Jerusha called from the depths of the house. Clearly, she had no idea who was visiting her or what was awaiting her.

The Constable had taken off his cap to reveal a close-shaven head of suggested dark hair. He had big brown eyes, which Sonia tried to fathom before remembering her manners and inviting him in. She took him into the sitting room, which she judged was the proper thing to do with a respected guest who didn't behave in the least like he was about to make an arrest. Perhaps he was here on some civic duty, or to warn them? Sonia noticed he was carrying a folder. Now her apprehension was turning to curiosity. What else could happen in this house?

'You're not from these parts?' he asked. She was not the only one who was curious.

'You can tell from my accent and my suntan,' she said.

'My guess is that you're from South Africa.'

'That's right. I arrived yesterday. I mean, not in this country. I arrived at Kirkfield yesterday.'

'My sister lives in South Africa. She has just built a house in Cape Town. Wouldn't live anywhere else, although the country has its problems . . .' Then he suddenly leapt to his feet.

'Aah, Constable Rutherford. Detective Inspector Drew said you were coming.' Jerusha had arrived. She negotiated the spaces between chairs to sit opposite the Constable who was now alert on the edge of the *chaise longue*. Does anyone ever know which is the owner's favourite chair? Or, do visitors sit in it deliberately? Jerusha was not in the least put out. She prided herself on being able to perform in any part of the house, or world, for that matter.

'Do be a dear and call the boys,' she said to Sonia.

'But, I can't,' said the girl.

'Why ever not?'

'Because it's their bedroom. They're in their bedroom.'

'You are a goof. Get the S.S. to do it. She's upstairs.'

Sonia went off to find the S.S. and Jerusha turned her full attention on her guest.

'You're Chris Rutherford's boy.'

'Aye. You ken my Dad?'

'Everybody kens your Dad. He's the best postmaster the village has ever had.' However, the compliment fell flat. Furthermore, her attempt to use Scots words only succeeded in encouraging the young policeman to speak the way she spoke. She carried on, 'You're the one who is mad about rugby.' With this, she tried another tactic. This time she was on target. She leaned back in her chair. She had found the pulse, as was her knack. If he was not in her thrall, he was in the thrall of the sport, which he talked about until Oswald and James appeared

Their appearance broke the spell and PC Rutherford remembered what he had come for. 'Detective Inspector Drew has asked me to get you to go over this joint statement relating to the events of yesterday and to get you all to sign it. If you wouldn't mind.'

'No problem,' said Jerusha. 'We'll go into the dining room to do it. If we have a table, we can all read it at once.' So they went through to the dining room, past the punished bunch of roses, and closed the door.

While they were going through the proceedings outlined by Constable Rutherford, Sonia was in her room, packing. The S.S. who was now away to her other job, in the village, had scrupulously cleaned the room. There wasn't much to pack, really. Sonia travelled light and, in this instance, she was a would-be traveller who couldn't, in her heart, decide whether to stay or go. Finding Jerusha living with homosexuals, blatantly, irreligiously; the flowers and her bloody hands; all those things made her question her motive for coming in the first place.

As she admitted to herself that she had come here to heal the rift between her father and Aunt Mary, now Jerusha Burnett, a small, lone tear trickled down one cheek. The rift between the adults had hovered over her childhood, both a frustration and a mystery. She longed for an aunt who would send her presents on her birthdays, who would write chatty letters, who would keep her in touch with the United Kingdom where her father came from. She tried asking her stepmother, Angela, what had happened but she told Sonia to ask her father. What she got was a tight-lipped response. Sometimes he refused even to denigrate his sister. If he had been more than human, he would have refused to acknowledge her existence. And Granny refused to say anything either. Even with all this stonewalling, Sonia had her own ideas. In her early teens, she was already fiercely religious. She would have told them if she had been brave enough that Christianity teaches people to hate the sin but love the sinner. She had no idea what Jerusha had done and the appearance of a policeman on the doorstep had succeeded in reinforcing her father's insinuations. She could not stay. And yet, she had found Jerusha warm, colourful, charismatic even. She had never met a person like her. She was creative and entertaining . . . She was in the doorway.

'Dear, sweet, Sonia, have you not finished unpacking yet?' asked Jerusha.

'No.' Sonia did not want to confront Jerusha so she lied. She also felt compelled to follow up and validate her lie. 'No. I'll just finish off.' She opened a drawer.

'Never mind that. You've got to come downstairs. We're going to play a game.'

'Don't any of you work?'

'Really, darling. I'm far too busy to work. Besides, it's Saturday. Time for fun.'

'What did the policeman want?' Sonia was abrupt because she was nervous about the answer.

'Oh, that.' Jerusha told her the story of poor Jocky's drowning. 'The Inspector sent word through young George Rutherford to the effect that it was an accidental death. I'm sorry I can't offer you a gruesome murder. Come on. Leave your things. Come and play.'

◠❧◠

Jerusha's seduction was such that Sonia followed her downstairs to the dining room where the game was to be played. The others were standing on one side of the dining table, reading the front page of one of the local weekly newspapers. Southleander had won its battle against the erection of a wind farm in the scenically renowned area. Oswald and James were applauding the victory.

'That'll please Sheena,' said Jerusha, dismissively. She went across to the games cabinet and opened it wide to reveal Monopoly, Cluedo and a number of other games. 'Here we have a banana.' She held it high, a fat yellow

48

cloth banana filled with tiles. She leisurely placed it on the table and pulled open the zip. She took out the plastic bag containing the tiles marked with letters of the alphabet and sprinkled them on the table. They were all still standing. James had put the newspaper on the sideboard. 'This game is like Scrabble, only you make up your own set. You don't score. You can be as uncompetitive or as competitive as you like. James and Oswald always play together,' said Jerusha.

'That's if you don't object,' said Oswald.

'No. If that's what you want to do. It's only a game,' replied Sonia.

'I think you object to a great many things about us,' said Oswald.

'Now, now, you two. We needn't start that way. I'll just find you a chair, Sonia, and a cushion.' Jerusha turned to the girl and, as if to her only, said, 'Don't mind Oswald. He can be very provocative. Here's your cushion. Make yourself comfy.'

They all went about sitting down, centre-table, only, when Sonia sat, a loud sound erupted underneath her. Jerusha had put a raspberry cushion on her chair. Hoots of laughter came from Oswald and James.

'Goodness me. And in public,' said Jerusha, smiling and then she, too, laughed.

After a moment of surprise and hesitation Sonia realized she was the subject of a practical joke. She hadn't farted in public. It was the cushion. She could do one of two things: either leave the room in tears or laugh with the joker. She decided that laughter was the best answer. And she roared and slapped her leg, then jumped up to remove the offending cushion. She flung it along to the end of the table then sat down again. 'It must have been the beans we had at breakfast,' she said, carrying on the joke.

'We didn't have any beans at breakfast,' said Jerusha.

'Gotcha,' retorted Sonia.

Somehow, Jerusha's little joke had succeeded in relieving some of the tension but when they'd sobered up, they remembered their game and started playing Bananagrams.

'Jerusha is always playing tricks,' James confided in Sonia as Oswald picked up their face down tiles for them. 'It's part of what makes her Jerusha and you get used to it.'

'I heard that,' said Jerusha but she was more interested in calling out "split" to start the game.

Jerusha and Sonia played in silence, making their tiles into crossword puzzles while James and Oswald whispered to each other about what words to put down and what to break up, usually concurring. Jerusha had a natural talent for word games and she was way ahead of the others. Feeling confident, she got up and had a look at what they were doing. 'Well, I'll be damned. That's a first,' she exclaimed.

'What are you on about, now, Jerusha?' asked Oswald.

'Each of us has the word "love" . . . 'All you need is love, love, love,' she sang briefly.

'You must admit the odds are against the same word appearing in three sets. We must have love on the brain. I don't know about Sonia, but we were talking about unconditional love yesterday at the picnic . . . before all the rest happened . . .' said James, faltering when he remembered falling in the river.

'Yes, we thought that unconditional love was very rare, if not non-existent,' said Jerusha. 'What do you think, Sonia?'

'That's easy,' said Sonia.

'If it's easy, tell us,' said Jerusha, now seated again. She leaned back in her chair. This was going to be interesting. What did a youngster like this know about the great topic of love? She, Jerusha, after all had vast experience of love, marriage and divorce. Sonia had only just left her childhood home and she hadn't mentioned having a boyfriend.

However, Sonia was away. 'First of all, there is the unconditional love of a mother for her child . . .'

'My mother only loved me for what she wanted me to be. That's hardly unconditional,' said Jerusha.

'But it is possible. Although my mother died when I was eight. There was hardly time for her to express her love,' said Sonia.

'My mother would have thrown herself in front of a train to save me whatever I had or hadn't done,' said James, and Oswald had a similar belief in the courage and fidelity of his mother.

'That's two mothers out of the four of us. Unconditional love is possible. What was your next point?' asked Jerusha. She was enjoying listening to a fresh viewpoint.

'That was the first point. A mother's love for her child. There is also God's love for mankind and Christian love,' said Sonia.

'Love thy neighbours. Love the sinner, hate the sin,' said Oswald, flippantly. 'You must forgive me for not being sympathetic towards this turn of the discussion. I've had experience of Christians, particularly fundamentalists, that has been less than love-filled.'

Jerusha stepped in to save this conversation. "Above all, love each other deeply, because love covers over a multitude of sins." The quote was from 1 Peter 4:8.

'Aunt Jerusha, I didn't know you could quote the Bible.'

'Years of Sunday school classes and a mother who was rabidly religious. Now, I think we should get on with our game. Trying to understand love takes a lifetime.'

They were still playing when somebody knocked at the dining room door and a head popped around it. 'I hope you don't mind me walking in like this. The kitchen door was open.' Sheena was visibly ageing but she had the figure of a young girl. Her thick, grey hair was tied behind her head in a plait. She carried a basket.

'You're welcome any time, Sheena,' said Jerusha, getting up. 'This is Sonia, my niece from South Africa. We were just having an enlightening discussion about love. We haven't put the world to rights yet.'

'Gracious. I wouldn't want to get involved in such a deep discussion,' said Sheena.

'It's an ongoing discussion but we've wound up for the time being.'

'At least it's not about the Credit Crunch. That would be too depressing,' Sheena said.

'God, no. We don't think about things like that. Now, what can I do you for?'

'I've brought you a sugar-free apple pie made with organic apples, some organic carrot soup and some plain yoghurt which was on special offer.'

'Thank you, Sheena. I'm sure Sonia will appreciate your healthy food. I, myself, am a sugar queen. And the lads, they like something sweet and tasty,' said Jerusha. 'Shall we go through to the kitchen and have a cuppa?'

'What about your game?'

'When you arrived, I was just about to say "bananas" which means I've won.' Jerusha took the basket from Sheena and led her through to the kitchen.

When she was seated Sheena pursued her chosen vocation of promoting Green principles. 'I couldn't help noticing in your transparent recycling bag that you put glass bottles in with the plastic. You must take your glass bottles to the bottle bank at the supermarket. Plastic, paper, cardboard, cans, all those go in your recycling bin.'

'You have been doing your homework. I imagine everything gets muddled up at the tip.' Jerusha sat drinking a cup of hot tea although it was after lunchtime and the household hadn't had any lunch.

'There's another thing I noticed in your recycling bag. It's choc-a-bloc with fizzy drink cans and chocolate wrappings. You know these things are not good for you. Why do you do it?'

'You are sweet, Sheena. I could eat you up.'

'You're not taking me seriously,' answered Sheena. 'I'm not casting aspersions on your weight.'

Jerusha took a long, calculated sip of her tea. 'My dear Sheena, I am a lady of acquired tastes. The acquisition of these tastes has taken place over many years. I eat, drink, laugh, love in measure comfortable to my whole being. This is something I've worked on and achieved and will fight for the right to maintain.'

'I don't really understand what you're getting at, Jerusha, but I guess you know what's right for you.'

'Exactly.'

'I can't help wishing you good health.'

'Wish it. That's a very praiseworthy thing to do.'

'And I won't give up.' Sheena said this with a wicked twinkle in her eye.

'I can guess what you're going to get onto next.'

'Yes. The bluebell wood in your fields.'

'A haze of blue in the spring beneath birches and sycamores and the occasional oak. It's a very nice dream for my property and I haven't dismissed it. The old ruin of the church restored. Picnics. At least we would not have to cross the river. Parties and champagne.'

'A priceless peacefulness.'

'You've planted this in my imagination. We'll just have to see if it grows.'

'It's not just a dream, Jerusha. It would be based on improving the environment. Trees lock up carbon absorbed from carbon dioxide in the air and release oxygen via photosynthesis. This improves air quality. It would be good for the planet.'

'Right. I've decided what we're going to do. We're going to rearrange my recycling bag.' She was on her feet and laying newspaper on the floor. Before Sheena had time to agree, she had emptied the bag onto the newspaper. 'We're going to make piles. One for cans, one for paper etc. What's this teaspoon doing here? That goes in the sink.'

Sheena entered into the spirit of the operation and studiously began to help. Jerusha gave her rubber gloves like her own pink ones and they were on their knees, sorting when Sonia came in. She stood in the doorway, silently watching.

Jerusha saw her and said, 'I bet you never thought you'd see your aunt on her knees, scavenging, up to her elbows in rubbish. Come in. Come in. Here's a wine bottle. Take that, Sonia and put it in the general bin.'

'No, don't,' said Sheena. 'Wash it and put it somewhere you'll remember to take to the bottle bank.'

'Whose instructions do I listen to?' asked Sonia.

'Oh, Sheena's. She's the expert. Now, let us stuff these things back in . . . Oh, wait. Here's my little chopping knife. I've been looking for this everywhere. What a lucky day.'

'Jerusha, you do drink a lot of fizzy juice. Look at all these cans,' said Sonia.

'I've been telling her. And all the chocolate wrappings,' said Sheena.

'Usually, rubbish is a private affair. Mine says here is someone who lives for the day. That understood, the contents of my recycling bag remain confidential. I'm closing my bag and, with it, the subject. I've got something intriguing to tell you, Sheena. She stood up and dropped the bag on the floor beside the sink. Taking off her gloves, she said, 'Come, let us wash our hands and then we can have another cuppa.'

૭૱ૹ

Over the next cup of tea she told Sheena about Jocky.

'I knew Jocky,' said Sheena.

'Who, around these parts, did not know Jocky?' asked Jerusha.

'Hmmm . . . the police were here today,' said Sonia.

'Chris Rutherford's boy came to take a statement. The Inspector told him to tell us it was probably a case of accidental death. The dead man's blood was full of alcohol.'

'Why was he out there?' asked Sheena.

'He used to go to the big house for meals but they wouldn't feed him if he'd been drinking,' said Jerusha.

'Sounds as if he stumbled into the river, fell and was too drunk to save himself,' said Sonia.

'Poor soul,' said Sheena. 'What a lonely death.'

'What gets me,' said Sonia, 'is that people in this country don't realize that they've got to die alone. It's so densely populated and so dependent on groups.'

'That may be so, Sonia,' said Jerusha, 'But Jocky had so much alcohol in his system that he wouldn't have felt much.'

'If you want to say something about today's Britain, Sonia, it's that there is too much drinking, all round,' said Sheena.

'A little tipple never hurt anyone,' replied Jerusha.

'This country is drowning in it,' replied Sheena.

'I say, drink and be merry . . .' Jerusha raised the cup holding the last of her tea.

'You'll come around to my way of thinking, eventually. Now, I really must go. I've got a hundred and one things to do.'

'Dear Sheena. Always busy,' said Jerusha. 'Do be a darling . . . on your way out, can you put these tea bags in the compost bin?'

CRILLO

When Sheena had gone they had a late, light lunch, after which Oswald and James went to Galashiels to do some clothes shopping. Jerusha remarked that they would come back squabbling because Oswald wanted to break James' hunting, shooting, fishing image and James felt uncomfortable in anything more urban that Oswald suggested. He wouldn't give any reasons why he didn't want to change his image. He just did not. While on the subject of clothes, Jerusha introduced persuasive powers on a change for Sonia. She had seen the girl wearing light, warm, waterproof and comfortable travel clothes in greys, khaki and a little turquoise. Jerusha asked Sonia if she had brought a dress across with her and finding the answer was no, she sweetly bulldozed Sonia into letting her make a dress for her. Sonia was surprised, and reluctant at first, but then decided she should be grateful for the dress was to be a gift and Jerusha was undoubtedly a talented seamstress. Admittedly, she felt more comfortable in trousers but she did have one or two dresses at home. What she didn't say was that she just didn't see wearing dresses as part of her travel repertoire. The project was settled, rather easily, and Jerusha suggested that while she was out visiting Lorna, as arranged, Sonia could rummage in her workroom for some fabric.

Happy with this plan, Jerusha set off to see Lorna. She drove her four-wheel drive—"gas guzzler"—that Sheena did not approve of, out of the drive, heading in the direction of Selkirk. Taking a road out of the town she drove along a single-track, tarred road winding through the hills and valleys of Borders countryside. At a passing place she stopped and turned off the engine. Adjusting her rear-view mirror she proceeded to refresh her make-up. More mascara. More lipstick. Then she drew out of her capacious bag a nail varnish bottle. She painted each nail with total care and attention. They became a bright, pearly pink, which clashed daringly with the maroon and gold scarf she had flung around her shoulders, the maroon trousers and sweater, the gold slip-on shoes she was wearing. When her nails were dry she started up the engine and followed a lonely path to Lorna's house. This was a great white house with blue window frames and blue door, set in all wildness with a mini-loch on its doorstep. The loch was the territory of a family of swans, the father swan hissing and rearing at anyone who came too close. Today the swans were on the far side of the loch so Jerusha didn't have to contemplate father swan's threatening behaviour. She went up to the front door and rang the doorbell. There was no reply. Jerusha waited and then rang again. When there was still no reply from Lorna she went down the steps and into the rose garden, peering through the sitting room window that was laced with trailing pink roses. She could see the state of the room.

On the floor were piles of books and newspapers; on the tables were half-drunk cups of coffee. Lorna liked her coffee and drank it very strong and black with two spoons of sugar in a cup. There were newspapers, splayed, strewn on the sofa and blankets draped on its back. The high-shelved silver display cabinet was intact but the lower drawers were open, as if someone had been rummaging in them. She looked at the low coffee table. As well as books it was laden with a silver-cleaning dip and blue buffing cloths. Lorna had been cleaning the silver.

'What are you doing?'

Jerusha started . . . Soon she relaxed when she saw Lorna standing just outside the front door on the wide top step. 'I'm trying to see if you're in. I told you I was coming.'

'Of course you did,' snapped Lorna. 'I was just putting on my wig. Lorna was wearing a wig, as she had done since her late teens. Nobody quite knew why she should do so because she had lovely, natural brown hair which might well be grey by now. As if in a gesture of self-directed anger, she would cut it with sharp, hairdresser's scissors so short that it stood out in spikes around her head. Her hair might have grown used to being abused in this way but the wigs she used were identical, thick, blonde, shaped in a bob. Now, as well as her wig, she wore rosebud pyjamas and a cosy blue dressing gown. Her slippers were navy blue with a pink rose on each of the upper soles. Jerusha noted that she wasn't wearing her glasses.

'Come out of the rose bed and come inside. I haven't seen anyone for days,' said Lorna.

Jerusha followed her inside, understandably anxious about what might ensue. Jerusha was not surprised by Lorna's appearance in her pyjamas in the middle of the afternoon nor did the disarray of the house startle her. She knew Lorna's moods. One moment she was down, and the world was a gloomy place; the next moment she was high and full of grandiose schemes. What all that she saw on entry to the house signified was that Lorna had not been taking her medication. She would tackle that subject later. Meanwhile something was missing.

'Where is Rudy?' Jerusha asked. 'She usually barks.'

'I don't know. She's somewhere around. She's a bit deaf nowadays,' said Lorna. 'You find her.' They were hovering in the hallway listening for the dog but no sound came.

'You put the kettle on. I'll find Rudy,' said Jerusha. She climbed the curving staircase, guessing that she would find Rudy in Lorna's bedroom. And she found the elderly King Charles Cavalier spaniel on Lorna's dishevelled, unmade bed. The dog was sleeping on the satin coverlet but was quite happy to be woken and taken downstairs to the kitchen where Jerusha looked for signs that Rudy had been fed. She discovered a row of unwashed dog bowls lined up on the floor and a stack of used and unused cans of dog food on a work surface. Jerusha quickly washed the bowls, moving aside other dirty dishes, and fed the spaniel some jellied meat. Rudy ate this hungrily and went through to the sitting room to be beside her mistress who was slumped in a chair beside the window. She hadn't even had the energy to put the kettle on.

Jerusha's response to the chaos was not the conventional one. She did not start to tidy and clean and scrub. Instead, she made some coffee and sat down to talk to Lorna. 'Lorna, what's going on? It's a long time since I've seen you like this.'

'I feel I can't go on.'

'Why do you feel like that? Why now?'

'I've turned day into night. I wake up in the night with terrible, I mean horrendous, nightmares and I can't get back to sleep. So Rudy and I sleep all day.'

'What are your nightmares about?'

'You know. I've told you what that wretched man did to me all those years ago.'

'Still?'

'Yes, I still feel his sweaty body on top of me, the saliva drooling from his mouth. In my nightmares I can see his face. And the pain inside my young body.'

'I can't imagine how awful it must have been.' Jerusha didn't know what else to say. She was showing a gentle, compassionate side of herself, a side which had a habit of bubbling into exuberance and zest for life. She cared for Lorna who was still her strongest link with her beloved Hamish.

'It was the betrayal of trust. My father's friend who should have been a father figure. Oh, I don't know. When will the memory go away?'

'You've tried therapy.'

'The answer is that it will never go away. Even though he is dead. Never.'

'You must let it go or you will be admitting that the rape has ruined your life. He will have won.'

'He has won. The sign of that was when Hamish married his daughter, Françoise, your predecessor. The evil witch. They were a loathsome family.'

'And she's dead too.'

'Don't I know it. There's something else I should tell you. No. Not today. I haven't got the energy.'

'The dead have gone to face judgement. You are released.'

'I don't feel free. I feel guilty and ashamed.'

'Have you been taking sleeping pills?'

'They don't work.'

'What about your other pills?'

'The honest truth is I don't know.'

'Where do you keep them?'

'In a cupboard in the kitchen.'

Jerusha went through to get the pills. She found an empty dosset box, some bottles and boxes of tablets and brought these through for Lorna to count out. But there was a problem. Lorna had mislaid her reading glasses and could not see the labels. She remembered having them last in the bedroom so Jerusha mounted the stairs once more, this time with Rudy at her heels, and searched the bedroom for the glasses. She began by stripping the bed. As she shook the sheets a grisly dog bone fell out and a single book. Jerusha picked up the book. "West Coast" by Kate Muir. Jerusha had read it and remembered nothing depressing in its covers. She put it on a side table and flung the bone out of the window. The dressing table, with wigs slung over the mirror, was relatively bare compared with her own, which held a host of nail varnish, lipstick, eye make-up, deodorants, varnish remover bottle and perfumes. In fact, this bedroom was tidy compared with the rest of the house. No wonder Lorna wanted to hide in it. However, there were no spectacles of any description. She went down the stairs again; back straight, measuring each step on the regal staircase. Some people might have been afraid of Lorna's mood. Jerusha was not afraid for herself. She had seen Lorna like this before. Over the years she had watched bipolar affective disorder distort her sister-in-law's personality. If anything, she was worried because she understood that when depressed Lorna's anger had been turned inwards.

When she got downstairs, Lorna was in very much the same position as she had left her, hunched, the corners of her mouth turned down. Now, Rudy was at her feet and Lorna was stroking her head lethargically.

'No glasses, I'm afraid. So, I'm going to do it for you.' Jerusha sat on the edge of the chair and reached out for a box of medication. 'Olanzapine. One tablet at night.'

'I always start with the Lithium.'

'All right. Which one is that?'

'In the bottles. Camcolit. I don't really need my glasses for this. I've done it so often.'

Jerusha managed to get the tablets into the mini-drawers of the dosset box. 'Do you take them all at night?'

'Yes.'

'Take them now so that I can see you do it.'

'They don't work immediately, you know.'

But Jerusha was away for a glass of water. When she got back, she asked. 'Why don't they give you an anti-depressant?'

'Because anti-depressants might end up sending me high.' Lorna swallowed the pills one by one.

'So, you've just got to cope on your own?'

'The Olanzapine is a mood stabilizer.'

'Why haven't you been taking these wretched pills?'

'Because I felt like taking them all, so I decided not to take any.'

'Had I best take the dosset box and these other pills away and bring them back in the morning?'

'I don't think I have the energy to overdose. Besides, I could find another way to do away with myself.'

'Which brings me to the question of whether or not I should 'phone your doctor.'

'It's Saturday. He's not working this afternoon. In any case, he's coming here on Monday. He's one of the few shrinks who do house visits. I'll be all right, Jerusha. I just wish I could find my damned glasses.'

The loss of the glasses was worrying Lorna, no matter what she said. It was a small thing but it just compounded the fact that she could not cope. Jerusha made her think back to when she had them last. Lorna thought it had been in the bedroom when she'd read a paragraph of her book. Her new Polish home help was coming on Monday before the psychiatrist's visit. She resigned herself to letting her find the glasses. Then, through the fog of her thinking she remembered she had put the glasses on the top of her head. 'I know where they are,' she said.

'Where?' asked Jerusha, excited.

'They're under my wig. I thought I was having undue difficulty putting it on.'

Lorna snatched off her wig, to reveal the missing specs, resting askew on her head of cropped hair. Jerusha's eyes widened and she began to laugh. All the tension of the afternoon seized her. She doubled up in her seat. 'I'm sorry. It's just so funny.'

Even more amazing was that there was a faint, wry smile on Lorna's lips. 'And now I can go back to bed,' she said.

As Jerusha drove home she mused that the finding of the glasses under the wig was as good as one of her own tricks. As she went along between fields full of grazing sheep, a song came to her mind. It was "The Rose":

"Just remember in the winter

Far beneath the bitter snow

Lies the seed that with the sun's love

In the spring, becomes the rose."

Lorna would return to normality. She always did. Jerusha noticed that she had chipped her nail polish when, after Lorna had gone back to bed, she had cleaned and tidied Lorna's kitchen and had made sure there was food in the cupboards. She knew that the home help also did the grocery shopping and there was enough food and pet food to last until Monday. As she had said, Lorna had not felt like eating.

It was late when Jerusha got home and the others were in bed. She made herself a sandwich and climbed into her four-poster. The next day she was distracted. Oswald remarked that she was 'unlike Jerusha'. Sonia had chosen the fabric for her dress, a yellow crêpe de Chine, but even this could not arouse Jerusha. She wondered if depression is infectious. She 'phoned Lorna but there was no reply. She did not really expect Lorna to want to talk to anybody but she was plagued by a vague unease. What could she do? Should she have called the crisis team? Lorna had expressly said that she should not come back until after the doctor's visit. She wanted to be alone. To do what? At best she would stay in bed all day and all night. At worst? That didn't bear thinking about but it created a pit in Jerusha's stomach. She had tried to tell the others about Lorna's plight but they did not really understand. Sonia had made an inane remark about negative thoughts being a failure to understand God's infinite wisdom.

'Come on, Sonia. I'm going to show you something,' said Jerusha in response.

'Aren't we included?' asked James.

'No. I wish your thoughts were as grey as your tracksuit, Sonia. Not so black and white. Now, come along. You'll appreciate this.'

'Is this a trick?' asked Sonia.

'No. It's completely serious. Now, come.'

CRULO

She marched Sonia out of the house. They went over a stile and across the disputed fields to the old church. Drawing a bunch of keys out of her pocket, Jerusha, dressed all in blue that day and with the freshly painted fingernails, picked out a large key. Then she paused and waved her arms over the outline of the building, saying, 'This is all mine. I own it. Do you want to come inside?'

Sonia was filled with curiosity. All the same she remarked. 'Nobody owns a church'.

Jerusha guided her inside and shut the large oak door. The interior was cool and dim. 'Look at my title deeds. I'm the one who keeps this building from falling down, who keeps the lights working.'

She switched them on which was a little shock to the calm and stillness of the church. Now they could see the shell of its former presence. The plaques dedicated to former public figures; the golden eagle, frontage for the lectern was gone. There would be no altar cloths and communion cups. What remained were the pews, the simple altar, the pulpit and the font. Unadorned, unused, but resounding with the history of church activities. Disuse could not wipe out the memory of babies baptized, wine and bread taken, prayers said and sermons given. There was a single, small Bible lying on the hard un-cushioned front pew. The stained-glass windows, miraculously fugitive from vandals, captivated Sonia.

'You have a look around,' said Jerusha. 'I'm here to pray for Lorna. So, that's what I'm going to do.' She sat on the front pew, one hand on the Bible, the other cupping her chin, her elbow resting on her half-crossed legs. And closed her eyes. She must have been praying, bent in the same posture, for a full five minutes while Sonia lost herself in a study of the stained glass window, which illuminated several scenes from Christ's life. The story of Abraham's preparedness to sacrifice his son, Isaac; a depiction of the Samaritan woman at the well; the shepherds and their sighting of the star over Bethlehem.

'Hamish would say that Christians use prayer as an excuse for inaction.' Jerusha broke the silence, regardless of what Sonia was experiencing. 'What do you think of that, Sonia?'

'That's not my experience. But then I have a way to go yet.'

'You are young. I must say, though, that some of the ideas and thoughts I had when I was your age were on the right track. For instance . . .'

'Jerusha,' interrupted Sonia. 'Tell me, why don't you go to church in a conventional way?' She came to sit beside Jerusha in the front pew, but Jerusha sprang up and stood at the front of the altar.

'Sonia, look at me. I am large. When I was at school the other kids used to tease me, to call me fatty, or fatso. How many cream cakes have you had today, fatso? I was shy and ashamed. I wanted to hide, to die even. I hated my figure. I was always going on crash diets that worked for a while then only made me eat more. My mother told me that I was just born to be fat. She said that even as a baby I had plump little limbs. Born to be fat. My first husband, Arthur, translated that into born to be voluptuous and sexy. Through him I found my image of myself.'

'If you don't mind my saying, what has that got to do with church-going?'

'Because it's a matter of being accepted.' Jerusha was moving around, using her arms, as if she were on a stage. 'I don't think the worthies of the local church would accept me in their hearts. They'd be like the children at school, criticising, but behind my back. For God's sake, I've had three marriages and what few people know, I had an abortion that went wrong and meant I couldn't have any children. As if that weren't enough, I live with two practising homosexuals. How can they accept all that and honour their beliefs?' She came down to sit next to Sonia and spoke in a serious voice: 'I am proud of who I am and mostly proud of what I have done. These things make me unique. Jerusha, the perfect wife, only now it's the perfect widow.'

'You need to be careful of pride.'

'You, lass, need to be careful of dogma.'

'Without the Bible, I would not have had the courage to come across to Britain on my own, to come here and risk . . .' She paused.

'You were going to say, contamination by living in a house like mine.'

'What I am clinging to at the moment is a passage from 1 Peter (4:8). He says, 'Above all, love each other deeply, because love covers over a multitude of sins.'

'Bless you, Sonia.' Jerusha gave her a hug. 'As I understand it you have come to Kirkfield to try to reconcile your father and me. How is that going?'

'I came to see if what my father says about you is true and I'm hoping there will be forgiveness on both sides.'

'And, is it true, what he says?'

'He has been very clear on the matter. When he will talk about you at all he says he thinks that you are fickle, irresponsible and false.'

Jerusha didn't react. She knew her brother's opinions too well.

'I think you are a person who is guided by love and, more than anything, you love life. That is something Christians sometimes forget.'

'You are a dear.'

'But I do hope Oswald and James will see the error of their ways.'

'There had to be a sting in the tail. Now, go back a bit. You talked about forgiveness. I am a great champion of forgiveness because it overpowers bitterness. I forgive your father right now. Let's see if he will forgive me. I tell you what, I'll email him.'

'No. Don't email. Write a letter. It's more personal.'

They spent a few moments at peace in the church and agreed that everything they had said in there would remain confidential. Jerusha locked the door and they crossed the field to go back to the house. After Jerusha had climbed over the stile she reached out a hand to help Sonia and the touch of their palms lightly warmed the fledgling family bond between them.

3

REVEALING SECRETS

Len came to collect Jerusha in his blue BMW, one of three vehicles he owned. The others were a pick-up truck and a large lorry, which he used to transport bulky building materials. Oswald, James and Sonia were watching through the window, unseen they thought, as Len opened the front passenger door and Jerusha swept into her seat. She had spent hours choosing what to wear. First it was the gold top with black trousers, and after that it was the navy dress. Finally, she had chosen the turquoise and gold caftan, which she now arranged around her legs in the car, her gold shoes peeping out and the gold purse resting in her lap. On her arms were rings of bangles and around her shoulders a navy cape. She smelled of lavender. She always wore lavender eau de toilette. She sized Len up as he got in behind the wheel. He was wearing a cream linen suit and a pink shirt, open at the neck revealing a provocative spread of dark hair. He seemed to her to be trying to be something he was not—subtle. She stared at his great, chunky, rough hands on the wheel and wondered if they would feel like sandpaper or an emery board. The car was also contradictory. Cream, plush leather seats and shiny, fake wood trimmings. It was an automatic, which implied a way of driving that was measured, leisurely. And this was a man who had made millions in the building trade, working his way from the bottom up. It was the same with the gifts and little niceties. The red roses, for instance, or opening the car door for her. It was as if he had learned these things in maturity. Jerusha wondered how old he was.

'Now, you're quite happy with the restaurant I've chosen?' Len asked.

'Quite happy.'

'Melrose it is, then.'

When they got to the restaurant it was only half-full. The smiling *maître-d'* showed them to their table.

'You're looking very lovely tonight, Mrs Burnett. But I've told you that already,' said Len.

At the beginning of the evening he seemed to know how to press the right buttons. Just as she loved to be called Jerusha, she loved being called Mrs Burnett because it reminded her that she was still linked to her late husband. She played with the long, gold pendant that Hamish had given her.

'Thank you. You clean up nicely yourself.'

'Oh, this is Patricia's doing. She dresses me.'

'I would like to meet your wife.'

'Actually, Patricia is all around you.'

'What do you mean?'

'I mean that most of the paintings on these walls are hers. She's a landscape painter.'

Jerusha took a look around her. The restaurant walls were covered with oils on canvas showing the wilder parts of the Borders.

'Well. They're different.'

'I know what you mean. There's nothing restful or peaceful about her style.'

'Where is she tonight?'

'She's gone to the Lake District for a couple of weeks, to paint there.'

'So, you're off the leash?'

'Something like that.'

This news gave Jerusha a little thrill of excitement; to think he had played such a royal card so early on in the evening. She steadied herself and asked, 'How did you meet Patricia?'

'We both went to an evening class in photography. Apart from property development, photography is my great love.'

'So, you have that in common.'

'That's about all we have in common.' He had played a second royal card. 'But we're not here to talk about my wife. I would like to photograph you, Jerusha. You'd make a fantastic subject. You'd be lying on your front, leaning on an elbow and one hand holding, like a cigarette, a single rose which is also resting between your pearly white teeth.' He looked at her as if he were re-arranging her right then.

'Sounds as if you've given it some thought.' She wriggled in her seat, vaguely embarrassed, vaguely intruded upon. Fortunately, the starters arrived at just that moment. 'So you photograph people?'

'Mostly, people. I leave the landscapes to Patricia.'

'I thought we weren't going to talk about your wife.'

'Well, hell, I live with her, don't I?'

'Let me tell you about Hamish. He was my third husband and the most important in my mind, in my life. He was quite a bit older than me. He was highborn, the son of an earl, and very dignified. He had this wonderful voice and he never raised it in anger, all the time I knew him. He had two children by his first wife, Jean and Claude. So, I have two stepchildren. Their mother was half-French. Her name was Françoise. Now, there's a story.

'After three marriages you have no children?'

'That's another story, a very private one. How about you?'

'No children. Too busy earning a living.'

'Well, that's certainly been successful.'

'I drive myself hard. I've earned every penny.'

'Hamish was born into a mega-wealthy family and inherited a fortune. That's the money I'm living off today. That's the land you want to build your houses on.'

'Don't lets talk business tonight, fair Jerusha. I brought you here to have a good time.'

'Brought me here? Let's get this straight. I am not somebody who can be brought or bought. If you want to get to know me, as you seem to, you will find that I am fiercely independent.'

'You'll be picking up the bill, then?' he joked, risking a provocative question to save a decaying conversation.

And it worked. Jerusha prized humour as someone else would prize kindness or gentleness. Generally speaking, she was kind rather by default than intention. As they ate their main course and chatted on a more superficial level, probably about food, she looked at him and saw that they had something in common and that was the precarious climb up the social ladder. The way he had dressed tonight, the smart casual clothes, the male *décolletage* belied a child brought up in a rough neighbourhood, she guessed. He'd have been a child with a deep, belly-hurting experience of hunger. She had come from the lower middle classes and joined the nobility by marriage. *En route*, she had learned her lessons well. The appreciation of art, the knowledge of fine food, the attempts at wit, the constant reference to servants, the cloak of leisure.

She aped the way the upper classes spoke and let up on her act only occasionally and that would always tend to be when she was alone. She wondered if Len saw these things but didn't voice them. To find out, she decided to play a trick on him. 'Excuse me Len, darling, but you have a half a pea sticking to your cheek. I thought I should tell you.'

He looked horrified and embarrassed. He slung his knife and fork into one hand and with the other took up his napkin and rubbed at his cheek. The knife and fork were pointed up in the air in a socially disgraceful way. 'Has it gone?' he asked, looking into Jerusha's eyes, helplessly.

'Gotcha,' she said, laughing.

He realized he'd been had and was briefly annoyed. When she continued to laugh, he saw the funny side and began to laugh too. They were sharing a silly joke and this broke the tension of pretension.

'I'm not even eating peas,' he said.

But someone coming up to their table interrupted their mirth. It was Tilda Morrison who lived in the village. She pulled herself up to full height, which wasn't very high, and said, 'I ken what you two are up to.'

'Can I help you?' asked Len.

'What we're up to, as you put it, is having a quiet meal.' Jerusha interrupted.

'The day you do anything quietly, Jerusha, I'll eat my hat,' said Tilda.

'It would be a long, drawn-out meal because you have plenty of those,' replied Jerusha. 'Len, do you know Tilda? Tilda Morrison. Len Robson.'

'I ken ye by reputation,' said Tilda. 'You build ugly new houses and spoil beautiful countryside. That's what property developers have done throughout Britain. Built on our natural heritage. It's sheer greed. Where do all the animals go, the squirrels and the birds? Even foxes take refuge in cities nowadays. It's always people who want more and more money. The one good thing about this Recession is that people like you, Mr Robson, will have their building work curtailed. And what of Kirkfield Village? Have you asked us? We don't want a bigger village with commuters moving in. We want to retain our character, our history and . . .'

'If I could just interrupt a minute, Tilda, we're here for a private dinner. We're not doing any sort of deal,' said Jerusha.

'Mark my words, you'll be bought by this man,' said Tilda, pink with anger.

'This is enough. You shouldn't say such things. It's libel. I will not be bought by anyone. I am my own woman.'

'Can't you see that it is not in anyone's interests, yours as well, to have ugly houses on those fields?'

'There are two things you need to consider right now Mrs Morrison. A) My houses are not ugly and B) You look beautiful when you are angry.'

The little woman with mouse-coloured hair and clothes from a charity shop was almost caught out by this second remark. Then she rallied, but her fervour had been undermined. 'See what I mean?' she asked tamely. Immediately afterwards she pulled herself up to full height and said, 'You haven't heard the last from me.' She left their table.

'Enjoy your meal, too,' Jerusha said to her retreating back.

'That's what you get for dining locally,' said Len. 'Next time, we'll go to Edinburgh. What an uptight, trite woman.' He was angry but he didn't want the evening to topple over this one encounter. 'People can be self-righteous and short-sighted. I choose to ignore her type. What are we going to have for dessert?'

Jerusha hardly heard what he was saying. For a while she was confused. On the one hand, she admired Len for getting rid of Tilda and, on the other hand, she had been alerted. Alerted to the way Len had silenced Tilda and aware that his technique just reinforced what Tilda was saying. She knew Len was trying to use his charm to get her to sell the fields but she had thought of it as a game. She'd seen going out with him as a diversion, a bit of fun. Now, she wasn't so sure. In her confusion, she did what she always did when life disconcerted her. She ate. She had not one, but two desserts, the second with the excuse that Len didn't like his *crêpe suzette*. And then she had biscuits and cheese. She began to feel more relaxed and Len was determined to maintain the equilibrium of the occasion.

'Tell me the story of Françoise,' he said.

In between mouthfuls, Jerusha told him what she knew about Hamish's first wife. She had gleaned her information mainly from Lorna as Jerusha, herself, had met Françoise only twice. Françoise was reportedly sharp-tongued, critical and imperious. She had needled Hamish mercilessly. She had endless lovers.

'That in itself might make her oversexed but it doesn't make her a bad person,' commented Len.

'It depends on what type of marriage she was in. Hamish believed in total commitment. As his wife, I went along with this.'

There was a consciousness at that table that they were both experienced lovers but Jerusha had rules about sex of her own making. She disapproved of Françoise betraying Hamish in this way.

'My marriage is an open one,' confessed Len. 'Both Patricia and I have affairs but, because of our attitude to this, they don't de-stabilize the marriage.'

'Each to his own tastes,' said Jerusha. '*Chacun a son gout.*' Yet it was a raw moment in their conversation because it resonated with the possibilities of what they would do after the meal. Jerusha switched the subject back to Françoise and it was the climax of her death that most intrigued Len. There had been a midsummer party. It was held outside, in one of the fields with a band and a marquee. Hamish wanted Scottish reels but Françoise insisted upon the contemporary dance of the time and an up-to-date band. No squeezeboxes for her. About eighty people came to the party, Hamish and Françoise's friends, including the landed gentry. 'I was there,' added Jerusha. It was after the party, in the early hours of the morning, that the mystery happened.

'Françoise just took off and walked out, into the sea.'

'. . . Bathing? With her friends?' Len couldn't quite get his head around the tragedy that was being described to him.

'I mean, like drowning. She simply drove to the beach at Coldingham, took off her clothes and waded in, never to return.'

'That's awful.'

'The police found her car and her clothes folded neatly and lying on the beach. There was no note, no indication that she would do such a thing. They never found her body. Hamish and their two children were distraught. First the worry of not knowing where she was and then the news of suicide.'

'Suicide doesn't sound in character,' said Len.

'That's what they all thought. Seven years later she was declared dead. Hamish turned to me and we married just before he died. And that's the end of my tale, for tonight.'

'And when did you say she died?'

'She walked out to sea in 1996. Why?

'Just wondered. Now, young lady, shall we go?'

Len insisted on paying the bill and she let him after a minor argument. Jerusha didn't want to be indebted to him but he was adamant. The truth be told, Jerusha considered herself above arguing over money and what with all the flowers and the chocolates etc. one teeny-weeny meal would not make much difference.

They walked across the road to the car park, Jerusha cuddling into her cape and Len, manfully, seeing out the cold. They stood by the car and looked at the night sky with its half moon and array of stars. Len didn't attempt to touch Jerusha, which left her guessing if or when he was going to make a move.

'Tilda is wrong if she thinks I don't appreciate nature,' he said. 'It's just that I like to make best use of land. I'm creative and practical at the same time.'

'Forgive me for saying so, Len, but your houses do all look pretty much the same,' said Jerusha.

'There is a formula for comfort and security. But I don't see how they can all look the same because some of them are five—or six-bedroomed and some have two bedrooms. The latter are the affordable housing everyone is on about.'

'I must say, you wouldn't have been so successful if your houses had not been what people want. Yes, there is, at present, a shortage of affordable housing in the Borders. I personally like weathered, old houses like Kirkfield. Can you take me home now, please?'

He gave her a deep look from his brown eyes, then ushered her around to her car door and opened it for her. The conjecture about what would happen after dinner, with the message that his wife was away, had seemingly come to an end. He got in and started the engine. If they had had wine with their meal, all this could have happened very differently. As it was, he didn't drink because he was driving and she didn't drink because she did not feel safe enough. However, she was wrong in thinking that he would let her go untouched.

Before pulling out of the parking place, he said, 'Look in the glove box. There's a surprise in there.'

'For me?' Jerusha loved nice surprises.

'For you.'

She opened the glove box and drew out a gold, casket-shaped box. Undoing the ribbon, she opened it up to discover truffles. With girlish delight, she asked, 'Can I have one now?'

'Of course. Whenever you like.' He drove to Kirkfield while she popped truffles into her mouth as if she had never had them before and as if she had not just eaten a large meal. As he drew into the driveway, she stopped, feeling that she must look like a glutton. He turned off the engine and swivelled towards her. The cape had by this time fallen off her shoulders and he took one of her hands. One by one, he put her fingers in his mouth, licking, lightly sucking. Then he placed the hand down on her lap and began on the fingers of the other hand. He paused. 'This is how I like my truffles,' he said.

After that he turned her face towards him and kissed her on the lips. Jerusha was melting. Len, however, made a mistake. He started to murmur in her ear and, as he felt her responding, he got carried away, asking her outright something that aroused his curiosity: 'What is your secret, Jerusha? Tell me your secret.'

'I don't know what you mean. What secret?'

'Your name is not really Jerusha is it? What is your real name?'

Jerusha pushed him away, sprang out of the car, truffles flying. 'I am Jerusha,' she shouted and ran into the house.

Left in the driveway, Len tried not to feel deflated, demoralized or even humiliated. Picking up the truffles one by one he found a way to salvage his ego by generalizing, by labelling all women as irrational. 'Women!' he exclaimed, stuffing the chocolate into the gold box. 'They're all the same.' But, even as he said it, he realized that Jerusha wasn't like all women. Her outburst had been sudden and dramatic and, by questioning her name, he had in fact found her Achilles heel. Future approaches to her would be based on this understanding and he wouldn't give up. There was too much at stake. Len wasn't used to losing. He drove off.

By the time Jerusha reached the kitchen, where Oswald and James were huddled at one corner of the table, her anger had dissolved into tears. When James and Oswald saw her standing in the doorway in distress, in unison, they jumped up and went to hug her, temporarily forgetting their own woes. One on either side of her, they entangled her in a group hug.

'What is it?' asked James, his voice soft and with timbre.

'It's nothing,' said Jerusha.

'It can't be nothing,' said Oswald. 'Look at you. If he has done anything to hurt you, he will have me to answer to. What did he do?'

'He didn't do anything,' she sobbed. 'At least, he didn't get the chance. It's what he said.'

'You can tell us,' said James.

'He tried to expose me.' She almost choked on the words.

'You mean he tried to have his way with you? I'll get him,' said Oswald.

'No. You don't understand and I'd rather not say. Would somebody please get me a whisky,' she said in a more normal voice. 'And stop throttling me,' she laughed.

'That's better. Whisky all round.' Oswald went to get the drinks.

Jerusha sat down at the table and looked at the fingers of her hands. She could see Len licking them one by one and remembered her own sensual delight. Him wanting to know her real name had been so crass by comparison. Jerusha had no idea until that moment how important the name was to her. It represented her identity, the identity she had forged when she married Hamish. The perfect wife. Somehow the name kept Hamish alive. This lifestyle, her widowhood, all this at Kirkfield did not belong to Mary Louise Patterson, as she had been called at birth. It belonged to Jerusha Burnett and all that entailed. She would not tell Oswald and James what had really happened. She would keep the incident in her store of private memories. She buried it, then and there. Instead, there was a superficial memory that sprang to her lips. 'Oh my God, I've left my cape in his car.'

'We will get it back for you, tomorrow,' offered Oswald.

'No. He will bring it back. I'm quite sure of it.' There was, after all, lurking, the feeling of his lips on hers, the excitement that Len had so clumsily trodden on. Yet, there remained the excitement. She felt alone, even with her two chums in the room. She gulped down some whisky and braced herself because she sensed what they were going to tell her about their evening. 'Sonia has been preaching at you, hasn't she?'

'You are a mind reader, Jerusha. We've had a very difficult time with her,' said Oswald.

'Where is she?'

'Gone to bed,' said James.

'She has been Bible-thumping. She wants us to mend our evil ways. She wants no less than that James and I split up. She says it is not the feelings she objects to. James and I are loving and that is good. James and I are living together and that is bad. It is the behaviour that counts. She is living in the Dark Ages.'

'And she won't let up,' added James.

'Who does she think she is? A twenty two-year-old with all the answers.' Oswald slugged back his whisky and thumped the glass back on the table.

'The whole thing is so unnecessary. I'll talk to her tomorrow.' Jerusha felt too tired to get involved in what was a huge debate, especially knowing that the conclusions to the debate would have such an enormous effect on life at Kirkfield.

'There is another thing,' said James. 'You know that this arrangement, our living here, was only ever going to be temporary while I look for a house to buy.'

'Today we saw a house that we like. James wants to put in an offer,' said Oswald.

Jerusha was silent. Her thoughts had begun to spin. She knew that the arrangement, as James put it, was temporary but the thought of life at Kirkfield without them was fearful. She felt a violent cramping in her stomach. And Sonia would go, too. She would be alone with the knowledge that her husband was dead. The S.S. would come and Sheena would visit but, on a day-to-day basis, who else would there be to talk to? 'I don't want to hear this tonight. Tell me, tomorrow. I think I ought to go to bed. Lock up, will you James?'

She slept well and late. It was eleven o'clock by the time she opened her eyes. She got up, showered in her *en suite* bathroom and dressed in a loose-fitting top, grey and green, with black trousers. She sat at her dressing table in front of the mirror and drew her Mason Pearson brush through her thick hair. She brushed it to the top of her head, twisted a band around it and she had what she called her helicopter style. Then she delved in the drawer and drew out her jewellery box. Inside, in a separate velvety compartment, were her wedding rings, the gold band and the cluster of diamonds. She put them on and admired them in the mirror. Of course, Jerusha had had other wedding rings but she had made a practice of returning them to each ex-husband. One of them, given back to Arthur, was just a plain wedding band but the engagement ring she gave back to Bert was a beautiful emerald with diamond surround that his mother had given him. These thoughts passed through her mind. She did not dwell on them. Widowhood was quite different from divorce. As a widow, she was allowed to have fond memories and to voice them. It's awkward for divorcees to talk about the good times, even although they were part of the history of a failed marriage. She didn't linger because today she was trying to focus on the present although, symbolically, she wanted Hamish with her. She went downstairs.

'That's a beautiful diamond ring you're wearing, Jerusha,' said Sonia. 'I haven't seen you wear it before.'

'Yes, it's lovely, isn't it,' said Jerusha and changed the subject.

As it was, she did not have much time to talk to Sonia because the phone kept ringing, right through what was left of the morning and into the early afternoon. The first call was from Lorna saying thank you for the visit and the answer phone messages. She was glad to report that she'd had a full six hours of sleep and no nightmares. She was going to do what the psychiatrist had suggested and normalize her waking hours, not sleeping so much during the day. Agnieska had gone to do her grocery shopping. Jerusha was relieved. She put down the phone, making a mental note to go and see Lorna soon.

The second call was a difficult one. At least, she thought it was going to be difficult when she heard his voice. Len wanted to apologize for upsetting her last night. It was not his intention. Jerusha didn't say then that she had forgiven him, nor that she had Sheena's vision of bluebell woods uppermost in her mind. She didn't tell him that but let him give his long-winded apology with the vested interest that lay behind it. However, Jerusha never could sustain bad feelings and she accepted when he said he would bring the cape around sometime. He was very busy on a site in Peebles but he would get it to her as soon as possible.

Jerusha was still holding the 'phone, musing, when it rang a third time. It was Claude, her stepson, who didn't 'phone very often. He and his sister, Jean, wanted to come and visit, for a weekend in November. 'Terrific,' said Jerusha, thinking the opposite. Jean was all right but Claude was like his mother, sharp and calculating. He rang off without asking how she was or, even, telling her how he and Jean were. They shared a flat in London. He was in computers and she was a dental nurse. Jean was twenty-five and she couldn't remember how old Claude was. He was a little older than Jean. Not an ideal stepson, he had always resented her marriage to Hamish, two years after his mother, Françoise, was declared dead. But he was that sort of character—critical, suspicious, money-minded. She thought of how she'd cater for seven people in the house for the weekend. And the thought came to her that she would perhaps, finally, clear the bedroom Hamish died in. He had moved into a bedroom of his own because, by that stage, he didn't sleep well at night. She had kept the room intact, the pyjamas he was wearing tucked under the pillows, the slippers beside his bed, the watch on his bedside cabinet. The wardrobe was full of his clothes. The tweed jackets. The corduroy trousers. Apart from her, only the S.S. went in there but no one else. The shutters were closed, the curtains too and she was the only one to possess a key to the door. The S.S. would borrow it, and then give it back. Jerusha would go in there, sit on the floor so as not to rumple the bed, and sense the feeling of the life of her husband, although sometimes the facts of his death were overwhelming.

ᠻᠣᡉᠣ

Another room in the house that brought her closer to Hamish was the study downstairs. She went there now to write a letter to her brother, Saul. The study was a large room opening off the passage, which led to the utility room. It was snugly carpeted in fawn. The centrepiece was a great wooden desk with a green leather top bordered with lines of gold patterning. She had married the things he had left behind with her business needs as the new owner of Kirkfield. On the top of the low bookshelves that lined the room she had displayed his fountain pens, a rubber stamp, a full letter rack, an even fuller pipe rack. The stand-up calendar and the diary were open at the date of his death, twenty—third of March 2005. She allowed the S.S. to dust these treasures. Hamish was a man of simple tastes. He heartily rejected computers and television. There was still no such thing as a television supper at Kirkfield. Jerusha had bought the TV and the computer with some pangs. She felt she was betraying his principles but, as she was twelve years younger than him, she thought he would understand her wanting to tackle technology, as she put it.

The thing about Hamish, she mused sitting in front of the computer, which took up a large portion of the desk, was that he was so desperately shy. It coloured everything he did. That's where she came in. Her apparent confidence made him feel that everything was all right. He had suffered deeply when married to the critical but beautiful Françoise. Her Hamish was happy when he was out shooting or fishing. He would come back ruddy-cheeked, invigorated, refreshed, alive.

Jerusha let her thoughts pass over memories of Hamish. She had learned not to try and stop them. He was still part of her. However, she now had a mission and that was to write to her tyrannical brother Saul who had refused to speak to her for over ten years. She started up the PC and opened Microsoft Word. The blank page. 'Dear Saul', she typed. Or, maybe she should address it to his wife, Angela, too? And what about mother? No, as she had advanced Alzheimer's she was hardly likely to understand or register the quarrel between her children. Saul had fetched her to go and live in Johannesburg about seven years ago. Mother lived in their granny flat and, according to Sonia, it was very difficult to care for her. It was only the security fence and the guard in the violence-torn city that stopped her wandering off through the suburbs in search of something in her head. No. Not mother. Not Angela. She would address the letter to Saul but, when she came to write her first sentence, she dithered. She decided to draft the letter by hand, first. She took out some A4 sheets and wrote, 'I have forgiven you' because she had, the other day in the church in the field with Sonia. She continued, 'Can you forgive me?' Her mind fudged this.

A hundred questions were crowding in, the main one being what was there to forgive? She was very clear about what she was asking him to forgive. She knew that her behaviour during her second marriage, to Bert, had made Saul angry. She had had an affair that broke up not only her marriage but the marriage of her lover. And then, it was pointless because she and her lover did not stay together. Jerusha wondered if she should try to make Saul sympathize with the boredom and loneliness of her life with Bert. Saul thought Bert irreproachable and thought her fickle. So, how would time have changed that? He probably never even thought of her now. No. He must think of her because of Sonia. Why had he let Sonia, young, vulnerable, impressionable, visit her? This could be a sign that he was coming round to a little understanding of her way of thinking.

Jerusha had, in her way, forgiven Saul for being judgemental but there were things she could not forget. Even although he was younger, he had bullied her when she was little and teased her for being fat

One day, after school, she was summonsed to see her mother in her workroom where she was sewing a new school uniform for Mary. This was in the days when Jerusha was still called Mary. She was unable to buy uniforms big enough for her daughter.

'It's a good thing you like sewing, Mum,' said Mary.

'It's a bad thing that you eat so much. When is it going to stop?' Her mother stared at her over her specss. 'What happened to that diet I put you on? My guess is that you've been getting your friends to give you sweets. Look at Saul. He is the perfect weight.'

Mary had been getting sweets and doughnuts from her friends but she wasn't going to confess to her severe mother. She felt embarrassed and frustrated that she couldn't lose weight. Every night she prayed to God that he would make her slim, then she could please her mother and not have to cringe every time someone looked at her. 'I'm trying, Mum,' she said. 'It's very difficult. I feel faint on that diet.'

'So, you do scrounge food from elsewhere. This has got to stop. It shouldn't be as difficult as you say. Your father, Saul and I are all a normal size. What's wrong with you? We give you all you need, make sure you get exercise, take you to church. After all I've done for you this is how you repay me, by eating a disgusting amount.'

Mary had heard this all before. She peered over to see how the pleated black skirt was progressing. It was nearly finished. Her mother began sewing the waistband and when she had finished, she said, 'Here it is. Look at it. Big enough to fit an elephant.' She held it up.

Mary was crying now.

'That won't get you very far,' said her mother. 'You don't want pity, Mary. You want to face up to life and exercise discipline. So the next time you want a cream doughnut or a chocolate, hold back, and restrain yourself. The Lord will do the rest.'

'Do you think I like myself like this? I hate myself. No-one ever felt so awful.'

Her mother stopped her from running out of the room. She held Mary's arm in a tight grip. 'There is another matter I want to speak to you about.'

Mary had stopped crying now. She was on the defensive. She knew what was coming.

'At the parent teachers meeting last night, they all had one refrain about you. It was "could do better". What am I to think? Are you lazy as well as . . . ?'

'. . . As well as what?' Mary asked.

'You know. What I've been talking about.' Her mother was running out of steam and Mary seized her chance.

'Mum, I have to go to my hockey match.'

'Goodness. When?'

'In about three quarters of an hour. I have to change. Are you coming to watch?'

'Not today. I'm very busy today. Remember; don't let this go to your head. Being chosen as goalie for the second team is not the same as being chosen for the first team.'

'I'll remember,' said Mary. She just wanted to get out of there.

'Before you go, I just want you to know I've been saying these things for your own good.'

'I know, Mum.' Mary kissed her on the cheek, which had the intended effect of being disarming.

'Good luck,' said her mother.

Mary raced upstairs and washed her face, tied her hair in bunches and dressed in her burgundy gym tunic, plimsolls and burgundy blazer with the gold braid; she went downstairs to get her hockey stick from the cupboard under the stairs. Little did she know that Saul was lying in wait. She was ferreting for the stick amongst golf clubs and umbrellas when she heard the door shut behind her and she was alone in the dark, dank cupboard. She tried the handle of the door but it was hopeless. Saul had locked her in. She cried and ranted but no one heard her. Her mother must have still been upstairs. She felt for her watch but she couldn't see the time. It slowly, agonizingly became apparent to her that she had missed the match. The reserve would be playing in her place. Her place, at the goal.

In the hours that followed, she periodically banged on the door but no one came. She found some newspaper and tried to slip it under the door, hoping to knock the key onto it on the floor. However, the door was flush with the floor and the newspaper would not fit under it. The cupboard smelled fusty. Years later, Jerusha, as Mary had become, would remember that smell and the feel of the winter coats touching her head as she crouched down in despair.

It was her father who discovered her. He had come for his golf clubs. By that time it was definitely too late for the hockey match. 'Daddy!' She rushed out and clung to him. Her father was half-inclined to believe that Saul had deliberately locked her in so that she missed her match but her mother couldn't see anything wrong in Saul. Everyone in the household knew that the door of the cupboard had to be kept locked or else it flew open. Saul was just being conscientious, if indeed he had locked it at all. Saul denied locking the cupboard and said how sad he was that his sister had missed the match she had been looking forward to so much. Father declared the incident a mystery and, watched disapprovingly by his wife, gave Mary an extra helping of roast chicken that night. And the potatoes, crispy potatoes. She was almost consoled.

❦

Now, father was dead and mother was with her beloved son in South Africa. Jerusha had been staring into the memory of malice and misjudgement. She cast off the anger the memory evoked and, opening one of the desk drawers, reached into her stash of chocolates.

As she had been staring into space, remembering a childhood of a girl called Mary who didn't have the courage and aplomb of the woman who had re-named herself Jerusha, she hadn't got very far with her letter.

However, her subconscious had been on the go. She had decided what to write and did so on the computer, going over the two-page document to clear up typing errors and misspellings. She signed the letter and put it in a good-quality envelope, which she addressed to Saul in South Africa.

Jerusha showed the letter to Sonia later that afternoon in her workroom where she was measuring Sonia for the yellow dress. 'I must get this right,' she muttered and Sonia thought she was talking about the measuring but Jerusha was also thinking hard about how to tackle Sonia's behaviour towards Oswald and James. This thrust of her thoughts had, temporarily, to be put aside because Sonia, understandably, wanted to talk about her father.

'Dad has changed, you know.' She held up her arms to have her bust measured. 'He's not so strict since Granny became ill. He loves your mum and he is so sad to see her losing her faculties. I remember grandpa. His death didn't affect my father so much.'

'It was at his funeral that I last spoke to Saul.'

'Have you tried?'

'Yes. He would not answer my 'phone messages, even put the 'phone down on me. I received no reply to my emails. What was his reaction when you said you were coming here?'

'I haven't actually told him I was coming to see you,' confessed Sonia.

'You little fibber. Well, he'll know after he gets this letter.'

'He wants me to find a job and settle in Britain, maybe go back to university and study maths this time. Being a banker he is very supportive of my interest in mathematics.'

'And Angela?'

'She wants me to get out of South Africa because of the way things are going there. And she is South African born.'

'I hope I've got my maths right in these measurements. You can put your fleece back on.'

The measuring done, Jerusha was flipping through boxes of patterns. She knew the one she wanted. She had used it many years ago to make a dress for herself, one that had now been passed on. If she could find it, she would adapt it for Sonia who was now fingering the yellow crepe de Chine in anticipation. Like Jerusha, she was in two minds about something. It was very kind of her aunt to spend time making a dress for her but she didn't usually wear dresses; she wondered when there would be an occasion for it. She wouldn't tell Jerusha this, for the world. She was completely taken in by Jerusha's charisma and creativity. She desperately wanted her only aunt to be accepted by her rather severe and rule-bound father.

As if she had read Sonia's mind, still searching for the pattern, Jerusha said abruptly, 'In this country we champion tolerance and freedom of expression.'

'I've been to Speakers' Corner in Hyde Park in London. It is great.'

'A bit closer to home. And I have to say this because the peace of the household depends on it. You have been somewhat intolerant of Oswald and James' relationship.'

'The Bible is the only authority,' said Sonia.

'What they are doing is not illegal, or anti-social. They are just people and, for a short time, they will be your neighbours. If you can't love them, like I do, at least let them be.'

'I'm afraid of becoming de-sensitised.'

'That's not likely to happen, is it?' Jerusha looked up. 'Is it?'

Sonia did not answer. Instead, after a pause, she said, 'I'll stop trying to save them and I'll pray for them instead. After all, we're all sinners. Me, too.'

'What, pray, are the sins you have committed in your young life?'

'Oh goodness, too many to recount.' She giggled in embarrassment. 'Mainly the sin of going my own way, of taking risks and disobeying my parents. The Bible is always my only authority, not my dad, not governments, not preachers nor teachers. The question is, do I read it well? Have I understood?'

'Do you regard it as sinful to have come here?'

'To try to heal the rift between brother and sister. That can only be good.'

'It's a bit presumptuous, if I may say so. What if I had not wanted to speak to your father?'

'Then I would have gone back to London and continued looking for a job. I can see by the way you're studying it that you've found the pattern.'

'Yes. I will have to check that all the pieces are here. Look. It's ideal.'

The picture of the dress had a rounded neckband and gathered in folds at the bodice, coming in at the waist and falling to the hemline. There followed a discussion about what length to have and they decided just above the knee. A further discussion ensued about what shoes she would wear. They discovered they wore the same size shoe and Jerusha took Sonia through to her bedroom to choose from the dozens of pairs that she owned. They found a yellow pair, almost identical to the colour of the cloth.

They left girlie things behind and set off for the village to post the letter. They grabbed their coats and as they went outside the front door, down the steps where the driveway swept around before them, they saw a figure standing beside the gateless gateway. Tilda was pacing, holding a placard that said, 'Keep Kirkfield Village green' and on the other side it said 'No property developers here'. She looked defiantly at Jerusha and Sonia, neglecting to greet them. They stopped.

Jerusha, also, missed out the greeting. 'You're jumping the gun, Tilda,' she said.

Sonia kept quiet, not knowing exactly what this was about.

'Tilda, it's coming on to rain. Are you still going to stand there? I can't think who would see you, anyway.'

'Somebody has got to stand up for our rights. Or, the whole countryside, our natural heritage, will be spoiled.'

'I can see where you're coming from . . .' said Jerusha.

'Can you? I don't think so,' snapped Tilda. 'You don't care. All your type care about is money. It's always money.'

'Tilda, you must understand, I haven't decided what to do with the fields yet. It depends on many things and these are not easy times. For instance, I have to have the slates on the roof replaced soon. Scaffolding costs a lot of money and they will be doing the whole roof, which is over a hundred years old. That's just one expense.'

'Do you expect me to feel sorry for you? No. I will not rest until you've said no to Len Robson. He is just trying to charm you into agreeing. He will not have any time for you once you've agreed. Mark my words.'

'Thank you for thinking of my welfare,' said Jerusha, 'But I can look after myself. Come on, Sonia.

⟨∾⟩

They walked down the road and into the village. As they went past Sheena's house, past the pub, past the village green, Jerusha joked about the wording on Tilda's placard. Each slogan could have more than one meaning if you thought about it. 'Keep Kirkfield Village green' could refer to the green used by villagers that they were passing, as if that were under threat. Then, 'No property developers here' could mean that the said developers did not exist in this area. Jerusha had to laugh because she was suffering a little discomfort. She liked to keep the villagers on her side. When she had first come here they had been very frosty towards her. It was only by winning around people like Sheena and Chris Rutherford that she had genuinely started to feel at ease in her environment. Of course, she always acted as if she were at home in the village.

Just as they reached the post office the rain began. A bell tinkled and they closed the door behind them.

'Ah, Mrs Burnett, just in time afore the rain.'

Now, it was not just drizzling, it was pelting down against the door and the post office windows. Inside, by the counter, there was a blazing Calor Gas heater. There were rows of sweets and newspapers and a whole section devoted to stationery and cards. The room was small and the shelves cramped, the produce squashed together. The post office service was carried out behind a slatted glass cubicle. The post box was outside.

'Mr Rutherford, let me introduce you to my niece, Sonia Patterson, from South Africa.'

'How do you do, lassie,' said Chris Rutherford.

'Your son, George, was up at the house recently. He's a fine lad,' said Jerusha.

'Aye, to do with that tramp what drowned.'

'Yes, Jocky, the homeless man.'

'If you ask me he was worse the wear for drink and couldnae save hiself.'

'There's a lot of drinking goes on in Britain,' said Sonia.

Jerusha wanted to prevent her getting on her soapbox but could not quite think how to do that. Fortunately, Chris cut in, 'There's nae harm in a dram or two but folks just dinnae seem to leave it at that. Now, young ladies I have my own introductions to do.' As if from the shadows, a man appeared beside Chris. 'This is Mr Rachid Khan who will be taking over from me as I'm retiring.'

'Pleased to meet you,' said Mr Khan. It turned out that his family originally came from Mumbai but he himself had been born in England. He was moving his family up from Luton in Bedfordshire to get some space and country air. They all chatted about where each of them came from and the merits of the beautiful Scottish Borders.

'And what's the gossip, Mr Rutherford?' asked Jerusha.

'Tilda is up in arms and making a nuisance of herself. But, ye ken that. The wee one in Harris Grove was poorly with suspected swine flu but he turned out to have pneumonia, nothing to do with swine flu.'

'Is he all right?' asked Sonia.

'He is on the mend. Dinnae trouble yourself, lass. Nothing much else at the moment.

When the rain eased, they said goodbye and went to post the stamped letter. Jerusha thought the stamp cost an extortionate amount but she duly posted it in the post box outside. Chris had told them they had missed that night's post but that it would go the next day. Both women said a silent prayer as the letter disappeared through the mouth of the box. Jerusha could now not change her mind, could not withdraw her petition to her brother so that all she could do, she felt, was brace herself for no reply, a hostile reply or, if the timing were good, a note of forgiveness.

4

FALLING LEAVES AND AUTUMN SHADES

'Oh my God!' Jerusha called upon Heaven as she stared into the large fridge. 'We've forgotten about Sheena's apple pie.'

'What do you mean we? You have forgotten about it,' said Oswald who never cooked, never looked in the fridge, except for milk for his breakfast cereal.

'Doesn't matter who,' said Jerusha. 'The fact is that somebody has put it at the back, at the bottom of the fridge. We haven't touched it and Sheena is coming around this pm.' She bent down and pulled out the pie, deftly made using brown flour, and fruit from Sheena's apple tree. Jerusha took a sharp knife and vigourously stabbed the defensive pastry, curling around a foil tray and decorated with pastry flowers. The knife would hardly dent the pie. 'It has got rigor mortis,' said Jerusha.

'Here, let me try,' said Oswald but the pie defeated him too.

'There's only one thing for it. The bin,' Jerusha said as if she were pronouncing a death sentence.

'I hate waste,' said James who had so far been strictly observing.

'Well, I wouldn't try and bite into it. It would crack your teeth,' said Jerusha. 'No. It has to go.' She took the whole thing and dumped it in the swing bin for non-recyclable waste. Then she crumpled up some newspaper and stuffed it in, on top. This was in case Sheena happened to use the bin. She needn't have worried because by the time Sheena arrived the bin bag had been filled, taken away outside and a new bag had settled in. This was the result of a surprise for Jerusha that Oswald and James had thought up. More about this later. Jerusha was oblivious to what was going on in the kitchen, the room she thought of as the heart of the home, for she went upstairs to get on with Sonia's dress. Sewing was something she took very seriously. It came under the umbrella of work. She put a DO NOT DISTURB sign on the outer door handle, a sign she had picked up from a hotel during her world travel with Hamish. The problem for anyone other than Jerusha was that the words were in Arabic. The rest of the household, however, soon learned to treat the sign as an English equivalent and they left her in peace.

It was the apple pie incident that prompted James to think up the idea of clearing the food shelves. He had a vested interest because he was a competent cook and produced dinner every second night, according to a rota that seemed to please everyone, even Sonia who was very much an amateur in the kitchen but eager to learn. Now that, through the passing of time, she was on course to treat Oswald and James as individuals, not defined by their 'gayness', she was to become hungry to learn from James about preparing food.

That morning, Oswald and James were a little disgruntled. They had heard that their offer for the house they wanted had been rejected because it was not high enough. James insisted that he'd offered what he thought the house was worth. They were having an emotional time of it because looking for a house is tied up with knowing yourself. How do you want to live? Who are you? After all, Oswald came from a terraced house in Edinburgh and James came from a stately home in the Highlands of Scotland. They had formed a relationship out of two seemingly different characters

Yes, they had things in common. Neither of them liked football or rugby. Both would be glued to the TV during the Wimbledon tennis. Oswald had played tennis, himself, before the heart attack. And squash. In general he had been a keen sportsman. James must have been the last person on this planet to get his first pair of denim jeans. He imagined they were permanently starched and would stiffly peer at his backside in the mirror. James was old-fashioned and his shining quality was gentleness. He worried about Oswald's heart, especially when Oswald went out jogging. Now that they were to set up home together, they discovered similar likes and dissimilar dislikes. James had always wanted to write a book, a biography of someone still to be specified. So, he wanted a home with space and silence. Oswald wanted space and grounds in which to walk. He fancied having some animals, such as a dog or cat and also chickens and, perhaps, bees. Their tastes were definitely country tastes. The Borders could satisfy these.

James had a lot of money. Oswald had some left after his marriage broke up and the kids were catered for. But it was James who was going to buy the house. As he did not want to commit his funds, Oswald agreed with this even although if he and James were ever to split up he would be homeless. He had no knowledge of James' will that left everything he owned, capital and property, to Oswald. Furthermore, they were toying with the idea of a civil partnership. This would most likely follow once they had set up home.

Now, they had begun the task of clearing the shelves. They were pulling everything out of the cupboards and the larder and putting them on the worktops so that the kitchen looked like a sale room. When that was finished, they had the presence of mind to clean the cupboard shelves. While they were waiting for these to dry they raked through the produce to see what was there. 'Look at this. Two packets of Angel Delight,' said James. 'I've never had Angel Delight under this roof.'

'You're meant to look at the use-by dates. And then we can bin the out-of-date stuff.'

December 2006. That was the curry paste. August 2008. That was the tin of green beans. April 2006. That was the mixed herbs that had been stuffed at the back of the cupboard. They went through all the refill boxes of herbs and most of the rest were in date.

'This flour is well past its use-by date,' said James holding it in the air. 'I bet you it's full of weevils.'

'Watch out. You're spilling it,' warned Oswald, but he was too late. James in his eagerness to get the flour to the bin had left a trail across the tiled floor. He hastily dumped the torn packet into the bulging bin. They were sweeping the floor when James suddenly remembered he had to collect his suit from the dry cleaner so that he could wear it to Jocky's memorial service the next day.

That was why, when she came downstairs, Jerusha found the kitchen vandalized with Oswald and James nowhere to be seen. 'Men!' she exclaimed and looked with sinking heart at the mess. This was how Sheena found her, Sheena having kept up her bad habit of coming in the back door without knocking.

'You look as if you could do with some help,' Sheena said.

So they set to, rehousing the food stuffs, roughly in the order Jerusha knew and trusted. 'Looking on the bright side,' she said, 'If they had put everything back I would not have been able to find anything.'

'You see this de-caffeinated tea?' asked Sheena, holding up a box. 'It's no good. They use so many chemicals to get out the caffeine and it doesn't work anyway. You'd be better drinking herbal teas.'

'Not now, Sheena. I'm putting up with enough change as it is.'

In the short-term Sheena decided to censor herself, all the while taking Jerusha's lead about where to put products in the cupboards and the larder. She said something neutral. 'I've been making marmalade this morning.'

'Oh.'

'Jerusha, if you want me to go . . .'

'Och, Sheena. It's not you. I'm annoyed with Oswald and James.' She did not say so but she was aware that her mood had to do with the shock of human contact coming straight after three hours of silently creating a garment, hours of self-expression and aloneness. 'You're a good soul, Sheena. Please stay for a cuppa when we've finished this.'

Sheena, who had been poised to go, relaxed. 'I was making this marmalade with pink grapefruit and lemons when my husband came into the kitchen, which is not as big as yours but equally as nice. The mixture was boiling rapidly while I waited for it to reach the setting point. Anyway, Derek came in and asked how I was, which I thought rather an odd question for a husband to ask a wife. It's more a question that is already stated in a marriage relationship. Still I answered him. I said I was happy. That was the very word I used. Happy. And I was, busy in my own home with my dog and making pink marmalade that Derek would like and that I could give to friends.'

'What was his reaction?'

'His face broke into a warm but patronizing smile, as if I were a child who had unwittingly said something endearing.'

'People aren't enquiring about your emotional health when they ask how you are.' Jerusha was getting a little breathless with all this reaching up and into cupboards but they were nearly finished. 'They are expecting a description of your physical health, if that.'

'I don't know why people are so gloomy. If the weather is bad it is not news. The weather in this country is predictably unpredictable. Take today. It's cool but the sunshine is glorious. Why not say that? And the autumn colours are magical. The most people can muster, occasionally, is that it is a grand day. Bless them for trying. But I'm wittering on . . .'

'Not at all. I agree with everything you've just said. The sunshine is glorious today. I'll put on the kettle.'

They sat at the table in the bay window, lit by a shaft of light. Jerusha emptied a packet of biscuits onto a plate. Sheena allowed herself one only. Jerusha had more. She looked at her friend and saw predominantly grey hair. Sheena was, at a guess, nine years older than Jerusha who hadn't a single grey hair. Jerusha was forty-two and had not yet begun to feel the inevitable grasp of time running out.

'I'll give you some marmalade when I've labelled the jars,' said Sheena. 'Oh, here is Sonia.'

⟨oⅢo⟩

Sonia flipped off her borrowed wellies in the back porch and walked in wearing thick socks. By now Jerusha's feeling of solitary productivity, the aftermath of it, had dissipated and she was able to genuinely welcome Sonia to the table. Sonia did not drink tea, so she had juice and biscuits. Her cheeks were rosy and she had grass in her hair. When Jerusha pointed this out Sonia told her she always liked to lie down on the grass and look up at the sky, watching the clouds change shape. Making pictures out of those shapes. She had done that since she was a little girl. She picked the grass out of her hair, a little self-conscious.

'You are happy today,' said Jerusha.

'Where did you go?' asked Sheena, ignoring Jerusha's remark.

'Jerusha said I could use her car so I went over to Tweedbank and walked by the river.'

'If you like walking so much, you could take my dog for a walk sometime,' said Sheena.

'That would be great,' said Sonia. 'I miss the dogs back home.'

'She'd have to get to know you, first.'

'She's a collie called Tammy. Jerusha will vouch for her.'

'Tammy is a darling,' said Jerusha.

'Come around tomorrow and meet her.'

'I'd like that,' said Sonia.

'Wait a minute. You're coming to Jocky's memorial tomorrow.'

'Do I have to, Aunt Jerusha? I didn't even know this Jocky character,' argued Sonia.

'The more people there to show their sympathy, the better. I can't make you come but I would like you to.'

'After the memorial then, Sheena.' They fixed a time and Sheena's active mind moved on. 'I've been meaning to ask you, Jerusha, whether or not you've met the new postmaster?'

'If that is a question the answer is yes,' said Jerusha.

'We met him yesterday,' said Sonia.

'I don't know if he'll have more difficulties stemming from his family coming from Mumbai or from being born in England,' said Sheena.

'Any incomer has difficulties, as you put it. My guess is that most villagers will be charmed by the novelty,' said Jerusha.

'He is most charming,' said Sheena, a statement which did not require an answer, a good thing because the front doorbell rang at that moment. Jerusha went to answer it. Opening the door, she found herself facing a *femme fatale*, carefully holding in two hands the cape she had left in Len's car. The woman, who had dyed red hair worn in a bob, was all in black, right down to skin-tight leggings tucked into high-heeled boots to the black sweater she wore under a black leather jacket. Although Jerusha tried to hide it, anyone could clearly note her surprise. 'I'm Patricia,' said the woman, helpfully.

'Len's wife? The artist?'

'What's the matter? Just because I'm an artist, do I have to wear clogs and snagged sweaters?'

'Dear Patricia, how rude of me. I did have you fixed in a stereotype. I guess I'm not the only one. You've brought my cape. How kind of you. Do come in.'

'Can't stay, however much I would like to. I have to get back to the studio. I have a painting on commission,' said Patricia.

'I thought you were meant to be in the Lake District?' Jerusha was emboldened now and curious.

'I was but the weather was foul and the light was all wrong. To tell you the truth, I had an argument with my friend and companion. The trip was a disaster.'

Jerusha was puzzled. Perhaps both Len and his wife were lying about Patricia being away? To what purpose. She had thought the absent wife to be part of his botched seduction. Now, here she was in person delivering the cape when Len could have delivered it himself. Jerusha was genuinely intrigued by this couple. She smiled broadly at Patricia, in command, bold, positive. The round-bodied and the tight-waisted looked at each other, sizing up each other. Len's business card, which had been resting on top of the folded cape, slipped and fell to the ground. Who was going to pick it up? After a little hesitation, Patricia bent down and retrieved the brown and orange card.

'Oh, I almost forgot,' she said, handing the card to Jerusha, 'Len has three tickets for the ballet at the Edinburgh Festival Theatre. He wondered if you would like to come?'

'Three tickets.'

'You, me and him.'

'I didn't know Len liked ballet. I wouldn't have thought . . .'

'Len has many sides to his character. Even I am kept guessing. Must go. Let him know about the ballet.' She strode to her car and drove off, waving at Tilda through the window.

Jerusha stood on the doorstep for some moments, looking through the protesting Tilda. She liked a puzzle. Her first conclusion was that Len was protecting himself from their aborted intimacy and her outburst. He was putting his wife between him and her so that he could still be in line to buy her land, without any awkward analysis or threat of a repetition of what happened after their dinner in Melrose. On the other hand, he might be thinking of her, might be trying to reassure her that if his wife were around he would not go too far. She vaguely looked at Tilda standing in the cold. She wondered if she should offer her a hot drink. Tilda would have known who Mrs Robson was and was no doubt seething. Might it not be best if Jerusha gave in now and stopped seeing the Robsons altogether? Mature woods, silver birches perhaps, would be a haven for birds and animals. Not many people can claim that they have their own bluebell woods. Hamish would have liked this. He detested modern housing. But Hamish did not have to do the accounts any more and she had worries even if she did not substantiate them or do anything about them. She wished him back with her. Len Robson wasn't a patch on Hamish.

Yet Jerusha was always on the lookout for something novel and she had found enough clues to stimulate her interest in Len and Patricia. First of all, their relationship appeared to be loose and free. Yet, she was suspected that they were so deeply joined together that no-one could tear them asunder. Yes, they might have affairs and entanglements but, ultimately, the ones who really lost out were not Len and Patricia, but rather the third parties. Secondly, this being established, Jerusha was convinced that Len actually fancied her, apart from what he could get out of her. What emerged was a cocktail of excitement and stimulation that Jerusha, at this moment, could not resist. She would go to the ballet. She would contact Len. She looked at the business card and flipped it over. On the back, in handwriting, were the words: 'A rose by any other name would smell as sweet'. She suspected Patricia hadn't noticed this because the card had fallen face-up on the step. Jerusha smiled to herself and went over to Tilda.

'It's not all as simple as it seems, Tilda. Would you like a cup of coffee?' But Tilda was not talking to her. It was not only her stare that was frozen. She did not show a flicker when a silver car came through the gateway and into the drive. Jerusha went over to see who it was, expecting a stranger as she did not recognize the car. It was Lorna in a brand new Toyota. Her wig was firmly in place as she got out of the driver's seat but she was wearing not one, but two cardigans, orange and black respectively and a light blue polo neck sweater with a large stain on the front. The tweed skirt and sensible shoes were Lorna's usual style.

She did not greet Jerusha, but said, 'Isn't it fantastic? Brand new and paid for.'

Jerusha had a look around the car, admiring it, not knowing much about the mechanics. She knew about miles to the gallon but carburettors and, even, batteries were out of her domain.

'The last one was ten years old,' Lorna said. 'It has gone for scrap.'

That seemed sensible but then Jerusha noticed a set of golf clubs on the back seat. 'Who are they for?' she asked.

'Me, of course. Don't be silly,' Lorna said.

'But you don't play golf,' protested Jerusha.

'I do now,' smiled Lorna. 'Anyone can change. I've changed. I'm not dead yet. No more the frumpy old depressed Lorna. I've only got one life. I intend to live it. And this is my starting point.' She stroked the car.

At that point Oswald and James returned, complete with dry-cleaned suit and up-to-date property guide. They spent some time admiring Lorna's new car and then all four of them went inside the house. With six people, including herself, in her kitchen, Jerusha felt content. She loved to gather people around her and to offer them hospitality. She wondered what Sonia and Sheena had had to talk about in her absence—marmalade, the evil of plastic bags, recycling, dogs,—whatever it was, they were interrupted. Lorna marched them outside to see the car, which gave Jerusha a chance to confide in Oswald and James. 'Does Lorna seem strange to you?'

'Everyone gets excited when they buy a new car,' said Oswald.

'It's not just the car. She has bought herself a set of golf clubs and heaven knows what else.'

'That's strange. I didn't know she was learning to play golf,' said James.

'Lorna can afford it. She's rolling,' said Oswald.

'That's not the point,' Jerusha replied and then they had to change the subject because the three women returned.

'As I was saying,' said Jerusha, 'Sheena and I cleared up your mess. We put everything back in the cupboards. You'll thank us for that.'

'Really, Jerusha, some of those food stuffs were way out of date. The cupboards badly needed a clear-out.'

'You should not leave a job half done,' said Jerusha.

'We had to go into town,' said James.

'So, I gathered,' said Jerusha.

'Jerusha, it was no problem. It is done now,' said Sheena, trying to keep the peace.

'It's just not nice confronting the wreckage of your kitchen.'

'Would anyone like a cigarette?' asked Lorna, changed the subject more by accident than design. Jerusha stopped berating James and Oswald and focused entirely on her dear Lorna. She was now convinced, based on what was happening now and on previous occasions, that Lorna was going high.

'No one else smokes,' she said and seeing Lorna take out a packet of cigarettes, preparing to light up, she took her gently outside. 'Most people smoke outside, nowadays,' she said.

Jerusha stayed with Lorna while she coughed and spluttered her way through a cigarette outside the back door. 'Lorna, you are going high,' she said.

'I know.'

'That's a mercy. And what do you do when you're going high?'

'Act like a rag doll.'

'Do you want to give me your cheque book and credit cards. Remember, like we arranged?'

'It's too late'

'No. It's not. I'll look after them for you.'

'They are in my handbag in the kitchen.'

'Okay. The other thing is that I want you to stay here tonight.'

'No. I want to go home. I'd just disturb everyone here with my waking in the night.'

'If that's the case, I'm going to get Oswald and James to drive you home.'

Lorna agreed to this plan and they went back in to get the handbag, and to talk to James and Oswald. Sheena sensed that the household needed privacy and she left after arranging to introduce her dog to Sonia after the memorial service the next day. Sonia went into the sitting room to watch TV. Oswald and James rallied. They would take Lorna home. When they were so compliant, Jerusha decided to forget the matter of the messy kitchen and she started to make dinner. Oswald would drive the new car on the way there and join James in their car on the way back. Lorna got into the front seat and allowed Jerusha to do up her seatbelt. As they were driving off, she said to James, 'They didn't tell me they were going to give me a chauffeur with the car. Jolly good thing. What ho!'

'Do you know who I am, Lorna?' asked James.

'Home, James. Yes, of course I know who you are. You're James, my half-brother. Only we don't say half. You're my brother. Same father. Hamish was my real brother. I wonder when he'll be back.'

'Hamish is dead, Lorna.'

'Can't hear what you're saying. Speak up.'

'Hamish is not coming back.'

'He'll be here. Now, if you don't mind, I'm meditating. It's all to do with the breath, you know.' Lorna pretended to

125

meditate for the rest of the journey. In reality, her mind was spinning with all sorts of conversations but she was still clinging to sanity and she was still aware that she was heading for the mania side of bipolar. Later that evening, she was to become totally unaware that she was ill but, for now, there were moments of lucidity.

They reached the house in its setting in the hills with the small loch a calm pool of water at its doorstep. Oswald was already there. Lorna snapped open her seatbelt and rushed into the house, telling them to bring in the things from the boot of her new car. They opened the boot and found three more sets of golf clubs.

'My God, is she crazy or something.'

'That's probably it,' said James. This was not the first time he had seen his sister in a manic phase. What he felt now was utter helplessness. Oswald lugged the golf clubs into the house and set them down in the hallway.

Lorna insisted upon giving them mugs of lukewarm coffee. She was determined to show them she was all right, that she could give them hospitality. Rudy rushed around at her heels, then promptly urinated on the carpet. Lorna made no attempt to mop this up but, too late, did she let the dog go outside. Lorna kept tugging at her cardies and at the neck of her stained sweater. In between, she made an effort to be a good hostess, interested in her guests. Oswald and James were perplexed, clutching at anything that seemed to them normal. They began to talk about house hunting and Lorna latched onto this in an astounding way: 'You want a house. Buy this one. I'll be moving out. One of the changes to my new life,' she said.

'Wait until you are well, Lorna' said James.

Lorna ignored that and continued: 'It would be ideal for you. No neighbours. Just the sheep and the hills and the loch. There's no price on privacy.' She was talking very quickly.' 'We could do a deal, without estate agents.'

'Sounds a great idea,' said Oswald, forgetting to suspend disbelief.

'We'll think about it,' said James with a warning signal to Oswald. 'We have to sleep on these things.'

'Sleep. You talk about sleep. I haven't had a decent night's sleep in months. I long for . . .'

She was interrupted when the 'phone rang. James answered.

'Good to have servants to answer the 'phone.' Lorna winked at Oswald.

It was Jerusha on the 'phone, saying the crisis team was on its way. The men should stay until the team arrived. James was not to tell Lorna. That might have proved a problem and James imagined that they would have to spin out their chat but Lorna had other ideas. She behaved as if they had already gone. She got up and went through to the hall. Choosing a golf club, she began to practise her swing. Apparently, she did not have any golf balls, which was a mercy. Not too long afterwards, the crisis team arrived and Lorna tried to ignore them too until it became apparent to her that she must entertain her 'guests' who had come a long way to see her. These people were different. They refused coffee and one of them mopped up the dog urine.

Oswald and James were relieved when they at last travelled down the rutted road and thereon to Kirkfield, away from the confusions and distortions of Lorna's illness. Oswald remained detached to an extent but James had found himself caught up and spinning, and he let Oswald drive home. James was particularly concerned because Lorna had said, 'Goodbye, young man' as if she no longer knew who he was.

Jerusha was worried. Should she have insisted that Lorna stay the night? Should she have gone to stay the night with her? She had seen Lorna having episodes of illness before and this was a serious one. And so, Jerusha was relieved when the local mental hospital 'phoned late that night to say that Lorna had been sectioned, compulsorily detained. She had completely lost sight of who she was and where she was. No more moments of lucidity. She was over the edge. The nurse explained to Jerusha that Lorna had been stopped when she went out to her car, on her way to look for a golf course at midnight. The hospital charge nurse was there at the time and, after initial protestations, Lorna had gone docilely in the ambulance. She had been sedated and was now lying quietly on her bed, apparently hallucinating. The nurse was telling her this because Jerusha was Lorna's 'named person'. That is someone Lorna had elected to protect her rights and to see that her 'advanced statement' of how she wanted to be treated was adhered to.

Jerusha was satisfied that Lorna was now under constant care and determined to visit Lorna as soon as possible. However, she was tense when she went to bed and could not sleep. Her voluminous nightie twisted around her flesh as she tossed and turned. Jerusha knew Lorna's illness well but she couldn't help but be troubled. At least it would have an end. All she could do was be there when Lorna returned to normality. She finally fell asleep

⁓

The next morning she felt thick-headed and sluggish but she jollied herself through breakfast until she felt almost ready for the day's events, whatever life might throw at her. After breakfast she dashed into Galashiels to the florist and bought a large bouquet of chrysanthemums in autumn shades and contrasting daisies. Back at Kirkfield she set about dressing in a dramatic black outfit with a deep *décolletage*, bordered with lace. The memorial service was to start at eleven. At least, they called it a memorial service. In fact it was to be a celebration of Jocky's life with no priest present. Hazel Gifford had issued an invitation in the local press where there had been a story about Jocky's accidental drowning. His funeral had already taken place in Glasgow. Jerusha tried to forget about the body she had seen lying in the water and to remember Jocky, the vendor with the banter.

James, Oswald and Sonia were all ready and they piled into the four-wheel drive, letting Jerusha take the wheel.

'I hope it's not going to be morbid,' said James. He was feeling as drained by Lorna's behaviour as Jerusha and he slouched in the back seat, holding the bouquet of flowers.

'We're going to celebrate a life,' Jerusha said, 'But, of course it will be morbid. The man is dead.'

'I don't know anything about Jocky,' said Sonia.

'That makes two of us. Perhaps they will tell us about his history?' suggested Oswald.

As Jerusha drove over the bridge and entered the long avenue leading to Sir Iain's stately home she was humming to herself. She was trying to motivate herself to lift her spirits. Whatever she said, she too was willing this to be a light-hearted occasion. She parked beside several other cars in the front driveway and the four of them headed across the grass and towards the river. The scene they walked into was full of expectant faces. There must have been about thirty people, mainly dressed in dark clothing, gathered together with a sense of belonging that had been Jocky's doing. They all shared a common feeling of sadness and a need for solace. Among this group, four magazine vendors stood out, a multicoloured collection wearing handouts or charity shop clothing. Hazel Gifford had collected them from town and had brought them here. They had already begun to tuck into the sandwiches on two white-clothed trestle tables, along with coffee and tea.

The gathering circled a small hole in the manicured grass beside which lay a sapling, a plaque and a spade. Hazel Gifford stepped in front of these to start proceedings and the general talk eased away.

'Welcome,' she said, going on to make a few more introductory remarks. Then she said, 'Jocky was a big man, Big in stature, big-hearted with a big sense of humour. This copper beech that we will soon be planting, young though it is today, will itself grow big, a reminder of growth and expansiveness and all the better things in life. This river behind me, that you can hear rushing on, is both beautiful and treacherous and I hope that Jocky's sad death is a reminder of both these things. Beauty and danger are a given when water flows.'

James cleared his throat.

'Jocky was among the people who are homeless, some of whom are here today. I must confess that my interest in them is not purely altruistic. By inviting Jocky in for a good meal on occasion I was doing the proverbial good deed but I was also re-assuring myself that I was not homeless. It could happen to anyone and I can't think of much that is worse. Perhaps you have similar feelings. Apart from, just liking the guy.'

There was a relieved titter.

'And now before we get William to plant the tree and hammer in the plaque, Annie wants to say a few words.'

Annie came forward in little, timorous steps. She was muffled in a large ginger coat and on her feet were well-worn, ankle-length boots. She had a nest of black hair. Her eyes were on the ground as she spoke softly about what she felt for Jocky. Her voice was so soft that it was difficult to hear her. 'He was my friend,' she seemed to be saying. Her audience was absolutely still. 'He knew what I had been through. I could talk to him. He didn't judge me. I will miss him. I am already missing him.' She stepped back abruptly, tears wetting her face.

Only the very determined had dry eyes after that. Jerusha dished out tissues to James, Oswald and Sonia. It was a few minutes before Hazel took command. She asked William, the gardener to plant the tree and when he had done this, tipping in the earth with spade and pressing it down flat around the slender trunk, everyone clapped. 'The plaque reads *Home at Last*. I hope everyone likes that choice of words,' said Hazel. William hammered the plaque firmly in the ground.

Jerusha began to look for familiar faces amongt the gathering on the riverbank. Tea, coffee and sandwiches were being served. She greeted a few acquaintances and then met up with Chris Rutherford, the postmaster.

'Good ceremony,' he commented and then, as if he were proud of the knowledge, said, 'I hear that Lorna has been taken into hospital.'

'Who told you that?' Jerusha was surprised and annoyed.

'You know what the post office is like. I hope she is all right.'

'She'll get some rest. Won't you have some coffee?' She had seen Sheena. She wanted to talk to *her* about Lorna.

'I thought I'd come and show some support' said Sheena. She didn't make it clear whom she was supporting. Jocky? Beyond support. The homeless? Could be. Hazel? She didn't mix in her circles. Ultimately, it was fear of homelessness. Sheena, like Hazel, had a dread of falling to the bottom of human endeavour. 'I notice no one mentioned alcohol. Beautiful and dangerous was the closest Ms Gifford came to mentioning the river of drink.'

'That would have sullied his memory. You must allow people their sentimentality, Sheena,' said Jerusha.

'It looks as if Sonia is at a loose end. Let's go and speak to her.' Chris was by now talking to someone else. They went over to where Sonia was standing on the fringes of a group.

'Thought you could do with someone to talk to,' said Jerusha.

'I feel as if I've made a new friend,' said Sonia. Her eyes were shining.

'Who is that?' asked Sheena.

'Jocky,' replied the girl.

'Come on. Come and meet my dog. I'll take you home,' said Sheena.

5

IN A SPIN

The dress was finished and the scaffolding was being put up for repairs to the roof at Kirkfield. The simultaneity of these events may seem of no consequence but, as it happened, they combined to bring a radiant change to life at Kirkfield and, in particular, a change to Sonia. What occurred was to lead her to ask Jerusha for an extension to her stay and was to distract her from her moral battle with homosexuality, or from her homophobia.

Jerusha had risen early to finish the hem of the dress and to iron it. This accomplished, she had taken the completed garment to Sonia's bedroom. She knocked on the door and when there was no reply, she opened the door a fraction and called in. Sonia was in the *en suite* shower. Jerusha pushed open the door and strode in, laying the dress on Sonia's unmade bed. She was excited by her achievement and keen to see the dress on Sonia. 'I've put your dress on your bed. Try it on and come and show me,' she called.

'Okay,' came the watery reply.

Then Jerusha descended the sweeping staircase, put on her purple anorak and went outside to see how the scaffolding was going. She was fascinated by the Meccano-type procedure; the way the poles were erected vertically, then horizontally and then wrenched together, platform and ladders fixed at various stages. 'Do you think I can go up there?' she asked Callum Thomson, the young man in charge of erecting the scaffolding.

'Sure thing,' he replied. He was wearing a blue hard hat, an orange luminous waistcoat, baggy trousers with pockets and dusty boots. The workmanlike nature of his clothing didn't stop Jerusha from noting that he was a very handsome man. He had laughing blue eyes and blond hair that licked the edges of the hard hat. He was one of those people who seem to approach everything from a positive angle.

'Are you not afraid of falling?' she asked.

'We do this every day. It's all secured so it's a calculated risk. Changing your mind?' He challenged her.

'I'm just wondering if it will bear my weight.'

'We winch up some heavy equipment. Not that I want to compare you . . .'

'Never mind.'

'You'll be all right, Ma'am.'

They were standing near the front door looking up at the scaffolding. When they looked down they saw Sonia come out, barefoot, wearing the yellow dress. Jerusha had never seen her in a dress, except for trying-on sessions, and she was startled at the transformation. Callum was transfixed. There was immediately something between Sonia and Callum. Jerusha saw the chemistry. Put another way, it was as if each of them had thrown a small ball and, acting together, they had each caught the other's ball at exactly the same moment. The perfect catch. This was not just attraction. In split seconds, they had fallen in love.

Forgotten, but nonetheless entangled, Jerusha wanted to do something to reduce the intensity of the moment. She made the introductions and Sonia and Callum were only too pleased to shake hands.

'You suit the dress,' said Callum, getting things the wrong way around. The dress suits you, is the way that Jerusha would have put it.

'Thank you,' said Sonia, without taking her eyes off him.

'Mrs Burnett is going to come up on the roof sometime. Maybe you'd like to come up too. It's a grand view from up there.'

'I'd like that,' said Sonia, unable to summon up the courage to say more than just a few words.

'The dress is a success,' said Jerusha. 'Let us go and show Oswald and James. Leave Callum to get on with his work. His mates must be wondering what he's doing. Come on, darling.'

⁂

Meanwhile James and Oswald had been planning their own bit of sorcery. They started off by lounging in the sitting room after breakfast, discussing Lorna's house.

'Don't forget, she was not all here when she offered it to us She might sing a different tune when she's well,' said James.

'But it would be nice. It's a fantastic property. Out in the wilds, with the loch and . . .'

'You are not bearing in mind that I don't like water.'

'That shouldn't be a problem. You need never go near it. You could just watch the birds from a distance. I wonder if there are fish down there?'

'You don't get it. I would worry about you fishing that water. I'm not just self-centred.'

'The loch aside,' said Oswald, 'Think of the house. It's a splendid design. That awesome hallway with the fantastic staircase. The views from the windows. We would have enough room to spread ourselves. And the garden is great.

Roses climbing around the window frames. Mature plants but room for new seedlings. I always fancied gardening.'

'I can see you now, in your wellies, turning the soil. Then in winter we would make a log fire. And sit. And read. Or, you can watch television, with no one to bother you. We could have the space all to ourselves. No one to pry or protest. I'm getting the idea now, aren't I?' James was tapping his imagination.

'Yes, but, as you say, we'll have to wait until Lorna gets out of hospital,' said Oswald.

'We'll have to wait a lot longer than that. She has really shot up high this time,' said James.

'Cocktails on the lawn, walks in the hills, watching the sun go down. We could invite Jerusha around when we get tired of each other's company,' said Oswald.

'I'll never get tired of your company,' said James.

'Thanks. The feeling is mutual. We can invite Jerusha for cocktails and meals, anyway,' said Oswald.

'She has been suspiciously serious recently. We haven't had one of her tricks for ages.'

'I tell you what,' said Oswald, 'Let's play a trick on her. Turn the tables as it were.'

James sat up. He had been reclining on the *chaise longue*. 'Good idea,' he said.

'She'll be coming in from talking to the roofer shortly. What if she was to have an encounter with some water? It's that trick she used on us,' replied Oswald. 'It's simple. All we need is a plastic cup filled with water.'

'We balance it on the top of the inter-leading door which is slightly ajar,' continued James.

'She opens it, dislodging the cup and, hey presto, she is soaked!'

'Masterful.' James lay back. 'You go and get the cup.'

Oswald went to the kitchen and soon found what he needed. He positioned the door and placed the full cup on top. He then settled back in a chair to await the arrival of the master trickster. They had seen Jerusha from the window but Sonia was out of sight on the doorstep. They were not to know that Sonia had had a life-changing experience on that doorstep.

Callum had gone back up the scaffolding, climbing up the ladders with a feeling of elation and a look in his eyes which puzzled his fellow workmen. For some moments, Sonia was rooted to the spot but Jerusha put her arm around her and led her into the house. She did not refer to the scene she had witnessed but said, 'The dress is a wow, I think.'

'Oh, yes,' said Sonia, eyes sparkling.

'Let's go and show the others,' said Jerusha, taking off her jacket. 'I think they're in the sitting room.' She guided

Sonia, ahead of her into the room, like a mother caring for a numb daughter. Thus, Sonia was the first to appear before a horrified Oswald and James. As she pushed the door open the cup wobbled indecisively then fell and knocked Sonia on the head before tumbling to the floor. Its contents, the water, spilled through her hair and dripped down onto the bodice of her new dress. There was a hush. Three pairs of eyes waited to see Sonia's reaction. However, they need not have worried because nothing could spoil her mood.

'I guess this was meant for Jerusha. I thought she was the one who went in for practical jokes.' Then, to their relief, she laughed. 'It's the second shower I've had today,' she said.

'A little water never hurt anyone,' said Jerusha, secretly triumphant that the joke had backfired. She was still mistress of the tricks.

Sonia went off to hang up the dress on her cupboard door and to dry her hair. She sprang up the steep stairs like a person immune to interruptions, motivated by emotions that were new to her.

Picking up the empty cup, Jerusha left Oswald and James in the sitting room and when she'd thrown the cup into the kitchen sink she, too, climbed the stairs. With no one watching, she was able to give in to her own emotions. The vibes between Sonia and Callum had stirred old feelings to do with a relationship she had lost. Hamish. She could never forget Hamish. She went into his bedroom, the room where he had died, took up one of his cloth caps and put it on her head. She slithered into a sitting position on the floor beside his bed. Now, for her, Hamish was alive. In her mind's eye. In her memories. She let him come to her.

⟨~~~⟩

Jerusha had first set eyes on Hamish at the Midsummer Night's party he and Françoise threw at Kirkfield. 'Pleased to meet you' were the first words he had spoken to her. He put out a hand and shook hers with a strong grasp. He was sitting in the open night by the marquee in a semi-circle of chairs, second chair from the end. He sat, with winged collar, black bow tie and kilt, tartan unknown to Jerusha at the time, a wine glass in one hand, as if he were holding court. His presence was comfortable, comforting and warm. Jerusha didn't then realize how shy he was without alcohol. He was not drunk but nicely mellow. Later, she was to treasure the memory of that handshake, so honestly given, so auspicious. If his were an act, he was very good at making her feel pleased to be met. James had introduced them and slipped away.

'This is my good friend, Derek. Oh. He seems to have departed.' Jerusha had noticed a dark-haired man get up and walk away. 'Never mind. You will meet him sometime. Lives in the village. His wife's name is Sheena. Lovely person. But, do tell me about yourself. You've come with James?'

Jerusha sat down next to him. 'Yes. I met him in Edinburgh. Friend of a friend,' said Jerusha, not deterred by the fact that this was the brother of an Earl. She saw that he prided himself on being able to talk to anybody, titled or humble, and she wondered which class he had her in. On her part, at that point, she was determined to be herself. Yet, he surprised her in what he said next. It was so direct.

'You know that James is gay?'

'Of course. Why?'

'Just so long as you're not heading for disappointment. Such a waste, I think. A good thing he came out after my father and stepmother had passed away. They would have been heart broken.'

'He is a brave man.' Jerusha defended James.

'And you, Mary, you live in Edinburgh?' asked Hamish.

'Yes and I'm not really Mary any more.'

'Oh. This gets interesting. You are changing your name?'

'I've lived the life of Mary for far too long.' Jerusha drew deeply on her wine.

'You're not that old, surely?' smiled Hamish.

'No. But I've lived through many experiences. For instance, two marriages.'

'Oh dear, I'd like to hear about that sometime.'

'It's not just that. I seem to have careered through life. I want to hold it still. I want to be Jerusha, which means the perfect wife.'

'And, is there anyone in the offing?'

'Not at present.'

'It's a lovely name. Are you going to pronounce it Yerusha?'

No. For me it has a hard 'J'. I want to be Jerusha.'

'I'll forget I've known you by any other name. To be the perfect wife, particularly if you haven't a husband is a great challenge, indeed.'

'Now, you're laughing at me,' protested Jerusha.

'My dear, forget my little joke. I sense that you have noble intentions but, seriously, you'll not hold life still. One, because it's impossible and, two, because you're too full of zest. Marriage both constrains and tantalizes. I wonder if you've met my wife, yet. She is Françoise and half-French. The latter excuses a lot of misdemeanours. People tend to find her tantalizing.'

Their conversation was interrupted by the arrival of Hamish's children. The twelve-year-old Claude dressed in a kilt and Jean in white with a sash. Jean crawled onto her father's lap, almost knocking over his drink.

143

As Jean tumbled onto her father's lap—sitting on his sporran must have been pretty uncomfortable—Jerusha realized she had been cocooned in talking to this dignified man. With the midsummer's day sky above and the house looming large nearby; the open fields lying fallow, leading to the river; the church then still in use, distant but not distant; she had felt strangely grounded, strangely safe. She would remember these feelings, remember liking Hamish but not yet loving him. The children insisted he go and dance.

'You know I only do reels,' he said.

'Mummy likes disco. Come on, Daddy.' Jean tugged at his cuff.

The four of them, Hamish, Jerusha, Claude and Jean, went onto the dance floor. Francçoise had insisted they have guitars and drums, with a squash box for the reels. They made a space among the gyrating revellers and held hands, the children between the adults. Jean started jumping up and down. Claude was more controlled. For Jerusha, ever after, Claude was to give the impression he did not want to be where he was. It made him appear disdainful. Enthusiastic, energetic Jean, her little hand was sticky. It was quite hard to dance in this manner and the group soon split up. Jerusha found herself dancing with a stranger, Vernon Brown, a lawyer from Edinburgh. She lost sight of Hamish.

'I've looked after Hamish's legal and financial interests ever since he came to the Borders,' said Vernon. 'And we go fishing together. The Tweed is renowned for salmon.'

'Why did Hamish and Françoise come to the Borders?' asked Jerusha.

'Didn't want to live in the shadow of the Old Pile. That is his parents' stately home in the Highlands which Ewan, his brother the Earl, now owns. Apparently he has divided a section of it into flats. Those old building are beastly to keep going.' Vernon was also wearing a kilt but he wore a jabot, a frilly collar.

Among her fellow revellers were men dressed in black tie. The women, without exception, wore flowing long dresses, some in white with tartan sashes. It took her a little while to work out that the party was divided into Françoise followers and Hamish followers.

She turned, from contemplating the company, back to Vernon, 'Is there a Mrs Brown?' she asked.

'She's an invalid, not up to parties. I have a young son.'

'I'm sorry to hear about your wife but it's nice that you've got a son. You haven't got a Scottish accent. Where were you born?'

'Auld Reekie. Born and bred in Edinburgh. Wouldn't have it otherwise. And you? Where were you born?'

'Surrey. I'm one of the dreaded English. Or, should I say dreadful? I'm in Scotland trying to decide what to do next after a messy divorce.'

'The number of divorces these days is tragic,' said Vernon, above the music.

He would be one of those who considered divorce an easy option, she thought.

'Pity I'm not a divorce lawyer,' he said.

I hazard a guess that you're raking it in anyway, she thought.

'You wouldn't want to go there. It's all about money and sex, so they say,' she said.

'You're right. I wouldn't want to go there,' he said, shying away from the subject.

'My ex-husbands have taught me an awful lot.' She would have gone on but Vernon made an excuse to leave the dance floor. He clearly did not want to hear what Jerusha had to say about marriage and its aftermath. His marriage would be rock-solid, inviolable except for the onslaught of illness, happy despite her being an invalid, she thought with a little bitterness. She would not try that topic of conversation again that night.

During dinner she sat next to a pleasant woman called Sheena. In those days, Sheena was a Twiggy type, all bones and angles. Jerusha's first husband, Arthur, had taught her to love her own plumpness, to present her rounded flesh with pride. She had given up any thought of dieting long ago, during that first marriage. Nonetheless, it was a case of the plump and the hungry-looking talking at dinner.

The emaciated Sheena and her husband, Derek, were both trained teachers. He taught Maths while Sheena was an English teacher. Jerusha had taught at Primary schools although she was not sure she wanted to go back into the classroom. She loved children and the long holidays but she did not care for the staff room politics. Sheena, herself, was thinking of leaving her school. Derek wanted her to be at home. He wanted a wife who would have his supper ready and waiting when he came home after a hard day's work. He coached sports teams in the afternoons. Sheena talked a lot about Derek, his likes and dislikes and Jerusha found herself willing Sheena to say something about Sheena. Eventually, she said, 'I'm awfully ordinary, really.'

'That you can say that, makes you extraordinary,' said Jerusha.

'She is extraordinary.' Derek, who had been eating and listening in the seat next to Sheena, contributed. 'She is ex . . .' he hesitated as if he had heard a drum roll. Françoise was making a late entrance. Talk subsided as the lady of the manor stood elegantly in the entrance to the marquee. She was wearing a scarlet, clinging long gown. Her hair fell in jet-black curls against the light. It was apparent to everyone that she was loving this. One arm moved upward, a hand cradling the back of her head, then down again. She paused. Then, as if in response to some unheard signal, she began to move. She swaggered, red net petticoats undulating and swirling, past the band instruments, along the dance platform, over the grass and came to a standstill in front of her husband. Hamish stood up out of politeness. Françoise came to rest on the chair reserved for her and the murmur of voices took up its refrain.

'That was spectacular,' said Jerusha to her neighbour.

'Yes. Françoise likes to make an impression,' said Sheena, ostensibly without judgement.

Derek was silent. He appeared to find his food very interesting that evening.

Jerusha went over and over her reaction to her first glimpse of Françoise. She did not get a chance to talk to her for Françoise came late and left early and it was only in retrospect that Jerusha learned that she had completely disappeared. If she'd been particularly astute she would have noticed when the night was still young that Derek went absent too. It was only afterwards that Hamish told her about Françoise's lovers and told her that, at that time, Derek was one of them. Hamish told her this with sadness because Derek was one of his closest friends. They went fishing together, drank and talked together and Sheena was a good friend also. Hamish appeared to feel no animosity towards Derek. Any bitterness he felt was directed at his wife. She ensnared men, played with them and then tossed them aside. According to Hamish, Sheena felt the same way. She thought Françoise used people, not just men, and she forgave her husband his aberration. Françoise would not be allowed to break up their marriage. They still loved each other. A part of Sheena could not forgive herself for not being as glamorous as Françoise but, as she became older, she grew in self-esteem and the relationship between her and Derek deepened.

After dinner Jerusha danced and she reeled, and she couldn't tell afterwards who her partners were. She thoroughly indulged in the present moment. The concatenation of divorce, the guilt and recrimination, were drowned by the music. She was still ready for more when, at half past midnight, James came to tell he he wanted to go home. After midnight, couples had been drifting off, leaving empty wine glasses, vanquished bottles and full ashtrays. Discarded, used napkins littered the tables. Yet, the band was to play until two and there were several stalwarts though the hosts had gone. A nanny had sent off the children to bed at eleven o'clock precisely. Jerusha was sorry that she wouldn't have a chance to say goodbye to Hamish for he had captured her imagination. She pictured him as the perfect husband—to a wild and wayward wife.

It was James who later told her that Françoise had disappeared that very midsummer's night. Some said she was missing; some said she had committed suicide. James was of the opinion that she was swanning around in Europe under a different name. Police were investigating. They had found Françoise's car at Coldingham beach car park. Her clothes had been left lying on the beach and a set of footprints led into the sea. Police had questioned Hamish, Lorna and James. It seemed to Jerusha that they could not question all of the eighty odd people who had been at the party. Jerusha tried to think what she would say if they asked her to act as a witness. All she could think to say, if they asked her, was that she had seen a self-confident, fickle woman who would not in a million years commit suicide. How could they even contemplate it? After all, there was no body.

Some years later, Hamish told her about the diary. Françoise had made a last entry in it the day she disappeared. It was ambiguous but could have indicated that she was going to end her life.

⟨⟨⟨⟩⟩⟩

It was about a year after the party when Jerusha was still in Edinburgh, working in a pub, that Hamish contacted her. She came home to her flat in Bruntsfield and found an answer phone message saying: 'This is Hamish Burnett. Do you remember me? I remember you. Can we meet?'

Of course, she remembered him. Hamish had remained seated in her mind over the year that had passed. She 'phoned him. 'I was sorry to hear about your tragedy. Is there still no word of your wife's whereabouts?'

'Thank you. No. No word from Françoise. To tell you the truth, I'm trying to forget all that.'

'Let me help you to forget,' said Jerusha. 'Meet me in the pub where I work when I'm off duty and we can have a chat.'

'I've got a better idea. You come out to Kirkfield for the weekend and we'll go to the Goat and Lamb pub in the village.'

'Sounds all right.'

'I've got a confession to make.'

'What's that?' She was expecting something serious.

'I've never been in a pub in my life.'

'Where have you been hiding? You're kidding me?'

'No. Really. But I want to do things differently now. Want to catch up a bit.'

She had arrived at Kirkfield with far too much luggage. She had not known what she would be required to wear. He definitely had posh friends so she might be required to dress for dinner. This thought excited her. She loved dressing up and for some time she had been making her own clothes. Yet, if he wanted to go to a pub, did he want to dress casual? Was that part of the catching up bit? The start of her relationship with Hamish was full of questions. He seemed to see her as someone who could help change his way of life and then he had very definite boundaries which to some extent were unconscious, in-bred, like the way to toss a salad and when to eat it during a meal. He was old-fashioned about the way to treat women. He was compelled to rise when a woman, or man, for that matter, came into the room. He would help her on with her coat and open the car door for her. All this Jerusha found enchanting. She began to act the part of a countess. After meeting several of his friends, she began to mimic them and she started to adopt Hamish's boundaries. For her, the 'lounge' became the 'sitting room'; the 'couch' became the 'sofa' and 'dessert' became plain 'pud'. Her adoption of a new persona happened quickly and indelibly but there were also parts of her lifestyle that impressed him and he changed, too. They were giving and taking customs and principles.

It was a big step for Hamish to set foot in a pub. He did so like a kitten, awake and aware when it is first let out in the open air. The Goat and Lamb was a traditional country pub with red velvet seating arranged in sections, small stools and tables and bar stools. It had a red-patterned, carpeted floor. The draught beer was at the bar and the spirits lined up behind it, in front of a large mirror. On either side of the mirror were large models, one of a goat and one of a lamb. On the walls were sepia photographs of the Kirkfield Village of the past. These interested Hamish and he examined a couple of them, letting Jerusha go and get their drinks. He then sat hesitantly on one of the padded seats. He could not see the whole pub from where he sat but he noticed that it was quite full. Customers sat in semi-circles around the walls and there were some on the bar stools; also, some standing waiting to order drinks. This was the part he'd been apprehensive about. Who would he know?

Who would witness his initiation into pub culture?

'The barman says he never thought to see you here,' said Jerusha, putting their drinks on the table. 'Recognize anyone?'

'There are some familiar faces. I'm so bad at names.'

'So, how come you've never been in a pub before? I know you drink at home.'

'Mummy, God rest her soul, always said they were inferior places. Frequented by low life . . . that sort of thing.'

'And you did not question her judgement?'

'Never thought to, on that score. Preferred to drink at home or at friends' houses.'

'So, what do you think of the sleaze?'

'The what?'

'This pub experience.'

'Jolly good, actually.' He smiled 'Let me freshen your glass. I think I'll make mine a Scotch this time.' They had both been drinking draught beer. She watched him gather courage and pretend he did this all the time. She was struck by his dignified movements. His breeding showed wherever he was. Hamish joined a queue at the bar, a throng of townies who had come to this country pub to prime themselves for going clubbing in Galashiels. They were young and noisy and sexily dressed. Hamish got chatting to them and one of them pushed him through to the front of the queue. 'I've got all night,' she said. He ordered their drinks from Iona, an outgoing, convivial woman with an outspoken cleavage who had the knack of letting a customer think he or she was the only one in the world, the only one who mattered. 'Never thought I'd live to see the laird in here,' she said. 'You're very welcome. You must make it a habit. We treat our regulars well,' she said. 'We're all very sorry about your wife going missing like that.' Hamish nodded a thank you, as he always did whenever anyone mentioned Françoise's disappearance. 'Who is that with you?' Now Iona was being nosey.

'She's a friend. Her name is Jerusha,' he said, paying for the drinks and taking the glasses back to where Jerusha was sitting, smiling.

'Great to be served, rather than serving,' she said.

Hamish was surprised but Jerusha wasn't when they were joined by several different people as they sipped their drinks. They were there to be sociable and everyone wanted a piece of Hamish's tragedy. Jerusha saw him becoming hot and bothered but he was always polite. He tried to deflect talk of Françoise and get them to talk about themselves. He behaved as if it were essential that he gather information about the villagers, not because he wanted gossip, like Iona, but because each human being is important. He was above being critical and suspicious.

Then, just as the stools around them were empty once more, Derek, who had been drinking on his own behind the partition, so that they had not known he was there, joined them. He wasn't drunk but he'd had a few.

'Mind if I join you?' Derek asked, sitting down in reply to his own question. 'I miss our chats, Hamish.'

'I've been a bit of a recluse since Françoise went missing,' said Hamish.

'We both know she is dead. You know she's dead and I know she's dead,' said Derek.

'You've had too much to drink. Mind what you say Derek.' Hamish's reply was sharp and then he toned it down. 'You'll think differently in the morning.'

'But, we . . .' said Derek

'We are waiting to see if she turns up. If she does not it will be seven years before she is pronounced dead. Six years, now. She has gone, Derek, and it is all over.'

'But, we . . .'

'We have to get on with our lives.'

'Have it your way. No doubt, the truth will out some day. I'm not drunk enough to argue with you,' said Derek.

'Jerusha, here, is helping me get on with my life. You remember Jerusha?'

'From the party. Yes. Hello.'

'How is your wife? Sheena, is it?' asked Jerusha, a little mystified by the conversation between the two men. There was an urgency to it and it seemed to need de-coding although it could have been the alcohol they'd all had making it sound artificial.

'Yes, how is your lovely wife?' Hamish seemed to think this was a good topic of conversation. 'Is she not with you tonight?'

'She doesn't like pubs. Horrible, smoky atmosphere, she says, and you come out smelling like a brewery.' Hamish, who had been puffing on his pipe all evening, looked abashed.

'Oh, don't mind me. I find the smell of tobacco quite attractive. So, what are you doing to bring him out of himself, Jerusha?'

'Well . . . the pub is one thing. Also, Hamish has never been on a bus. We're going to take a bus ride to some as yet to be decided destination.'

'We must go fishing again, sometime, Hamish. Like in the old days.'

'Yes. We could do that,' said Hamish, more out of politeness than anything.

'And the children? How are they?' asked Derek.

'Claude is a little withdrawn but then he has always been a deep child. He is entering puberty, of course. And Jean, well, she's my little kitten. Full of hugs and giggles. She is convinced her mother will appear in her bedroom one day. That's why she doesn't like going back to boarding school. They both go. She always says, now, remember Daddy, be sure to 'phone me when Mummy gets back.'

'Poor things. I cannot begin to say how sorry I am.' Derek looked heartbroken as if he were somehow to blame.

'Won't Sheena be waiting for you?' asked Hamish, his way of trying to end the conversation.

Derek, however, was becoming maudlin. 'We decided not to have our own children as I have so many at school. In any case, this is not a world I'd like to bring anyone into.'

'Oh, I don't know about that,' said Jerusha, hoping to lighten the conversation. 'The world is full of new mercies, every day. We saw a heron catch a fish in the water today. It had its eye on the fish for some time before it plunged and scooped the fish up in its beak.' She also wanted to deflect the conversation, guessing that Derek would ask her if she had children. She would not have talked to him about the abortion and resultant infertility but it was difficult to explain otherwise.

Their attempts to change the course of the conversation worked, so much so that Derek made moves to leave. 'Think about some fishing, Hamish,' he said as he made his exit. 'We will meet again, Jerusha.' He was gone.

She turned to Hamish. 'Another drink?'

'A last one would be nice.' He let her go up to the bar and order more drinks.

As he drank the whisky he said, 'Derek was a good friend at one time, a very good friend. It's just that since Françoise went missing I find him a reminder.' He paused,

157

as if not sure whether or not to say what followed. He took a breath. 'He was also one of Françoise's lovers.'

'Good heavens. He doesn't look the type. And Sheena. She worships him.'

'Don't be mislead by appearances. Sheena is a canny soul. Françoise, now, she was shrewd. She cut through people to find their Achilles heels. Then she cut and thrust until they squirmed. She used to call me the dormouse and she would humiliate me in front of the children.'

'Are you sure you want to talk about your wife?' asked Jerusha, unsettled by this confession. She was outspoken herself but she wasn't comfortable with other people speaking out or confessing.

'You may as well know that I don't miss her. Except for the children's sakes, I'm glad she has gone.' If Hamish were the swearing type he would have sworn now. 'She used her wit to hurt people and her body, a very beautiful body, to use men and then toss them aside. Françoise had many lovers and the police questioned as many of them as they could rally, including Derek. Sheena found out during the whole ghastly business but she had an understanding of Françoise's personality that made the affair seem inconsequential and Derek a victim. He was just one of a long line of discarded lovers.'

'Why did you marry her?' asked Jerusha. This direct question was almost a protest.

'She was the daughter of a friend of my father, Henri Simpson, who had French origins. It seemed to be a stable thing to do—marry the daughter of family friends. Mummy and Daddy were all for it. I thought I'd made the catch of a lifetime. She was so beautiful and so witty. On her part, I think she fancied being related to an Earl and Countess. Then it all went wrong. About two years into the marriage . . . at least, I mean to say, two children later, we discovered the reality of each other. Neither was the person we expected. We settled in to an uncomfortable dislike of each other. You have experienced what a bad marriage is like, Jerusha?'

'There was nothing wrong with my ex-husbands. There was something wrong with our decision to marry. A touch of midsummer madness comes out to play,' said Jerusha.

'You would never do anything like that to me, Jerusha?' He hadn't been listening carefully.

'Like what?'

'Undermine me. If someone expects another to be stupid that other will act stupid.'

'Of course not. You appear to be the dearest man, the most dignified.'

'I'll have more of that.' He laughed.

He did have more of that because, over the next few years, she grew to love him. He took the relationship very slowly which, at first, perplexed her. Didn't he even want to kiss her? It was partly because of the children, she thought. They were very suspicious of her, especially Claude.

Once, when they were sitting at the dining table with food Jerusha had cooked, Hamish, Jean and Jerusha tucked in but Claude remained detached, stirring the food with a fork.

'Come on, old man, eat up,' said Hamish. It's delicious.'

'I'm not hungry,' said Claude, continuing to stir. His voice had not yet broken.

'You will have to eat if you are to grow up big and strong.'

'Like you, Daddy.' Claude was sarcastic even then. 'Mummy called you a dormouse. That's what you are. A dormouse. And when you wake up you eat too much.'

'Daddy is not a dormouse,' said Jean, going over to Hamish and hugging him. 'Mummy was only joking.'

'Jerusha is doing all the joking around here now. As if Mummy wasn't going to come back. Like the raspberry cushion and the spider in your shoe, Jeanie. Do you remember that? Funny, ha ha. Who is laughing?'

'That's good food in front of you, Claude. Now, eat it. Jerusha was only having a bit of fun,' said Hamish.

'We can't have fun around here whilst Mummy is gone. It's not allowed. I won't allow it.' He stood up and gave Jerusha a piercing, withering look. 'When Mummy comes back, you will have to go Jerusha. Do you hear me? I insist on it.' Claude scraped back his chair and left the room.

Jean burst into tears and went to Jerusha, snuggling into her ample bosom. 'It's all right, little one. He's sad because your Mummy is not here.'

'I miss Mummy too.' The child cried. 'But I'm not rude, like he is.'

'He'll get over it,' Hamish said. 'Now let's finish off our meal. Jerusha is going to take you to the donkey sanctuary.'

'Claude won't come. I hope he doesn't. He spoils things.' Jean went back to her chair and resumed eating her food.

Hamish was wrong about Claude. He wasn't ever going to get over losing his mother. When he was home from school and Jerusha was there he continued to make snide comments about her. It was as if he had muddled up in his mind the sequence of events, as if Jerusha had come before his mother's disappearance. The two things were nastily entangled in his mind. At one point, they thought of getting him to see a counsellor but he recoiled when Hamish suggested it to him so Hamish let the idea go. Jerusha began by being hurt but became inured to the barbs and pricks Claude inflicted. Claude, although he never forgot to try and hurt Jerusha, toughened up a little too when it became clear that Françoise was not coming back soon and that Hamish and Jerusha were falling in love.

ᏬᏙᏯ

Hamish remained respectful of her, touching her, holding her hand but never more intimate than that until about a year later he finally kissed her. It was in deepest winter. Great quantities of snow had fallen and the branches of the trees were coated with snow, fresh, wet, white on dark glistening boughs. Jerusha always became very excited by snow. It was a signal to play. Hamish caught the infection of her excitement. He was starting to awaken to life without Françoise and was peeling away the guilt he felt about not missing her, the guilt that he could not have prevented what had happened. Jerusha had seen him through bad times and that day, as she was bundling up in scarves and a woolly cap, he realized he loved her. He was not in love with her but he deeply, tenderly loved her. She was his soul mate. Jerusha was far too active and buoyant to realize what he was feeling in those moments. She wanted to run out into the snow and career down hillsides on her toboggan. She needed him to come alive with her.

And he did. They tackled treacherous roads to get to a friend's farm and parked the car at the top of a field whose slope was ideal for tobogganing. She pulled out her toboggan and raced ahead of him to slide down the hillside on her plastic ship. He followed soon after, churning and jolting down the hillside. Breathlessly, they began the trudge back up. At the top again, she dared him. 'Race you,' she said. 'Okay. One. Two. Three.' They were off. It was neck and neck but Jerusha won by a small margin. Gleeful, she lay on the toboggan, panting. Then she rolled over, off the toboggan and into thick snow. She lay on her back, trying to talk. Soon there was another reason why she couldn't breath. Hamish, who had crawled over next to her, placed his lips on hers and they kissed, lovingly, longingly. It had been a long time in coming and she would always remember it. For days afterwards, years, she would touch her lips to see if she could induce the feeling of this first kiss

⊙⫘⊙

As well as Claude's jibes, there was a cloud, which might have cast a great shadow over her happiness if she had let it. Any day, at any one moment, Françoise could walk in, she thought. Françoise had the power to claim she was there first. What power for one person to hold over another. She found herself wishing that Françoise were well and truly dead but it would take five more years before Françoise would legally be pronounced dead. It had been two years since she disappeared. Jerusha could remember the glamorous figure in scarlet as she made her entrance into the marquee at the midsummer night's party. She was beautiful and bold and she cared for no one but herself. Jerusha could imagine her making another entrance at Kirkfield. She would stride in through the back door, nonchalant, imperious and threatening. Jerusha consoled herself that if Françoise were to return Hamish would firmly demand a divorce. However, Françoise, ever quick-witted, might have anticipated that. She might persuade him she should stay, and then seek her revenge.

Jerusha's vivid fear of Françoise re-appearing made her value every moment she spent with Hamish. He, on the other hand, appeared more phlegmatic. 'It's the children I feel sorry for,' he said. 'She never did think of them.'

It was winter 2001, only just, the week between Christmas and New Year when everything and nothing can happen. Jerusha was in the sitting room sewing name tapes on Jean's school blouses. They were white blouses worn with a purple and navy kilted skirt and navy, v-necked sweater. She had been growing out of her old blouses steadily over the past few years. Now, she came up to Jerusha and admired her handiwork. 'I never get it so neat,' she said. 'Mine always look as if some dog has chewed the name tapes.'

Jerusha, who was always very serious when she was sewing, looked up over her glasses and said, 'Perhaps matron will appreciate what I've done? No one else will notice.'

'Saves me having to do it. But, listen. Daddy has got a question he's going to ask you. I can't tell you what he is going to say. It's very exciting,' said Jean, bubbling over with suppressed information.

Jerusha held the needle in mid-air lest, in talking, she break the chain of tiny stitches. With her eyes, she followed Jean as she flitted from chair to chair with apparently vacant intention. The girl was more effervescent than usual. Jerusha wondered what Hamish was going to say to her. 'Perhaps he's going to tell me he is thinking of buying a computer? That would be thrilling. Or, perhaps he is going to ask me to do the meal tonight? My cooking is always adventurous.'

'You are on the wrong tack but that's okay because I shouldn't have said anything. So, I'll change the subject. Do you know, Jerusha, that I've told my friends at school that you are my stepmother?'

'If you have need of a stepmother, then so be it.'

Jerusha still had her job in the pub but she had been visiting Kirkfield on her days off for four years. Her relationship with Hamish had deepened and she had become very fond of Jean. Claude was different. He would not let her come near him emotionally. However, his initial antagonism had lightened and his attention to her or subversion of her had lessened as he grew up and became obsessed with the very things his father feared—computers. So, Jerusha snuggled into the family unit and also came to love Kirkfield itself. Some of its familiarity came from working within its walls. Jerusha was not just a house guest. She washed and ironed, prepared guest rooms, cooked meals, cleaned, washed up, put away dishes. She did this for Hamish. She wanted to make his life more comfortable.

He came in now and Jean ostentatiously left, with a giggle. Hamish was carrying a basket of logs and pushed the door closed with his foot. He went over to the fireplace and put down the basket next to the hearth. He was wearing a red waistcoat and his cheeks reflected the colour. His shirt sleeves were rolled up and he was covered in sawdust. Jerusha would often remember him like that. When he saw what she was doing, he said, 'You don't need to do that, Jerusha. Jean can sew on her own name tapes.'

'You don't need to chop logs. Luke Junior can do it,' she replied.

'When you are rich, as I am, you don't need to do anything.'

'That begs the question of other motivation. I can think of a few. Love, self-esteem, feeling useful, sex even,' said Jerusha.

'Now, I know that you love me for my body.'

'Don't flatter yourself.'

'You mean you don't love my body?'

'I love every part of you.'

'And I you. Which brings me to the point . . .'

'The other things that motivate people are the immoral ones like greed, hatred, revenge. Then there is guilt. But I'm sure you've never felt any of these.'

'No. Yes. I'll light the fire.' He set about laying down newspaper and kindling in the grate. When he had finished and the fire had taken, bringing a warm glow to the room, he went over to Jerusha and knelt at her feet.

'Rise, Sir Hamish, Knight of the Realm.' She pointed the needle at his head as if it were a sword.

'Put that needle away, woman. I have something to ask you. In fact, put all that sewing on the side table and take my hand.'

She did as he bid her, feeling the warmth of his large, comfortable hand. 'Jean said you had something exciting to tell me.'

'To ask you. Yes, I've spoken to the youngsters.'

'That serious?'

'Yes. Now, I can't think how to broach the subject.'

'Be honest.'

'I'll try. I've said, I have spoken to Claude and Jean and they approve.'

'Approve of what?'

'Your coming to live at Kirkfield, on a permanent basis. I've given it a lot of thought. As you know, I can't marry until Françoise is pronounced dead. Otherwise, I would ask you to marry me. Now. At this very moment. I can't do that so I would like to ask you to be my partner. We would live together in love, 'til death do us part. And in 2003 we will be free to marry. This is a ring of my mother's which I would like you to have.'

He took out of his trouser pocket a small box containing a diamond and sapphire ring. He took the ring and held it between thumb and forefinger. The expression on his face was inviting Jerusha into his life. Yet, did she see a beam of fear of rejection in his eyes? Or, was it guilt that he was betraying his first wife, the unaccounted for wife, the wife who had disappeared under mysterious circumstances? He was still in this pose of supplication, like a leaf bereft of breeze.

Jerusha's emotions welled up inside her. Her immediate, impulsive answer was yes, yes, yes. Then quickly she sized up her position of live-in lover. It would be insecure. If the relationship went wrong, as her marriages had done twice before, she would be rudderless. Accepting his offer of a lifetime of love would mean risk. And yet, this was Hamish she was thinking about, Hamish kneeling before her and offering her a precious ring. 'You mean I'd give up the bar job?' she whispered.

'Yes. I'd give you an allowance. Don't be afraid, Jerusha. Based on trust, you'll be the perfect wife and I'll be the perfect husband.'

'Oh, I love you,' she said, launching into a huge hug, forgetting about the ring which she knocked out of his hand. It went rolling under the chair and they spent the next minutes on hands and knees looking for it. Finally, he announced that he had got it. He helped her up and they stood facing each other.

'I do,' said Jerusha. 'I will.'

'Until death do us part,' he said.

He slipped the ring onto her finger, on her right hand.

⟨⟨⟨⟩⟩⟩

Jerusha got up and put the cloth cap on the top shelf of the cupboard along with the deerstalker, top hat and several other hats and caps. 'The primary aim is to keep your head warm,' he used to say, putting on a cap. She went out of the room, shutting the door with exaggerated gentleness. Her *aim* now was to see her greatest living link with Hamish, Lorna. Yes, James was his half-brother. However, James had been so much younger than Hamish and, having a different mother, he'd had a different upbringing. Lorna was Hamish's blood sister and she had been closer to him than his older brother, Ewan, the Earl. Jerusha had overheard a conversation between Ewan and his wife, Elizabeth, that had set her against them. It took place one day when they were visiting. They were in the sitting room and clearly thought that they were alone. Unknown to them, Jerusha was standing at the door, about to enter. When she heard her name, she stopped, a hand on the doorknob.

'I've thought about this,' said Elizabeth, crossing her legs and leaning forward. 'From all my dealings with the woman I've come to the conclusion that she is a fraud. I mean, who goes around with a name like Jerusha. The rumour is that she is actually called Mary and is from a humble background. She purports to talk like an aristocrat

169

but she actually worked in a pub. For God's sake. I'd say she's a first class actress,' she said.

'It's my guess that there are two things she is after,' said Ewan.

'And that is money and the prospect of a title.'

'My brother gives her an allowance but there's no contract. Can't be, because of poor old Françoise not turning up. Pitiful business. Damned shame . . .'

Jerusha decided to terminate their conversation by walking into the room but she had never forgotten their hypocrisy. However, at least she could count on Lorna to be straight with her.

❦

Lorna was halfway between hospital and home, in a hospital linked—halfway house. The unit had previously been a cottage hospital, which had closed down and still had an atmosphere redolent of a hospital. The communal area was a former waiting room and was now peopled by patients waiting for their psychiatrists and for their visitors. Lorna was over in the corner, knees together, trying to snooze. Jerusha took a deep breath and strode over to her. She merely touched her arm but Lorna looked startled. 'You look pretty today,' Jerusha said, although Lorna looked an echo of herself.

'Do you see, they washed my wig? Practically tore it off me. I had no choice. I guess they've made a good job. I don't feel pretty, mind you. I feel exhausted and drained and I can't concentrate. I'm drugged up to the eyeballs.'

'You've progressed since I last saw you.'

'What did I say? What did I say to you when you first visited me in hospital?'

'You seemed very keen on one hallucination you'd been having. It was of a Madonna and child. You told me you lay and gazed at it for hours. But when the nurses encouraged you to mix with the other patients you became frightened. You said you were in a jungle where people were wild animals. And you said that Myra Hindley, child murderess, was there on the ward. It was all to do with children. Isn't that strange?'

'It's like the golf clubs. Why I went and bought them I don't understand. I don't play golf. What am I going to do with them? And the car? Is that all right?'

'Perfectly fine. Garaged at home. We'll turn the engine over for you periodically.'

'I hope I'm not going to be here that long.'

'Just take your time. They won't let you go home until you can manage on your own.'

'Tell me, what else did I say?' asked Lorna and Jerusha saw she was becoming agitated. She put her hand on Lorna's own. They were sitting side by side.

'You seem to be very anxious about how you appeared to me. You must not worry. I have treated anything you said at the time as confidential. You were ill, my dear. Don't upset yourself.' She noticed Lorna had clenched her fists.

'Did I say anything about . . . falling down some stairs?'

'Yes. Come to think of it.'

'What?' Lorna was shaking.

'It wasn't very clear. I gathered you'd taken a tumble down the hospital stairs. Bump, bump, bump you kept repeating. I spoke to the nurse afterwards and she said you'd reported falling down the stairs but that you had been examined and there were no bones broken.'

'That must be it. It was me who fell down the stairs. A woman can break her neck falling down stairs. Bumpity bump. I think I ought to pack my bags, now.'

'Lorna, you're not going anywhere today.' She restrained Lorna who had started to rise from her chair. 'You'll come home when you are feeling better. Lorna, don't cry.'

'You have no idea what these people are like. Someone could get killed.'

'Nobody is trying to kill you, Lorna.' Jerusha pleaded with her. 'Myra Hindley is not here.'

'I know that now,' sobbed Lorna. 'But some of these people just don't make sense. There is one woman who cuts herself at any opportunity. If she can get hold of a knife or a piece of broken glass she'll tear herself to shreds.'

'That's her problem,' said Jerusha. 'Your aim is to get yourself better, never mind the others.'

'I'm just a silly billy,' said Lorna, drying her tears with a tissue. 'My brain is not right yet, you know, Jerusha. It was very nice of you to come and visit me.' She got up abruptly, as if she had switched to a different time and place. She left Jerusha sitting there, leaning over a vacant chair.

6

FALLING LIKE CONFETTI

Jerusha was sorting through that day's post when she found one with South African stamps. Startled, she looked again to make sure what she'd seen was true. Yes, definitely South African and that was Saul's handwriting. She took it away to read in her workroom. She found her hands trembling as she opened the envelope and unfolded the sheets of paper from inside. It read:

Jerusha (Mary Louise),

I can't really say thank you for your letter. It gave me an unpleasant surprise. Nevertheless, I read it and was further surprised by its contents. You talk about forgiveness when, as far as I am concerned, you have nothing to forgive. I have never quarrelled with you as you imply. I have merely withdrawn my attention, casting it instead on our ageing mother and on getting on with life in South Africa. I, on the other hand, have plenty to forgive, in particular your breaking up two marriages by having an affair with a married man while you were still married to Bert. It was the last straw. What happened to the morality our parents taught us? It seems to me that you are either amoral or just plain cruel. Granted, you seem to have remained faithful to Hamish since his death but isn't widowhood easier than a long-term commitment? And, more dramatic.'

Jerusha put the letter down on top of a bolt of fabric and started playing with a pair of large, sharp scissors. In her mind's eye she could see the blue paper fluttering in shreds to the floor. So far, Saul's reply was not what she had expected. Somehow, she had begun to anticipate that he would write in brotherly love and goodwill. Anyone can be criticized, she thought. We all have our good points and our bad points. So much depended on the person who viewed the subject. For instance, she could be viewed as either fat or sensual, depending on the viewer's willingness to befriend, love or admire. Early on in her life she had decided to love herself so that reading the first part of this letter was dangerous. She got so far as to nick the margin of the first blue page with her scissors but then stopped, thinking of Sonia. What was she to tell the girl if she didn't reveal the full contents of the letter? She began to read again:

I notice you do think to enquire after mother. She is ill, thank you. She is in the advanced stages of

Alzheimer's and most of the time doesn't know where she is or who she is. She would wander off but, fortunately, we have a security fence (to keep out armed robbers) that stops her going very far. It's no good my telling her I've heard from you because she wouldn't know who you are, I'm afraid. What a way to go. At least she is not aware of how difficult she has become.

I am responding to your letter for the sole reason that you have my daughter with you. I understand she has fond ideas about peacemaking between you and me. She is young and the young cannot grasp the full implications of the history of adults. As you will have gathered, she has a strong Faith and a faith in Christian love that errs on the side of the romantic. It is because of her Faith that I have entrusted her to you. Neither your lifestyle nor your opinions will overwhelm her. She is pure Sonia. She seems to have a firm base in London so I wouldn't want her to dally in your household.

May God guide you and help you,

Saul

There was a knock on the door. It was Sonia. 'I saw the envelope and came to find out what he had to say.' She came into the room and began fingering some cloth, part of an outfit Jerusha was making for herself.

'He is not very forgiving,' said Jerusha.

'Can I read it?' asked Sonia.

'I'd rather you didn't. He thinks I'm a bad influence on you. He wants you to go back to London.'

'He doesn't know I'm perfectly all right here. There is a greater reason why I am here.'

'You have an ulterior motive?'

'What do you mean?'

'Sonia, everyone knows that you're in love with Callum.'

'I love him. That's different. He's a born again Christian.'

'That makes it all right, does it? What would your father think?'

'He would not approve because Callum is a roofer and not a lawyer or accountant.' She was sobbing now. 'He has got to let me live my own life. He and Mum. They've got to let me go.'

Jerusha made to put her arm around Sonia but the girl shrugged her off, snatched up the letter and started reading it. After a while, she said, 'How can you put up with such character assassination? What is he thinking of?'

177

'It's all right,' said Jerusha, trying to soothe her.

'It's not all right,' said Sonia. 'I wanted you two to be friends. I saw the letter you sent him. It was okay. I mean, kind of compassionate. Why can't he bury his grudges? That's what I like about you, Jerusha. You don't hate anybody. That is why I'm staying. Because of you . . . and Callum.'

'Callum seems a fine person but is he right for you if, as you suspect, your father won't approve?'

'He is a Christian. That is better than any number of degrees or qualifications.' She was dipping in and out of tears.

'What would your stepmother say?'

'Mom. She'd go along with Dad.'

'Do you and Callum really love each other? How do you know so soon?'

'I know it's a lot for people to take in. I love my parents too.'

Jerusha had seen them the day she and Sonia had climbed the scaffolding with Callum. They were on the rooftop, surrounded by a whole vista of Borders hills, and all the young pair could do was gaze at each other. Now, she was before her, torn between her family and her boyfriend, in tears, upset because of her father's accusations against Jerusha, angry enough to tear up the letter. She crumpled it and tugged at it, then tore it to shreds. It was a symbol. She had started on the path of defying her father.

'I could have done that myself,' said Jerusha. 'Some letters are made to be destroyed. Now, come let us go and get a cup of tea.'

'I'm going to walk Sheena's dog.'

'Dry your eyes, then.'

'Going to walk Sheena's dog' had, in this case, become a particular euphemism. Oswald and James joked about it. Yes, she was going to walk the dog but she was also going to meet Callum. It was a well-walked dog.

Sonia's coy subterfuge was well and truly expressed when one evening she announced again that she was going to walk Sheena's dog. Nobody said anything. Jerusha, James and Oswald all stifled giggles because, in fact, *they* were going to walk Sheena's dog. They were going for a night walk with Sheena and Derek. Afterwards there would be soup and board games. Or, as Claude was in the habit of calling them, bored games. Jerusha thought that he missed out on the fun.

The dog, a collie called Tammy, came bounding up to them as they walked along the short drive and they knocked on Sheena's door. Sheena welcomed them in her prim fashion and took their jackets. 'Come in,' she said.

'Thank goodness it's not raining,' said Jerusha. It was October and it was getting dark at about six thirty in the evening.

She, Oswald and James were dressed in layer upon layer of informal clothing and they wore walking boots. It turned out that Oswald and James did not need the boots in the end. They had a group consultation. Derek was by now also present, and they decided to drive to Tweedbank, on the outskirts of Galashiels, and then walk from there to Melrose along the river. Someone was needed to drive the car and meet them in Melrose. Oswald and James volunteered for this enthusiastically. Neither really fancied a walk in the dark. That having been decided, they had to choose whose car to take. In the end, they waited while James went to fetch his hatchback that had room for four passengers and the dog in the boot. It was a good thing, he thought, that he had not had a drink that evening before they came.

Sheena busied herself finding head torches, leaving her guests with Derek in the sitting room.

'How is the teaching going, then, Derek?' asked Oswald.

'How is it ever going? The little blighters get more unruly by the minute. Can't say I blame that teacher who lashed out at one of his pupils. Did some damage. It was on the news. Not that I could ever condone murder, but I could murder one or two of them sometimes.'

'Murder will out,' said Jerusha vaguely.

'What do you mean by that, Jerusha?' asked Derek, looking suddenly perturbed.

'It's just that there is no point in committing murder unless one is prepared to take the punishment.'

'It was just a turn of phrase,' said Derek. 'I would not dream of killing one of the little darlings. Instead, I might take early retirement. Stay at home with Sheena. And tend to the garden. I'm afraid it is thoroughly neglected at the moment.'

'What is neglected?' Sheena came into the room. 'Your wife?'

'And that, too,' said Derek. 'No. We were talking about the garden, amongst other things.'

James drove them to Tweedbank, less than a mile away, with its small loch where swans and ducks swam and jostled for crumbs of bread. Derek leading, Sheena and Jerusha walked around to the far side of the loch, along a path beside an empty children's play area, across a field and through some trees. Derek knew the way well, and so did Sheena and Tammy. It was when they got into the trees that Jerusha felt unnerved by the brooding silhouettes of trunks and branches. If she had not trusted Sheena and Derek she would have turned back. The head torch only a minimal beam, enough to stop her tripping on tree roots and stones. There was an unhelpfully small moon and they could see few stars.

They walked on, over a small bridge. They could hear the water running to their left. Derek walked fast and Jerusha had to double her normal pace. She was panting when they reached a steep incline and gasping when she got to the top of it.

Aware of her friend's struggle, Sheena called to Derek to stop for a minute for them to catch their breath. He came to see what was up, his torch casting a ghoulish light over his wrinkled face. His dark hair, which was peppered with grey, fell into a thick fringe over his forehead. When he spoke, Jerusha could not make out the movement of his lips. Just the shape and furrows of his face showed; his body was a dark form in the night. Perhaps because she knew Sheena better, she didn't look quite as eerie. They continued to walk, coming up to a small gate. When they opened it a rough path led them on, with the river still on the left and trees and scrub to their right. They could see the lights of a house set back on that side too. They were no longer crowded in by trees but felt space in the night air. They kept walking until they came to a bench where they sat while Sheena poured cups of tea from a thermos she had brought in her backpack. For Jerusha, never had tea tasted so good as when drunk in the cold night air. Derek was impatient with what he saw as an interruption to the walk but he accepted a cup of tea. They could hear Tammy wading into the water. Then another sound reached them. Human footsteps behind them. Voices surrounding a hand-held torch.

Jerusha would know that voice anywhere. It was Sonia and it must be Callum with her. He shone his torch on them in an challenging way. He was out to protect Sonia. Then he recognized Mrs Burnett and he dipped it. 'It's you, Mrs Burnett,' he said. 'Now, that's a coincidence.' What he wanted to ask was what they had in their flask, tea or something stronger, but he had to defer to a customer so he left it at that. In fact, he repeated 'a coincidence'. He wondered whether or not they could see he was holding Sonia's hand. He gripped it tightly. Sonia felt this and returned the squeeze.

'Jerusha, what are you doing drinking tea, or whatever, by the water in the dark? Wouldn't it be more comfortable at home?' asked Sonia in a high-pitched voice which betrayed the fact that she was nervous about having been found out. Her questions were designed to put the spotlight on Jerusha's group and take it away from her own presence here. Just then Tammy, who had come out of the water, recognized Sonia and came racing up to her, then stopped and shook his whole body so that water sprayed all over her and Callum. Careless of the wet, Sonia let go of Callum's hand and hugged and stroked the collie.

'You're his friend,' remarked Derek.

'Mind you don't get too wet,' said Sheena.

They spent five minutes talking about Tammy's exploits and Sonia's actual dog-walking after which Jerusha interrupted with an abrupt question. 'Sonia. Callum. Why does Sonia have to pretend she is walking Tammy when she is actually seeing you? You could come to Kirkfield. As you say, it is much more comfortable there. I'm aware that you have been seeing each other frequently. Why try to keep it a secret? Sonia has already confided in me that she feels something for you Callum.'

'It's kind of private. And besides, Sonia's father would not approve. Me being a roofer, and all.'

'But I am not my brother,' Jerusha retorted. 'Nor have I any intention of telling Saul about you two. But, in the Borders, anyway, I'm sure it would be healthier for your relationship to be out in the open. Don't you think so, Sheena?'

'It is up to these two young people to decide whether they want to continue to walk in the dark or face the social glare. Jerusha's brother lives a long way away,' said Sheena.

'Can't you try telling him, instead of pre-judging what he will say?' asked Derek.

'You don't know my dad, I love him to bits but he is the one who pre-judges,' said Sonia.

'You don't need to talk about that now,' cut in Jerusha, repeating her invitation. 'Callum, I want you to know that you are very welcome as a guest at Kirkfield. You needn't resort to meetings under cover of darkness. Unless, that is, you want to. Come tomorrow. Come any time that suits Sonia.'

'Thank you, Mrs Burnett.'

'Call me Jerusha.'

'Jerusha, I think we ought to get on,' said Derek. 'Oswald and James will be wondering what has happened to us. Are you two going home?'

'Take him back to Kirkfield. Light a fire . . .' said Jerusha.

'We'll be all right. Come on, Callum.'

They moved off along the dark path with the light from Callum's torch bobbing ahead. Sheena took up her backpack and the three adults walked in the opposite direction, Derek leading, then Sheena, followed by Jerusha. The dark did not seem so black to her now. She began to feel the space of the night air freeing her. Some way along, she stopped and took off her head torch, holding it loosely in one hand. She turned full circle to see the sky. There was a fragment of moon, now surrounded by stars. She thought she could make out Orion's Belt, the only constellation she was familiar with. She turned again until she became dizzy. That passed and she stood still. She became aware of an unbearable happiness, as if Hamish were with her. A light breeze shifted wisps of hair across her face. She imagined Hamish holding her and stroking away the hair. She heard her name being called. 'Jerusha.'

However, it was Sheena who had come to find out why she had been left behind. 'We have to stick together, Jerusha. What's up? Is your torch not working?'

'It was a little scratchy so I took it off.'

'You need to keep it on. We don't want to lose you,' said Sheena.

'No chance of that,' laughed Jerusha, putting the torch back on her head and following Sheena. She was not going to confess to Sheena that she'd been communing with the ghost of Hamish. She wanted to keep that experience to herself.

They caught up with Derek, who had waited for them, and soon saw the lights of Melrose. Oswald and James were in Nibs Hotel in the proud, upmarket town. The hotel was well-known and popular and had been for many years. Its tapestry replica covered chairs were welcoming and warm. There was a fire in the grate. Black and white photographs of old Melrose covered the walls. Relaxed by the cease of exercise, they joined Oswald and James around their table. Derek ordered a round of drinks. Orange juice for Sheena and coffee for James, who was driving. Sheena wished that Derek would become teetotal but at least he was not drinking as much as he did at one point. Jerusha and her household consumed far too much alcohol for her liking. Sheena had had to get used to the relationship between Oswald and James, almost as much so as Sonia, but she now got on with them quite happily.

They had just one drink at The Nibs before moving on to Derek and Sheena's home where courgette and spinach soup was waiting to be heated up and a dollop of cream thrown in. They were to eat while they played a board game. That way the evening wouldn't end too late. Sheena gave them the choice of Rummikub, Monopoly, Boggle or Cluedo. Boggle, a word game, was not strictly a board game and it could be played in combination with something else. The five would-be players opted for Cluedo and they all sat down around the dining table except for Jerusha. She was waiting to see where the piece representing Miss Scarlett landed on the table. Jerusha always liked to be Miss Scarlett, one of the suspected murderers, because it was this character who started the game. As luck would have it, Miss Scarlett was positioned on the part of the board nearest the vacant chair and Jerusha sat down.

To play the game they had to solve the murder of Dr Black whose body has been found at the foot of the stairs leading to the cellar. The group had to discover in which part of the house the murder was committed, by whom it was committed, using what weapon. A classic murder mystery game, one that the five players knew well. Jerusha threw a six on the dice to move Miss Scarlett along the board. She was heading for the hall.

'If the crime was committed in one of these rooms, how did the murderer move the body to the cellar?' asked Jerusha. 'Dead bodies are very heavy.'

'How do you know, Jerusha?' asked Oswald.

'She knows from TV. She is always watching whodunits. Not to mention reading crime fiction,' said James.

'I expect there was an accomplice,' said Derek. 'There usually is.'

'And how do you know that?' queried Sheena.

'It's only a game,' Derek said to his wife. 'Come on. It's your turn. Throw the dice.'

But Sheena hesitated. 'It is rather an old-fashioned thing. A board game to entertain one's friends. Think what options young people have these days. Computer games, I-pods, I-players, Wiis. They hardly have any time left to communicate with each other, let alone their parents.'

'I don't know, dear. They still have the odd word to say to each other. There is hardly a hush when the bell goes to end classes. I don't buy this end of childhood idea,' said Derek.

'It's their parents who are left behind,' said Jerusha.

'Parents have to leave it to their children to solve technological problems. It's humiliating and disempowering. Also, as you say, look at Face Book and Twitter or Tweeter, whatever it's called. These seem odd ways of communicating,' said Jerusha.

'Would you like to communicate with my wife?' said Derek. 'Tell her to throw the dice so that we can get on with the game.'

'I suppose people have always had communication problems,' said Sheena as she threw the dice and moved her Mrs Peacock into the conservatory.

Jerusha was keen to win for she regarded herself as an amateur sleuth. She was the first to move and quick to eliminate possibilities. She kept throwing double sixes and using the secret passages to move around the board. She was the first to make 'an accusation'. She accused Derek's piece, Colonel Mustard, of committing the murder in the study with the dagger. And she was right. Game won.

'Pity he couldn't have just fallen down the stairs,' said Derek.

'Then we would have had no murder and no game,' said Sheena.

'We would if Dr Black were pushed,' said Oswald.

'The weapon is part of the fun,' said James. 'Jerusha, how did you work it out so soon? I had only guessed the place.'

'She has a nose for sleuthing,' said Sheena, packing up the game and putting it away. 'Anyone for more soup? There's plenty of it.'

'Thanks. But, no. We must go,' said Jerusha, presuming Oswald and James did not want any more soup. When they got back to Kirkfield the house was in darkness and there was no sign that Sonia had returned. A glass with a residue of milk or a warm kettle would have been a clue. Jerusha bid the others goodnight and went upstairs. She went up to Sonia's lightly closed door and nudged it open. Putting her head around the door she saw the girl's form under the bedclothes. She was relieved but not altogether surprised. Sonia wasn't one to sleep out at night. Jerusha was about to withdraw when the bedclothes moved and Sonia said, 'Yes, I'm here.'

'Just checking,' said Jerusha.

'I'm not sleeping with him, if that's what you think.'

'I didn't know whether or not to lock the front door.'

'You must remember that Callum and I are both Christians. We wait until we're married.'

'I don't want to pry into your private life but you're not thinking of marriage already?'

'It's a possibility,' she whispered.

'But you have only known him a few weeks'

' The happiest time of my life.'

'Promise me that you'll go easy.'

'What do you mean by that?'

'Take your time.'

'Jerusha, I'm young and I believe in love. You want to change me and I can't promise you that.'

'People do change, whether they like it or not.'

'Are you speaking with the voice of experience?'

'Yes. Now, go to sleep. Tomorrow is another day. Sleep well.' Jerusha shut the door and went to her own bed. Foremost in her mind was what Saul would say about this latest development. If he didn't like it, and he would not, he would blame her and her bad influence.

Jerusha didn't sleep well that night. She tried to return to her experience of happiness on the dark path by the river but it had been spontaneous, seeming to come from outside herself. She could not conjure it up. So she lay in her bed, worrying about Sonia and Saul until she finally fell asleep. The next day she was feeling dull-witted and quick-tempered and she was obliged to take a nip of brandy to get her through the day.

'No tricks from Jerusha, today. We can be grateful. You'd think she'd be pleased that her Miss Scarlett won the game,' said Oswald to James.

'Maybe she has got the bill for the roof,' suggested James.

They kept out of her way.

James was, indeed, right. Not only had Jerusha slept badly but also the invoice for the roof, amounting to several thousand pounds, had arrived. She had expected it but when it came, it was painful. She didn't want any more large bills. This led her to thinking about Len and his offer to buy the fields. Perhaps it was the best thing to do? Why shouldn't prospective buyers be sold a slice of Kirkfield? There are always people who are against progress. Take Tilda, for instance. What had it got to do with her that Len wanted to buy the fields. People like her always latched onto some protest, people who grew up in the sixties who couldn't be happy without a cause. She had noticed that Tilda had not been at her post outside the house recently and she had asked Chris Rutherford what was up with her. It turned out that Tilda had flu, not swine flu though. It was not surprising, thought Jerusha, her standing still at the gate in all weathers. She wondered how long Tilda could keep up her protest. She had very little power but her opinions might spread. The real crunch would come when Len applied for planning permission to build houses. Perhaps the best idea would be to sell the land swiftly and let the resultant furore play itself out. If she weren't bothered by a conscience and a vision of bluebell woods she could dispatch part of the problem and benefit from the cash injection. She would be seeing Len at the weekend.

Len and Patricia arrived at quarter to six, as arranged, on that Saturday when they were going to the ballet in Edinburgh. Patricia came to the door to collect Jerusha. The artist was all in grey, even her boots were grey, and she had dyed her hair blue. 'You look great, Jerusha.' Jerusha was dressed in her peach outfit, with a cape of peach and loose, cascading peach trousers. She carried a box of chocolates, to make up for the ones she had spilled over the driveway when Len had taken her out to dinner. 'Hi,' said Len, standing between the open door and the car itself. He leaned an elbow on the top of the roof. At that moment, although rain was forecast, the sun was shining and he had sunglasses resting on his head, nestling into his dark hair. She went with Patricia across to the car and the latter made a great display of letting Jerusha have the front passenger seat. This always seems to be regarded as the second in the pecking order of car seats, the first being the driver's.

'I see our lone, arch protester is absent today,' said Len.

'She's ill. She has not given up,' replied Jerusha.

'Probably made herself ill, standing there in all weathers,' remarked Patricia.

'Let us leave her behind us,' said Len. He drove off, heading for the A7, the road to Edinburgh. The journey would take not much more than an hour. For the first part of it they passed the time talking about the weather—it was beginning to rain; the state of the Borders' roads; the ballets they had seen in the past. Then Len said abruptly, 'before we go any further, I think you ought to know that I'm having second thoughts about buying your land. It's not just buying it that is entailed. It's also the cost of building houses. These are tough times. The Credit Crunch has hit hard. I don't want to rule it out but there is a chance I might have to withdraw my offer.'

'Len has given it a lot of thought,' said Patricia from the back seat. 'It's not easy making these decisions.'

Jerusha was taken aback and deflated but she wasn't going to let it show. She had enjoyed being a person who had something others wanted. It had been a position of power and she had seen herself as the one to make the big decisions. Not, of course, that Len was the only potential buyer but he had seemed so certain of his intentions. She did not need the money urgently but it would have helped. 'So, bluebell woods, here we come.'

'What are you talking about?' asked Len.

'The alternative to houses on that land is to plant trees and bluebells.'

'That would please Tilda and the likes of her.'

'Not to please Tilda. To please me. I've got a very green friend who is making me eco-minded. What's left of the countryside should be treasured and nurtured.'

'I'm not saying a definite no,' said Len.

'I understand that but I'm changing my way of thinking. I . . .'

'Watch out,' called Patricia. She had seen the car driving out of a side road, directly in their path. Len was doing a legal speed. The driver of the other car clearly had not registered their existence. It was a purple Allegro driven, as they were to find out, by an elderly man with three passengers. Len reacted quickly. He swerved and the BMW careered into the middle of the road. He had avoided any impact but their car was almost out of his control. It went shuddering on and he put his foot on the brakes. They were heading for a bridge but before they got there the BMW did a complete spin and they finally came to rest, facing the wrong way on a busy road. Len sat still, in a state of shock.

'Get this fucking car off the road,' yelled Jerusha. She only ever swore out of extreme emotion. Up until then, all three had been silent. They could have smashed through the side of the bridge and landed in the water, upside down. They could have smashed into cars coming the other way.

But it was not meant to be. They were meant to be sitting there, shaken. Yet, if Len did not get the car off the road there could be another, worse accident. Fortunately he registered Jerusha's instruction, given crudely in the heat of the moment, and he slowly drove into the side road, next to where the Allegro was now parked. The Allegro had remained intact and under the driver's control but he was severely shaken and his passengers were quivering.

'He realizes it is his fault. Don't you speak to him, Len. I will,' said Jerusha and she was out of the car before he had a chance to reply. It was still raining and she had no coat. She went up to the Allegro driver's window. 'Are you all right?' she asked. The window was half open, as though the man wanted a barrier between them.

His eyes filled with tears. 'I'm sorry,' he said. 'I didn't see you.'

'What are we? Invisible?'

'I ken the road so weel,' he said.

'If you know the road so well, you would know to look out for cars coming either way.'

'Are you going to report this?'

'No. We are are not but I want an admission that it was your fault and a promise that you'll be more careful in the future, if only for your passengers' sakes.'

'Aye, it was my fault. I will drive more carefully.'

Jerusha stepped back and took in the frightened looks of his passengers before walking away. She was wet and now hungry. Patricia was in the front seat next to her husband who had recovered his composure. Jerusha insisted on getting into the back.

'Are you going to turn around and go back home?' asked Jerusha.

'Not likely,' said Patricia.

'Come on, we've got a bally ballet to go to,' said Len, starting up the car.

The Allegro was standing still as they drove off, the elderly offenders taking time to recover.

The rest of their short journey went uneventfully. Jerusha admired Len for getting back in the saddle. He had a determination about him that wrestled with the shock of the near accident. Patricia was talking incessantly but Jerusha switched off from what she was saying. It wasn't easy to hear from the back what the front seat passengers were saying, anyway. However, Jerusha was working out how to play the trick she'd prepared in advance. It would relieve the tension. It was very simple. All it required was the small bag of confetti she'd brought, concealed in the pocket of her trousers and, also, Patricia's umbrella. They drove on in the pouring rain and arrived in Edinburgh with half an hour to spare. They had difficulty finding parking near The Festival Theatre but eventually found one. Jerusha handed Patricia her closed and bound umbrella and her grey handbag that she had left on the back seat. She leapt out of the car to see her trick come to fruition.

In the now light rain, Patricia quickly, and unthinkingly, put up her umbrella, hastily covering her body with it. The result was a flutter, a flaking, a falling of confetti over her hair and shoulders. Jerusha doubled up with laughter. 'Just married,' she spluttered. There was a moment of confusion when Len and Patricia were working out what was going on. And then a pause, while they decided whether or not to join in the joke. Fortunately for Jerusha, they decided to find it funny although Len was not so amused when he had to spend the next ten minutes picking confetti out of Patricia's blue hair in the drizzling rain. Patricia cleared her umbrella of the offending bits and they walked off to the theatre, leaving a trail of confetti behind them.

7

FAMILY

For weeks, the success of the umbrella trick rivalled the near accident in Jerusha's conversation. Lorna thought it was funny. Sheena found it endearing. Claude, who had arrived for the weekend, sneered and said, 'typical.'

Jerusha had become very excited as her stepson and stepdaughter's visit grew closer. She had stocked the freezer and made new curtains for their bedrooms. She had decided not to clear out Hamish's bedroom, the one where he died, because she needed it there intact. So, Jean was to keep her old, small room at the end of the passage. Except, Jean wasn't coming after all. She 'phoned to say that a man she had 'been cultivating for years' had asked her out. What could she do? She couldn't refuse. Jerusha was disappointed. If pressed, she would have said that Jean was her favourite of the two. Most of the time she ignored Claude's sarcasm but, every now and then, it got to her.

At twenty four, he was cynical beyond his years. She did wonder why he was coming this weekend because he had been avoiding Kirkfield since his father died and the will had been read out leaving the bulk of Hamish's fortune and the house to Jerusha. The property and any remaining capital and stocks and shares were to be divided between Claude and Jean on Jerusha's death. Jerusha herself found this an odd way of doing things because, if she allowed herself to think that way, it provided a perfect motive for murder. She tried hard to keep her relationship with her stepchildren amiable but Claude was impervious.

He arrived in his second-hand Mercedes Benz and with very little luggage. The message was that he was there under duress for a very short duration. He ignored Jerusha's attempt to hug him and pushed his way past her into the house.

'Where have you put me this time? Where am I to put my bags?' he asked.

'Your old room,' she said.

'It's hardly my old room when you have cleared out all my stuff. And where are the terrible two? They surely must be one of your better jokes.'

'Oswald and James are not a joke. They've gone, very seriously, into town. They're still looking for a house to buy.'

'Good thing they are taking their time or you would be rattling around in Kirkfield House. How is the old place going? Costing a fortune in upkeep, I'll bet. And what's this about a niece staying? It could be that she is my step-cousin, could it not?'

'One question at a time,' said Jerusha. 'Yes, the house is costing a lot in upkeep. I've just had the slates replaced on the entire roof. Hopefully, that's it done for the next hundred years. Secondly, you asked about Sonia. She is my brother's daughter. I don't know what her relationship is to you.' She couldn't help adding, 'She has fallen in love.'

'Now, that is interesting.' His eyes brightly gleaned this bit of information. 'Who with?'

Jerusha thought she had at last found a topic with which he could engage. 'With Callum Thomson.'

'And who might this Callum be? How did she meet him? Don't tell me it was your doing?'

'Not really. It was love at first sight. He's a roofer.'

'A roofer.' He said this with imperious emphasis.

'Yes. And they are both Christians.'

'My, my. A Christian roofer. Well, certainly, he'll be close to heaven.'

'They are madly in love. You'll meet them. Now, let us get your bags upstairs.'

'I can do that. You do whatever it is that you do.'

'Notice the new curtains, Claude,' she said to his retreating back.

What she was doing was baking a chocolate cake for afternoon tea and it should be nearly ready. She took a skewer and, opening up the Aga, she pricked the brown sponge. When she withdrew the skewer there was some moisture on the tip so she put the cake in for a little longer.

Claude was a strange one. She couldn't please him. If she tried to mother him he pushed her away. If she tried to treat him as an adult he rejoined with extra-adult cynicism. He had never got over losing his mother and his reaction to his father's death was frightening. Claude was only ten when Françoise went missing and in all the long seven years before she was pronounced dead he always believed she would come back. He dismissed any suggestions that she was dead as 'stories'. Jerusha imagined that he still believed that, at any moment, she would come in the door at Kirkfield, as beautiful and glamorous as she had been when she vanished, oust Jerusha and take over Kirkfield as her right. As Jerusha, herself, sometimes imagined this, even now. Nobody as magnetic as Françoise could go without a pull. The whole sad affair had made Claude grow up faster than he should. It made Jean vulnerable but it toughened up Claude. And when his father died he was at first angry and then outwardly stoical. Physically, he tensed and emotionally he hardened. It was as if the little boy in him was saying, 'No more, please' and the adult in him tightened and toughened.

Eventually, Claude accepted Jerusha as inevitable but there was always a hard edge to his treatment of her. Would he be violent towards her? Sometimes she thought he would and, despite her compassion towards him, she never slept well when he was in the house. She would often think, though, that his verbal abuse of humankind was so sustained that all his violent feelings would be going into that. He was constantly channelling his aggression and, thereby, attempting to maintain control.

'Gosh you gave me a fright!' said Jerusha, swinging around. Sonia and Callum had come in the back door without noise. They had been standing behind her while she put the cake in the oven. It could have been Claude.

'You are the one with the vicious weapon, Jerusha,' said Sonia.

Jerusha put the skewer down on the worktop. 'Anyone would think there was to be a murder in this household. We're all so jumpy.'

'You've got to be joking, Jerusha,' said Callum.

'I am. What can I do you for?' She deliberately muddled the sequence of the words to cover up her nervousness. Getting a fright was not a Jerusha thing to do.

'We're going to climb the Eildon Hills and we wondered if you wanted to come with us?' asked Sonia.

'I've got too much to do here, but I know who would like to come with you. Claude would. He is just getting organized.' Jerusha did not really have that much to do in the house. It had all been done, with the help of the S.S.,

202

but she didn't fancy keeping up their pace on a hill walk. Her size had its disadvantages.

Claude came in and agreed in a lacklustre manner to go with Sonia and Callum. 'I've nothing better to do,' he said.

'See you in a few hours,' said Sonia. The three of them were gone.

Left to her own devices, Jerusha found the cake baked to her satisfaction and put it on a wire tray. She then took off for the old church. She wanted to thank God for their escape from harm in the near accident on the way to the ballet. She had forgotten up until now. That was the extent of her prayer life. Erratic. There were large spells of life when she forgot God altogether. At other times she was feverish in her faithfulness. She had entered the church and sat down in a pew when the door swung open and Oswald and James came in. Their arrival was the equivalent of an invasion in the quietness of the church. They were clearly in good humour. So much so, that Oswald rushed up ahead of James to the pulpit. 'Beware the wrath of God,' he intoned. 'The end is nigh. Doomsday is upon us.'

'Come down here. And don't you ever make fun of the Christian Faith, again,' shouted Jerusha. She had seen Christianity mocked and parodied too often to let it happen in the sanctity of her 'own' church. She was aware that there were many detractors of religion in today's British society and she usually kept her own Faith hidden but not here and not by way of an assault by Oswald.

'He didn't mean it, Jerusha,' said James. 'He's just excited.'

'Yes. Sorry, Jerusha. I'm going to see my children this afternoon. I got carried away. Besides, many Christians will not accept James and me so why should we not play their game?'

'It's not a game,' replied Jerusha.

'Since when have you taken life so seriously?' asked Oswald.

'In private, I am a very serious person.' But she could not contain her giggles. 'Deadly serious.' She couldn't keep a straight face. Her playfulness was re-emerging just because her two best friends were there.

'Am I forgiven then?'

'Say he is forgiven, Jerusha. He won't do it again.'

'Almost. If you promise not to do it again. And remember, there are Christians who accept you and your lifestyle,' said Jerusha.

'And are you a Christian, Jerusha?' asked Oswald.

'I believe in God but I don't go to a conventional church.'

'That is not much of an answer,' said James.

'I don't expect them to accept me either, to be honest. What with three marriages and other things you know nothing about.'

'The last marriage ending wasn't your fault,' said James.

'You are implying the first two were my fault.' Some of her annoyance re-surfaced.

'I'm sure it's very complex,' said James, retreating.

'Quite right,' said Jerusha. 'Now, you had better go, if you're going to see the children.

They went, leaving her restless and incapable of communing with God. She went to Hamish's room, to commune with him instead.

⟊⟊⟊

It was not a long, drawn-out illness. It was quick and brutal. The cancer took nine months to consume him, once it had been diagnosed. Not years. They first noticed he was not well when he began to tire easily. He went off his usual Scotch in the evenings and complained about the food Jerusha prepared for him. He was pale and withdrawn. She persuaded him to go to the doctor who had xrays taken that showed there was something wrong with his liver. An appointment for a scan at an Edinburgh hospital was made for two weeks later. While he waited, he became increasingly weak. She remembered that the day she took him for the scan it was snowing. It was February 2005. She had great difficulty getting the car out of the driveway because it was iced over. She remembered, also, what he had said to her. 'It's cancer,' he had said, in a matter-of-fact way. He knew before the doctors confirmed the diagnosis. 'Promise me, you won't let me die in one of those wretched hospitals,' Hamish had said. 'I want to die, if I must, at Kirkfield.'

'Don't be silly. You're not going to die,' she had said. 'Positive thinking is what it's all about, Hamish.'

'Not with terminal cancer. I'm sorry, my love.'

He was right, of course. After the scan results were in he was admitted to another Edinburgh hospital for an operation. They were going to open him up and examine him, particularly his liver.

After the operation she drove from the Borders to see him. Lorna went with her.

'I don't think it's as bad as he would have it,' she said to Lorna.

'He's so certain of the worst,' said Lorna. 'But his instincts must count for something.'

'Cancer is such a ghastly word,' said Jerusha. 'It's so final. It sounds so terminal.'

'Well, it is, in many cases. I wonder what the doctors are going to tell you?'

'I wonder.'

It turned out that it wasn't the doctors who told her the diagnosis and prognosis but Hamish himself. He was numbed and frank. 'They opened up my liver and found it so riddled with cancer that they simply closed it back up again. I've got weeks, perhaps months.'

'You are telling me that is it?'

'You need to know the truth.'

'You seem so . . . stoical.'

'I don't want to die, Jerusha.'

'Maybe they can do something? Give you a transplant. Something?'

'It is not just the liver. The cancer has spread. No. My time is up and you can help me by accepting that.'

'Oh, my love. I'll do anything. Lorna is here, waiting in the car. Do you want to see her?'

'No. Tell her what I've said. I'm tired now. Give me a kiss and go back to Kirkfield. I'll be there soon.'

Jerusha was in a state of shock and the nurses outside the private ward saw this and gave her a cup of hot, strong tea. Not only did she appreciate the comfort of the tea but it gave her a reprieve from having to tell Lorna. It was while she was sitting sipping tea that she decided not to tell Lorna until they got home. The only way she could bear the drive back was to pretend everything was going to be all right. She needed to pretend that the operation had been a success and that Hamish would recover. He would be back amongst them soon.

'He'll be out of there in no time,' she said, getting into the driver's seat.

'Doesn't he want to see me?' asked Lorna. She had been on edge, expecting the worst. She was still tense, despite Jerusha's words.

'He is tired tonight. He'll be home soon. You can see him then.'

'Okay. Did you give him my card and the flowers?'

'Yes. He says to tell you thank you. Now I've got to negotiate my way out of this city.' She had not lied. She just hadn't told Lorna the truth. They drove in silence until they got back to Kirkfield where Lorna's car was parked. Lorna was unsettled. She kept adjusting her wig. She sensed that Jerusha was not telling her everything. She knew well what she was like when she was lying by omission. Bright. Chirpy. Or vague. Jerusha was an honest person and couldn't keep up the deception. As soon as she had turned the engine off in the driveway, she turned to Lorna and said, 'what I told you is true. He will be out soon but he is not going to be with us for very long.'

'You mean the cancer is terminal?' asked Lorna.

'He is dying, Lorna.'

'What . . . days, weeks, months?'

'Months.'

'And he knows this?'

'He is the one who told me. I didn't see a doctor.' Both women were dry-eyed. It was as if they were sharing a secret so deep and dark that they were stunned. Jerusha wondered if Lorna's mental constitution could tolerate the news that her brother had been given months to live. 'Do you want to stay the night?'

'No. I'll go. We can talk tomorrow. How are you going to tell the children?'

'He will tell them. When he is back they need to come home from school. Claude wouldn't take the news from me.'

Lorna walked numbly to her car and Jerusha went inside and poured herself a stiff whisky. She had the house to herself. The tears came. She went and looked at herself crying, in the mirror. 'The perfect wife,' she sobbed to her reflection. Then she turned and lay down on the *chaise longue*, glass in hand. But she found her hand shaking so much that she had to put down the glass on a small side table. She buried her head in her hands. Hamish was being taken from her, after all that they'd lived through together. They had planned to marry after Françoise was declared dead but somehow hadn't got around to it. Unless they were to marry soon, there would be no groom. Her cries became louder and her whole body shook. After some minutes she was able to lift up her glass and gulp down some whisky. When the glass was drained she went to bed, exhausted.

ᏫᎢᏒᏍᎤᎧᎧᎤ

The weeks blurred into months once Hamish was home. He had to get over a major operation and was very weak. He ate little but he liked Marmite on toast and she fed him copious quantities of this, most of which remained half-eaten. He also liked cups of tea with spoonfuls of sugar, which he never liked before. The district nurse came in morning and night, mainly to adjust the amount of morphine the doctor was prescribing and to see that he was comfortable. A Macmillan nurse came and counselled both Hamish and Jerusha. Jerusha had never before been cast in the role of carer and it didn't suit her particularly well. To begin with, the house had to be kept spotlessly clean or the nurses were unhappy. At the time, there was no home help. After about a month of this Jerusha put the word out that she needed home help and she employed Sarah Sharp, the S.S. That left her free to wait on her beloved Hamish who could be restless and demanding. He was still able to get out of bed and sit in a chair. He insisted that only she make his bed and clean and tidy his bedroom. She had moved out of the once-shared bedroom before he came home from hospital. She took to keeping fresh flowers by his bedside—fuchsias and carnations, mainly small bunches—but he told her to stop this because he had been brought up to believe that men did not appreciate flowers the way women did. He said she was doing it for herself. At night there was no respite for she had to answer dozens of 'phone calls from family and friends, many of whom were in tears and, although she tried to play up the little positive things, they succeeded in pulling her down.

The children were different. She felt a need to mother them, although Claude resisted. After the operation they had come home to hear the news. Claude took his laptop into his bedroom and did not come out for several hours. Jean nestled into Jerusha's comfortable form and allowed her to stroke her hair while she wept. They struggled to get used to the fact that their father was dying. Then one day Hamish called them in for a 'conference' from which Jerusha was excluded. She sat at the kitchen table painting her fingernails a rosebud pink. It was a long time since she had felt so fat and useless. In fact, the last time was before Arthur unveiled her sexiness. And at school, under the merciless teasing of the other children, with her mother's criticism thrown in. Her lover, a dying man, was having a family conference and he did not want her there. All the stress of caring for him mesmerised her. She was too tired to take her emotion into her own body so she disengaged in this way, automatically putting brush to nail in the oft-repeated stroke. She was blowing on them to dry them when Claude and Jean came downstairs.

Claude stood in the doorway and said, 'you've won.' That was all and then he left the room.

Jean came and put her arm around Jerusha's neck, standing behind her. 'I'm not allowed to tell you what he said. He did say to tell you that he would speak to you tomorrow, if there is a tomorrow for him,' she said. 'He has gone to sleep.'

Jerusha knew what that would be like. Hamish could not sleep well at all, even with the morphine. He would wake with the pain and cry out; his body bathed in sweat. She would hurry through and wipe his brow, talking him back into sleep. That night, however, he was quiet, so quiet that she wondered if he were dead. Then she wouldn't hear from him the contents of his conversation with his children. Death had to come. When? It was teasing them like some gruesome joker. She had to be constantly ready for it. She tiptoed through to his bedroom and stared in the half-light at his torso where he had pushed the duvet away. There was no doubt that there was a rise and fall as he breathed in and out, his eyes closed. She left as silently as she had come.

The next morning he was drowsy, especially after the district nurse had been, and it wasn't until she was eating some lunch in the kitchen that he called through the intercom, 'Come on up, Jerusha.' She had another mouthful and was eating as she went upstairs. It was a cold day and they had the heating on. She had climbed those stairs a million times over the past month but never with such trepidation. Who knew what she could expect from his call? Was she to be given her marching orders? After all they had been together for only seven years. They had known each other for seven years. Now what? How did he really feel about her under the pressure of certain death?

She went in and sat beside his bed. They didn't touch.

'I've been giving some thought to your suggestion that we marry anyway, even although I'm not much good to you. I've been thinking as much as I can under the circumstances.'

'I don't want to tire you. I just want to show my love for you.'

'Hush. Hear what I've got to say. I think it's a good idea . . .'

'A good idea?'

'Yes. The sooner the better so you can be Mrs Hamish Burnett before I pop my clogs.'

'That's wonderful.'

'That way I can do my best by you. Show my love for you. My lawyer, Vernon Brown, you've met him, is drawing up my new will and he has promised to come here for me to sign it. You can let him come up. All this is urgent.' He was breathless.

'Do you want me to organize the wedding?'

'Well, I'm not going to do it, am I?' He asked this with the suggestion of a shudder.

But they laughed. Jerusha was now feeling rounder, more buxom, sexier than she had for months. She was Jerusha. She was wanted. 'Do you want a priest?'

'Absolutely. Let us say Wednesday, if I last that long. I think I can do it.' He sank back into the pillows.

'I'm onto to it,' said Jerusha, giving him a kiss on the forehead.

They clasped hands before she let him go and hurried out of the room to start organizing a small wedding. She returned just as quickly to stand at the door. 'I love you,' she called.

'I love you, too. Now, get to it, woman.' But there was little strength in these words.

She counted the days in a very special way. Not only was she counting towards a special occasion but she was holding on to each day that he was still alive. Counting forwards and backwards.

The local minister agreed to conduct the ceremony provided divorce and other paperwork were forthcoming. And he could do it on the Wednesday afternoon. After that was fixed she told the children who, of course, knew already that they were getting married. That is what the secret conference had been about. How could she have been so wrong about it? This now explained Claude's caustic remark that she'd won. She was surprised that Claude had not put up a fight. All she could think was that he wanted to comply with his dying father's wishes. Jean was happy and excited. As well as the children, Jerusha wanted to invite Lorna and James. They had to be told the news and booked for Wednesday afternoon. James hadn't yet met Oswald and was living in Edinburgh at the time. They could both come.

Jerusha dashed into Edinburgh and bought the peach outfit that she was to treasure for many years. She bought a cake, locally, and shopped for a celebratory meal for the guests, the children and herself. She engaged the S.S. to come and do a super-clean of the whole house. She filled it with flowers, apart from Hamish's bedroom.

'You'll want to prepare yourself spiritually,' he said, seeing her dashing away. She went to the old church and prayed that he would still be alive in the morning. She was marrying Hamish, the living person, not just a terminally ill man. It was to be her one last declaration of love. She would carry on their marriage into a world without him. She would love him always. She would keep the memories. The tobogganing when he had first kissed her, the Christmases, the birthdays, the jokes. She would never stop loving him. There would be no children between them, even if it were possible that he should live. God bless this man. The perfect husband and the perfect wife.

On the day the priest, or rather a Church of Scotland Minister, Reverend Frank Giles, arrived early, while Jerusha was still getting ready. Lorna was there and she gave him a mug of coffee. The ceremony was to take place at eleven o'clock, or thereabouts, at a time when they thought the patient could cope. It was to be some time after the nurse had given him morphine but not too long afterwards, when he would be in pain. Jerusha had bought him a new beige dressing gown and new brown silk pyjamas and she dry shampooed his hair, his lovely grey hair. When she was ready herself, in peach with flowers in her hair, she re-arranged his pillows so that, propped up, he could sign the register. He was looking pale and serious. There were dark rings under his eyes and his hands were shaky.

'Are you going to be able to go through with this?' she asked.

'Wouldn't miss it,' he mumbled, trying to form a smile.

'Then I'll get the others.'

They trooped into the bedroom: Reverend Giles in a suit with dog collar; Vernon with his briefcase; Lorna looking pert in a light blue suit; James in a grey suit and tie; Claude and Jean were dazzling. Jerusha was unaccustomed to seeing them in anything other than denim jeans or, in Jean's case, school uniform. Claude did look uncomfortable in his suit but Jean fitted happily into an emerald green dress with petticoats making the skirt flounce. Solemnly, they arranged themselves around the bed. Hamish's eyes were barely open but he was awake. The Macmillan nurse had asked if they wanted her there but Jerusha said no. She would watch Hamish to see that it wasn't all too much.

'Is it okay to start, Hamish?' Jerusha whispered.

He waved a hand and the minister took this as a signal to begin. 'Dearly beloved, we are gathered together . . .' He went on through a shortened version of the marriage service.

When it came to Hamish's turn to say 'I do', he appeared to be asleep and there was a pause when everyone looked at everyone else. Jerusha wondered if this was it. Under the pretence of holding his hand she felt his pulse on his wrist. He was still alive. She nodded to Reverend Giles. He repeated the words: 'Do you promise to love and honour this woman as long as you both shall live?'

'I do,' said Hamish with terrible effort.

'I now pronounce you husband and wife,' said the minister with some glee in his voice.

The couple had exchanged rings, the wedding band joining the sapphire and diamond ring he had given her so long ago. Jerusha remembered them scrabbling on the floor to find it after she had dropped it. Hamish clasped her wrist, a weak gesture. 'We have been the perfect husband and wife,' he said.

She kissed him on his dry, caked lips.

With one accord, the guests and the professionals left the couple alone. But it was an uncertain aloneness for Hamish had apparently gone to sleep. She tried to feel his pulse and again he groaned. She was afraid the occasion had worn him out and she hovered by his bedside. Would a perfect wife stay with him? Or, go to be with her guests?

'Go now, woman,' he said.' He was not truly asleep after all. 'And when you come back I've something to tell you.' He lapsed back into silence.

Jerusha insisted on re-arranging his pillows to that he could sleep and then she went downstairs.

'To the new Mrs Burnett.' They raised their glasses, even Claude. 'Congratulations,' said Vernon. 'I'll have the certificate to you in the post within the next couple of weeks.'

Jerusha felt as if she had come from a darkened room into light, which she had. Yes, she had. A darkened room that contained the most precious person in her life. To a room of light where her friends wanted a party. She was briefly thrown and then she took a glass of champagne. 'To the groom,' she said. She put some music on, softly so that it would not disturb her husband. She would celebrate for two.

Reverend Giles left but the rest remained to eat the magnificent buffet Jerusha had prepared. She had intended that they eat on laps but the six of them ended up eating from plates on the table edges surrounding the buffet, reaching out to help themselves to more. They went on to puds—lots of cream and fruit and a biscuit-based cheesecake—before the cutting of the cake. Jerusha posed for photographs holding the knife, then she cut into the two-tiered cake with the figure of a bride and groom resting on its centre. Jerusha made sure everyone had a piece of cake and cut two more, one for herself and one for Hamish. She excused herself and went up with the cake to his bedroom.

She came back very quickly, without the cake, which she had dropped onto his bedside table. She stood in the dining room doorway. 'I think he's dead,' she said.

'Wait there, Mrs Burnett,' said Vernon. 'I'll go up' He went and was back again after what seemed a long time. 'Yes, he has gone,' he said.

Jerusha often wondered what Hamish had wanted to say to her before he died. She wondered if she would ever find out.

She was coming downstairs as Claude, Sonia and Callum were coming off the hill. It took Sonia and Callum less than ten minutes to drive to Kirkfield. 'Darlings. How was it?' Jerusha greeted Claude and Sonia as they walked in the kitchen door.

'A hill is just a hill is just a hill,' said Claude.

'Come on, Claude,' said Sonia. 'It was brilliant. The views were spectacular.'

'Where is Callum?' asked Jerusha.

'Gone home to shower and change for dinner,' said Sonia.

Jerusha would wear one of her saris that night but she would change only just before the food was ready. A couple of hours later she went to get some sprigs of rosemary for the lamb from the greenhouse. She found the glass sliding door already open. She went in and there, at the end of a corridor of plants, were Sonia and Callum in a close embrace. They stepped apart when she cleared her throat but still held hands.

'Sorry to interrupt. I need some rosemary,' said Jerusha. She was not embarrassed. She just wanted to get what she had come for and leave them to it. She held a pair of scissors in one hand. The rosemary plant was right beside Callum.

'You're always holding lethal weapons,' joked Sonia.

'You are always holding hands,' replied Jerusha.

'We want to be together, always,' said Callum.

'Yes, Jerusha. We'll let you into our secret. If you promise not to tell,' said Sonia.

'This must be something I should not tell Saul?' asked Jerusha.

'It is. Promise?'

'Tell me first and then I'll see.'

'No. Promise now.' Sonia was firm.

Jerusha looked vaguely around as if for support and then came to a conclusion, 'I promise.' It had taken seconds for her to decide to give her word but, once given, she was very unlikely to go back on it. Jerusha was loyal and trusting but even she was not prepared for what came next.

'We are going to be married. Tomorrow we're going to Gretna Green where we will marry and go to live in Paris. Callum will find work there and I will, too.'

'You're still young. Why the hurry? And I am not to tell Saul about this?'

'We know our own minds. Sonia's father would not understand that,' said Callum.

'You haven't asked him.'

'Auntie Jerusha, you promised not to tell.'

'You never know, he might give his blessing. And then you could have a conventional wedding.'

'Do you think that's likely?' asked Sonia, her head on one side. 'If you don't think it's a good idea how much more will Daddy object?'

'It's not that I don't think it is a good idea. I just think it's a bit hasty. You've known each other a short time. Sonia, you have become like a daughter to me. I can't stand by and let you . . .'

'What? Do something rash? We'll be doing something spontaneous and romantic.'

'Marriage is for life.' It was the adult in Jerusha talking. She felt she had to take a stand, even although she sympathised with these two young people.

'And you have a good record,' said Sonia.

'There were reasons why my marriages did not last.'

There is no reason why this one won't last,' said Callum.

'What about your parents, Callum?'

'They just want to see us happy. It's not the groom's parents who put on the usual wedding performance. They would not try to stop me, if they were in on this.'

'Will you have an address in Paris so that I can contact you?' Jerusha saw that they were going to do this thing, with or without her permission. At least they could keep in touch.

'We'll send you that once we're organized,' said Sonia.

'What about your religion? Doesn't the Bible say you should honour your father and your mother?'

'I do honour my father and my mother. It's up to them whether they understand that.'

'Marrying without his knowledge is a serious thing to do.'

'It's better than the rumpus that would occur if I told him. Besides, Callum is a Christian.'

'We have God's blessing,' said Callum

'How can you know that?'

'We know,' said Callum, giving Sonia's hand a squeeze. They were beginning to trust that Jerusha now felt the romance of their intentions.

It *was* a romantic thing to do, to run away to be married at Gretna Green and then go to live in France. If she had been their age she might have done the same thing. She saw now that any argument against it was stale and negative. She wanted them to defy Saul and his prejudices. She wanted them to be young and impulsive. And she had promised to keep the secret. Suddenly, searching for rosemary for the roast lamb seemed a very mundane thing to be doing.

The next day, Sonia and Callum were gone. Claude went too but for different reasons. He said he would go before someone suggested charades. Oswald and James were on a high after seeing Oswald's children; so much so that they didn't realize Sonia had packed and left. They would notice later and question Jerusha about it. She said something vague about Sonia having gone to South Africa in a hurry because there was a crisis. They were doubtful. 'But she didn't say goodbye,' said Oswald. 'Shows what she thinks of us.' However, they did not ask any more questions at that point.

APRIL FOOLS' DAY 2010 IS OVER

8

JOKE UNCOVERED

Jerusha's favourite day was April Fools' Day and this year she had carried out a '*coup de fools*', which had kept Oswald and James guessing for weeks. **Did she or did she not bury a body? Was that Sonia's corpse that went into the ground?** They still discussed going to the police. However, the second part of the trick had yet to come—the exhumation of the dressmaker's dummy. Jerusha was stringing out the fun and could have done so indefinitely were it not for a very unfortunate turn of events.

Jerusha's least favourite day of the year 2010 to date was the day that Saul turned up on her doorstep. She opened the door to see him standing there, greyer, more lined but still her brother. 'Darling.' She automatically used the now stale term of affection. 'Come in.'

'Don't darling me, Mary.' He pushed past her. 'Where is my daughter?' He called for Sonia.

'She is not here,' said Jerusha, afraid of his manner and intentions. She awaited his questions, thinking she would have to make up her answers as she went along.

'Then where is she? Why haven't I heard from her for months? We've been worried sick. And now I've had to come all the way from South Africa to find out what you've done with her.'

'You could have 'phoned.'

'And got some cock and bull story. I wanted . . . want to see for myself.'

'Will you be staying? I'll make up a bed.'

'No. Not likely. I'm booked into a B&B in Galashiels and I'm here for as long as it takes.'

Hearing his loud voice, Oswald and James came into the hall. In unison, they reckoned that Jerusha needed protecting.

'Oh, here you are,' said Jerusha with relief. 'This is James and this is Oswald. My brother, Saul. Can I offer you a cup of tea or a coffee, Saul? I've got some cake to give you. You must be tired after your journey.'

'You talk of tea and cake while I'm trying to find my missing daughter. What can you tell me?' He looked at Oswald and James.

'I understand why you are upset,' said James, 'but I can't think you're going to make matters better by yelling at Jerusha.'

'All right. Look, if I call you Jerusha will you tell me where Sonia went?'

'She said goodbye in October,' said Jerusha.

'That's just it. She did not say goodbye,' said Oswald,' not to us she didn't.'

'So, you think there's something mysterious about her departure?' asked Saul. His eyes were bulging with suppressed anger and he looked as if he might grab Oswald by the T-shirt and pin him against a wall.

'I did not say that.' Oswald was starting to get angry himself. 'You have no right to behave in this aggressive manner, no matter what your problem.'

'If everyone could just calm down,' said Jerusha.

'All right,' said Saul again. 'Let's start afresh.'

'Come through to the kitchen and take a seat.' She ushered him through and James and Oswald followed. 'There now. Make yourself comfortable.' She sat, herself. 'The truth is, Saul, we don't know where Sonia is. That's the gospel truth. No amount of bullying can help to give you your answers.'

'Then I must call in the police. You do have such people around here?'

'You're welcome to use the 'phone,' said Jerusha. 'I'll fetch it for you and the number.'

While Saul was on the 'phone, the three of them went into the kitchen.

'You know where she is, don't you Jerusha?' whispered Oswald. 'You must know. You were the last one to see her that night when Callum was here. And Claude.' James also kept his voice down. Neither of the two men were mentioning the burial. It was a subject too gruesome to contemplate. But it was in the back of their minds. 'No one will blame you, Jerusha.'

'That is because I am not to blame for anything.' She put the kettle on.

'But, we thought . . .'

'No matter what you think, I don't know where Sonia is exactly, any more than you do.'

'What do you mean, exactly?' asked Oswald. 'You're not talking about Heaven and Hell are you?'

Just then Saul came through and put an end to their conversation. 'The police will be here in half an hour,' he said. 'A Detective Inspector Fergus Drew is coming.'

'The copper with the long nose,' said Oswald, irreverently to break the tension.

'What's that got to do with his performance as a policeman. You seem to be familiar with him,' Saul remarked.

'We've had dealings with him recently. A tramp drowned in the river and we found him,' explained Jerusha.

'Things seem to happen around here. I mean bad things.'

'What do you mean?' Jerusha was annoyed.

'Just a hunch,' said Saul.

Inspector Drew arrived and he brought PC Rutherford with him. Confronted by four pairs of eyes he chose to forestall any contradictions. 'I'll see Mr Saul Patterson first and then, one at a time, you others. Where would you like us to go, Mrs Burnett?'

'Call me Jerusha. Everyone else does. You can go into the sitting room. That would be the most comfortable. This way.'

'We will find our way,' said the Inspector with authority. 'Mr Patterson, could you step this way, sir?' They went into the sitting room and found two chairs where they could be seated opposite one another with PC Rutherford sitting to one side.

'You have reported your daughter missing. I am here to find out what basis you have for saying that.'

'And to find her.'

'Yes. I've no doubt we will find her. When did you last see her?'

'Before she came to the UK. About a year ago. I last heard from her in September last year. I got a letter from her, in South Africa where I live.'

'And was there anything to alarm you in this letter?'

'No. I'm sorry, that wasn't the last time I heard from her. I got an email asking me, us, to send her some more money. I received it at the end of September. Here, I have it here.'

'Did you send her more money?'

'Yes.'

'Have you any idea what she wanted it for?'

'She said she wanted to do more travelling.'

'That is your answer. She has gone travelling.'

'Look here, Inspector. It's not as easy as that. It's definitely not like her to fail to send some sort of communication. A postcard, even.'

'In her last letter, did she mention any people? People she might be with?'

'It was all about what she had been doing with my sister, who you call Jerusha, and about Oswald and James.'

What do you call your sister?'

'Mary. She was christened Mary Louise. She has changed her name.'

'Why did she do that?'

'I don't know. Grandiose ideas?'

'You don't get on with your sister.'

'We had not spoken for many years and then, out of the blue, I get a letter from her all about forgiveness. But hang on, this is about my daughter, not about Jerusha.'

'The two may be interconnected.'

'I see what you mean. I knew it. Jerusha is somehow responsible for Sonia disappearing.' He moved to the front of his chair to indicate action.

Inspector Drew put out a hand. 'Patience, Mr Patterson.'

George sat silent. It was not his place to ask questions, aloud at any rate.

The Inspector continued. 'Now, tell me what the letter said, Mr Patterson.'

'If she has done anything to Sonia I swear I'll kill her.'

'The letter.' Inspector Drew raised an eyebrow and Saul sat back in his seat.

'Oh, it was all about how she had forgiven me. Asking if I could forgive her. How pleased she was to have Sonia with her. I'm afraid I wrote quite a nasty reply.'

'A reply that might have motivated her to somehow engineer Sonia's disappearance?'

'Yes. I'm sure she knows something.'

'We will find out. I will speak to her now. You can go for the time being.' He paused as Saul got up. 'Be warned, Mr Patterson, we'll have no violence in this house. Send her in.'

Jerusha came in looking self-assured and, she hoped, innocent. Although she had done nothing to Sonia, she was well aware that her joke might be uncovered and might not seem funny to some. All it would take was Oswald or James, probably Oswald, to mention a grave and an unidentifiable body. Of murder, she was innocent. Of colluding with Sonia and Callum, she was not to blame. They had told her their plan and she had tried to stop them. She had nothing to do with their getting away. She had merely looked in a different direction. Also, she could safely say she didn't know where they were because she had not yet received their address. Paris is a big city. She sat down on a seat warm from Saul's occupancy.

'I'll not beat about the bush, Jerusha,' said the Inspector.

'Thank you.'

'Do you know where Sonia Patterson is?'

'No' Paris is a big city, she thought to herself. 'No. I don't, but I would like to. Inspector, I have had nothing to do with this, Sonia has become a friend and I would like to see her safe, as much as Saul would. You will have gathered that my brother and I don't always see eye to eye.'

'This could cloud the issue but it also might be a motive.'

'A motive for what?'

'For revenge. He has told us that he sent you what he called a nasty letter after you wrote asking for forgiveness.'

'Yes, but Sonia tore that up.'

'Then, we can't see this letter?'

'No. It went in the bin. She did it. I did not.' She was starting to feel as if she had been handed a load of suspicion. The policeman could not really believe that she had harmed Sonia. For a moment, she contemplated telling the truth but she remembered her promise to keep it a secret. She would not be forced into betraying Sonia and Callum.

'When exactly did you last see Sonia?'

She told him about the weekend with Claude and even added a bit about finding Sonia and Callum in the greenhouse.

'So, these two were an item?' The Inspector pushed away some strands of fringe, pleased with himself for using a modern phrase for the relationship between the pair. PC George Rutherford cleared his throat and then resumed silence.

'You could say so. They fell in love the moment they met.' Jerusha was conscious that she was starting to give too much away. 'Sonia has a very independent spirit and very definite ideas. For instance, she didn't approve of the relationship between Oswald and James, the gay couple you met when you arrived.' She was gabbling, trying to divert attention from Callum and his influence on Sonia. However, the Inspector was not fooled.

This Callum. Can we contact him?'

'You can try. He did the scaffolding when we had the roof repaired so I've probably got the number. Sonia also used to walk Sheena's dog frequently and Sheena might be able to be of help.' Jerusha was still trying to lay a false trail. Sheena would know nothing. 'Claude was one of the last to see her. I can give you his contact number.'

'Yes. All this would be helpful, particularly the number of the scaffolder.' He was making notes all the time and he began to make Jerusha feel uneasy. Inspector Drew wasn't easily deceived. Then he said something that ruffled her further. 'It seems this house makes a habit of reporting missing women. Your late husband's first wife went missing from Kirkfield in June 1996. My predecessor dealt with the case but I have heard about it. I read about it in the press, as well. I believe she was never found. Strange that.'

'It's just a coincidence. In any case, I met her only once so I don't know much more than you.'

'As you say, it must be a coincidence. It's no use dwelling in the past, as fascinating as it may be. We have to focus on the present. We must find Sonia.'

George showed Jerusha out and, on instructions from his superior, brought Oswald and James in together. Privately, the Inspector did not have much time for these two and thought he was to make short shrift of what they had to say. He was to be surprised. He asked the standard question about when they last saw Sonia.

'It was that weekend in October when Claude was here. I can't remember the date,' said Oswald, the more vocal of the two as usual. 'She was there and then she wasn't. We were mystified by her sudden departure,' he continued. 'We realized she didn't like us . . . our situation . . . but she could at least have said goodbye.'

'You didn't think to report her missing?'

'Jerusha said she had gone back to South Africa,' said James.

'Clearly not.'

'It wasn't so clear then,' said Oswald.

'No. We are used to being snubbed,' said James.

'Your relationship is your affair. What I'm interested in is a young girl who is missing now. Today. And she was last seen in this house.'

'I can tell you something that James and I have been worrying about. On April Fools' Day, Jerusha got James and me to dig a hole.' He was fumbling for words because he felt he was betraying Jerusha. But he had to speak up, to throw light on the case if what he had to say was relevant. James and he had discussed it in the hall, waiting to be interviewed. They would voice their suspicions because what they suspected was too serious to ignore. When it came to something like murder, loyalty and love were not unconditional.

Inspector Drew took Oswald's hesitation the wrong way 'Tell me another one,' he said.

'No. You must listen. The hole was big enough to be a grave. We got drunk while we were digging. We did it to please her, as we always do. Jerusha is a dear friend but if she has done what I think she has, I must report it,' said Oswald.

'Afterwards, from the window, we saw her burying something. It could have been a body. Only, as Oswald said, we were drunk. What happened is not clear,' said James.

'Where is this hole?' Inspector Drew was now alert to a new possibility.

'At the side of the house, near the veggie garden,' said James.

'We can show you,' offered Oswald, relieved that he had now spoken out.

'PC Rutherford, get two men from the station. You and they need to do a bit of digging. Don't look stupefied young man. Get PC Anderson and PC Kier and tell them to bring some spades. Oswald will show them where to dig.' He had opened the door and was starting to leave. 'I have to attend to another case but will be back as soon as I can. Don't go anywhere, any of you.' He looked at the fraught faces of Oswald, James, Saul and Jerusha in the hall. 'And you, Mr Patterson, keep a lid on your anger. We don't know whether or not we'll find anything.'

Jerusha was worried. She judged that the mood in the group was not right for the climax of an elaborate joke. Oswald and James, perhaps, but not Saul. She could not blame him for he was desperate to find his daughter. She thought of confessing all but decided to let events take their course. At the very least, they would prove that she did not bury Sonia. Why would she let a hoax that she had painstakingly planned go unnoticed? Sonia would write with her address and she would give it to Saul or, anyway, leave it where he would find it. She didn't want to see her brother in this state of misery but he had brought it on himself. One thing at a time. Out of the window, she saw Saul take a spade from Luke Junior and start digging when Oswald showed him the fatal spot. Oswald and James then disappeared to their bedroom, hiding from their betrayal of her.

It wasn't long before the three policemen, armed with spades came to help Saul and work began in earnest. Luke Junior rang the doorbell. 'I told them Mr Burnett said never to dig in that spot. I told them, Mrs Burnett, but they wouldn't listen.'

'Some strange things are happening in this house. You take the afternoon off Luke Junior. Mr Burnett would have understood. Go and take Zilla out for the afternoon, or something.'

'Aye, Mrs Burnett. It's a sad day when Mr Burnett's instructions aren't followed.' He went away to his house, shaking his head.

Jerusha gave a passing thought to why Hamish had forbidden digging in that spot. Not knowing his wishes, she had already done so, to no ill effect. She went into the kitchen to find something to eat. James and Oswald seemed to have forgotten lunch. Enjoying a bacon roll, she wondered which one, Oswald or James, had told the Inspector about the hoax grave. She was quite aware that they thought she had buried a human corpse but it must have taken a lot for them to expose her. That was why they could not now face her. They would see.

A couple of hours later, when the Inspector was back, they saw. Everyone saw. All inhabitants of the house and visitors gathered around the grave as the digging got deeper. The PC's and Saul were sweating with the exertion of flinging earth out, creating mounds on the grass.

Jerusha was very calm as she saw PC Keir's spade hit the dummy. The men scrabbled with their hands. Out it came. The dressmaker's dummy. There was a perplexed silence and Jerusha held back nervous gigles.

'What the devil!' exclaimed Inspector Drew.

'It was an April Fools' prank,' said Jerusha proudly.

'And you think this is funny, Jerusha,' said Saul, wet with sweat, with earth in his pores and in his fingernails.

'My men have spent all afternoon digging, to find this?' The Inspector was more than exasperated. 'I've a good mind to have you up for wasting police time.'

'At least it is not Sonia,' said Oswald.

'I knew you could not have harmed her,' said James. 'It's just your sense of humour. We still love you, no matter what we might have thought.' He hugged her and Oswald joined in. They were immensely relieved and had forgotten all the hard labour that went into digging the hole on April first.

However, the police inspector had not forgotten what he saw as a waste of time. 'I'm afraid I can't offer to let my men re-fill the hole.'

'Then, where is Sonia, Inspector? Interrupted Saul.

'I can understand your impatience, Mr Patterson, and we will mount a search for her . . .'

He was again interrupted, but this time by Jerusha. 'She's in France. That's all I know.'

'Why didn't you say so?' Saul accused her. 'You let us go through with this dig when you knew all the time.'

'I promised her and Callum that I would not say anything. I gave them my word and they trusted me.'

'That's withholding information,' said the Inspector.

'I only withheld it because they wanted it to be a secret. They didn't think Saul would approve.'

'Approve of what? A holiday in France?' asked Saul.

'They left to get married. They did not think you would accept Callum because he is a humble roofer.'

'You allowed this? I knew I should not have let her come here.'

'They are in love.'

'She is young, for God's sake.'

'You would understand if you saw them together. They're a lovely couple.' Jerusha was not convinced that Saul understood any of this but she was braving it out.

'We'll want that address as soon as you have it,' said the Inspector. 'And no concealing it. The secret is well and truly out.'

Ꙩ𝕿𝖂Ꙩ

'Sir.' It was PC Rutherford.

'Not now, Rutherford'

'But Sir, this is important. We've found some bones to the side of the hole. We have found the skeleton of a hand with a wedding ring on it. Do you want us to dig some more, Sir?'

'What have we here? Is this indeed a grave?', said the Inspector, running his hands through his hair.

The men dug carefully so as not to damage the bones. Then they scraped away the soil, revealing the skeleton of a woman.

'Before you get excited, Mr Patterson, this could not be your daughter. This body has lain in the ground for several years.' The Inspector was adamant.

The PC's placed the bones in the shape of a skeleton to one side of the grave.

'Take off that ring and pass it to me,' said the Inspector to PC Rutherford. He took the ring that had been carefully extracted by his officer. He held it up and examined the inner curve. *Françoise love Hamish*, he read. 'So this is the body of Françoise Burnett,' he said, 'after all these years.'

9

ARRIVALS

The household was in a state of shock. Oswald, who had no contact with Françoise while she was alive, was the least affected but he felt for James, who took to his bed and would not eat. Jerusha, at first, could not comprehend what finding Françoise's remains meant. She was overwhelmed to discover that Hamish's first wife, who had been missing for fourteen years, had, in fact, been under the ground at Kirkfield. Hamish and she had been sleeping beside a corpse. The perfect husband and the perfect wife? She wished those old bones back in the earth. For days, she listened to Inspector Drew's questions without comprehending, without seeing him at all. He was somewhere out there, telling her that a Detective Superintendent Clive Drummond from Edinburgh had been brought in to head this case. It had become a murder enquiry. Inspector Drew might still be involved and he would follow up the case of the missing South

African. 'Yes,' she said. 'Yes.' She blotted out the thought of Saul waiting at the B & B for an address in Paris. Saul did not want to get involved with this earlier crime and he did not like the atmosphere at Kirkfield. Jerusha had to surface enough to tell Claude and Jean. They would both be coming out the following day. Not that they could do much, except examine the grave. The police had taken the skeleton, with the telltale engraved ring, away to their forensics laboratory.

Jerusha began to get an idea of what all this meant. She kept remembering Hamish wanting to tell her something before he died. He was not granted time. Did this mean that Hamish knew all along that Françoise was dead? She wouldn't go a stage further and ask whether or not he killed his wife. It was inconceivable. If he knew that Françoise was buried in the garden, what a mighty secret he had kept. From her. From the children. She tried to remember back to occasions when he might have been about to tell her. On the toboggan ride. The first kiss. Thoughts of death and maybe murder were nowhere near their happiness. She would not believe he had lied to her by omission and, if he did, he must have had very good reasons. She even began to think that Françoise's death might affect the legitimacy of their marriage. However, now it was clear that Françoise was dead, dead, dead when they married. They could have married earlier, before Françoise, suspected missing for seven years, was declared dead. He still would have been a widower. He had not told her that. Perhaps he didn't know she was buried in the garden? If so, who would have buried her there? Whichever way she looked at it, or tried to distort it, she sensed that

Hamish had known what had happened to Françoise. And he had not told her.

She wouldn't admit these thoughts to anyone and particularly not to Superintendent Clive Drummond who had a very brusque manner and did not seem sympathetic to her position. He was a grey-haired man with bulging eyes and a very penetrating voice.

'We'll put aside the incident of the dressmaker's dummy but we will not forget it. For the time being we have more serious matters to concentrate on,' said the Superintendent. The police had taken over the sitting room for interviewing. Files and newspaper cuttings lay on the small table next to Superintendent Drummond. She could make out the headline of one of the cuttings from fourteen years ago. 'Local Woman goes Missing, Feared Dead'. She could not take her eyes off it. Superintendent Drummond saw this and covered up the cutting with a blue file. 'Careless of me. These documents, remaining from the original case, are on their way to the Galashiels Police Station where they will be kept in a secure place, but so that I can have ready access to them. You are aware that I am commuting from Edinburgh?' He didn't seem to expect a reply to that but, instead, looked straight into Jerusha's eyes. 'I said concentrate. That means answering my questions, not gawping at sensationalist headlines. I didn't use the word lightly.'

'What are your questions? I did not ever meet Françoise formally. I saw her but . . .'

'When did you see her, as you put it?'

'She made an entrance at the Midsummer Night's party. I was there, sitting at a table.' She was now totally transfixed by the Superintendent's bulging eyes and challenged by his harsh manner.

'Ah, yes, the party. You and a thousand other people.'

'About eighty. About eighty people came.'

'Some of them, I suspect, came long distances. Some, I suspect, are no longer contactable.' He was telling her something about his methods of investigation.

'You're not going to interview all those people?'

'Just the relevant ones. Who do you remember being there?'

'Well, there was James. He took me to the party and introduced me to his stepbrother, Hamish, who later became my husband. He died five years ago.'

'Yes, I've got James on the list. I believe he has taken to his bed. He will just have to get out of it to speak to me. Who else?

'There was Lorna, Hamish's sister.'

'And is she available?'

She lives near Selkirk. She's not always well either.'

'And what's her problem?'

'She has bipolar disorder which means she has ups and downs.'

'I know what it means. In my work, you come across all sorts.'

'Also, Sheena and Derek. They live in the village.'

'And how are they connected?'

'Just friends. At one time Hamish and Derek were very close.'

'What other relations, people related to Françoise and Hamish?'

'Ewan, Hamish's brother, the Earl, and his wife, the Countess Elizabeth. I knew very little of Françoise's family, except she had a father called Henri. Her close relatives are all dead now, otherwise we would have contacted them immediately the body was found. Except, there is an aunt who lives in Edinburgh.'

'That'll do on that topic for the moment. Tell me about your husband.'

'He was kind and gentle and he couldn't hurt anyone.'

'You're not biased by any chance?'

'No, honestly . . .'

'You didn't have secrets from each other?'

'Hamish would never kill his wife, no matter how awful she was. He told me about her rudeness, her sharp tongue and her promiscuity. She angered him but he was never angry enough to murder her.'

'The lady doth protest too much,' the Superintendent said to himself. He said to her, 'That's not what I asked. I wanted to know if you had any secrets from each other.'

Jerusha was busy thinking about whether or not to tell him about Hamish's last words to her. Spontaneously, she decided not to for this, she judged, was a detective who would twist her words, twist Hamish's words. 'We were always open and honest with each other,' she said.

'I'll take that as a no. Is there anything you can tell me that would shed light on this mystery?'

'To begin with, my husband, sadly, is dead so he is not here to defend himself.'

'I'm not accusing your husband. I'm just trying to ascertain facts. In case you aren't aware, a body has been found in your garden. Everyone connected to the household is a suspect.'

'Even me?' asked Jerusha.

'Even you, Mrs Burnett. What better motive could there be than wanting to marry the deceased's husband?'

'I told you I only met Hamish that night. I did not dream that one day I was going to marry him.'

'And yet you had had several husbands before. With that record, anything could happen.'

'Two. I'd had two husbands. Who has been telling you these things?'

'George Rutherford has been filling me in on some of the background.'

'And you believe him?'

'He is a good copper and his father has been postmaster, heading a gossip network, for many years.'

'Did he tell you, too, that his father, Chris Rutherford, was one of Françoise's lovers? Did he say that?'

'Was he now?' He clearly appreciated this bit of information and almost visibly filed it in his head for future use.

'He was at the party. I was only at it for a limited time. James took me home at midnight. Ask James.'

'I will when I've got through talking to Claude and Jean. I'll speak to Claude now. You can go.'

She got up as if obeying an order, which was not like Jerusha. She was used to giving the orders. Then paused, wanting to take control of the closure of the interview. 'When you speak to Claude, you must understand that he does not like me. Never has. He is bound to say something against me.'

'Probably never got over losing his mother.' In his more mellow moments, the Superintendent could be perceptive. And he was mellow, now that he had finished rattling Jerusha.

'Exactly.'

'Send him in, won't you? There's a good girl.'

Claude ignored Jerusha as he came into the sitting room and she left to be with Jean in the kitchen. Sheena was there, too. She had brought some freshly baked scones and, having spread these with butter and jam, they all tucked in.

'How did it go?' asked Jean, nervous about her turn to come.

'Not good. He has a mind like a cesspool and he twisted my words,' said Jerusha.

'Detectives are like that,' said Sheena. 'Have another scone.'

'Jean, I just don't see how he can think I had anything to do with your mother's death. I had not even been introduced to her. I did not know her. I didn't even really know your father at that point.'

'You're all right, Jerusha,' said Jean, giving her a peck on the cheek. 'I don't know how I'm supposed to know anything, either. I was too young. It is just so awful,

Mummy's body being in the ground all that time and Daddy not here to see it discovered.'

'It's probably better for him that he doesn't know any of this,' said Sheena. 'I believe the Superintendent is going to interview Derek as well. On account of that little fling that he had. We thought we could forget about it.' She could not elaborate on the affair between Françoise and Derek because of Jean's presence. She had already said too much.

'Little fling? What do you mean?' asked Jean.

'Just something that happened a long time ago' She changed the subject. 'Have you thought of what the Superintendent might ask you, Jean?'

'He will ask what we did that night before Mummy went missing. He will ask who we were with when we went to bed and I will say that we were with our nanny, Miss Ross. Daddy usually read us our bedtime story but that night she did.'

'He will ask when you last saw your mother,' added Jerusha.

'I never saw her at all the day after the party. She was just gone. At the party Mummy was wearing that lovely scarlet dress and she smelled of a perfume I can't name. I'm still searching for it. When she entered the marquee everyone turned their heads.' Tears were running down Jean's face. 'I can't stand the thought that someone killed her. Daddy would hate it too. And Claude is cold-hearted.'

During his interview Claude was, in fact, being cold and sarcastic. 'I can't understand why the original investigation did not turn up my mother's body. It would have been much easier to find the killer when the case was fresh,' he told the Superintendent.

'We have to work with what we have, young man.'

'Calling me young man is a put down. I'm old enough to know when mistakes have been made. Granted, at the time of my mother's death I was too young to fasten on to any clues. But I do know who I suspect.'

'We are the ones to bring forward the suspects. You just tell me what you remember.'

'I was ten at the time. My parents had invited a lot of people to celebrate Midsummer's Night. On the whole, they were boring old farts, although some of the women were very pretty. However, my mother was the star of the show. She loved a party and she loved to show off her beautiful figure. But, I'm going off the point. The last thing I saw of her was when we were eating at our table in the marquee. The top table. Jean was being obnoxious as usual. She wanted to climb on mother's lap while she was eating. Mother told her to go and sit down so she went onto father's lap instead and ate his food. When mother had finished eating, she began dancing with Derek Whatshisface and then she had a whole lot of different partners after that, including Daddy. I watched her moving around the dance floor. She was beautiful and vivacious. Then Miss Ross started tugging at my sleeve. She took us to bed. Nobody thought that we'd like to say goodnight to mother. If they had, I would have the memory of a goodnight kiss. I thought then, especially once mother was gone, that grown-ups can be so stupid and insensitive.'

'You've been very helpful.'

'I did not mean to be helpful. You asked me a question and I answered it. Let's hope you find the bastard who did it.'

'We will.'

The interview over, Claude called Jean through then took his laptop into Jerusha's study or, as he preferred to call it, his father's study. With Jean occupied, Jerusha and Sheena could now talk openly about Derek's relationship with Françoise.

'She was a wicked woman,' said Sheena. 'She would entice men away from their wives and, once she thought she had them, she would drop them and walk away from the chaos she'd created. Derek was just one of them and he has sworn to me he regrets what he did. It took me a while but I have forgiven him. I wouldn't say that, God rest her soul, I forgive her. Her actions were too much of a pattern, too cruel and unfeeling. Sometimes, Derek and I speak of it now and we can see how Françoise entrapped men to boost her own ego. Not that it needed boosting. She was immensely sure of herself.'

'I want to speak to Derek. For Hamish's sake.' Jerusha resolved to do some investigating herself, alongside Superintendent Drummond. 'Would he do that? Speak to me about Françoise?'

'I can ask him. He is pretty shocked by the discovery of Françoise's remains. He is very low at the moment.'

Just then the doorbell rang and Jerusha went to answer it. She came face to face with Saul. He had clearly just had a shower because his hair was wet. It was a bit late in the day to be having a shower. It was almost three o'clock. He didn't say hello. He merely asked, 'Any news?' She had not looked at the post today. Oswald had put it on the hall table where it remained, neglected.

'Come in. Come through to the kitchen.' She introduced Sheena and Saul.

It became apparent that Saul was going to be civil, if impatient to be gone. He still felt he did not want to be involved with what he saw as the drama at Kirkfield. It was typical of Jerusha to become entangled in such a mess. What he did not want was for that mess to divert attention from the plight of his daughter. Now that he had a lead on where to find Sonia he had decided that he would confront her situation once he had found her. What he needed was her address. He thought he could get this from Jerusha by being nice to her.

He was right. She would not have given him the address if he had continued to bully her. As it was, she was having trouble with the feeling that she was about to betray Sonia and Callum. She found herself wishing that Sonia's letter would not arrive and then the decision would be made for her. She made her excuses and went through to check the post, leaving Sheena and Saul to make polite conversation. The truth be told, Jerusha, for all her show of bonhomie, was finding it difficult to keep the Jerusha act going. Was it only yesterday that they had found Françoise? Thoughts of Hamish were uppermost in her mind, dulling her senses. She felt as though she had a hangover, which was not possible because she hadn't touched alcohol for days. This whole question of what to do with Sonia was struggling to surface. One part of her wanted to do the dirty deed, betray her niece to her brother and let father, daughter and son-in-law get on with it. Another part of her said that, if she gave him the address, Saul would bully and hound Sonia and Callum—and it would be her fault. How was she to face Sonia if she did this?

'Is it there?' asked a voice at her elbow. It was Oswald.

'Darling. Don't creep up on me. I'm just looking.'

'You're looking without seeing. I've been watching you.'

'Be a sweetie. Don't.' Jerusha chucked him under the chin.

'That's it, isn't it?'

She was holding a letter, addressed to her, with a French postmark. 'I guess it is. Now, I've got to hand it over.'

'You don't have to. Here, give it to me, I'll hide it.' He made as if to take it from her.

'No more secrets. They come to no good.' She snatched it away. Then she opened it. It contained the address and an effusive note about how happy Sonia was to be married and what a lovely life they were making for themselves in France. Just then Jean came out of the sitting room in tears, brushed past them and, saying she wanted to be alone, ran upstairs.

'You know, this is all your fault, Oswald. You and James. If you hadn't told the police about the dressmaker's dummy they would not have started digging and found the skeleton. None of this unearthing of forgotten secrets would have happened. You did not seriously think I could have harmed Sonia?'

'That's what you are contemplating doing now.'

'She can't avoid her father forever.'

'Perhaps you think she will thank you?'

'Yes I do. Her Bible teaches her to honour her father and her mother. You never know, he may like Callum.'

'That's an about turn.'

'Well, you betrayed me, didn't you? That was an about turn.'

'We've said we're sorry for doubting you, Jerusha. James is ill with all this.'

'All this is enough to make anyone ill. I simply cannot deal with these two things at once. Be a dear, you give this letter to Saul.'

'Much as I love you, Jerusha, there is no way I'll do that. Even if she doesn't approve of gay relationships, Sonia became a part of this household. I can't be a part of breaking up her relationship.'

'We don't know he'll do that. In any case, I've thought of the solution. Come with me into the kitchen.'

She put down the letter on the table and then went through and found Saul telling an appreciative Sheena about life in South Africa. Saul broke off what he was saying. 'You've got it. I can tell.'

'Saul, go through to the hall on your own and snoop. Without my knowledge, you will find what you came for. Copy out the address and tell no one you have done so. Sheena, Oswald and I will stay in the kitchen and you will do this behind our backs.'

'Can't we do this without the drama?' asked Saul, his anger rising.

'Those are my terms. It's that or nothing,' replied Jerusha, standing to her full height and weight.

'Okay. Will someone give me a pen and a piece of paper?'

'Give the man a pen, someone,' said Jerusha. 'And Saul, let Inspector Drew have your findings, as well.'

10

INVESTIGATING THE DEAD

The next few days saw Jerusha gather force. If she had felt confused and overwhelmed she now felt determined to prove Hamish's innocence. She would not rely on the police to do this. She, herself, would investigate. Sitting in her workroom, she made a list of all the people she wanted to question: James who was still ill in bed; Françoise's lovers who included Derek and Chris Rutherford; Jean and maybe Claude; Lorna who used to be close to Hamish; the nanny, Miss Ross; Vernon Brown, the lawyer. Oswald wasn't around when the murder took place. For that's what it was, a murder. And, at Kirkfield. She wracked her memory for clues. Something she might have heard that night or might have seen. Mainly, she remembered Hamish and how avuncular he was. She remembered, also, Françoise's grand entrance to the marquee. She came in like a model on a catwalk, slim, lithe, superior, deadly. She paraded herself in front of friend and foe. No wonder nemesis came. She would ask Lorna for the names of anyone else who might have wanted to harm Françoise. First of all, she would speak to James and then Derek, if she could get him on his own, without Sheena. Derek had been captivated by Françoise. So, thought Jerusha, was she. She hadn't thought beyond the grand entrance. Why was Françoise late? It was the time that Françoise was not there in the marquee which was important. Who else was absent with her? Enthused by these thoughts, she rushed up to James' bedroom and burst in.

'Hush, Jerusha. He is sleeping.' Oswald was standing at the window looking down on the grave. The young constables, Keir, Anderson and Rutherford, were still digging, sifting the earth for more evicence.

'I'm awake,' said a frail voice from the bed.

'I'm glad to hear it. You need to be well, James. We've got work to do.'

'I'm not putting this on, you know. I simply haven't the energy to eat or get out of bed.' He clutched the duvet to his chin.

'What did the doctor say?'

'What doctor?'

'He has not seen any doctor. Won't hear of it,' said Oswald.

'It has all been too much for you. Finding Françoise like that after all these years,' said Jerusha.

'The family implicated in a murder. I never thought I'd see the day when such scandal has overtaken a proud and upright family. A noble family.'

'James, you knew Hamish as well as, if not better than I did. You will be aware that he could not have been involved in Françoise's death.'

James groaned. 'But, Jerusha, how could he not know about the body in the garden? It was his garden?'

'He loved to travel. Perhaps somebody buried it there while he was abroad?'

'And his instruction to Luke Junior not to dig in that patch?'

'He simply wanted it to be grass. Vegetables there and grass there. He planned the garden. That's the positive way of looking at it. Everything can look negative if you let it. You're depressed. You are not seeing things clearly.'

'Without Hamish to answer our questions, how can we proceed?' asked Oswald.

'That's just it. We will proceed. We can begin by asking people who were at the party what he was doing, and when. I was talking to him for a short while before the dinner and there was nothing abnormal about his mood or behaviour.'

261

'Well, I saw him before the party and he was angry. He and Françoise had had a quarrel,' said James.

'Murderously angry?'

'Ruffled. You of all people understand that he didn't often lose his temper.'

'So, he was ruffled. What was the quarrel about?'

'The children, of course. Hamish felt that Claude was growing up too fast and Jean, too slowly. Hamish also felt that Françoise had a negative influence on Claude. She was teaching him sarcasm at an early age. And neglecting Jean.'

'All parents argue about their children. What about Françoise's behaviour otherwise? Her affairs?'

'He was used to those. He had to accept that he could not change her as far as lovers were concerned.'

'But she humiliated him.'

'He was resigned.'

'It was a measure of his good temper. Did you and he discuss this?'

'Often. At first he was distressed but as the affairs continued he came to terms with this aspect of his wife's behaviour. I think he believed he had married her for better or for worse.'

'Darling Hamish. He was so phenomenally sympathetic. So loving. He accepted her outrageous behaviour and put himself aside.'

'He accepted that she could not help herself. Françoise wasn't all bad. She was a splendid cook and, in conversation, very entertaining. However, she did neglect Jean. She saw herself in Claude.'

'It's not Françoise we are defending. It's Hamish and we've got to protect him from whatever happened.'

'I'm tired now,' said James.

'You can take your questions somewhere else, Jerusha,' said Oswald.

As she left James' and Oswald's room something drew her to Hamish's room. Glad that she had not got as far as clearing out his belongings, she went there to look for clues. She had no idea what she was looking for and she said a little prayer to Hamish that he would forgive her for rifling through his belongings. As if following some invisible divining rod she headed for his large wardrobe. She felt and probed under the hats. Nothing. She opened the drawers one by one. Socks in pairs neatly arranged. Nothing among the underwear. She passed her fingers under the drawers to see if there was anything like a key taped underneath. No such thing. She turned to a drawer full of sweaters. There was nothing but cashmere and wool. He was so neat. Hamish took great care of his clothes. She went to sit on the bed, flummoxed. Casting her eye around she lit on the bedside cabinets.

She sprang up and tried the handle of the one nearest her. It was locked. She tried the other which opened easily to reveal a few books, an alarm clock and a magnifying glass that was protected by a man's woollen stocking. These things did not interest Jerusha. She had to find a way to unlock the other cabinet. She felt all around both cabinets for a key but all she discovered was smooth wood. Then, being the amateur sleuth that she was, she decided she had been too dismissive of the second, open cabinet. She went back to it and examined each item carefully. There was a small tin box but all it contained were buttons and spare key rings and paper clips. She examined the inside cover of each book, without luck. She came to the magnifying glass and took it out of the stocking. She was just about to put it back when she felt something hard in the toe of the woollen stocking. It was the key.

Enthusiastically, Jerusha took the small key over to the other cabinet and it fitted perfectly. She opened the door. Inside were papers and a book that looked like a journal. Jerusha flicked through the pile of papers, most of which were letters to and from Hamish's lawyer, Vernon Brown. One letter caught her attention. It was dated September 9, 1995. Jerusha was transfixed by one sentence. It was from Vernon to Hamish and it read: 'My dear chap, if you really want to pursue a divorce, knowing that your wife cannot touch your inherited income, please contact my colleague, Ignatious Dwyer, who specialises in these things.'

So, Hamish had thought of divorce. He had never told her that. What more secrets did he have from her? Why did he not speak to her about his intended divorce? It had obviously come to nothing but he had gone as far as to approach Vernon about it. Come to think of it, he hardly spoke about Françoise at all. A remark here or there, a description of her cutting tongue, a reference to Claude being like his mother, these things were all that she remembered. The big things, her disappearance, the police investigation, the possibility of divorce, these he had kept to himself. What was she to do with this new information? She decided that if Hamish could get a divorce without losing his fortune he had no motive for killing Françoise. He could rid himself of her through the divorce courts. Jerusha scrabbled through the correspondence looking for a follow-up to the letter of September 1995. She found only dry notes about finances. Vernon would be able to reveal the outcome. She resolved to speak to him.

She turned to the fat, red, embossed book. On the inside cover was written in clear, sure writing: 'Françoise Burnett. Death to anyone who spies'. Jerusha ignored this and instead felt a surge of excitement. Here were Françoise's private writings. Surely, they would hold a clue. She settled down to read, scanning the pages. It soon became apparent to her that it was all about men, men she had met, men she had made love to, every man but the one she had married. What was Hamish doing with this in his locked bedside cabinet? When he read it, it must have hurt. It must be that this was evidence for divorce. That's why he kept it. She did not name names. Every man was called by a letter of the alphabet, randomly it seemed. There was a 'Z' and a 'Q' and Jerusha couldn't think of any first names that began with those letters. 'Q' for Quentas, perhaps? Jerusha left that question for another time. She came to the last entry in the journal. This was about 'X' It was dated 18th June, 1996. The last part of it read:

'So X has become very clingy and the one thing I can't stand is men who cling. Behaviour like his is enough to make me want to commit suicide. I have no choice but to end it.'

Here was proof. Françoise was suicidal. She had committed suicide. Jerusha had found the answer. She would show Superintendent Drummond. Jerusha was reading very fast and thinking with her emotions. She did not yet have the habit of cool detection. All she knew was that she was onto something and she must share the information.

She knocked, finding it strange to knock at her own sitting room door.

'Come in, Constable,' called Superintendent Drummond.

'It's me' Jerusha stepped into the room.

'Not another of your little jokes, I hope.'

'No Super, this is deadly serious.' Jerusha proffered the book and the letter. 'I have been looking through Hamish's things and I've found some evidence.'

The Super took the journal and the letter and tucked them under one arm.

'I hope you didn't disturb or remove anything. My men will want to do a search. Incidentally, this is Brenda Smith one of Françoise's friends. I bet you did not think Françoise had any women friends. She seems to have been universally disliked. Apart from by her children, of course.'

'Counsellor and friend,' said the woman sitting in a chair opposite the Super. Jerusha could see little but drapes of cloth and bangles for the wings of the chair hid her head. The Super flicked through the journal and scanned the letter. He was aware, with a little helplessness, of Jerusha's naïve anticipation.

'Well, come and sit down.' Jerusha moved forward and sat on the edge of the *chaise longue* in eager anticipation but she got an unexpected reaction to the journal. 'Oh, no. Not this diary. We've got photocopies of extracts in our files.'

'Don't you see,' pleaded Jerusha. 'She could have committed suicide. It says she wanted to end it and that she felt suicidal.'

'You are referring to this last entry.' He turned the pages to the place Jerusha was referring to. 'This, and its connotations, is what led the original investigation astray. That is why she remained a missing person for so long. But, tell me, Jerusha, how she could have buried herself. Unless, whoever found her wanted to cover up the scandal. It's my guess that there is more than one person involved. Such an elaborate ruse. Some people went to an awful lot of trouble to take her car and clothes to the beach and to dig a grave. There are at least three people involved in this cover-up. Fourteen years is a long time to keep silent and we've little chance of finding new evidence at this stage. We're now appealing to people's consciences.'

'Then you don't think it could have been suicide?' asked Jerusha, disappointed.

'I know for certain it was not suicide. Forensics have came back with their report. I'm afraid there is no DNA to assist us with our enquiries. However, judging by the damage to the vertebrae, her neck was broken. She could not do that to herself.'

Jerusha was devastated and trying hard not to show it. She had nursed the idea of suicide as a solution that would exonerate Hamish. She wanted her solution to been the right one.

'Look at the letter, then. Please,' said Jerusha. 'Hamish didn't need to kill her. He could have divorced her without losing his inherited possessions and income. He had no motive.'

'Except jealousy,' said the Super. 'But I grant you, this does throw light on his attitude. I'll keep this.'

Jerusha took this as praise. At last something she had shown him was of value to the case.

'Françoise didn't want a divorce,' said Brenda. 'She knew she was difficult to live with. She was addicted to sex, you see. I tell you that in confidence. And I tell you because she was very misunderstood.'

'So misunderstood that some people wanted her dead,' said the Super.

'She was a highly intelligent woman who could detect people's faults and shortcomings straightaway. Her sardonic humour was the result of her extraordinary perceptiveness,' said Brenda.

'And deep down there was a little girl crying for attention,' added the Super. He sounded jaded and didn't expect a reply.

'If you want to put it that way,' said Brenda, equally world weary.

Jerusha saw her chance to add a new piece of information. 'I know that her father, Henri, was not a very nice person,' she said.

'How so?' asked Superintendent Drummond. He was still no more than tolerating Jerusha. He had had his share of amateur sleuthing.

'Ask Lorna,' was all Jerusha would say.

'Yes, I want to speak to Lorna. Do you think you can arrange it for me, Jerusha?'

'Certainly.'

There was a knock at the door.

'Enter,' said the Super. It was PC Keir and PC Anderson, muddied, sweating, straight from the site of the grave. Yet, beneath the dirt they were triumphant.

'We have something for you, Sir.' PC Keir handed over a gold cufflink.

'From the site?' asked the Super.

'Yes, Sir. Amazing that we actually found it.' It was apparent that PC Keir was going to be the spokesman in this instance.

'Who found it?'

'PC Rutherford, Sir.'

'Why isn't he here, then?'

'If you look at the initials, C.G.R., you'll see that in all likeliehood it belongs to his father, Sir,' said PC Anderson.

'Is that so? Well, he can come off the case while we investigate this. Tell him to go back to the station. This was found in the soil where the body was buried?'

'Yes, Sir. In the earth that was dug up when we found the remains. It's so small we must have missed it before.'

'We must talk to Chris Rutherford. We will go down to his house this afternoon. I want you, Constables, with me. Be here at 2pm. I guess we could all do with some lunch.' Then he seemed to remember that the two women were still there. 'All right, ladies. You can go.'

'Would it be okay if I come along this afternoon?' asked Jerusha. 'I'm a friend of Chris. I might be able to get him to talk.'

'I can't see any harm in it. You can show us the way.' The Super was deceptively compliant, indicating that he had an ulterior motive.

Unaware of this, Jerusha was pleased.'And I can give you some lunch, if you like, Sir.'

'No, thanks. I've got a packed lunch. I'll do a bit of thinking while I'm eating. Thank you, all the same.'

'Brenda, you will come and have some lunch with us. Come on.'

⌒▨▨▨⌒

Brenda went with Jerusha through to the kitchen. Claude and Jean were there, eating bacon rolls. They were acquainted with 'Mrs Smith' from the past so no introductions were necessary.

'Is the Superintendent any further forward?' asked Claude, putting down his half-eaten roll.

'He has found a new piece of evidence but I don't think we are supposed to talk about it,' said Jerusha, starting to ferret in the fridge.

'At least, that's something. I can't see how he expects to find anything, the way he sits and talks. Acts like a confession is bound to come to him.' Claude's voice was harsh and critical.

'He is an experienced policeman,' said Jean, her large eyes shooting Claude a look.

'Can't say I've noticed. I would have searched this house by now,' said Claude.

'That's a thing,' said Jerusha. 'Claude, Jean, what happened to your mother's belongings?'

'Ever wondered why the garage was not used for cars?'

'So, that is where they are,' said Jerusha.

'Locked up,' said Jean. 'She had two wardrobes full of lovely dresses. She used to let me dress up in them sometimes and . . . .' She would have gone on but she was interrupted.

'Did you ever receive counselling after your mother's death?' Brenda asked as if this question had been preoccupying her. She was always working, always analysing, always questioning.

'We were packed off to boarding school and just had to get on with it,' said Claude.

'Oh, it wasn't quite like that,' said Jean. 'Daddy talked to me about it but he was so upset himself. He tried to talk to you, Claude, but you would not listen.'

'I was sent off to boarding school at the age of seven. I had to become independent. What could he expect?'

'At a time like that, counselling would have helped,' insisted Brenda.

'You're only saying that because you're a counsellor. I had friends,' said Claude.

'You did not have any friends. That's just it. You've never had any friends. You are too sharp and sarcastic. Anyone near to you gets stabbed with words.'

'It's just a defensive mechanism,' suggested Brenda, not averse to butting into a family quarrel. Her insistence on having a say was fuelled by hunger. Jerusha was taking a long time to decide on lunch.

'I'll thank you not to analyse my personality or I'll have a go at yours. That wouldn't be too pleasant.' Claude did not seem to know what niceties were and Brenda stopped herself from replying.

Jerusha changed the subject. 'I could think of worse things than bacon rolls, Brenda.'

'That sounds lovely.' Lunch at last but she was not going to be diverted. She had a hard core of experience and she was not going to let Claude chip away at it. She turned her attention to Jean. 'What did the adults do for you the day after your mother's disappearance, Jean?'

'We were sent off with Miss Ross to the Edinburgh Zoo and then to bed early at Grandpa's in Edinburgh. Again, Miss Ross read the story. Miss Ross was a nice nanny. I liked her,' said Jean, ever looking at the positive side of things. She was wistful, not really engaging with the main thrust of the conversation.

'Where is she now? Do you keep in touch?' asked Jerusha.

'She's old now. She lives in Galashiels in sheltered accommodation.'

'Do you ever see her?'

'Sometimes,' said Jean.

'Claude, we weren't packed off to boarding school. We went there to get a better education. Mummy and Daddy didn't want to get rid of us, as you are implying. They were wonderful people and now they're gone.'

'You mean somebody did her in right under our noses. Sent us to the zoo and to stay overnight in Edinburgh while they were digging the grave. How ironic can ironic be?'

'Claude, your father had nothing to do with it,' said Jerusha.

'Jerusha, how can you be so naïve? He wasn't at the zoo with us, and Miss Ross. He was at home, at Kirkfield. How could he not be aware a grave was being dug in the garden?' asked Claude.

'I believe he is innocent and I intend to prove it,' vowed Jerusha.

'The Super does not need an amateur sleuth. He'll make enough mistakes on his own. Just like they did in the original investigation,' Claude snorted.

'If you really want to know, I'm going with him to an interview this afternoon.'

'He must have an ulterior motive. By the way, have you seen this?' He unfolded a newspaper that had been lying on the worktop.

'Claude, she doesn't want to see that,' said Jean, trying to grab it from him.

'This will bring you out of cloud cuckooland. Here, let me read it to you.' He read the headline. 'The remains of Françoise Burnett, who has been missing for fourteen years, were exhumed yesterday at Kirkfield, the manor house in Kirkfield Village where she lived with her husband, Hamish Burnett and their two children, Claude and Jean.'

'The remains, along with an engraved wedding ring were found as a result of an April Fools' prank instigated by the second Mrs Burnett, which involved digging in the vegetable garden. The second Mrs Burnett, Jerusha, had thought to bury a dressmaker's dummy as a joke. Now, nobody is laughing.'

'I could continue but you know the story. My mother was thought to have disappeared when her clothes and car were found at the beach on 22 June 1996, after a lavish Midsummer Night's party etc., etc. You're in the limelight, Jerusha. I notice we haven't had any of your little jokes recently.'

'Never mind that, Claude. He is innocent. How can anyone think anything else?'

'You always thought of him as a cuddly teddy bear. Would the real Hamish Burnett step forward,' said Claude.

'He was a loving, caring man. Good to me. Good to his friends,' said Jerusha.

'Claude, you are so cruel,' said Jean, snatching the paper from him and tearing out the front page story.

'I'm only telling you what the local newspapers are saying about our story. It's unlike them to get anything right.'

'They have got it wrong. You'd be the first to criticise the local press. I don't want any more newspapers in this house. I will burn them,' protested Jerusha.

'Any action like that shows a troubled conscience. In any case, don't you have to go to your interview?'

'I must be going, too,' said Brenda, hurriedly eating the last of her bacon roll.

⟨✺⟩

They left Claude gloating at the damage he'd done and Jean hurting. Jerusha went to the sitting room to meet up with the Super. He was there with PC Keir and PC Anderson. The Super was at his most brusque. 'Good thing you've arrived. Good for you, that is. We were about to go without you. Now, who has the cufflink?'

'It's bagged and on the desk, Sir.'

'Good. Can't lose this vital piece of evidence, can we?' He put it deep in his jacket pocket.

'No, Sir.'

'Enough of that yes Sir, no Sir, PC Keir. Shall we proceed?'

'Yes, Sir.'

'Oh, come on the lot of you.'

They walked down the road to the Post Office where they found Chris and Ena Rutherford packing to move. 'I'm retiring,' explained Chris. 'The house went with the job.' Ena stood behind him, a gentle, quiet woman who would seemingly never think ill of anybody.

'We'll see if the retirement goes according to plan. I want to ask you some questions. Would you prefer to do that here, or down at the station?'

'Here, if you don't mind sitting on packing cases,' said Chris.

'We can stand and ask questions, can't we constables? I know . . . Yes, Sir.' The Super chuckled. 'And while we are about it, ask your missus to take Mrs Burnett into the kitchen for a cup of tea. She has been through a very trying time recently.'

Jerusha felt as if she had been slapped in the face. So that was why he had allowed her to come along, to keep the wife occupied while he interviewed Chris.

'I presume you still have a kettle,' continued the Super. 'That's always the last thing to go when one is moving. In my experience, anyhow.'

Jerusha had no choice but to go through to the kitchen with Ena.

'I'm sorry, Mrs Burnett, I haven't baked today.'

'Nobody would expect you to, Ena. Call me Jerusha.'

'Jerusha. I don't know what all this is about?' A plain, grey-haired woman wearing glasses, she was clearly in love with her husband and horrified by the turn of events. 'Chris has never done anything wrong in his life. He has always been very good to the boys and me. We'll be celebrating our ruby wedding anniversary soon. Do you know, my son, George, is a policeman?'

'A fine young man.'

'You've met him? Then ye ken. But here I am wittering on while what you need is tea and sympathy. It must have been an awful shock, them finding the remains. So sad for the children. I remember when the first Mrs Burnett went missing. That was bad enough.'

'What do you remember about when she went missing?' Jerusha seized her chance.

'I remember there was a big party and we were not invited. Chris was annoyed, a little bit, about that but I said what would them grand folk want with the likes of us, anyway. I've been brought up to know my place. I never thought I'd be offering you a cup of tea in my kitchen of all places, what with all the boxes. Here it is. Drink up. That will make you feel better.'

Jerusha drank but she did not want the subject to change for she was hungry for clues. 'If you did not go to the party, what did you do? Were you together?'

'We were together all night. I remember watching something on telly but I can't remember whether George was in that night. He was eighteen at the time. I think that's right. I do get muddled with my boys' ages. They grow up so fast. Don't you get muddled?'

'I haven't got any children.'

'Oh, my dear, I'm so sorry. Me and my size nines.'

'It's all right. I used to worry about it but I don't any more. I always say my three husbands were my children.'

'Quite right. Men can be bairns at times.' Ena sighed. 'Me. I'm surrounded by men. Three boys and a husband. No little girl to dress up and have secrets with.'

'I'm good at dressing up myself. I sew, you see. I make national costumes and other outfits which I wear to dinner every night.' She chatted on. She had got what she wanted. An alibi for Chris. Not only his wife but also possibly his policeman son were with him on the night of the murder. Chris could not have done it, no matter the evidence of the cufflink.

⚬〰〰⚬

Sitting on packing cases in a stripped room, Superintendent Drummond was coming to a similar conclusion. He had begun by saying to Chris: 'It can't have escaped your notice Mr Rutherford, that the remains of Mrs Françoise Burnett were found at Kirkfield this week.'

'It's news isn't it? They say Hamish Burnett was implicated. But I don't see what the goings on at the big hoose have got to do with me,' said Chris, trying to get comfortable on an uncomfortable packing case.

The Super continued, 'What I'd like to know is what your relationship with the deceased was?'

'I didn't have any relationship with the deceased, God rest her soul.'

'Come on, Mr Rutherford. Rumour has it that you had an affair with Françoise, even although you were only one of a long string of affairs.'

'Superintendent, my wife and I celebrate our ruby wedding anniversary next month. I would not want you to spoil the celebrations.'

'Mr Rutherford, this is a murder enquiry and your cufflink, this one here, was found at the grave of the first and late Mrs Burnett. Can you tell me how this came to be there?' He was good at keeping people to the point.

Chris shifted his position. 'The short answer is no. However, I will tell you about my brief affair with Françoise if you will keep it from Ena. She's a very trusting person.'

'I will be discreet.'

'Let me think. I met Françoise when she came into the post office. That must have been about ten or so years before she disappeared . . .'

'She was new to the area and pregnant with Jean. You could tell from the things she said that she didn't like being pregnant. And the little boy, Claude, was entrusted to the care of a nanny. She was beautiful by any standards. After that, I'd known her as a customer for, it must have been, seven years when she started to come on to me.'

'Her hand brushing mine when exchanging an envelope or some postage stamps. A secretive chuckle. Touching my face when she was talking to me outside. These were little thrills, little invitations. Then the real thrill came one night when both Ena and Hamish and his family were away. No, we did not use the marital beds. I wouldn't allow it. We checked in at a rather posh hotel near Jedburgh. I was wearing my best suit and a shirt with the engraved cufflinks Ena had given me on our tenth anniversary. We wined and dined. She talked about all sorts. She was an educated woman. She was charismatic with long, wavy hair, dark but not black. Like a mane. She had a liking for red but that night she wore green. To match her eyes. That night I was captivated. For those brief hours I loved her. We had booked a room and after dinner we went upstairs. We made love like I had never made love before. She was on fire. Afterwards, she pleaded with me to give her a token, something to remember me by. From that, I understood that the party was over. We weren't going to remain secret lovers. We would go back to being the postmaster and his customer. I had had my pleasure. Disappointed but still mesmerised, I gave her my cufflinks. I was flattered that she wanted to keep something of me. Now I see that they were a trophy. Another man conquered. She was not a goddess but a whore.'

'You sound very angry about it now,' said the Super. 'How long did it take for you to change your opinion of her?'

'About a year. I kept hearing rumours of her escapades. The post office is a fine place for rumours. I felt angry that she had taken what she wanted from me and led me to betray my beloved and loyal wife. That was my first and last affair. I love my wife and, given my time over, would never betray her.'

'Did you feel strongly enough to kill Françoise?'

'I did not kill her. I thought of it but I didn't do it.'

'Your cufflink was found in her grave. How do you explain that?'

'I can't. I swear to you I didn't do it.'

'I'll be candid with you Mr Rutherford. I think there was more than one person involved in this. It involved an elaborate ruse. The car and the clothes at the beach. It involved digging a grave. That doesn't, however, let you off the hook. You are high on my list of suspects. So much so that I want you to come to the police station with me for further questioning. My constables have a car outside. They will take you. Constable Keir, will you call the women in here.'

Jerusha and Ena came in to a room that looked forlorn with people perched on packing cases. Jerusha looked expectant. She wanted to know what conversation had passed in this room yet it soon became very clear she wasn't going to.

'Ena, I want you to think back to June 21 1996, Midsummer night and the following day.

Ena blushed. This was not an indication that she was about to lie but an indication of her shyness. She clasped her hands together. 'I was just telling Mrs Burnett, Chris and I were not invited to the party at the big hoose. I don't know why we should have been but we were a little offended. That's why I remember that night. We stayed in and watched telly and went to bed early, even though it was still daylight.'

'And your husband was in bed with you all night?'

'Naturally.' Ena was easily offended. 'I can't tell you what we did the next day. I can't remember what day of the week Midsummer Night was that year.'

'So, your memory is hazy but you remember your husband being by your side?'

'Yes, Sir. Is everything all right, Chris?'

'Your husband is helping us with our enquiries. He's coming to the police station with us. There is no need for you to come.'

'He'll need to be back for his tea.'

'We will just see how things go,' said the Super.

'Ena will be fine. Won't you Ena? Chris is just doing his civic duty,' said Jerusha.

'Do you think so? I hope he won't be gone long. It's not right for him to miss his tea.'

Chris gave his wife a hug. 'Whatever happens, remember I love you.' Then he turned and went with the policeman to his car.

'We'll be celebrating our ruby wedding anniversary soon,' Ena said tearfully to the two who were left, Jerusha and the Super.

'And you're moving house. You've got a lot to look forward to,' said Jerusha.

⊙⟫⟪⊙

The Super and Jerusha walked up the road towards Kirkfield House.

'We'll want to search your house and the garage. I believe the garage is where Françoise's effects are stored. Would you like me to get a warrant, or do I have your permission?'

'Go ahead. We have nothing to hide. Do you have a confession?' asked Jerusha, bristling with curiosity.

'Confession?'

'Did Chris confess to the murder?'

'Oh, no and he has an alibi.'

'You found the cufflink in the grave.'

'Circumstantial evidence.'

'So, you have nothing on him?'

'Not as yet.'

As they were walking they became aware that there was a commotion going on further up the road. A little further on they saw that it was Kirkfield House at the centre of attention. Several villagers had gathered in the driveway and beyond them there was a bright light. Jerusha started running, thinking the house was on fire. It was not the house. It was the garage and a fire engine was slewed across the driveway, firemen with hoses attempting to put out the blaze.

'My God, it's Françoise's things,' said Jerusha to anyone who would listen.

'Don't go too close.' Tilda came up to her. 'You're too late to save anything. It's a good thing it wasn't the house.' She would be in on the action, thought Jerusha.

'Did you see what started it, Tilda?'

'Nope. There was just smoke and then the blaze. Good thing nobody was in there.'

'I understand that you are looking for positives, Tilda, but there were clues in there, clues that could have proved Hamish's innocence.'

'The truth will out,' said Tilda.

'The key to the truth may have just gone up in flames,' Jerusha retorted.

'There's nothing you can do, Jerusha. They have got it under control. Come inside,' said a voice at her elbow. Lorna motioned her inside.

'Wait a bit, Lorna. I have to talk to the fire chief. After all, I *am* the owner of this property.' She went over to where the Super was talking to the fire chief.

'It was most definitely arson,' said the fireman. 'Very clumsy too. Whoever did it left an empty petrol can outside the door.'

'The garage held the deceased's personal effects. It could have held vital clues,' said the Super.

'Someone didn't want you to investigate.'

'I am the owner,' interjected Jerusha. 'Has anything been saved?'

'You can't go inside Madam but you can see from here that there's very little left. It's a good thing it wasn't the house.'

'It's just the one garage. The other houses Françoise's car,' she said.

It was the Super's turn to speak. 'That was searched and dusted for fingerprints during the original investigation. They found nothing. Only fingerprints that appeared to belong to the deceased. However, we might as well give it another going over. The trouble is that whoever is responsible for all this might not only be destroying genuine clues but also planting false clues. I want this cordoned off as a crime scene, just as we have done with the grave. I'll have a constable guarding the house tonight. We'll have it searched tomorrow. Now, I have to get back to interview Mr Rutherford who clearly had nothing to do with the fire.'

'Doesn't that tend to suggest his innocence?' asked Jerusha.

'I have been maintaining all along that there was more than one person involved in the demise of the first Mrs Burnett. Rutherford might not have started the fire but he might have been involved in the elaborate ruse whereby the clothes and the car were planted at the beach.'

'You have no proof and that cufflink could have been planted by anybody, intentionally to incriminate him.'

'My thoughts exactly, Jerusha, but I must investigate every possibility.'

'I wish that my husband could be here to defend his honour.'

'I'm sure you will do that for him

BLUEBELL WOODS:
THE TURNING POINT

11

OUT OF THE ASHES

On the evening of the fire, when the garage was a mess of wet ashes, Claude and Jean were due to go back to London in Claude's car. Jean, however, asked if Jerusha wanted her to stay, to give her support. Jerusha refused the offer but was touched by it. 'Nothing else is going to happen,' she told Jean. 'Nothing can happen. We've had our share of disasters.'

'What if the police start arresting people now, for arson as well as murder?' asked Jean.

'The Super will be pretty sure of himself before he does that. He's a cautious character in the main and so far, he has nothing to go on. Chris isn't his man, I'm sure of it. He has a watertight alibi, never mind the cufflink. That was planted to incriminate him, you mark my words.'

'The police should have had someone standing guard by the grave overnight,' said Jean.

'They're a small police station unused to uncovering dead bodies. Murders just don't happen in the Borders.'

'Then, how could it happen to my Mum?' Her eyes filled with tears.

'You go. Get away from this for a while. We'll give your Mum a decent funeral as soon as the police release . . .'

'Whatever is left of her.' Jean finished off Jerusha's sentence.

'It'll do you good to get some space, away from this tragedy.'

'I'll 'phone.' Jean took her luggage and went to the car where Claude was waiting in the driver's seat, the engine running. Brother and sister drove off. Jerusha was pleased to see Claude go. As always, his attitude threatened to undermine her. It was a relief to be in a house with only Lorna, Oswald and James. She went to her bedroom to change for dinner. It would be the Chinese tunic and trousers again tonight, red and gold. She was not going to let a small garage fire prevent her from expressing herself the best way she knew how. Her sewing and dressing up were her creativity. Anybody who did not understand that didn't understand Jerusha. As she combed her hair she saw a worried look on her face which she attempted to upturn with her fingers. After all, the fire had destroyed possible vital clues about Françoise and her death and it had been very close to the house. What if somebody saw fit to set fire to Kirkfield House? While they were sleeping? Now there were two crime scenes on her property—the grave and the garage. If she had allowed herself she would have felt frightened. But she was Jerusha. Unassailable. She would present a good front to the family, especially James. She applied some lipstick and smiled at herself in the mirror.

After dinner, they gathered at James' bedside. Jerusha's idea was to galvanize the group into action. She really did not see James' illness as anything other than depression brought on by Hamish's seeming implication in the murder of his first wife. If she could convince him that he had a role to play in proving Hamish's innocence she felt he would rally.

James was lying, propped up by pillows, on his side of the bed, looking pale and listless, a tray of uneaten food at his side. 'I don't know what you all want?' He plucked at the duvet.

'We want you to get better. What did the doctor say?'

Oswald had taken James to see his GP that afternoon. When they returned, the fire was at its height, flames shooting out of the wooden garage door, threatening to leap over to the house. James had just turned, wanly, and struggled upstairs to their bed. He had changed back into his pyjamas and hidden under the duvet. That's how he stayed until he was interrupted by Oswald bringing a tray of dinner that he didn't want.

293

'The doctor says he is suffering from depression brought on by recent tragic events. He has given him some anti-depressants but it will be a couple of weeks before they take effect,' said Oswald.

'You know what depression is, Lorna. You tell them,' said James, summoning up a little irritation. 'And then you can all go away.'

'But we can't go. We need your help,' interrupted Jerusha. 'Please, James. You've got to pull yourself together.'

'It's no use telling him that,' said Lorna. 'That's exactly what he can't do.'

'I'm sorry, James. It's just that we've all got to stick together in building a case for Hamish's innocence.'

'You've said that before. What exactly do you want me to do?'

'Invent something. A visit. A telephone call. Something that proves he was not planting clothes on a beach or digging a hole. Something that shows his distress about his missing wife.'

'Well, I did talk to him on the 'phone that day after the party.' James was sitting up now with a gap between his back and the pillows.

'What did he say?' Lorna was now intense.

'And how is your own health, Lorna?' Oswald asked.

'Don't distract him. I'm on an even keel at the moment, thank you. James, what did Hamish say?'

'Let me think. He said he was very busy clearing up. That he didn't know where Françoise was but, as she had slept out overnight before, he was not too worried. That Miss Ross had taken Claude and Jean to the Edinburgh zoo. Then he said something very strange. He said he wanted me to trust him, no matter what happened. Friends were essential. Brothers were vital.' James fell back on his pillows, exhausted. He contributed very little to the rest of the conversation.

'You see,' said Jerusha. 'Hamish said he didn't know where Francoise was. You've got to tell that to the Super. James, you're a star. Tell that, never mind the bit about friends and brothers, to Superintendent Drummond. Now, what about you, Lorna?'

'Yes. You tell us what you were doing on the night of the murder,' said Oswald.

'I'm not accusing Lorna,' said Jerusha, 'I want her to give Hamish an alibi.'

'I told the police in the original investigation that I went home but that isn't strictly true. I stayed overnight.'

'Why did you lie?' asked Oswald, looming over her.

'Can't say, exactly.' She tugged at her wig. 'I guess I wanted to protect myself. Now, I want to protect Hamish. Sisters are vital, too.'

'What if the Super doesn't believe you?' asked Jerusha, flushed with the idea of an alibi for Hamish.

'I could say I was ill when they interviewed me.'

'And how are you to prove you're not ill now?' Oswald was playing the devil's advocate.

'He can ask my doctor or my community psychiatric nurse.'

'And then he can ask them how ill you were all those years ago?' asked Oswald.

'I was in the beginning stages of a high. I was in hospital soon after that.'

'So, that at least is true,' said Oswald.

'Your illness is not on trial here, Lorna. Tell us what Hamish was doing that night after the party,' said Jerusha.

'Umm. Mostly, clearing up and worrying about his wife,' said Lorna.

'You tell that to the Super and Hamish's name will be cleared,' said Jerusha. 'I knew you two could do it. You and James can clear him of suspicion. You are darlings.'

'I hope you are right, Jerusha,' said James. He had been listening, after all. He turned his head to one side on the pillows and closed his eyes as a signal that they should go. As Jerusha and Lorna were leaving the bedroom, Oswald pulled at Lorna's sleeve and spoke in a low voice. 'Aren't you rather hiding behind your illness?'

She laughed. 'Yes, probably. The illness has got to have some advantages.' She walked out of the room.

Drinking hot chocolate at the kitchen table, Jerusha and Lorna were surprised by a visit from Chris. He looked haggard and dishevelled, not his usual debonair self. He hurtled through the front door and then turned as if he'd hit a barrier, and pleaded, 'you've got to believe me, Jerusha. I said nothing to incriminate Hamish.'

'You can't have because he is not guilty,' she said. 'Now come and sit down. You can have a cup of hot chocolate and tell us what the Super is thinking . . .'

Chris moved in a daze to the kitchen table, not bothering to say hello to Lorna. 'First of all, he questioned my alibi. He eventually gave up on that. Ena was with me on the night of the party and the following day and there was nothing he could do to change that fact. He asked me if Ena and I had seen Françoise or Hamish at all during that time and I had to say no. I said I presumed that Hamish was acting as host and that there were scores of witnesses. After the party, Hamish would have been helping to clear up. He pounced upon those words.'

'What, clear up?'

'Aye. Clear up or cover up, he said. Hamish was a good man. He would never cover up wrongdoing. He would never break his wife's neck and then bury her in the garden.'

'Hamish should never even be suspected of these things,' said Jerusha. 'What about the cufflink?

'The Superintendent seemed to think that somebody had planted that. I did not deny that I'd had an affair with Françoise, one night in a hotel many years ago. You can't even really call it an affair.'

'And you gave her the cufflinks?' asked Lorna, who had been quiet up until now.

'They were like a memento,' Chris said. 'She wanted something to remember me by.'

'Who finished the affair? You or Françoise?' asked Lorna.

'We both did. I saw that it was not right, our both being married, and she had another man in the wings.' 'Who was that?' asked Jerusha.

'I don't know. Listen, I've been answering questions all day, ye ken. I think I'd better go now.'

'What if the cufflink wasn't planted? Did the Super question you on that?' asked Lorna, pressing the point.

'Then, I have a cast iron alibi. Ena. I must get back to her. She will be worried sick.' He stood up, having finished his drink. 'I just came to tell you that I had not betrayed Hamish.'

'It's all right,' said Jerusha. 'We have alibis for him as well.'

'That's a mercy. You ken what the papers are saying.'

'We have decided not to read the newspapers,' said Jerusha.

'I'll tell Khan not to sell them.'

When he had gone, Lorna expressed her thoughts about him. 'Guilty as sin. That little wife of his would swear anything for him.'

'I'm not so sure,' said Jerusha. 'I think he is honest. Foolish, but honest. Either that or we've just been entertaining a murderer. You get so that you suspect everybody.'

'That's how the police operate,' said Lorna.

Jerusha took these thoughts to bed with her. They tumbled around in her mind as she threw off her duvet and then pulled it up again, pummelled her pillows into shape, sipped from the glass of water at her bedside. Her new alarm clock seemed abnormally loud and she kept looking at the clock face, pressing the night light. She didn't know whom to trust. Chris was an old friend but, if he were innocent, he wouldn't have been so battered by the police interview. Yet, she knew what it was like being fired with questions. James and Lorna would be interviewed in the morning. What if either of them had broken Françoise's neck? Or, both? The Super seemed to think it was a group of people. Dead bodies are heavy to lift. Everybody knows that. What if Hamish had been involved? She flung off the duvet and punched her top pillow.

Then she stopped and in the renewed silence she heard faint footsteps in the passage. It could not be Oswald and James because they had an *en suite* bathroom. She lay very still. It might be the person who had started the fire starting another fire? Or, somebody looking for clues? Quietly she slipped out of bed and gingerly opened her bedside drawer. There was the torch she kept for power cuts. She pulled on her dressing gown and eased open the door. She was afraid. Whoever had committed one murder might commit another. However, she was not cowed. She had locked all the outer doors. There must be a simple explanation for this. She heard a rustling noise coming from downstairs. A door squeaked open and shut.

Jerusha crept down the steep stairs, shining her torch ahead of her lest she slip, not thinking that she was revealing her presence. As she tip-toed down she succumbed to a fond imagining. The footsteps outside her bedroom door made her suspect that whoever it was in the house had been in Hamish's room before going downstairs. There was a lamp on in the sitting room. Perhaps it was the spirit of Hamish returning. Excitement welled up in her. 'Hamish,' she called. 'Hamish'. She entered the sitting room and, as she did so, the door moved behind her but she did not have time to swing around. She did not see the intruder who shoved her from behind so that she lay, winded, and sprawled on the carpet in her dressing gown. It took her a while to catch her breath and in that time her assailant fled into the hall and out of the front door.

Jerusha started to pull herself together. She heaved herself up, not knowing whether she was alone. She turned on the lights in the sitting room and the hall, noticing that the front door was ajar. She shut it. The shove onto the floor had extinguished any idea that Hamish come back. Those were human hands that had pushed her so forcibly. She went through every room on the ground floor, turning on every light. There was nobody there. She went back to the sitting room and saw the bookshelves had been ransacked. While she was looking at this mess she became aware of someone in the doorway. She started . . . but it was Oswald who had come to investigate.

'What are you doing, Jerusha?'

'There was someone in the house. They shoved me from behind and then they fled.'

'Oh my God. Are you all right?

'I'm not hurt but they have been going through these books and the papers in the office. What's a bet my computer has been interfered with.'

'We'd better call the police.'

'First, Oswald, can you check there is nobody upstairs.'

'You call the police. I'll check upstairs.'

It was Constables Keir and Anderson who came within ten minutes. They first ascertained that nobody had been hurt. Then they looked at the disarray of the house before checking the doors. There were no locks on the interior doors but the front outer door had been opened with a key. They presumed the intruder had used the front door for entry, going on what Jerusha told them about finding it ajar.

'Has anyone other than yourselves a key to this front door?' asked PC Keir.

'No . . . yes. Sheena has a spare, in case we lock ourselves out.'

'Who is Sheena?'

'A friend in the village. Sheena McPherson.'

'I'll want to contact her. Can you give me the address?'

Jerusha gave him Sheena's address. 'It's impossible that Sheena, or Derek, broke into the house. It's inconceivable.'

'They might have been careless with the key. You never know, they might have mislaid it.'

'I suppose so,' said Jerusha. 'The Super is going to be furious about all this.'

'Aye. I wouldnae like to be there when he hears.'

The Superintendent wasn't just angry about the break-in. He was incensed. The next morning when he heard about it he paced the hall at Kirkfield, barking orders at his officers. 'Someone, very badly, doesn't want us to continue with this investigation. We shall see about that. I want the whole house searched and the garages, what remains of them. The guilty party is clearly panicking. We're looking for a murderer, or murderess, who can probably also be charged with arson, if not with breaking and entering. And possibly theft. I want the search to start now and I want it thorough.'

'What are we looking for Superintendent?'

'Seeing as you needed to ask, PC Keir, you are looking for anything belonging to Françoise Burnett. Anything that betrays whoever broke her neck and dumped her in the garden. And anything that will indicate involvement in the elaborate ruse whereby some conspirators left her garments on the beach and her car in a nearby car park. I want this whole shoddy cover-up exposed.' He seemed to calm down a little after his officers had begun the task.

'If you don't mind my saying so, Superintendent, isn't it a bit late to start searching the premises?'

'And you are?'

'Oswald, James' partner. If you had done it before, there might not have been the fire and the break-in.'

'You are right to point this out, my good man. I will explain. Because this is a cold case all the evidence has been recorded or else is now contaminated. For instance, Françoise's car was dusted for fingerprints during the original investigation. It showed one set of fingerprints only, which were presumed to be hers. However, once the car was moved and brought back to Kirkfield there would have been a new set, or sets, of fingerprints unrelated to the crime. Therefore, you will see why I thought a search of low priority and have been concentrating on getting confessions. However, events have disclosed that someone, or some people, are worried that there is evidence that could implicate them.'

'You have the journal,' said Jerusha who had been avidly listening.

'Ah, Mrs Burnett, Jerusha, I'm sorry about your fright of last night. I will do my best to ensure that nothing like that happens again. You're quite sure you did not see the intruders?'

'Quite sure, but I think it was only one,' said Jerusha.

'If that was the murderer, she was lucky all he did was push her down,' said Oswald.

'I couldn't have put it better myself. We may have made mistakes, Oswald, but we'll get it right I'll have a man outside your door, day and night. I'll also confiscate your spare key from the McPhersons. I'm on my way there now. Is there anything else you want to say?'

'I'm not too keen on the house being searched. It's an invasion of privacy and there are valuables,' said Jerusha.

'Do you want to catch the killers, or not?'

'Yes.'

'There you are, then. My men will be careful.'

'I thought you were going to interview James and Lorna,' said Oswald, something Jerusha would have liked to have said herself.

'All in good time,' said the Super as he left them to go and speak to the McPhersons.

Oswald and Jerusha were left a little dizzy at the forcefulness of the Super's actions and words. They stood in the hall feeling stranded, invaded by the tide of the law. Jerusha was worried about her workroom, her precious sewing machine, the trinkets, the shiny and specially chosen ornaments. She could imagine clumsy hands unravelling multi-coloured bolts of fabric. She thought of Hamish's room, kept as he liked it. And how would James take this?

'James,' she said and with one accord they raced up the stairs to his bedroom. They made it in time. The police had not yet entered. James was lying, gazing into space.

'James, you've got to get up. The police are coming,' said Oswald.

'I'm ready for my interview,' said James.

'It's not the interview we're talking about,' said Jerusha. 'They're searching the whole house and they'll be coming in here.'

James surprised them both by throwing back the bedclothes to reveal that he was fully clothed. Oswald supported James and the three of them moved slowly downstairs.

'I can manage now,' said James as they reached the kitchen door. 'Is that coffee I smell? Nothing like freshly ground coffee.'

'The antidepressants have started to work,' Oswald whispered.

'It's wonderful,' said Jerusha.

'Hello. I'm with you. I can hear you,' said James.

'It's terrific weather we've been having.' Jerusha tried to cover up. But it was wonderful seeing James start to pick up; to take an interest in a cup of freshly ground coffee. He was still hesitant and they could expect his recovery to be patchy but here, in essence, was the old James. 'I think I'll go for a wander,' he said, putting down his mug.

'We'll come too,' Jerusha enthused.

'If you want to,' he replied. 'I want to see the garden in late Spring but I'm not going anywhere near that grave.'

'We will avoid the veggie garden,' said Oswald. 'Better take a jacket, James.'

'Don't mollycoddle me. You're not wearing jackets.' He stood up and made his way down the passage, past the utility room and through the outer door, which they called the garden door. What they called the back door was really the side door and had direct access to the kitchen. The garden door was in fact the back door and opened directly onto the garden.

James blinked in the light, which he had had shut out for weeks. He was drawn by the open space and the fresh air, onto the lawn, highly manicured by Luke Junior. He gasped and breathed in deeply. Then he noticed the lacing of cerulean blue around the burgeoning rhododendron bushes. Luke Junior had been planting bluebells.

Jerusha was reminded of the bluebell woods of her imagining, inspired by Sheena. Len hadn't been in touch recently. He must be aware of events at Kirkfield and consequently was keeping away. He had said he might not be in a position to buy the fields but now, looking at the bluebells against a backdrop of strong green leaves, she made an independent decision. She would plant trees with bluebells at their base and she would open up the land to villagers. Such visions would lift the depression of more than just James. She blurted out her plans to her companions who were busy examining the web of a spider on one of the rhododendron bushes.

'Jerusha, you've seen the light. This calls for a celebration. Your decision and James being with us, and everything. How about it James? A sip of the old champers?'

'Make mine a soda,' said James. 'And then I'm going back to bed.'

'As you wish,' said Oswald.

'You had better make mine a soft drink, too,' said Jerusha. 'I have business to attend to this afternoon.'

As it turned out, they drank orange and mango juice from fluted glasses at the kitchen table. Then James did indeed go back to bed.

'Seems quite a lot better,' said Oswald to Jerusha.'What's this business you have on this afternoon?'

'I'm going to see Derek and Sheena.'

'That's hardly business.'

'Oh, but it is.'

❧

The police were still searching the house, the greenhouse and the sheds when she left to visit Derek and Sheena. Derek was the one she wanted to talk to and she did not know quite how to engineer this. First and foremost she was a friend to Sheena and had avoided Derek, whom she found declamatory and pedantic. She didn't know much about him. She understood that he'd gone through a rough time in his forties when he had started to drink a lot and drag Sheena down. However, he was through that, had just taken early retirement from school teaching and had become a fitness fanatic. He jogged. He cycled. He walked. All of which didn't stop him going prematurely grey. He was evangelical about keeping fit and Jerusha did not appreciate his efforts to get her to take exercise. She was energetic enough about things that mattered to her. When she got to their house she discovered they had just taken delivery of a treadmill, Sheena's present to Derek on his fiftieth birthday. He was on it and running. He waved to her, joyfully.

'How long has he been on that thing?' she asked Sheena.

'He has another fifteen minutes to go,' said Sheena.

They sat, to the sound of the machine whirring and Derek's feet thumping.

'Did you get a visit from the Super?' asked Jerusha, pretending not to show more than a mild interest.

'Uhuh. Nice man but rather brusque.'

'He was furious about the break-in, coming on top of the fire.'

'I don't know if he got what he came for? We couldn't help him very much.'

'I saw you at the party. What did you do after that?'

'We told all this to the Super.' Sheena bristled.

'But I want to hear it. For Hamish's sake.' Jerusha was treading very carefully as if she would cajole Sheena into telling her.

'What a pity Hamish is not here to defend himself.'

'I am his representative. Tell me.'

However, she wasn't to hear straight away because Derek came off the treadmill, leaving it running.

'Have a go, Jerusha. It will do you good.'

'I haven't got the right shoes,' said Jerusha, looking at her maroon, patent leather high heels. She was wearing maroon more and more these days. It sort of merged black and red, to her mind. The shoes, however, were totally unsuitable for a treadmill.

'You can go barefoot or Sheena can lend you a pair of trainers. Can't you Sheena?'

'I don't think Jerusha wants to go on the treadmill.'

'No. I don't,' said Jerusha, hugging her cardigan to her and wiggling further back in her chair.

'It's your loss. It's great exercise. You only have to do half an hour every day. And that's you. Fit and ready for anything. Perhaps next time, when you are wearing more suitable footwear?'

Jerusha shook her head and smiled. She wanted to cross-examine Derek but she did not want to buy his time by using his new toy. He stood there dripping with sweat, in a white T-shirt and black tracksuit bottoms and she wondered what secrets his sports exhilaration was hiding. She hoped that he would sit down and open up to questions but he had other ideas. He turned off the treadmill then went to shower and change. Sheena put the kettle on. Alone in the sitting room, Jerusha felt tense, as if she were waiting for a special telephone call, or waiting to spot her luggage on a conveyor belt at an airport. She didn't wait long for Sheena came through with a tray of tea and cake.

'I've opted for planting trees and bluebells,' she said, knowing this news would make Sheena happy.

'I *am* glad,' said Sheena, going pink with pleasure.

'What are you so glad about?' asked Derek coming in wearing fresh clothes. His grey hair was wet and combed. He had developed strong arm muscles.

'Jerusha is not going to sell her land to that property developer.'

'Good to do something for the planet,' he said.

'I thought I'd tell you that but I also want you to tell me some things,' said Jerusha, tucking in to the cake. 'What did you do after the midsummer night party when Françoise disappeared?'

'We've told all this to the Super,' said Derek.

'But I want to hear it from you. I need to protect Hamish's good name.'

'Mmn, the newspapers have latched onto Hamish as the culprit. But we all know how they get things wrong,' said Derek. 'I can provide Hamish with the perfect alibi. I was with him.'

'What happened was that I came home to bed at about 1am while Derek stayed to help clear up after the guests.' Sheena spoke up. 'He went back to Kirkfield early in the morning to do some more clearing up and then to help Hamish search for his missing wife. He and Hamish were close friends. Derek kept 'phoning me to tell me how things were progressing. I said I would go and help but he advised me not to. So, I stayed here. Derek was back for supper that evening. So, you see, Hamish and Derek were both alibis. I believe Lorna was there, too.'

'I can vouch for Hamish. He was no killer.' Derek said this with some aggression.

'I never, for one minute, thought Hamish had harmed Françoise, although she might have deserved it. Now Hamish has two alibis. One is you, Derek, and one is Lorna.'

'You mustn't worry, Jerusha,' said Sheena. 'The truth will come out.'

'The truth is that Françoise had friends but she had more enemies,' said Derek. 'She was wayward. That having been said, to all accounts, her parents, Henri and Rhona, were distraught when she went missing. I guess Henri and Françoise both had the same dry wit. He is dead now, of course, and so is Rhona. They never knew what happened to their daughter.'

'You must be exhausted, Jerusha, with all the goings on,' said Sheena.

'I'm all right. I'm pleased that James is feeling a bit better.' Jerusha desperately wanted to ask about Derek's affair with Francoise but she didn't know how to broach the subject. Derek himself raised the subject.

'The Super wanted to find out about me and Françoise. My guess is that you do too.' He looked directly at her, as if challenging her. 'Sheena is aware that I had a brief affair with Françoise and that it nearly sent me off the rails. She was a tantalizing woman and completely amoral. I was betraying both my wife and my best friend by having a relationship with her. I thought I loved her but I was merely a pawn in her game. She ended it. And I started to drink to numb the hurt. However, I came through that and thank God for my wonderful wife and her understanding.'

Sheena looked down at the floor, then up at Jerusha. 'My husband is a good man, Jerusha. And he is respected in the community. He has overcome a drink problem, which was a test of his character.'

'I'm sorry to ask you to go over things that hurt you,' said Jerusha.

Sheena and Derek were silent. So much had been wrung from them about a period of their lives that they would rather forget. She pitied them and, at the same time, felt triumphant that Hamish had another alibi. She sensed that Derek had more to say about the day after the party but he wasn't going to say it then. It was going to be difficult to get him on his own but she would do it. 'By the way, have you still got my spare front door key?'

'The Super asked the very same thing. In fact, I gave it to him to take away. It has been hanging in the key cupboard ever since you left it with me,' said Sheena.

The Super was at the house when she got home. On the other hand, the police car with his officers was just pulling out of the drive.

'Here, you'd better keep this.' He handed her the spare key to the front door. 'It's not necessary to take fingerprints. My guess is that there will be many, including yours. Might I have a word with you, in private?' They went into the sitting room and Jerusha shut the door. They both sat in armchairs but neither was relaxed.

'It has come to my attention that you have been questioning suspects yourself.'

'I want to clear Hamish's name.' How many times did she have to say this, to make people understand, she thought.

'I'm not questioning your motive, just wondering why you will not leave it to me. My methods are very thorough.'

'I, in turn, am not criticizing you or your methods. I think that people might say things to me that they won't say to you.'

'How far have you got in your so-called investigation?'

She noted the sarcasm in this question but plunged on. 'I have established that Hamish had two alibis, three if you count James' telephone call.'

'The two, Derek and Lorna, both talk about clearing up. Surely Hamish and Françoise would have paid the catering company, or someone, to clear up? What do they mean by clearing up?'

'Taking away plates and rubbish; dismantling trestle tables; taking down the marquee. The band would have removed their instruments, themselves. Dealing with uneaten food. Then all the empty bottles had to be recycled and the leftover drink to be stored in the cellar. It's a morning's work.'

'Put that way, I see that it could take time but I'm not so sure that the work would not have been done by paid help. Miss Ross, for instance.'

'She was in Edinburgh at the zoo with the children.'

'So she was. Then Luke Junior. He would know.'

'Yes, but he would not have done it on his own. And you don't just pluck out help from thin air.' Jerusha was starting to get annoyed.

'Just some thoughts I've had after speaking to Lorna and James. Lorna, in particular, has changed her story.'

'Lorna is not always well.'

'Does that make her a trustworthy alibi?'

'Lorna is well now. That's all that counts. What did you find in your search?'

'Only one thing of any note. Your husband had two sgiandubhs, two ceremonial daggers worn in the sock in highland dress. Surely, he would need only one? Is the second one his or does it belong to someone else?'

'There was no sign in the post mortem that Françoise was wounded by a dagger.'

'Maybe not but it could have been a flesh wound?'

'The search has not given you very much to go on?'

'No. What I'm looking for is a confession, or confessions. I'll see Lorna again and find out if her story stays the same. I'll also speak to Luke Junior tomorrow. Now, I must get back to the station. Thank you for your time.'

Jerusha wandered into the kitchen, her mind on the case. She did not like the way the Super was thinking. Was it possible that clearing up meant covering up? Lorna or Derek could be using words to hide their real actions. How would it be possible for someone to dig a grave without being seen while people were dismantling a marquee nearby?

She found Oswald and James in the kitchen, making savoury pancakes. 'We thought we'd have an informal supper at the kitchen table tonight,' said Oswald.

Jerusha was relieved to have the meal preparation taken out of her hands and also to see James up and doing things. 'Would you say it's possible for someone to dig a grave in the veggie garden while people were dismantling a marquee?'

'Jerusha, I don't think James wants to talk about these things. You have nothing else on your mind.'

'It's all right, Ossie,' said James. 'I've thought about this and I do think it's possible because of the hedge separating the veggie garden from the lawns. Digging would take time, as we know, Oswald. And perhaps it would have been done by two people. Where they would have kept the body during the digging, I do not know. And, how would they have kept it from the children?'

'The children were in Edinburgh. They stayed overnight in Edinburgh with their grandparents,' said Jerusha. 'When Henri heard the next day that his daughter was missing, he rushed down here, with the children. Hamish told me how distraught he was. He worshipped Françoise.'

'So, there was time to bury a body before he arrived.' This was more of a statement than a question from Oswald.

'What makes me despair, is that I don't see how Hamish could not have been aware of it,' said James, sharply cracking an eggshell.

'Hamish would have told me,' said Jerusha. She had to believe in Hamish, even when the evidence was against it. The perfection of their marriage depended on it. She left the kitchen abruptly and ran down to the church. Even food could not comfort her. Inside, the church was cold and there was a mist of her own making. Her eyes were brimming with tears. She felt that God was angry. It was an oppressive wrath but a wrath that left her to explain the wrongdoings at Kirkfield. James had pointed a finger at Hamish when she believed her husband had never done anything wrong in his life. What happened the night that Françoise died and what did Hamish want to tell her before he also died? That was it. He had wanted to explain everything to her. He had wanted to be honest with her but he never got the chance. What secret had he held all those years? And, why? He could not have killed his wife. That was out of the question. Jerusha simply could not countenance it. Yet, if he knew who did kill her he must have had a very good reason to keep this knowledge from the police. And, from her. He was a deeply loyal man. He must have been protecting someone he admired, respected, loved. But, who? She had been kneeling and now she banged her head against a pew, in anger, in frustration, in disappointment. She loved Hamish. Nothing he had done would take that away. She cherished his memory. She saw him now, in her mind's eye. He was warm. He was comforting. He was moving towards her, coming to kiss her. She tilted her head upwards but the slight movement made the vision evaporate.

'This is sweet madness.' She spoke softly, getting up and sitting in the pew. 'Hamish is dead and I can conjure up his presence. Death did not part us. I am still wedded to him five years after his death. And here I am, talking to myself. The loneliness of his going is insufferable. I miss you, Hamish.'

The church quietly absorbed her words. There was a palpable silence. The mist had lifted. All that surrounded her was a small building with an altar, a humble lectern, a pulpit and enough pews to accommodate eighty or so people. She kicked a wooden pew and heard the noise sound out in the emptiness. Then, she left.

12

─────────────☙❦☙─────────────

SONIA AND CALLUM RETURN

The next day Jerusha dressed all in blue. Baby blue and contrasting navy blue, shoes with a little heel. The weather was hesitant. The month of May not as warm as it usually was. Or, that's how it seemed to the Borderers. She tripped down the stairs to the kitchen where she started to make a fry-up, something to keep them going. She was happy preparing a meal for friends, apron tied around her wide waist, her hair brushed back and up into a helicopter ponytail. She was determined to be positive and expect only the best, for Hamish's sake. Oswald and James were more than just friends, she thought. They were family; not exactly brothers, but close to it. She thought of Saul and how stern he was, always missing the good points in life, always castigating her. She wondered how his visit to Sonia and Callum had gone. She felt guilty about letting Saul find their address but Sonia seemed to have forgotten that when she 'phoned. Sonia and Callum were due on the two o'clock bus from Edinburgh that afternoon. She was going to meet them.

Breakfast went well. Oswald ate heartily—bacon, eggs, mushrooms, tomatoes, fried bread—and James ate a good portion from his plate, which was more than he would have done a few days ago. They were just finishing up at the kitchen table when Zilla came to the back door. Jerusha sensed that something was wrong because Zilla never came to the house and certainly would never step inside. The bird-like woman stood in the back porch, the sun gently behind her, a wet handkerchief in her hand and her face blotchy with tears. She was bashful at the best of times. Now she was made brave by her plight.

'Bad news, Mrs Burnett.'

'What is it?' asked Jerusha who had answered the door. 'Come in and sit down. You look dreadful.'

'Oh no, Mrs Burnett. I've come to tell you that Luke Junior died last night.'

'I'm so sorry. You poor thing. Can't I give you something? Tea?'

'Oh no, Mrs Burnett. He died in his sleep. They think it was a heart attack. The police are doing a post mortem. I just thought I'd tell you so you know.'

'Poor Luke Junior. He was a wonderful man. Unique. Can't I do anything?'

'There is nothing to do while the police have his body. I can't see to a funeral or nothing. I must go now.'

'Can I come with you, perhaps make you a cup of tea at home?'

'Oh no, Mrs Burnett. I can manage. My sister is coming.'

Jerusha let Zilla go. She felt helpless and shocked. The house seemed full of death and dying. She told Oswald and James the news.

'He was an old man,' said Oswald, 'And he worked so hard.'

'How old do you think he was?' asked James of nobody in particular. 'Seventy? Eighty?'

'Late seventies, I would have thought,' said Jerusha. 'Poor Zilla. She is so shy. I don't know how she is going to get along without him.'

'She won't accept help from us,' said James. 'She's old-fashioned. She thinks the big house is above the likes of her.'

'I wonder if we'll be invited to the funeral?' asked Oswald.

'She can't do anything while the pathologist is conducting a post mortem,' said James.

'You don't mean to say . . . ?' Oswald couldn't get the words out.

'You're right. This is too much,' said James.

'The Super was due to interview Luke Junior today. Maybe someone wanted to shut the old man up,' said Jerusha.

'This is too much,' repeated James. 'No one would want to hurt an old man like Luke Junior. I've had enough of this.'

'Now, James, don't let it get to you,' said Oswald.

'Zilla said she thought it was a heart attack. The timing is co-incidental. Don't fret, James,' said Jerusha.

The 'phone rang and Jerusha went to answer it, expecting it to be Sonia confirming their time of arrival but it was the Super. Due to the 'convenient' death of a key witness he was postponing the day's interviews until the post mortem results were out. He wanted Jerusha to tell Lorna as he did not have her telephone number, or to give him the number and he would do it. She undertook to 'phone Lorna, giving him the number for future reference. She had just spoken to Lorna when the 'phone rang again. It was the Countess Elizabeth who wanted them to know that her husband was on his way. Sir Ewan thought the situation at Kirkfield was getting out of hand and he wanted to sort it out. He did not have much time to spare but they could expect him to stay overnight.

'My brother thinks his authority is sacrosanct,' said James when he heard this piece of news.

'I can't see how he thinks he is going to change things,' said Jerusha.

'It's worth a try,' said Oswald.

Oswald and James had temporarily stopped looking for property whilst this house was in turmoil and James, during that time, had been confined to his bed. However, today they were going house hunting again.

'Kirkfield will never be the same again,' Oswald confided in James when Jerusha was out of the room.

'We can get a fresh start but what about Jerusha?' asked James.

'Is there anything in the will to stop her selling?

'She would never do that. It would be like leaving Hamish. She will get through this and bounce back. You know what she is like.'

While they were talking thus, Jerusha was arranging a meeting between the Super and Sir Ewan. It was to be at six o'clock at Kirkfield. The Super couldn't make it much later and Sir Ewan would have arrived by then. Jerusha hoped everyone would be satisfied with the arrangement. Now for the house. The S.S. arrived and began a thorough cleaning operation. She was to make up beds for Sonia and Callum and for Sir Ewan. Jerusha disappeared into her room and began to cut out an African print tunic for herself. The African print had been a gift to her from a friend who had visited Zimbabwe and East Africa at Christmas. She had been longing to make it into something she could wear. With the summer coming she wanted to have it in her wardrobe. She spent a good couple of hours measuring and cutting and had begun to sew when she realized it was time to go and meet Sonia and Callum. They had flown from London to Edinburgh and had caught the bus from Edinburgh, arriving in Galashiels pretty shortly. She must go.

She drove into Galashiels and parked outside one of its superstores, then walked to the bus station. This was a small, shabby line of stances with an equally small waiting room and toilets. People waiting for buses ignored the no smoking signs. Jerusha couldn't work out which stance their bus would arrive at so she positioned herself centrally next to a woman with her baby in a buggy under the roofed area. Unfortnately, a man who was the worse for drink came and stood on her other side so she moved to stand next to an elderly couple. The drunken man swerved over in her direction again, now asking her the time in a slurred voice. She told him the time bluntly and, fortunately, that seemed to remind him that he had to be somewhere other than Galashiels Bus Station. She turned around from watching him go to see Sonia alight from a bus with Callum close behind her. They all hugged, Jerusha giving them an effusive welcome. They were relieved to be at the end of their journey.

'Jerusha, you haven't changed,' said Sonia, holding her hand.

'People always say that out of insecurity. How can one not have changed when time has passed?'

'Never mind that. You look wonderful. Doesn't she, Callum?'

He smiled in agreement, a little anxious about his position with Jerusha. After all, he had worked for her. Jerusha saw this and grabbed his hand, still holding on to Sonia. 'And you. You've tied the knot. Congratulations.'

'What is more, Daddy has come around. We're off to see them in South Africa in a few days time. Daddy thinks he can use his influence to find Callum a job. We know it's not easy for young Whites given that they have affirmative action in the country. Especially difficult for young White men. We'll live with Mummy and Daddy for a while and see how things go.'

'There is lots to say. I know of an Italian cafe near here that does delicious apple tart. Let's go and have a cup of tea.'

They went to the restaurant that was just over the bridge from the bus station and found a free table outside in the sunshine. Jerusha told them about all the happenings at Kirkfield, some of which she had told Sonia on the 'phone. Sonia understood what the slight to Hamish's good name meant to Jerusha. Callum listened intently but he didn't know what to say so he let Sonia do the talking. 'How awful for you. Poor Jerusha,' she said.

'There's nothing poor about me. I can withstand more than that. It is Hamish you need to feel sorry for,' Jerusha replied.

'But, he was your husband. Marriage is a uniting, a sharing, of spirits,' said Sonia. 'Isn't that right, Callum.'

'You're right. It is a bond.'

'But I believe I will live to see Hamish exonerated. I am determined to prove his innocence. I haven't given up,' said Jerusha. 'But what about you. You left and got married . . .' Jerusha listened to their story and told it to James and Oswald afterwards.

'We got married at Gretna Green. Look. Here are my rings.' Sonia showed Jerusha her left hand. On her ring finger was a small diamond engagement ring, and a wider wedding band. Callum also wore a wedding band. He put his hand on Sonia's and moved it to his thigh, clasping it with both of his hands. They were very aware of each other's movements and gestures. Jerusha felt a small pang of jealousy. If Hamish had lived they could have been holding hands together at this table, outside this restaurant, in the tempered sunshine of late May. They had been the perfect couple. She tried to empathise with the young couple. The story they had to tell that came from a different season and from the year before.

◖◖◖◖◗

The wedding ceremony was religious but not formal as in a church. It was only twenty minutes long. She wore the yellow dress and a single gardenia in her hair, carrying a bouquet of white, bronze and yellow roses, and gardenias. On her feet she wore the silver sandals that Jerusha had encouraged her to buy because they might come in handy. Callum wore a silvery grey suit with a white shirt and blue tie. He didn't wear a kilt because he wanted to save the money for Paris. They were going to need every penny. 'On a shoestring but happy' was how they described their financial state.

They spent the night in Gretna and then really enjoyed the journey to Paris. They took a train to Dover and then the ferry across to Calais. After that, they took a train to Paris. They loved every minute of the journey. They were free. United. They had done what they wanted: what they had set out to do. These were grand statements, which expressed what they felt. New, fresh, exciting. Paris is a city for lovers. They found René's flat quite easily and he was in. He gave them a great welcome and showed them the tiny, box-like room he was to let to them. René was a character that Sonia thought Jerusha would like. He was not French but Irish. His real name was Sean but he adopted the name of René because he thought it would make him blend in with the French.

'Some hope,' Callum said, and laughed.

Callum soon got a job as a waiter working for the proprietor of a pavement café. Sonia would go and sit out of doors at one of the tables and her husband would serve her. She called him polite and efficient. 'Of course, he couldn't stay and talk to me. I would sit for hours and watch Parisians passing by.' She also visited some of the tourist attractions: the Eiffel Tower, the Louvre, Notre Dame, and the Pompidou Centre. It was quite cold by November and she bundled up in sweaters and an anorak, with a woolly cap on her head and the scarf that

Callum gave her. She was scarcely visible amongst all this paraphernalia.

Sonia got a cleaning job in a grand house with a very fussy employer, Madame Tousson

It gave them a little extra money and it meant Sonia was out of the house when Saul found the flat. It was only by coming back at night that he found them in. When Sonia opened the door to him she was flabbergasted. He just stood there looking angry. He did not make a move to hug her or to come in. She could have sworn he was grinding his teeth. She was the one to make the first move. She stepped out of the doorway and took one of his hands, expecting him to follow her in but he did not budge. He turned her hand palm down and examined the rings with distaste.

'So, you have done it,' he said.

'Yes, Dad. Be happy for me.'

'Why, Sonia? Why?'

'You wouldn't have approved,' she said.

'I don't approve.'

'You haven't even met Callum.'

'Precisely.'

'Come in and meet him.'

'It's you I've come to see.'

'I have no secrets from my husband.'

'How could you have secrets from your father?' He turned on his heel and walked off into the night.

'How did you find out where we live?' she called after him. She was trembling. She was certain she would see him again. She went inside and told Callum what had happened. He held her tight and they planned how to deal with a second visit from her father. They decided to share their love. Simply, to love him. It seemed the only way to deal with Saul. He did come back. This time he came inside and Sonia introduced him to Callum. He said nothing, not even 'how do you do' or 'hello'. He did not take Callum's extended hand.

Finally, after an unhealthy silence, during which he sat rigid in his chair, he asked, 'What am I to tell your mother?' It was a direct, loaded question. His lips hardly moved. A muscle in Saul's cheek would palpitate when he was anxious. It was flickering then. They had no idea how to answer him for whatever they said could prove to be a minefield. All they succeeded in doing was looking stupefied.

Saul repeated the question. 'What am I going to tell your mother?'

This time Sonia replied: 'That we, that I am happy. That this is what the Lord wants. He has brought Callum and me together. That I pray every day that my parents will understand, rejoice and love us.'

The palpitation in Saul's cheek was still in motion. After a pause, he said, 'It's because we love you that we are concerned that you have made the right decision.' There was pain in his eyes as he said that, a brief darkness and then he became stony again. 'Why all the secrecy, my girl? Have you got something to hide? Are you pregnant?'

It was Sonia's turn to be affronted. 'Don't be ridiculous, Daddy. You know my principles. We waited until we were married to have sex. It's not that I didn't want to include you and Mum. I just thought you wouldn't approve.'

'Why wouldn't I approve? What's wrong with you, Callum?' He was being brutally direct. 'Are you divorced? Do you have a prison record?'

'There's nothing wrong with me, sir,' said Callum.

'No bigamy? No history of failed engagements? No history of mental illness? What is wrong with you, young man, that you couldn't marry my daughter in the conventional way? He got up and started pacing the floor. He still had his coat on and a scarf wrapped around his neck. 'Are you a Christian?'

'I've told you, Dad. He is.'

'Then why the heck do you have to run off and get married and not tell anybody? Are your mother and I such ogres?' He gripped the back of a chair. 'And what do you do when you're not waiting on tables. I've seen you, bowing and scraping and collecting dirty dishes. That's no way for my daughter's husband to earn a living. I never thought I'd see the day when Sonia did cleaning jobs. What you are doing, both of you, is demeaning.'

'When he is not waiting on tables, Callum is a roofer.'

Saul paused for a minute. 'We can do something about that,' he said finally.

Now Callum was angry. 'We don't need to *do* anything about it, as you say. It's fact. It's what I do. I don't have a degree and letters after my name. I get my hands dirty. And it pays. We knew you would not approve.'

'Callum is good at his job,' Sonia said, trying to give him some support. It was almost possible to see Saul's brain working, trying to embrace this new revelation, this disappointment. He stood looking at them for a few moments, then left. The next time they saw him was at the café. Sonia was sitting having a cup of coffee after work when he came and formally asked if he could sit with her. 'Of course,' she said and ordered him a beer. He was looking more relaxed but she was still ready for a lecture.

'Sonia, you know that your mother and I love you and we want the best for you. We have to face up to the fact that you and Callum are married and that there is no way out except for divorce.

'Divorce is inconceivable.'

'Hear me out. I have spoken to your mother on the phone at length and she has persuaded me that we should give our blessing to your marriage. What we would like you to do is come back to South Africa and live with us for a start before you find alternative accommodation.'

'But . . .'

'I have not finished. Living in a poky flat in a foreign country doing menial jobs is no way to start married life. I think I could arrange a job for Callum in the bank and you could choose a career, go back to university or do something that will use your potential.'

'What if Callum doesn't want to work in a bank?'

'He could give it a try. He's an intelligent person and he could learn to be good with people, and he is certainly good-looking.'

Sonia could not understand where all the compliments were coming from. Saul had scarcely been able to look at Callum a few weeks ago. She suspected that he wanted reconciliation in order to get them to do what he wanted.

Later that night Callum and Sonia had their first quarrel. Strangely, Callum agreed with what Saul had proposed whereas Sonia was wary of it. What she did not fancy was living with her mum and dad, even as a start. She had tasted independence. 'You're very young,' her dad had kept saying and that put her on edge. She decided to pray about it and the Lord guided her to agree to the plan.

'One question remained. How had Dad got our address in Paris in the first place? The only person I gave the address to was you, Jerusha.'

'I didn't give him the address, Sonia. I promised you I wouldn't. He took it. He must have been rummaging through my post,' said Jerusha. It was only a half lie, an excuse.

'How like Dad to force his way into the arena.'

13

WHAT'S UP?

'I see what you mean about the garage. It's a mess,' said Sonia as they drew into the drive. Jerusha turned off the engine and they spent a moment looking at the burned-out shell of the garage with a police cordon flapping across the void that had been its door. They got out of the car and Callum and Sonia took their luggage into the house. 'Have you any idea who did it?' asked Sonia.

'Did what?' asked Jerusha.

'Burned down the garage. It could not have been an accident, with all Françoise's belongings in there.'

'I have my suspicions,' said Jerusha but she was not going to elaborate. 'Someone didn't want any evidence found.'

'Where was Tilda that day? She would have seen anybody pouring petrol on the site,' said Sonia.

'Yes, it was done with a can of petrol. The police found the empty can carelessly chucked next to the door. 'The door that used to be there, that is.' She went on to explain that Tilda had given up her post a long time ago. It was too arduous, standing there in self-righteous isolation. She kept getting chest infections. Instead, she started a petition that went around the village to stop Jerusha selling the fields to Len. It carried little weight and few took any notice. 'However, I have decided to turn two of the fields into a wood. This was my own decision and nothing to do with Tilda and her petition. Sheena did encourage me, furiously!'

'I'm so glad. You have done the right thing,' said Sonia.

'Not, financially speaking,' said Callum.

'In this case, money certainly does not grow on trees. I'll have to be satisfied with the leaves and the birds and other woodland creatures. We might even have some red squirrels.' Jerusha was feeling more buoyant now that the couple were there. They reminded her of a time when there were no police watching Kirkfield, when there was no suspicion hanging over her home. When they entered the kitchen she saw by the dirty dishes that Oswald and James had been in there.

'Where are Oswald and James,' asked Sonia, taking note of the wreckage.

'House hunting is my guess.'

'I thought they were going to buy Lorna's house.'

'Lorna is wavering. She wasn't well when she offered it to them. It's a pity. Lorna needs to move into a smaller house, with neighbours. Tell you what, you go and settle into your room and then we can go for a walk. Get some fresh, country air.'

'Suits me,' said Callum. Sonia gave him a light kiss on the cheek.

They walked into the village and were passing Sheena's house where Tammy was in the garden. The dog started barking a welcome to Sonia, presumably in memory of those many walks. Sonia put her hand through the gate and ruffled its head. Sheena waved from a window.

They were nearing the post office when they saw Chris coming out of it.

'I thought you were retired,' commented Jerusha.

'I may be retired but I'm not dead yet. Or in jail.' His manner was gruff, as if he bore a grudge.

'You remember Sonia and Callum.'

'Och, aye. How are you doing? Fine.' Chris answered his own question. 'I must be getting along. Ena will be wondering what has become of me.' He hurried off.

'There is someone who doesn't like the whole shoddy business,' said Jerusha. 'For a while, I suspected him of murdering Françoise. One of her lovers, you know. But he has a watertight alibi. His wife, Ena. She wouldn't lie, ever.'

'You've been doing your own sleuthing, Jerusha. Is there anyone you suspect now?'

'I agree with the Super that a group of people was involved and I have my suspicions, which I won't go into now. I've come to the conclusion that if Hamish were involved it was only for honourable reasons. He was so loyal.'

'To think that, must hurt you very badly,' said Sonia.

'As James says, Hamish could not have been ignorant of a grave in his garden. I have come around to that way of thinking. What a terrible secret. He wanted to tell me something before he died but he wasn't given the time. He wanted to divest himself of a burden that he had been carrying for so many years. Had he lived long enough, he could have told us what we need to know to solve the case. But let's not talk about this now. Whatever happened to idle chit chat?'

They walked on past the pub and out of the village. Ahead of them was a winding country lane, with fields of sheep on either side. They needed to watch out for cars even although they straddled the road. Sonia and Callum were holding hands. They must have walked for less than two kilometres when they saw ahead a silver car parked by a farm gate. A woman was standing outside the car talking to a man with a bicycle. They could make out Lorna and Derek.

'Oh, it's Lorna. And who is that with her?' asked Sonia. 'I've been wanting to see Lorna again.'

Jerusha pulled her back. 'Now is not the right time. I don't think they want to be seen. Turn around now and don't look back.' To oblige her, they all turned and walked away from the pair at the gate, back towards the village.

'This is a bit odd, Jerusha. She's your sister-in-law and Derek is a friend,' said Sonia.

'I'm just going on instinct, Sonia. Bear with me.'

They walked on almost guiltily. Sonia looked over her shoulder a couple of times to see that Lorna and Derek were still talking conspiratorially. Then the three rounded a bend and could no longer see Lorna's car or the two huddled around it. In Jerusha's brain a few things had fallen into place and she was silent, nursing her suspicions. Lorna and Derek were not close friends. In fact, they had little to do with each other. So why the secret assignation? Lorna was a complex person and Jerusha could well believe that she would keep some secrets, but to keep them while in a state of mental turmoil would take some doing. Derek had a troubled past and his obsession with keeping fit might indicate that he was running away from something. Yet, perhaps she was reading too much into what could have been a chance encounter?

When they got back to Kirkfield James' car was in the drive, so Oswald and James must be back. Alongside James' car was a white Saab, which belonged to Sir Ewan. However, he was not there when they went inside. Oswald and James greeted Sonia and Callum warmly, with no hard feelings, and then went on to grumble about the houses they had been viewing. They were either rambling and impractical or on the small side. Nothing in-between.

'I thought you were going to buy Lorna's house,' said Sonia.

' Lorna is dithering. She can't make that final decision to sell. James would buy it at the right price,' said Oswald.

'You have more interesting things to tell us. How was Paris?' asked James.

Jerusha left Sonia and Callum to describe their romantic escapade and went in search of Ewan who had apparently gone outside. She found him standing inside the police cordon beside the empty grave, deep in thought. Even in travelling clothes, he was noble in his bearing. He looked up when she greeted him, not returning the greeting but saying, 'Death is a great leveller. Probably the greatest leveller. To think she lay here for fourteen years.'

'And nobody knew.'

'Somebody must have known,' he corrected her. 'Tragic. How like Françoise to die that way. She lived on the wild side. I never understood why she and Hamish got together.

I put it down to the attraction of opposites. My dear brother was so tolerant and she was so passionate.'

'She had so many so-called admirers and in the end nobody loved her,' said Jerusha.

'There were people who loved her. Her children, for a start. I remember her coming up to the Highlands with them and enchanting all the children, mine included, with her Winnie the Pooh impressions. Or course, she wasn't much good at changing nappies or being with her children when they were ill. She was scarcely a conventional mother and she was an unfaithful wife, a flirt, and that's the sum total of it.'

'Her counsellor made that seem like an illness.'

'Could have been. But what is all this? The police cordons. The open grave. The charred garage. What has all this unwarranted police presence done to Kirkfield? Perhaps you can't see it? You're too close to it. The whole atmosphere is of suspicion and you, James and Oswald must be oppressed by it.'

'It won't last forever.'

'You were never one to be oppressed by anything, Jerusha, but, nevertheless, we could hasten the end of all this. I'll need to speak to the officer in charge.'

'Superintendent Clive Drummond. I've arranged for you to speak to him this evening.'

'I would like you to be present.'

Jerusha would very much like to be present. She had no idea what Ewan was going to say but she suspected there would be a clash of opinions, the laird against the law. Chatting to Oswald and James while Ewan changed into a suit, she discovered that he had already been talking to the press. A reporter and a photographer from the local weekly were parked outside the property when Ewan arrived and he welcomed an opportunity to defend the family name. Ewan was totally in charge of the interview and the reporter, a novice, heard only what Ewan wanted her to hear. This young woman thought she had a scoop, unaware that the national press were waiting on a press release from the Super. The Super, himself, was reticent but the press had sniffed a breakthrough. With patience, they would get their story.

The Super arrived on the dot of six o'clock and Sir Ewan kept him waiting for ten minutes. Then he made a grand entrance, in suit and tie, striding into the sitting room where the Super and Jerusha were seated, Jerusha with a tray of drinks next to her. Sir Ewan accepted a Scotch on the rocks and held it in one hand but he did not sit down. He strode around the room and paced up and down. The Super was determined not to be discombobulated. He accepted a soft drink from Jerusha and sat back in an armchair, smiling, as if he wanted to convey the impression of being at ease. In his work he dealt with all strata of society, from the humble to the titled. Yet, to tell the truth, he was made a little anxious by Sir Ewan's manner. He did not know what to expect. He didn't have to wait long to find out.

Sir Ewan turned to look directly at the Super. 'Look here,' he said, 'This thing has gone on long enough. Why don't you admit defeat, my good man, and call it a day? This is an old case. I believe you call it a cold case. All the evidence should have led to an arrest fourteen years ago. Nobody could solve the case then and now what evidence there was has disappeared into the mists of time. You really should call a halt. Let Françoise rest in peace.'

'You forget that we now have a body.'

'A skeleton with a ring on its finger. What of it?'

'There's a great deal to it, Sir Ewan. The ring is engraved. We have to find out why Françoise Burnett was buried in the grounds of this house. Who put her there and why? Who went to great lengths to cover up the death? Already feathers have been ruffled. We have had a fire and a break-in at Kirkfield. These are not matters to be dismissed lightly.'

Jerusha was listening intently, sipping a gin and tonic.

'No one could accuse me of treating the matter lightly,' said Sir Ewan. 'My family's reputation is involved and it has already been besmirched. A lot has to do with the way you have taken over Kirkfield as a site for your activities. My family, Superintendent, is an honourable one, with titles going back centuries. It is inconceivable that it should be treated with suspicion. My brother, Hamish, was a good man whose only fault was to marry a sharp-tongued, wayward woman. Françoise brought this tragedy on herself.'

'We've ruled out suicide,' said the Super.

'That's not what I meant. I mean her actions were an invitation to death. She had drama and sudden death written all over her.'

'She did indeed die a tragic death and it is our duty, as a police force, to solve murder cases.'

'You are not suggesting my brother killed her?' asked Ewan.

'Hamish would never have done it,' added Jerusha.

'I'm not suggesting he committed the murder but he might have helped cover it up. Some people went to elaborate, if not ludicrous, lengths to make her death look like a disappearance. The clothes on the beach. The abandoned car. This subterfuge was successful in covering up her death for fourteen long years. We have to put that right.'

'I'm not getting through to you. I want you to drop the case on the grounds of insufficient evidence.'

'A confession would count for something, Sir Ewan?'

'Who has confessed?' 'Nobody, so far.'

'Ewan is right. If you haven't got enough evidence and no one has confessed, why not let things be?' asked Jerusha.

'I said, I haven't a confession, *thus far.*'

'You know more than you're letting on,' said Jerusha. Her mind was spinning around all of the people who could possibly confess, people who had no alibis. There weren't that many.

'I had hoped to get some useful information from Luke Junior who, sadly, or conveniently, died. By the way, the pathologist's first impression is that he died of natural causes.'

'You are too slow,' said Sir Ewan. 'You are missing tricks all the time. Luke Junior knew the garden backwards. He would have been aware of any untoward digging that went on.'

'Loyalty to your brother might have kept him silent.'

'Well, perhaps not. You might have been able to prevent the fire.'

'That only shows how close we are getting,' said the Super.

'I still want you to close the case.'

'I understand, Sir Ewan, that you are used to issuing commands. However, in this case you are dealing with the law and it is my duty to track down the truth. I tell you what, though, I will make a deal with you.'

'I'm not sure that I want to make a deal,' said Sir Ewan.

'Listen to him,' urged Jerusha.

'If I have not extracted confessions within forty-eight hours, I will recommend that the case be closed. How does that sound?'

'It's a compromise but I will accept your deal.'

14

THE WHOLE STORY

The next morning Sir Ewan left for his estate early, making it clear that he was a very busy man and that it was good of him to have spared his time. He missed the celebration. It was Oswald's fifty first birthday and they were having a champagne breakfast to which they invited Lorna, and Sheena who brought the cake. The dining room was decked with a banner saying Happy Birthday, the napkins had been folded into fans and the candles in the silver candlesticks were lit, never mind the daylight. On the menu was cereal, one of Oswald's favourites, and smoked salmon with scrambled eggs and toast. Sonia had done most of the preparation and she was cooking. She felt sorry for Oswald, trying to celebrate his birthday when the predominant feeling among the members of the household, before the mid-morning interrogations, was seriousness. Everyone, but Jerusha, was putting on a good face. Jerusha was effervescent, over-flowing with good cheer. She was happy because Oswald and James had announced that they were to become civil partners. She had long seen it coming so she was not surprised, but pleased that two of her favourite people were going to commit themselves to each other. She brought out the champagne but there were few takers. Sonia and Callum did not drink. Lorna refused a glass because of her forthcoming interview, then changed her mind and sipped half a glass. Sheena, also, didn't drink. Oswald tucked in and James kept him company with a small glass. Jerusha was quite happy to drink a little and they all toasted Oswald with champagne or orange juice.

The cake was brought in with a nominal number of sparkling candles and when Oswald had blown them out, they sang 'happy birthday' Sheena put the cake, an orange and cranberry sponge, on the sideboard to be eaten later with coffee or tea. Oswald poured his favourite cereal into his bowl and called for the milk. Jerusha passed him a pottery jug containing the milk and he started to pour it out. Then he stopped abruptly.

'What the devil! Jerusha! You have turned the milk green. I'll get you.' He leapt up and made as if to strangle her.

'Don't you think we've had enough of murder recently,' Sheena joked.

'Who said anything about murder,' said Lorna. 'What about insufficient evidence or accidental death.'

'Murder is a word that is bandied about in the village in connection with Kirkfield,' replied Sheena who could be quite stubborn when she chose.

'It's all the fault of the press,' said Lorna.

'Come on. This is a party. We've got to have tricks,' pleaded Jerusha. Oswald was still standing over her, his hands now by his sides. 'Aren't you going to drink that, Oswald. It's only a little green colouring. Perfectly safe.'

'Not likely,' said Oswald, taking the bowl of sick cereal to the kitchen and getting a clean bowl and another jug of milk. He was the only one eating cereal. The others were waiting for their salmon. They had had a lucky escape from the green milk trick. Oswald munched on.

As it drew near the time for her interview with the Super Lorna became visibly agitated. She kept plucking at the hair of her wig and shifting in her chair. Eventually, she got up and went over to Jerusha. 'You will come in there with me, won't you?' she asked.

'Of course. If that is what you want. Don't worry. He's quite a nice guy,' said Jerusha.

'I am worried. I don't know why he wants to see me a second time. I don't know how I can help him.'

'Just tell the truth,' said Jerusha.

'How can you just sit there and say that? You weren't there.'

'Is there something you want to tell me, Lorna?'

'No. No. Just come with me.'

'Are you quite well at the moment?'

'As sane as the next person. It's a wonder what drugs can do.'

They broke off their conversation to say goodbye to Sheena who had some shopping to do. She left with heartfelt goodbyes, thanking them for making her feel a part of the family, Sonia gave her her cake tin which she had washed. Jerusha did not feel the least bit usurped by Sonia taking over the kitchen, cooking and washing up with Callum. She liked to think of the kitchen as a communal hub, an arena for sharing, a place where one cooked and was cooked for. Now, she sat, relaxed, in the dining room, idly playing with a fork and a table mat. Lorna had gone to the bathroom. Oswald and James were helping themselves to more champagne.

'Ewan wanted me to call in Vernon,' she said to Lorna on her return.

'I don't need a lawyer. I'll be quite all right without one. Thanks to Ewan for the thought. Shall we go?'

Lorna had apparently composed herself and now wanted to get the whole thing over with.

※

The interview began at half past ten sharp, in the sitting room. The Super seemed to have come to feel quite at home in the largest of the armchairs. He began by asking Lorna how she was and whether or not she was in a position to answer questions.

'You mean, am I all here? The answer to that is I'm fine. Why is everybody so concerned about my health? Am I acting strange?'

'I understand that you can't take pressure and some of the questions I have for you are pretty searching.'

'Sounds frightening.'

'I hope not.'

'I am ready for your questions. You ask Jerusha if I am.'

'She'll be all right. And, if she is not, you can stop,' said Jerusha.

'Right. I will start with the victim. You did not like Françoise much, did you?'

'That's a leading question,' said Jerusha.

'I'll rephrase it. Did you like your sister-in-law?'

Lorna thought for a minute. 'It was more her father that I didn't like.'

'Why is that?'

'What has this got to do with the case?'

'Just bear with me. Why did you dislike Henri?'

'Because he raped me when I was fourteen. Are you satisfied?'

'I'm sorry to hear that. What did you do after you were raped?'

'I cried buckets.'

'Yes, it must have been very distressing. Did you report it to the police?'

'No.'

'Why not?'

'Because no one believed me. I tried telling my mother but she accused me of making things up. Henri was father's friend.'

'So, he was never prosecuted in a court of law?'

'No.'

'And you had to watch your brother marry his daughter.'

'I didn't kill Françoise, if that's what you are getting at.'

'I'm not suggesting you did but I think you know who is guilty.'

'What makes you think that?'

The Super's voice was very steady and he held a straight-backed posture in his chair. If he had been holding a pen, it would have been totally still. He pressed on. 'Let's go back to the unfortunate incident of the rape. You were a young woman. It must have shattered your confidence, made you afraid of relationships, humiliated you.'

'It did all of that, and more. I can't tell you how awful it was.'

'Now, if you had gone to the police and Henri had been prosecuted, you would have had justice.'

'That's what my psychiatrist says. I think that would have been some kind of revenge.'

'The Law is here to serve society. That's what my job is all about.' Jerusha saw that the Super was trying to gain Lorna's confidence by talking about himself. 'I'm here to put the pieces of the jigsaw together, to see that people like Henri are punished.'

'Too late, now'

'But it's not too late to see justice done with regard to the murder of Françoise.'

'I think it might be. Ewan says it's an old case that is best buried.'

'Françoise was a woman in the prime of her life, the mother of two children . . .'

'She was cold, calculating and hard, just like her father.'

'I thought you said it was him you did not like.'

'Both of them.'

'Let's go back to the concept of justice. It isn't a matter of likes and dislikes. It's made up of a series of laws, many of which have stood the test of time.'

'You're the one who asked me if I liked Françoise.'

'Indeed, I did. And we'll get on to that. Let me take you back to the point at which you said you would have liked to have seen Henri prosecuted and imprisoned.'

'Hanged.'

'Now, you're going a little too far back in time. Ideally Henri would have been imprisoned. Does it not follow that the killer of Françoise Burnett should be put in jail for his crime?'

'You're assuming it was a man?'

'Now, you are playing games. I'll be frank with you, Lorna. I believe you know who murdered Françoise.'

'It wasn't murder. It was an accident,' Lorna blurted out.

'Tell me what happened.'

'You don't need to say any more, Lorna, without a lawyer,' interrupted Jerusha.

'It's all right, Jerusha. I can cope.'

'Take your time. Tell me about this accident, Lorna.' The Super said this very carefully, as if he might break the spell.

Jerusha slipped out of the room to phone the lawyer. Minutes later, she was back, having satisfied herself that Vernon Brown would be here as soon as possible. Jerusha's absence affected Lorna who paused nervously.

The Super was acutely aware that Lorna was on the brink of breaking the silence that had surrounded the case, the silence she had held all those years. It was a key point in his investigation. Speaking or interrupting Lorna would be to risk the loss of vitally important information.

'It was an accident,' she repeated. 'I will tell you how it happened.'

☙❧

Midsummer Night had turned into morning and the partying guests had gone, leaving a vacuum at Kirkfield. Lorna and Hamish thought all the guests had left but they were to discover there was one upstairs with Françoise in her bedroom. Lorna and Hamish made a vague attempt to straighten some of the chairs and stack a few plates. It was about three o'clock in the morning. The children had long since gone to sleep in their rooms at the back of the house. Miss Ross, a dedicated and devoted nanny, slept in Jean's room because Jean was frightened of the dark. After the music and laughter, the house seemed deafeningly quiet when brother and sister entered the hall. However, shouting in Françoise's bedroom soon broke the silence. Lorna and Hamish were at the foot of the stairs when Françoise and Derek appeared on the landing. She came out of the bedroom first, in the red dress. He was in his kilt. They gave the impression that they had been in the bedroom for some time.

'I can't understand why you men are so feeble,' said Françoise, tossing her mane of hair.

'Give me one more chance, Françoise. I don't see what I've done to make you like this'

'You can't let go, can you?'

'Why must things have to change? We are good in bed.'

'Don't fool yourself. You are not that good.'

This angered Derek. His manhood had been insulted. 'Were you lying then when you said I was the best lover you've ever had?'

'Naturally. One says these things in the heat of the moment. Passion can make liars of us all.'

'You lying bitch.'

'So why don't you go back to your little wife in your little house.'

'Sheena is not a little wife. She is worth ten of your sort.'

'Oh. I'm a sort of person, now, am I?'

'You don't deserve your husband or your children.'

'And you have no children to deserve. Poor Derek. Wanting in that department, were you?

If he had been angry before, now he was incensed. She knew how to find the bits that hurt. First of all, Derek was very sensitive about his prowess as a lover; secondly it still made him sad that he and Sheena could not have children. Françoise seemed to know how to wound him. He was standing on the landing, tensed, and she was standing at the top of the stairs. 'I've had enough of this. I don't know what I saw in you. It's finished,' he said.

'Before you go, dear Derek, could you do me a teensy weensy favour. I like to have something to remember my lovers by. This for instance.' She dangled a cufflink in the air. 'This came from someone in the village with whom I had a great deal of fun. He was also married. He gave me this and its pair to keep me quiet. Wouldn't want the wives hearing of their husbands' dalliances, would we? She lifted the cufflink high in the air and then dropped it down her cleavage. 'And so, my dear, you can give me something, a token of your appreciation. Your dagger would do.'

'I'll give you my dagger.' He took the dagger from his stocking and unsheathed it. It was razor sharp, a weapon of murder. He lunged at her in fury and, when she put up her arm to protect herself, the steel blade dug deep into her forearm so that blood oozed and dripped down to her elbow, running down like liquid, scarlet icicles. Derek was still incensed. Even now, when he wanted with all his being to exact revenge for her taunts, he had failed to master her. He pulled back the weapon and held it high above his head, intending to attack again. This was the fatal move.

In stepping back to avoid his onslaught, Françoise lost her footing and fell backwards down the steep stairs, knocking her head several times. She lay motionless at the foot of the stairs, her neck broken, lifeless. Lorna and Hamish, who had witnessed the whole scene, stood frozen. Then Hamish recovered enough to step forward and feel Françoise's pulse. There was no pulse. Françoise was dead.

Derek dropped the dagger and came racing down the stairs. 'I've killed her,' he said, in sudden realisation of what had happened. 'I've bloody killed her. I didn't mean to do it, Hamish. She was your wife.'

'She brought it on herself,' said Hamish. 'Besides, I saw what happened. She fell.'

'It was an accident,' said Lorna.

'What are we going to do? I'll lose my reputation, my job, my wife.'

'*My* wife was on a collision course with providence. Something like this was bound to happen. I'm only sorry it had to be you, Derek.'

Nobody touched the body, nobody wept in pain. Françoise's death was just a fact, an ending to all the hurt she had delivered. Moments passed and they were passive, overwhelmed by the enormity of sudden death. Then Derek crumpled. 'Look. I saw her eyelid flicker. She's not dead,' he said.

'You are imagining things, Derek. I'm one hundred percent certain she is dead. She'll be at peace now, something she never found in life.'

'Oh my God, what have I done?' He was kneeling down and stroking the dead woman's hair. 'I didn't mean it, Françoise. I am so sorry.'

❧

'Come. Get up, my friend. It wasn't your fault,' said Hamish, helping him up. 'I suppose we'd better get a doctor to certify her dead, and the police.'

'No. No police. They will never believe me. It will ruin me.'

Lorna spoke up. 'We don't have to call a doctor or the police. We can make it look as if she has disappeared.'

359

The other two listened intently as she outlined her plan.

'She was a cruel woman,' said Hamish after Lorna had finished. 'Let her be kind in death. Derek, my friend, I will do anything to stop Françoise wreaking havoc with your life. I will stand by you.'

'But I was poaching your wife.'

'If it weren't you, it would have been someone else. She was addicted and undiscriminating. She made nonsense of our marriage commitment. My feelings for her have long been as dead as she is now. And you were just a pawn.'

'I didn't see it like that but I do now,' said Derek. 'I've been so stupid.'

'Smarten up now,' said Lorna. 'Let's get on with the plan. Let's get Françoise's body out of the way before Miss Ross and the children come down for breakfast.'

'Before we begin, we must swear to secrecy,' said Hamish.

They solemnly swore, as if in blood, to a silence that was destined to last fourteen years. Derek handed Hamish the dagger in ceremonial fashion.

Having agreed a plan, they soberly went about executing it. They began by stifling the blood on the dead woman's arm and then moved the body out of sight. Hamish and Derek carried it into the utility room and laid it on the floor between the washing machines and the tool cupboard. Hamish took a long look at his lifeless wife, as beautiful in death as she was when alive. He felt a pang of remorse about what he was doing, which he suppressed by leaving the room and locking the door. Derek was jittery but he was by Hamish's side and the two embraced outside the utility room door.

Derek was to go back home to Sheena and act as if everything were normal. He was to go to bed and tell Sheena that he had to be up early to help clear up at Kirkfield. She was scarcely awake but sleepily nodded her assent. Sheena made a practice of having only good thoughts about people until it became impossible not to see their faults and she knew how close Derek and Hamish had been, so she did not question Derek's behaviour. He, on the other hand, went through torment. He couldn't sleep and, what was worse, he could not toss and turn as that might disturb Sheena. The true impact of the night dominated his thoughts like a clamp on a car wheel. Emotions of fear and horror tried to escape but they were pinioned by an unbearable pretence. He was to lie still and pretend to be asleep until it was a normal time to get up and go to Kirkfield. To dig a grave.

Hamish and Lorna banished thoughts of sleep. They were executing the cover-up. Lorna searched for some gloves in the coat cupboard and found an old pair. She wanted to avoid leaving fingerprints on Françoise's car, which she had elected to drive to the beach. Wearing the black leather gloves, she rifled through Françoise' wardrobe and drawers for some light clothes to leave on the beach. The idea was to make it look as if Françoise had gone for a swim and had never come back. Lorna took some pride in conceiving this drama.

Hamish waited for her at the front door, both sets of car keys in his hand. He would have waited outside but he was afraid of being seen. That was his fear as they drove off in convoy; that some early bird villager might take a note of what was going on in the big house. They took a road skirting the village, Hamish leading the way. There was little traffic on the road. It was four thirty in the morning and the journey would take roughly one hour. Both cars were full of petrol and well looked after. What they did not want was for one of the cars to break down. That would jeopardise their whole scheme. However, they reached the beach without mishap and both parked in the small car park. They got out and were soon on the sand, arranging Françoise's clothing in a pile near a sand dune. Lorna's *coup d'état* was the footprints she made leading into the sea. Hamish scuffed his own footprints. There was no one else on the beach. Except for the lapping of the waves, all was quiet and the sea air freshened their tired faces. They did not stay long, did not speak much. They had a small argument about where to leave Françoise's car keys. On the beach or in the ignition? Hamish thought they should be in the car as Françoise would not expect to use them. Lorna wanted to leave them in the small handbag, with some money in it, which she had left beside the bundle of clothes near the sand dune. In the end, they decided to leave them in Françoise's car. They were operating on nervous energy so that a decision like that became a big decision. Nevertheless, they kept their voices down as if non-existent ears could hear.

They were drawing out of the car park when an early dog-walker crossed in front of them. They pulled down their visors and waited for the dog-walker to get out of their way. Fortunately, the dog was distracting its owner and they were soon on their way. Hamish, who was driving, said, 'what we don't want is for her possessions and her car to be discovered too soon. She needs to be buried by the time they are found and treated as suspicious.'

'Derek said he'd be digging by seven o'clock.'

'He has plenty of time. This is a bold plan of yours, Lorna, and it requires strong nerves. What if we are caught?'

'We won't be, believe me.'

There were a few awkward moments over the children's breakfast table when they got back.

'If mother's not coming to the zoo with us, you could at least let me say goodbye to her, Father,' said Claude.

'Mummy had a late night. She's probably sleeping,' cut in Miss Ross. It was uncharacteristic of her to interfere between father and son but she, herself, had had a broken night. She had been woken by loud voices coming from the passage and she had spent some time getting back to sleep. She even thought she'd heard a scream but far be it for her to meddle in the private lives of her employers. Miss Ross usually knew her place and now regretted speaking out about Mrs Burnett having had a late night. She worried about her charges and about how much they missed the constant care of a mother. She should be there as a nanny and not a substitute mother. Mrs Burnett was fine and entertaining when she was there but she was not there very often.

'You should answer me, Father,' said Claude, digging his spoon into his bowl of cereal.

'What's this with Father and Mother, Claude? You don't need to be so formal,' said Hamish. 'I think Miss Ross has answered your question, if it was a question.' Hamish was feeling jagged; the strain of events and the affect of no sleep. He also felt the first onset of guilt. His children had just lost their mother and they were oblivious to the fact. Claude was instinctively suspicious. He sensed something was not right but he could not identify what was wrong. All he could do was make minor protests. Jean, on the other hand was very excited about their visit to the zoo and going to see grandma and grandpa. She sucked her thumb, wishing Claude would not be so grouchy. Her brother spoiled things. If Mummy could not be there she was just as happy with Miss Ross, who was kind and didn't scold her as Claude did.

Now Claude chose to be difficult. He wanted to wear his red socks. No other pair would do.

'Very well. I believe they are in the utility room with the other washing. I'll go and get them. You get on with your breakfast. We've got to go,' said Miss Ross, getting up.

'No,' Lorna said sharply. Then she changed her tone. 'I mean, I will get them for you. Just a tick.' And she left the room hastily.

Miss Ross was surprised but she didn't argue.

Lorna hurried down the passage to the utility room. She had the key and she turned it in the lock. She tried not to look at the corpse lying on the floor and, for a moment, imagined Françoise getting up and berating her. She could not help but look. Françoise's face was contorted, as if she had been fighting death. Lorna hastily found the red pair of socks and took several more, in case Claude changed his mind. She backed away from the room and all it contained, locked the door and returned to the kitchen, out of breath and red in the face.

Claude promptly pounced on the red socks and put them on. Within ten minutes, after they had brushed their teeth, the children were away to Edinburgh with Miss Ross, who had her own car.

Hamish and Lorna exchanged looks that said a little part of them was dying too. 'I don't think I can do this,' said Hamish.

'You can and you will,' she said, trying to bolster him.

'They are so innocent,' he said.

'So is Derek. That is what you've got to focus on.'

'It's a choice between betraying my children and betraying my friend. Have I chosen the right course?'

'You can't go back now. We're nearly through. Come. We must go and help Derek with the digging.'

'I've got to make an appearance in the marquee first. The caterers will be wondering where I've got to. Don't worry. I will be with you shortly. I will carry on with the plan. I will help dig Françoise's grave.'

Although the grave was ready by early evening, they decided to wait before they brought out the body. Hamish and Derek carried it, one at each end, while Lorna went ahead.

They eased the body down into the earth. Derek was the first to start shovelling earth into the grave.

Hamish stepped back, spade poised. 'May she rest in peace,' he said like a broken man. Then he braced himself to join in the burial.

When they had finished, they placed the turf carefully back on the earth and they put a bench on top of it to divert curious eyes. They were all sad and exhausted.

15

ARRESTS

'Have you told me everything, Lorna?' The Super's face was inscrutable but this time his voice was gentle. This suspect needed to be coaxed, not bullied. They had come a long way but there was something she was hiding. She had done her best to make Françoise's death look accidental. But was it? The cynic in him and years of experience made him pretty sure it was not.

'It was a long time ago,' said Lorna.

'And yet, events like those you have described have a way of staying vivid in your memory.'

'What I've told you is correct, but . . .' Lorna was sitting on the edge of her chair, looking at the door as if she would like to flee. She had betrayed Derek after all those years. She imagined the anguish she had heaped upon

Derek and Sheena. It wasn't so bad now he had retired. He hadn't a job to lose. Lorna was sure the Super was going to arrest both her and Derek. On what grounds? That was the important thing. She had to maintain that Derek never caused Françoise to fall down the stairs. She had omitted to tell the Super about the dagger.

'But, what, Lorna?' The Super was now stern. He had been immensely patient up until now. This little woman in a wig, with a history of mental illness, had hatched a plan that had defied the law for fourteen years.

'Nothing. What I've told you is what happened.'

'You'll have to repeat your tale in a court of law.'

'Yes.'

Then the Super seemed to lose patience. 'Stay where you are,' he ordered. He went outside to where his constables were parked, leaving Lorna and Jerusha alone together. He ordered PC Keir and PC Anderson to go to the McPherson's house and bring Derek up to Kirkfield. They took the police car, hoping to evade the press who had gathered in cars outside in the road. Some newspeople got out and surged into the driveway, gathering around the Superintendent. Somehow, with their nose for news, they had got wind of the fact that there was going to be an arrest. That is, all except the local weekly, which was stuck with the story of Sir Ewan defending Hamish.

'Sir, I believe there is going to be an arrest. Is that true?'

'Sir, who will you be arresting?'

Sir, have you arrested anyone already?'

'What comments have you on this case, Sir?'

'Will you be holding a press conference?'

They tried to hem him in but he broke free and yet they sprang up alongside him on the steps. At the front door he turned and said, 'I'll have something for you in about an hour's time.' With that, he went inside and shut the door. Superintendent Drummond did not despise the press. He believed in liaising with them to try and make sure their facts were right. They would write the story, anyway, press conference or no press conference. That was their obsession. Getting the story, without regard for morality.

Inside, Jerusha and Lorna had been whispering to each other to avoid being heard by the lone constable standing by the door.

'Is that really what happened, Lorna?'

'I'm afraid so.'

'That is what Hamish wanted to tell me from his deathbed. He wanted me to know and now I do. He did all that for a friend. He was a very loyal person.'

'He loved you, Jerusha. He loathed having a secret from you.'

'It must have tormented him.'

'He'd want you to forgive him.'

'How can I not forgive him? So that's what really happened. I thought there was something between you and Derek when I saw you together by the farm gate.'

'I hope Derek is not going to detest me for confessing.'

Just then the door opened. It was the Super followed by someone else. It was not Derek, but Vernon Brown, their lawyer. He went up to Lorna and said, 'You do not need to say anything more, Lorna. The less said the better.'

'I've already done the damage,' said Lorna.

☙ ❧

Vernon did not have a chance to caution her further at that point because the police constables ushered Derek in. The policemen went outside the room but Vernon stayed, with the Super's permission. Derek was given a chair directly in front of the Super. He was looking agitated and surly. He greeted no one and sat hunched up, his hands clasped around his knees. He knew this was a moment of truth but he still tried to hang on to the subterfuge, the fourteen-year-old lie.

'Lorna has told us what really happened on Midsummer's Night 1996. Are you going to corroborate her evidence?' the Super began.

'How would I know what she has told you?' Derek was almost insolent.

'She called it an accident. Françoise fell down the stairs in this very house and broke her neck.'

'Françoise Burnett disappeared. She went missing and was declared dead after seven years.'

'There is the small matter of the skeleton we found in the garden.'

'That could have been there for centuries.'

'Let's start again Mr McPherson. Were you and Françoise lovers?'

'Yes, briefly. My wife knows about that.'

'Presumably, what she doesn't know yet is that on the night in question you and Françoise had a lovers' quarrel and you pushed her down the stairs.'

'I did not say that,' Lorna intervened.

'Hush, Lorna,' said Vernon.

However, she continued. 'And I didn't tell him about the dagger.' She was momentarily privately uncertain about what she had or hadn't said and oblivious to who was listening, a sign of the strain of being under interrogation for hours.

'Lorna!' said Jerusha.

When Lorna realized she was muddling her story, she said, 'Oh,' and 'I'm sorry Derek.'

'I see,' said the Super, 'the second sgiandabh. So, am I to understand, Mr McPherson, that you stabbed your lover and pushed her down the long flight of stairs?'

'It's only a ceremonial knife. A lot of men carry them when they are dressed in kilts. In any case, to tell you the real truth, she wanted it as a token of our love making. She had this thing about keeping trophies to remind her of her lovers. With Chris, it was cufflinks.'

'Ah. The cufflinks. So, Françoise wanted a trophy. She was getting rid of you, then. Figuratively speaking, she was giving you the push.'

'Well, yes, but . . .'

'This made you angry and you attacked her, causing her to fall down the stairs and break her neck.'

'She fell, yes, but I didn't mean to kill her.'

'You admit, then, that you did, in fact, kill her?'

'I've asked myself that for fourteen long years . . .' Derek hunched over in his chair and clamped his hands against the sides of his head.

The Super was silent. He got up and went to the door. Opening it, he beckoned to his constables to come inside. He returned to stand by his chair. 'Derek McPherson, I'm arresting you on suspicion of murder. You do not have to say anything but what you do say may later be used in evidence against you.' He turned to face Lorna, who began to tremble. 'Lorna Burnett, I'm arresting you for acting as an accessory to murder.' Now he spoke to them both. 'There is also the matter of arson, and breaking and entering but we'll deal with these later. You can choose to come quietly or we can cuff you. Remember you'll have to face members of the press as you leave the house. My advice to you is to keep your heads down and say nothing. I will deal with the press. Take them away, Constables.'

They went quietly. You may even say they were relieved that the strain of keeping a secret for fourteen years was now over.

Jerusha watched them go and, herself, felt relieved, but for a different reason. It was a blessing that Hamish had not lived to face a trial for his part in covering up what she determinedly saw as the accidental death of Françoise Burnett.

DARLINGS

16

LORNA HOLDS THE KEYS AND JERUSHA AVOIDS THE TRUTH

Over the next months Jerusha had to call on all her acting skills. She would not let the world know how devastated she was by Hamish's actions. And the world was loud and critical in her ears. First it was the village gossip. She couldn't go down to the post office without being targeted by some villager.

'How does it feel, Mrs Burnett, to have been married to a criminal?'

'The laird had blood on his hands. You knew, didn't you? All this time.'

'Your sister-in-law should never have got bail. Free today, gone to prison tomorrow.'

'So much for the big hoose.'

They said things that she couldn't really answer, didn't want to answer lest she totally destroy her image of her husband. She couldn't put on a smile because that would make her look villainous. Instead she adopted a dignified, wounded expression, and bought some more chocolates. 'Hamish is innocent. He is not on trial,' she would retort, cold and aloof and magnificent.

With the press, she was a little less haughty. She tried to woo members of the press into thinking of her as a guilt-free, loyal wife, the widow of an admirable and loyal husband. It did not work. She still came across as the deluded widow of a husband who had deceived her. In any case, they were far more interested in Derek, who was to be tried for manslaughter and also in Lorna who was to be tried as an accessory to crime. Jerusha would not read newspapers or listen to any news. The case had captured the public's imagination and it was widely publicised. Jerusha had persuaded Sheena to go away, into hiding, until the trial was over. Sheena took Tammy and left home, keeping a low profile as best she could while still continuing to visit Derek in prison. After a while the press no longer overwhelmed Jerusha but she still had daily knocks on the door. She covered her ears. 'Actors don't read reviews,' she said.

Although Lorna, having been let out on bail, was going to have a tough struggle with publicity and harassment, the shock of being arrested and locked up in a cell, and the sense that she had already lost her privacy, had led her to make the final decision to leave her loch-side home.

Afterwards, Jerusha was always very proud of the fact that the house sale deal was struck over her kitchen table.

'We'll take it if you are sure you are being sensible about this,' said James to Lorna.

'I'm being perfectly rational. You can have the house at the right price. Deliberately, no one really mentioned Lorna's suspected participation in the cover-up of Françoise's death. Occasionally, they referred to 'the accident' but did not dwell on it. Finally buying a house was much more fun.

'And there's a lovely cottage for sale in the village for you, Lorna,' enthused Jerusha.

'I've put in an offer for that already,' said Lorna.

'We can be neighbours.' This was Jerusha acting. She had very mixed feelings towards Lorna these days. In her heart she judged her to have led Hamish astray with an elaborate ruse. But then her reasoning would come into play and she would say to herself that Hamish was not weak. He would never have been led by his sister.

'So, that's it. Champers?' said Oswald. 'Not for you, James, you'll be driving to our new home.'

'Just a moment, Oswald. I'm not so sure I want to celebrate your going. While I'm happy for you that you've found the house you want, I'm going to miss you,' said Jerusha.

'We won't be gone for good. We'll come and see you, I promise,' said James.

'And you can come and see us,' added Oswald as he popped the cork of the champagne bottle.

'I'll be close by, all things being well,' said Lorna.

Jerusha found her act. Snatching up a fluted champagne glass she said, '*Darlings*. Here's to you and your lovely homes.' She raised her glass and chinked those of the others. 'Darling Lorna, we can get together every day.'

'That's if I don't go to prison,' Lorna muttered.

'We won't talk about that now,' chirped Jerusha in an attempt to cut off serious conversation. She wanted them to stick to the superficial. She, herself, was depressed about the trial for Lorna and Derek's sake but also because she thought it would expose Hamish's actions. She was still fighting the reality of Lorna's confession. Even if she were going to miss James and Oswald desperately, it was far better that they talk about moving house. 'Rudy will like living in the village with neighbouring dogs. There are lots of walks around here, Lorna.'

'I'd better go and try to find out if my offer has been accepted.' Lorna proceeded to make a great display of looking for her handbag and, once she had found that, of looking for her car keys. 'One thing I should warn you of, James and Oswald, is that the press has been a nuisance out there.'

Nobody said anything about this until she had left. When she had gone, Oswald said, 'Don't worry, James, I will get rid of any press hounds. In any case, if I'm right, they are not allowed to do anything that prejudices a trial.'

'I feel sorry for her. It's bad enough having the trial hanging over her . . .'

'James. We promised not to talk about the trial while we're waiting for it. If I've got to pretend I'm not going to miss you, you'll need to stick to the rules,' said Jerusha.

'Just imagine not having any of these rules,' said Oswald, raising his glass in celebration.

'Here's to Lorna and the success of her bid for the cottage,' Jerusha said and sipped her champagne.

'We'll still have to have celebrations,' said James.

'Oh, we will. House warming, birthdays, Christmas, April Fools' Day and all the rest. You and me, and Lorna. But Lorna has hardly touched her glass.'

❦

Scarcely was a sale more straightforward. Lorna bought the cottage and the previous owners moved out in good time. She hardly got to know them and they didn't even try to mention her impending trial. They must have been aware of her potentially criminal status but everyone knows that the question of money can silence the most moral of souls. Lorna moved her furniture and other belongings into a meticulously decorated property with a neat garden on Sunday, the first of August and James and Oswald moved into their new house on Monday, the second of August. They were elated. No reflection on Jerusha but this was theirs. They strode through the space of empty rooms, whooping and chortling with the utter glee of having their own home, a little guilty when they thought of Jerusha and leaving her behind. Jerusha had wanted to come with them when they took possession of the house but James had persuaded her to wait until it was habitable. There wasn't even an armchair for her to sit on. Besides, Lorna needed her help.

Lorna was, in fact, staying with Jerusha until she had sorted out her belongings. She had much more of those than Oswald and James who were actively, and blissfully, camping out. It's a good thing it was summer. They had two deck chairs in the cavern of the sitting room; a futon they had managed to borrow in the master bedroom, with cushions for pillows and one of Jerusha's sheets. Casting aside depression, James was visibly blossoming. He never mentioned the trial and, instead, he had a clear sense of purpose about what he wanted to do with his new home. He intended furnishing it with second-hand furniture, which he would restore. He had started on a long pine kitchen table already, sanding it, making it ready to treat with a light coat of matt varnish. The six matching chairs he would give the same treatment. Not only was James interested in furniture restoration but he had also bought an easel and some watercolours and was planning to teach himself to paint the landscape.

Oswald was occupied in putting up a fence in front of the house, at the end of the loch, because James felt a little dizzy every time he looked at it. This vague unease did not detract from the happiness they were deriving from this exciting new project. When they were ready they would invite Jerusha in. The relief came not from leaving Jerusha, whom they still loved dearly, but from leaving behind the drama and sadness of Kirkfield House. The crime scene cordons were still in place, the garage still stood gutted. As far as James was concerned the grave was an open wound in the family. Jerusha would have agreed with him when she allowed herself to think of it. She blotted out thoughts of these things and she skated over the fact that her two best friends had gone, leaving a vacant hole almost as deep as the grave. She threw herself into helping Lorna dust, clean, arrange furniture, make beds, get the 'phone connected, test out appliances. However, Jerusha's artificial optimism could not help Lorna adjust to her new surroundings. She was mourning the loss of the belongings that had to be ditched because she was downsizing; mourning the loss of the house she had lived in for so long and the open space surrounding it; missing Rudy, who was in kennels for a few days.

They were standing on the doorstep of the cottage. Jerusha was about to go. 'Well, you've got a bed for the night so I guess you'll want to stay here. Just think of it, the first night in your new home. Lucky you.'

'There's something not quite right,' said Lorna.

'It is fabulously comfortable, don't you think? You've got everything you need at hand. Not like me, rattling around in a large house. I'll see you in the morning.'

'No, wait a moment, Jerusha. I'd rather spend another night with you, if that is all right?'

'No problem. I'd love to have you.' What Jerusha did not say was that Lorna made her think of Hamish, as if she needed reminding, and together they reminded her of the cover-up of Françoise's death. They did it to save Derek, but Lorna was going to be tried as an accessory to a crime or attempting to defeat the ends of justice, or some equally serious charge. Lorna was also going to be tried for arson. She was lucky to have been let out on bail. Jerusha was tied to Lorna by a family bond and, on the outside, staunchly defended her but inside was a little afraid of her, rather as she was afraid of Claude.

⟡

Lorna had a huge golden key ring, the size of a round coaster with two small keys on it; one for the front door and one for the back door. Now she locked the front door and she and Jerusha walked out of the driveway, leaving Lorna's car locked in the drive. They walked up the road, past the village church, past the pub—which was heaving by the sound of it—past Sheena's darkened house. No one, not even Jerusha, knew where Sheena had gone; probably not too far from the prison Derek was being held in. Sheena would never give up on her husband. In their last conversation before she went, Jerusha realised that Sheena adamantly blamed Françoise for provoking Derek, and Françoise's behaviour for bringing about the whole sad affair. Jerusha spoke of 'the accident' as a simple affair but, inside, she thought it more complex.

They reached Kirkfield House without meeting anyone and Jerusha let them in. 'These will be finished by tomorrow,' she said, the sewing machine singing its own personal song. They had eaten and repaired to Jerusha's workroom so that Jerusha could get on with the bedroom curtains she was making for Lorna. They were soft lilac with a deeper purple iris pattern—fabric Lorna had chosen when they went shopping in Edinburgh. The two women were dressed informally, in the clothes they had been wearing all day. Jerusha had dropped her habit of changing for dinner while there were so few people in the house. That did not mean she was going to give up sewing outfits for herself. The workroom was teeming with colour and texture and a bolt out of the blue was the black fabric she had bought to make a funeral suit. She didn't know whether or not she was going to Françoise's funeral when it happened after the trial. Jean was keen to persuade her to go. Claude, as ever, was sceptical.

'I wonder how Rudy is getting on? I've extended her stay in the kennels,' said Lorna.

'Whatever for?'

'She's getting on now and will be confused by the new environment, me moving furniture, hanging curtains and paintings.'

'She'll have to come home sometime.'

'That's just it. It's not home.'

'It can't be home if you are not there to make it one.'

'You want me to go?'

'No. Of course not. You are preventing me from rattling around in this big house now that Oswald and James have gone. I wonder how they are getting on? Perhaps they are missing me? No, you're fine Lorna.'

'I get the feeling you're a little nervous of me, Jerusha.'

'Tosh.' She was finishing sewing a long seam.

Lorna had been moving around, touching fabric, but now she sat in a basketweave chair in a corner of the room. The chair had a high back, making her look as if she were sitting on a stage throne.

'I'm serious, Jerusha.'

Jerusha stopped sewing and said, 'the last thing I want is to be serious, Lorna.'

'Well, you're going to have to be sometime. It's like me getting Rudy out of the kennels and moving into the cottage. Are you uneasy when you're with me? Ever since I confessed you've adopted a special tone with me.'

'*Darling!*

'You see what I mean. Let it drop, Jerusha. Tell me what you think.' Lorna clasped her hands together as a way of pleading.

Jerusha pushed her sewing aside and turned the machine light off. 'You make me uneasy because you are so unpredictable. I can't tell what you're going to do next. I know you can't help it but that's how it comes across.'

'My illness, you mean?'

'Yes. That was difficult before but with recent events, I just don't know . . .'

'I find myself unpredictable too.'

'When it comes to the crunch, I can understand what you and Hamish did for Derek but what worries me is the fire. You did set fire to the garage, didn't you?' Jerusha looked her squarely in the face.

Yes. I did.'

'Why?'

'The police were getting too close. I still hoped they would never find out the truth.'

'But Lorna, Kirkfield. Your brother's home. It could have spread. People could have been hurt.'

'I was not thinking straight.'

'What else could you do when you are not thinking straight?'

'Nothing. I promise. I will probably go to prison for what I've done.'

'That doesn't change the fact that you did it. It is a sore, a scar on Hamish's memory.' A real sense of drama was beginning to surge and bypass Jerusha's acting and it infected Lorna.

'I'm truly sorry. I'll never do anything like that again.'

'I love you, Lorna. You are my closest link to Hamish but it will take me a while to forgive you for that. You must understand my confusion.'

'I'll move into the cottage tomorrow.'

'That might be best.'

⚬⚬⚬

They went to bed with cups of hot chocolate but both were destined to have a broken night.

Lorna took off her wig and put it on the moulded head where it spent the nights. She examined her own head of stunted hair in the mirror and took up a pair of nail scissors. She snipped a bit here and there and ignored the locks that fell to the floor, a grey carpet. She hated her hair. When she was young she wore it long, when it was brunette, thick and admired. The trouble was that Henri had admired it. She could not get out of her mind the memory of him stroking it before he violated her. After that, she went for years putting up with compliments about her hair until finally she took a pair of large scissors and cut it to the scalp. Then she reasoned that her only recourse was to cover up the jagged tufts with a wig. Her trademark was born and she had destroyed Henri's fingerprints. Every time she cut it back she was protesting at what he had done all those years ago. It didn't help that he was dead. He had not released her when he went to his grave.

Usually, when she looked in a mirror, all she saw was hair but now she looked at her face. It was wrinkled. It was old. Her small eyes had a way of beaming out at whoever she was looking at, in this case, herself. They honed in on the lines across her brow. They criticized the lumpy chin. She wondered what she looked like when there was madness in her eyes—deep, angry, beams of fierce fear. They had been her eyes, sane and capable, when she had poured petrol around the garage at Kirkfield. She knew she had set fire to the garage when she was in her right mind. The trouble was that Vernon had persuaded her to plead insanity against all of the charges, even the fire. So, if she won her case, she was going to have to live with another secret for the rest of her life. A part of her would prefer to pay the price of prison.

These thoughts were too much for her. She got into bed where she lay restless, unable to sleep.

Jerusha, too, was having difficulty sleeping. She tossed and turned for about half an hour then put the bedside light on and started to read. She was reading the play 'Twelve Angry Men' by Reginald Rose, which traces a jury's verdict from guilty to not guilty. While she was reading it she imagined Hamish on trial, finding the steps to make him win the case. When she had finished the play she experienced a great feeling of exhilaration and was able to sleep, the book lying on her breast, the light still on.

While she was sleeping, Jerusha had a dream. She dreamed she was on a cliff top overlooking the sea. Hamish was beside her. They felt the wind through their hair and heard the waves thrashing onto the shore below, jetting up in between rocks. She kept this image for what seemed a long time. Then she made a mistake. She tried to touch him. She felt her hand go through him. He leapt up and stood behind her. She turned. She knew he was going. She scrambled up onto her knees, in supplication, before him. She was pleading with him to stay. 'Don't worry, my love. Everything will be all right,' he said before he vanished. And Jerusha woke up.

Lorna had not been to sleep at all. As soon as her tufty head hit the pillow she experienced that dry-eyed, wide-awake feeling of the insomniac. She started breathing deeply, concentrating on each breath but her thoughts plagued her. They were inevitably about the case, surrounded by guilt, fear and pessimism. Whenever she experienced insomnia, for whatever reason, she would get up and make a cup of tea. Usually, Rudy was there to comfort her. Now, she was aware that she was in for a long night of wakefulness. At home, by this she meant James and Oswald's new home, she would sneak a cigarette but she couldn't do that here. A cup of tea. She went downstairs in her nightgown, went into the kitchen and put on the kettle. This was a soothing ritual. It gave her something to do. She hoped not to disturb Jerusha but she had to put on the light.

After she had made her tea, she took her mug through to the sitting room where there was a thin glow coming from an outside light although the curtains were firmly shut. Her eyes soon acclimatized to the slight light. Lorna sat and imagined herself in prison. It was the other prisoners who worried her most. They would tease, or worse, they would attack her. She would not be like them and they would resent it. Poor Derek. She wondered what he was going through. She was lucky to have been granted bail. He must have been desperately disappointed when the judge refused him bail. He was in it. Rules and regulations. Stale, cold food. Sleeping in a small cell with, perhaps, a murderer. A hardened criminal, a rapist, a bank robber. He would have to toughen up, at his age.

Of course, Lorna's thoughts weren't as ordered as this. They came in flashes and tailed off and repeated themselves. It was three thirty in the morning. She had just taken a sip of tea when she started to feel she had company. She was convinced she wasn't alone in the room. The curtains moved. She tensed. Someone stepped through the parting in the curtains. She could make out the figure of a man radiating light. The ghostly body of Hamish was standing before her, empty-handed, severe. Her heart lurched and she started to get up. She wanted to touch him. Lorna believed in ghosts and she was not afraid. 'Don't get up,' said the ghost. 'I won't be here long'.

She sat again, mesmerised. Then she said, 'Hamish, you don't know what's going on. They know it all.'

'This is not news to me, Lorna. Don't worry. Everything will be all right.' And then he evaporated and the curtains rippled as if parted by a light breeze. The ghost of Hamish was gone, leaving Lorna sobbing with excitement, grief and awe. She stayed there, holding the moment of Hamish's appearance, letting her tea grow cold and that is how Jerusha found her when she came downstairs still encased in her dream.

'Are you all right, Lorna?' Jerusha had on her dressing gown, tied firmly at the waist.

'Strange things have been going on in this house tonight,' said Lorna.

'Hamish has been here.'

They told each other their experiences, quickly, urgently as though by voicing them they would lose them. When they had finished they looked at each other with joy and hugged and repeated like a mantra: 'don't worry. Everything will be all right'. They clasped each other as if there had been no rift, as if Lorna hadn't a prison sentence hanging over her. They had been cleansed and renewed. They longed for Hamish to appear to them again.

Jerusha left Lorna having a cigarette, allowable under the circumstances, and the moment her head hit the pillow she was asleep. Lorna took a while longer to drift off but she did eventually.

Cwwo

In the morning, or rather, later that morning, still elated, they got ready to go to Lorna's house to unpack some more cardboard boxes. The curtains were still not quite finished. They would go at a later time. Lorna was confidently contemplating spending the night at the cottage so she took an overnight bag. It's strange how confidence can be rewarded with disaster, Jerusha thought afterwards, because what they found challenged the cosy aftermath of the night's events. Walking into the drive they saw Lorna's car parked where it had been the night before, only there was a difference. Graffiti had been spray painted on its sides. One side, in red paint, spelt 'murderer' and the other side read 'madwoman'. Lorna reacted as if she had been slapped in the face. Jerusha looked at the angry words, back at Lorna, then again at the defaced car. They circled the vehicle several times, absorbing the venom of the words and then they walked around the cottage to see if there was any more graffiti. They found none. Then they went back to the car, Jerusha hoping they had imagined the foul words.

'It's no good,' said Lorna, finally. 'I should never have moved into this village.' She now looked as if she might run back to Kirkfield House.

'It's only some nutter,' said Jerusha.

'How do you know it's not what they all think?'

'You have as much right to be here as they have. And this . . . this is just slander.'

'What do we do?'

'We call the police. That's what we do.'

'You can't do that. They will ask what I can expect under the circumstances.'

'Lorna, you are not a murderer and you are not mad, although you have your moments.'

'This wretched illness is always tripping me up.'

'Come on. We'll go inside and call the police.'

It was Constable Keir who came out to the cottage. He arrived in a white, blue and yellow police car and sprang out of it to take a look at the offensive words. Then he rang the doorbell. Jerusha showed him in. 'Same case; different story,' she said.

'It's a shame this has happened. Someone with a steady hand and a grudge. Can you think of anyone who could do this, Miss Burnett?' He addressed Lorna.

'Could be anybody and everybody. We weren't here last night. I was staying up at Kirkfield House.'

'The trouble is, if you didn't see who did it there's not a lot we can do.' Constable Keir was holding his cap in his hands.

'Except if you find an aerosol spray can, with or without fingerprints,' said Jerusha.

'And the chances of that are minimal,' said the Constable. 'The best thing you can do is get the car resprayed and hope that it doesn't happen again. I will report this incident at the station. If you want someone to spray it quickly and expertly, you could do worse than to go to Micky in the village. MacManus Garage. He is your man.'

'Can't you give Lorna some protection?' asked Jerusha.

'Short of posting an officer outside your door, which we can't do, I'm afraid we won't be of much assistance. Now, I must go.' He got into the car and drove off, leaving them vulnerable and nervous.

'What about Hamish's words? Hamish assured us everything would be all right,' said Jerusha.

'Perhaps he meant in the long term?'

'Perhaps we don't know what all right is? It could be that we haven't come to any physical harm. It's just a car and a vicious piece of lettering. Whoever did it could have been angry enough to attack us personally.'

'Attack me, you mean. They're not getting at you, Jerusha. That's just it. I feel that little edge of fear every time I'm alone in this house. Who knows what the villagers are saying about me. They shun me when we pass in the street. Some of them even go so far as to cross the road to avoid me.'

'You're imagining it, Lorna.'

'What's this, if not proof?' She pointed at the car.

'We've got to go to the garage.'

⚬♒♒♒⚬

The car was soon silver again and there were no more incidents for some weeks. Jerusha persuaded Lorna to sleep at the cottage while she prayed to the walls at Kirkfield for Hamish to appear to her and give her some guidance. She wasn't sure what was the right thing to do by Lorna although she never told her that. Part of her wanted Lorna at Kirkfield but she dismissed this as selfish.

Rudy came back from kennels. Jerusha fetched her. She waddled in the door and let herself be petted and stroked by Lorna, whose mood visibly lifted the moment she saw her pet. She didn't notice at the time that the dog only walked, and slowly, whereas before she would have pranced and danced up to her owner. And then she would have jumped up against Lorna's legs in a way Jerusha found particularly annoying to watch. Jerusha noted this and noticed how the dog's back legs were weakened. Yet, there was something about Rudy's presence that brought

Lorna closer to feeling at home. Jerusha left them together and went back to Kirkfield where she sat and wondered whether she should get herself a dog. She missed James and Oswald and the fun they'd had together. She missed Sonia and Callum. And Sheena. And Jean. She even missed Lorna. Being alone did not come easily to Jerusha. An actress needs an audience and she constantly made herself feel better by giving out, or giving something to somebody else. Here she was in a big house with silence numbing her, with no one to talk to. She wondered if she should get herself onto Facebook or something like that. Or, she could turn to television for company. In her present mood, none of this could replace human beings. She could not telephone Sheena. She idly tried to imagine where her friend was. Sheena had kept her hideaway completely secret, even from Jerusha. However, she couldn't be far from Edinburgh because she was visiting Derek in prison. Jerusha contemplated visiting him herself but decided against it as he might want to talk to her about Hamish's involvement in Françoise's death. She didn't want to think about this. She was to deify her late husband. The longer she spent alone, the longer her thoughts dwelt with Hamish and the more wonderful he became in her sight. She longed for another dream where he would appear to her, so intimately, so vividly but her sleep had become dark, deep blanks in the night. Or, he might appear to her, ghostly, as he had to Lorna. But she was slightly afraid of that. In the quiet of Kirkfield, she might fear that she was losing her mind.

Jerusha didn't have long to feel lonely. One evening, after she had eaten and had settled down in front of television, there was a loud banging on the front door. The only people she knew who knocked so forcefully were the police. What crisis was she confronting? She opened the door a chair's length and saw a dog's nose sniffing at the gap.

'It's me,' said Lorna.

Jerusha let them in. Lorna was panting and weeping, her body bent, her wig askew.

'What on earth has happened?' asked Jerusha.

'They are after me again,' wailed Lorna. 'This time it's worse.' She collapsed into a fit of coughing and weeping.

'You poor thing. Come and get a glass of water and you can tell me all about it.' They went through to the kitchen and Jerusha helped Lorna to sit in one of the chairs around the table. 'What has happened to make you so upset?'

'Somebody has thrown a brick through my window. It missed me by inches.'

'But it didn't hurt you?'

'No,' Lorna sobbed. 'But there is glass everywhere and I can't tell you what a fright it gave me. I'm no longer safe, Jerusha.'

Jerusha put an arm around her sister-in-law. 'You can't have a gaping hole in your window. We'll have to get it fixed tonight. Would you like something stronger than water while I organise a repair?'

'Jerusha, Hamish said everything would be all right. That's not so. Everything is not all right. I can't cope any more. At this rate, I'm going to become ill.'

'You must not lose faith in what Hamish said. I think he meant in the end. Everything will be all right in the end.'

'When is the end? It's not just the window and the graffiti. They cut off all the heads of my beautiful roses. They keep ringing my doorbell and running away. Someone shovelled manure through my letter box. When I go into the village they shun me except for that nice Mr Khan. I have to go to Galashiels for just a bag of sugar because they won't serve me in the village shop. This was a mistake, Jerusha, my moving in to Kirkfield Village. I would have been better off in jail.'

'Don't say that. It will pass, Lorna. Give it time. Meanwhile, you and Rudy are moving back here.'

'What if they target Kirkfield House, instead?'

'They won't do that because I have an idea.'

A week went by and no further assault on Lorna took place. She was distracted because Rudy clearly wasn't well. The dog had slowed down even more; her hind legs were weak and she was urinating in the house. Jerusha was very patient but Lorna was anxious and made sure Rudy went outside into the garden every couple of hours. Often Jerusha and Lorna would take Rudy on a short walk through the village, when they would check the cottage for further damage. Whoever it was who was vandalizing it seemed to think that by driving Lorna out they had accomplished what they set out to do for there were no more incidents. However, most of the villagers went to great lengths to avoid and ignore Jerusha and Lorna when they passed them in the street.

❧

That day, in the kitchen, Jerusha unravelled a poster, smoothing and spreading it out on the table. It called for volunteers in the village to help plant bluebell woods in one of the fields at Kirkfield House. Jerusha had ordered the trees and bluebell bulbs and had briefed her newish gardener, Latimer Davis. Latimer was much younger than Luke Junior had been and he had the muscles of a weight-lifter. He was single but quite happy with the house Zilla had vacated to go and live with her sister in Melrose. Latimer was as good a gardener as Luke Junior had been. Jerusha thought him a little fierce and wondered if he would take to the tree planting scheme.

'It's okay by me, as long as there are enough volunteers,' he said.

Jerusha had her doubts about the number of villagers who would be prepared to join in. Trusting that the idea of bluebell woods, instead of new houses, would flush out their friends in the village, she had gone ahead and ordered the trees. Sycamore and beech and a couple of oaks. Volunteers were to sign up at the post office. Jerusha put up posters around the village and they waited. The first day there was one volunteer and that was Tilda. Three more days followed and Jerusha went down to the post office. Lorna was deliberately keeping a low profile.

'Nothing. I'm afraid no more signatures,' said Rashid Khan.

'That can't be. They must be pleased that there aren't going to be any houses in the field,' said Jerusha.

'You must be patient.'

'But I'm not patient. I've a lot riding on this scheme.'

'That's just it. They are suspicious.'

'I'm giving a great deal to the community.'

'They think you are trying to bribe them, after all that has happened at Kirkfield House.'

'In a way I am, but I'm sacrificing a lot as well. It's a peace offering.'

401

'I have two bits of advice, Mrs Burnett. First of all, liven up your posters and, second, get the community councillor, Rory Gibbons, on your side.'

'Oh no. He's the one I was supposed to meet some months ago and I forgot about it.'

'Leave it to me. I will speak to Rory. You attend to your posters.

'Would you?'

'If Rory signs, many signatures will follow. Believe me.'

Jerusha was excited and hopeful after she had spoken to Rashid Khan and she went straight away to take down all the posters. As luck would have it, James was at the house when she got back and he had his paints with him. 'Darling. Please . . .' He painted a quick colour scene of trees with bluebells at their base which they could photocopy. Meanwhile, Jerusha worked on additions to the text: 'Come create this Picnic Idyll for Villagers. Preserve our natural environment. An end to speculation. Work under a professional gardener. Free food while you work.' She got James to write all this out in his beautiful, calligraphic handwriting.

'They are masterpieces,' she said, rolling them up to take them to the village. 'You know what I've just thought, that even if the old posters didn't do the trick, they weren't defaced. The idea has not been chucked out, willy nilly.'

Rudy was peeing on the kitchen floor. Lorna mopped this up and took the dog outside. Jerusha made a mental note to get Lorna to take Rudy to the vet but she, herself, was pre-occupied. She wanted to put the posters up immediately.

The next day Rashid Khan phoned her at home and said he had Rory Gibbon's signature. 'Now, wait and see,' he said.

'You're a fast worker, Mr Khan. Thank you so much.'

'Not at all. By the way, I've signed up myself. So that makes three. My guess is that in three days time we'll have twenty signatures.'

He was right, except there were twenty one, enough to make the plan feasible. James and Oswald promised to come across and do some of what they called 'legitimate digging'. Lorna would be sitting this one out because she did not want to 'affect the atmosphere'. She would help Jerusha with the catering. Jerusha resolved to do all the catering using the village shop—to buy locally.

One of the highlights of these events was that Sheena came out of hiding. She appeared at the back door just as she used to do, wearing a light dress and a cardie and, uncharacteristically, without a basket. It was strange to see her appear empty-handed. The nothingness in her hands made her seem vulnerable. It was the day before the planting would begin. She opened the door without knocking, as she used to do.

'Sheena!' Jerusha pulled herself up from a chair and swamped her friend with a huge bear hug.

'I couldn't stay away. It was my idea, after all.'

'Your idea?'

'The bluebell woods. Remember when you were thinking of selling to Len?'

'It was a great idea. We're all set to start tomorrow. Get the trees growing before winter sets in.'

'And you've still got plenty of daylight to do the planting.'

'Are you moving back in?'

'Yes. Tammy is at home now. I heard that Lorna had trouble with vandals?'

'I'm staying here in the meantime,' said Lorna. 'But there has been no trouble since I moved out and since Jerusha started this natural healing exercise.'

'How is Derek?' asked Jerusha.

'Not good. Talk about a brutalizing experience. Prison is definitely no good for him. He is pinning his hopes on being acquitted at the trial. It's not long now.'

'Don't tell me,' said Lorna.

'I cannot say . . .' Sheena hesitated.

'If you don't want to talk about it that's okay,' said Jerusha.

'I've come to plant trees, to do something positive for the community. I notice those police cordons are still up. You should get them taken down.'

'You read my thoughts. I was on the 'phone to the Super today. He says men will take them down and the grave can be filled in. Latimer is doing it as we speak. And Lorna is paying for the repair of the garage, which will begin next week.'

'It must have been awful for you,' said Sheena. 'I just hope that no one is going to vandalize my property.'

'They've had plenty of chance up until now,' said Jerusha. 'Who knows how vandals' minds work. Anyway, we've now got a plus to rival their minus. Who knows, some of the tree planters could be vandals in disguise? Naughty turned nice.'

'I've always liked your optimism, Jerusha. But, to change the subject, have you taken your dog to a vet, Lorna? She looks ill, to me.'

'We are taking her on Monday,' said Jerusha. 'We've just had so much to do, getting ready for this weekend.'

The weekend sailed on the wings of a breeze to success. The saplings were delivered late on Friday afternoon in protective soil and hessian in case they were left above ground for any length of time. And it became apparent early on that the work was going to take more than two days. That early in September it was getting dark about quarter to eight in the evening so the workers did a twelve hour shift, unflinching, uncomplaining. They turned up in old clothes, in trainers and wellies. They came in different ages; from nine to sixty nine. Some were fit and muscular; some looked as if they had never lifted a spade before. Latimer was always in command. He had risen very early and had positioned the saplings in their planting places. He had staggered the different types of trees and had lain down the oaks at one end of the field.

'What about the bluebells?' asked Sheena.

'They come later. Latimer will see to them,' said Jerusha who had her time cut out feeding the masses. Lorna helped in the kitchen but refused to appear in the fledgling wood saying she was too controversial. In any case, she had to look after Rudy. Sheena took time off planting to help Jerusha.

'This is a dream come true,' she said, buttering some rolls.

'What? Ham and cheese baps?' joked Jerusha.

'No. The birth of a wood. You are so kind and wise to go ahead with this, Jerusha.'

'There might have been a little propaganda on your part.'

'But it captured your imagination and now you're doing it.'

'It's a good atmosphere isn't it? Constructive not destructive. These people have a sense of purpose. There now, two more trays of rolls for the hungry.'

⁊⁊⁊

The sense of purpose was sustained the whole weekend. Some people dropped out because of other commitments and a few found the going too hard. Some of them borrowed Sheena's head torches and carried on after dark. By the Sunday night the work force had made a real dent in the task at hand. Latimer had decided to put the oaks in the middle of the field and he planted those. He was fierce in his concentration, broken only by his need to supervise. He would continue planting the bluebells over the next few weeks. He would plant them at intervals. Some of the volunteers dropped out but some persevered. With or without them, it was Latimer's obsession.

Jerusha and Lorna took Rudy to the vet as planned. This particular Galashiels veterinary surgeon held surgeries in the morning and afternoon. They chose the morning, thinking there would not be such a queue. However they were disappointed in this. Ahead of them were a Labrador puppy, a poodle and a cat in a cage. The surgery was bare with a scrubbed floor and low seating around the walls and a few posters. A receptionist sat behind a glass window, an energetic young woman in a tracksuit, who knew Rudy from past visits and made a fuss of her. Rudy was trembling. After half an hour they were called in from the waiting room and the vet examined the spaniel. She was an efficient woman with a jaunty air and an attitude that said she would get things done. She decided to do some tests on Rudy and see her again in a week's time.

One of the tests required getting a urine sample. The vet suggested they use an old margarine tub. Getting the specimen would have been really amusing, keeping a watch out for the next pee and shoving the plastic tub under Rudy's rear end, if the dog had not been ill. Nine times out of ten they ended up with a dribble of pee and an indignant dog. However, they managed to get something to present to the vet at the next visit.

Lorna was distraught because Rudy was so busy dealing with whatever was wrong with her that she had no time for cuddles. The two of them were still at Kirkfield House, although there had been no recent acts of vandalism. One of the women checked on the cottage every day. However, it was Lorna's presence at Kirkfield House that was keeping Jean and Claude away.

'It doesn't seem quite right,' Jean said to Jerusha on the 'phone, 'with Auntie Lorna's involvement in covering up Mummy's death.'

'You mean, suspected involvement.' Jerusha had begun to juggle the facts of Lorna's confession so that neither her husband nor his sister could be ashamed or guilty. She had blotted out the beach scene with car and clothes and footprints in the sand. She pronounced Hamish and Lorna not guilty and thus, although she didn't say so to Sheena, the whole weight of the guilt fell on Derek's shoulders. 'But let's not talk about that. How are you? How is the love of your life?'

'Still brilliant. Rodger is wonderful. I can't believe I am so lucky.'

'You deserve a little luck.'

'That's what he says.'

Jerusha told her about the tree planting and Jean enthused because she was pleased. 'That will help to heal the wounds at Kirkfield,' she said.

This put Jerusha in a good mood and she went about some sewing. However, an hour later Claude was on the 'phone. He didn't say hello or enquire after her health. He was blunt. 'I hear you're acting as if money grows on trees.' Then, there was a silence.

'Claude, I can't think what you are talking about.'

'You can, Jerusha. You just don't want to.'

'I can only think you are talking about the bluebell wood. It's a great success.'

'Is that the way you should be spending our money? I mean, what income is there from a picnic site?'

'You'll have to come and see it to understand its full potential. In any case, what do you mean by our money? You know very well your father left his money to me.'

'And the residue comes to his children. There's not going to be much residue at this rate.'

'Claude, you've got to think of the planet. Natural beauty and wildlife are to be preserved.'

'You are under the influence of your buddy, Sheena.'

She ignored this remark. 'But, darling, there are the other fields.'

'Times are hard and you are going to make them harder by throwing money around.'

'You must come and see what we've done. You'll be convinced it's a good thing.'

'You know why I won't come up at the moment. We'll see what happens after the trial. I don't expect to be convinced.' He rang off.

Lorna was keeping her niece and nephew away and, even so, she was was hiding in her room, except for meals and to take Rudy out. She sometimes skipped the meals. Thus, she wasn't there when Oswald and Sheena came in one day from working in the field.

'Nearly finished?' asked Jerusha, pouring them mugs of tea.

'No. But it will be if Latimer has got anything to do with it. That man is focussed if not obsessed,' said Oswald.

'I hope he is not neglecting the garden,' said Jerusha.

'The garden will survive a little rest, what with all the work Luke Junior put into it,' said Oswald.

'Ah, dear Luke Junior. Quite different from Latimer. I wonder how Zilla is getting on at her sister's'. But there we are. Time brings change and Latimer's arrival was timely, to say the least,' said Jerusha.

'I haven't seen Lorna. How is she doing? asked Oswald.

'I'm a little worried about her. She closets herself in her room. Often, I'm the one to take Rudy out. And she says strange things like, 'Nature is golden' or 'Trees grow on money'. She inserts bizarre little phrases into ordinary conversation.'

'If she can just hang on. The trial is not far away now. I know Derek wants to get it over and done with. The anticipation is very stressful,' said Sheena.

'I hope Vernon is working on Derek's morale as well as preparing him for what to say in his defence,' said Jerusha.

'Vernon is a godsend,' said Sheena. 'But, you are right, Derek needs help with his morale. Poor darling.'

'He is a darling. And the court ought to see that,' said Jerusha. Yet, she wasn't going to let the conversation go over and over the 'terrible accident' that led to Françoise's death because she was in complete denial about Hamish's part in it. 'Rudy is going to have an operation next week, the day of the trial. Isn't it strange how things happen at once? We got the result of the x-ray yesterday. There is a dark mass on her liver. Her prospects don't appear to be too good.'

'I'm sorry to hear that. So you won't be coming to the trial?'

'No.' Jerusha had wanted an excuse to get out of going to the trial. She did not want to hear Hamish's name used in vain. He couldn't be tried after death but she didn't want to hear him cited as an accessory to crime in the course of the trial. She didn't want to hear challenged her version of the events of that Midsummer Night.

'But I had hoped you would give me support, Jerusha, said Sheena.'Can't you change the operation to another day?'

'I would if I could. Rudy is dying. She is practically starving herself to death. I've tried everything; cooked her pasta, rice, even casseroles. She can't eat and she is very weak. She cannot manage the stairs any more. She barely walks. She has taken to lying in the study on a mattress.

'And you are in loco parentis,' said Sheena, hardly hiding her sorrow. 'That reminds me, I've got to go and see to Tammy. He is still outside. I'm sorry about Rudy. Perhaps she will pull through?'

⌾⟋⟋⟋⟋⟍

The spaniel was desperately ill and Lorna didn't seem to register this. Jerusha did the slow, tortuous walk with her in the smallest patch of the garden; she cuddled her; she prepared the daintiest of dishes; she spoke to the vet who had come to treat her as the owner of the dog. All along, the vet had suspected that something was wrong with Rudy's liver and the x-rays seemed to endorse that. Rudy could have had a scan which entailed travelling some distance, but the vet, Julie, wanted to go ahead with an operation.

The day arrived; the day of the trial, the day of Rudy's op. Oswald and James were to collect Lorna. They were in suits and ties, neat and formal whilst Lorna wore a crumpled green suit and her best, blonde, wig. Jerusha offered to iron Lorna's suit but got a short-tempered response from her. 'It isn't as if I'm the star of the show,' she snapped and then herself crumpled, giving Jerusha a hug.

'You had better give Rudy a hug, too, darling.'

'Oh, Rudy. I'd forgotten about Rudy.' The dog suffered a squeezing and left hairs all over the front of Lorna's jacket.

Oswald and James arrived they didn't want to be late so the three of them left hurriedly. Jerusha went to find Rudy who had gone without food or water from six o'clock the night before, in preparation for her operation. She took her to the vet in Galashiels. There was no waiting to be done. The vet's assistant greeted the dog by name and asked Jerusha into the surgery where the vet was waiting. The vet had explained before that she was going to open up the dog and look at her liver. Now, she said that there was a chance that they would find that things had gone too far and that it would be kinder to let the dog go. Rudy's forehead was rumpled and her face told that she was suffering. Jerusha stroked her gently. To hug her would have been to threaten her balance.

Mercy killing. That's what this was going to be. Kinder. More humane. Jerusha, fleetingly, wondered why human beings could not be treated in the same way. She had no doubt that the dog was suffering. She also had no doubt she would be dead in a couple of hours.

She went home and buried herself in her workroom with the telephone by her side. To be honest, she wasn't really aware of doing this. She went from fabric to fabric, touching, stroking, taking the bolts and absent-mindedly, matching them with one another. She then started to sift through her bought patterns. She sometimes used them and sometimes cut her own patterns. She didn't find anything she wanted to use.

The 'phone rang and she snatched it up.

'Is that Jerusha?'

'Yes.'

'I've got Rudy on the operating table. Perhaps you'd like to sit down. It's not good news, I'm afraid.'

'Tell me.'

'The dark mass is more than likely cancer and the growth has spread from the liver to the gut. There's simply nothing we can do.'

'You want her put down?'

'With your permission, we can increase the doze of anaesthetic and she will just go to sleep.'

'Lorna and I have discussed it. We want her cremated individually.'

'We can get that done. I'd better get back to the operating table. Do you want her put to sleep?'

'Lorna and I want it.'

'I'll speak to you later.' The vet put down the 'phone and went to do her act of mercy.

All alone in the house, Jerusha let her tears run freely. These were partly for the dog, partly through the tension that the trial had created. Over the past few months she had developed an affection for the spaniel which she thought was returned. It was. When she was sitting Rudy would come up to her, put her paws on her legs and climb onto her lap or she would just nuzzle her. Jerusha would stroke and cuddle her and this, as is the way with petting dogs, would relieve any tension she as feeling. Rudy had definitely been one of her darlings.

Jerusha would have gone to the old church but was put off because a furious wind raged through the country. She had opened the garden door and it had snapped back against her nose. She feared for the saplings out in the field but comforted herself that they were encased in plastic shields. She wondered how long the wind would continue; well into the night if the weather forecasts were accurate. Jerusha hated wind. It created turmoil in her whole being. It drove itself into her emotions and left her short-tempered and uneasy. She went from room to room, making sure the windows were shut. Of course, there was the possibility of a power cut. She lined up candles along the dining room table. The windows were rattling as the wind tore its way around the house, around every house, building and barn and it howled through the chimneys. Small wonder Jerusha didn't hear a knock at the front door. She had just time to see Sheena burst in before the lights went out.

'Sheena. Shut the door woman. Just a sec and I'll get some candles. My what a night.' She went through to the dining room and lit two candles in metal holders and took these through, her shadow alongside her. Sheena looked exhausted and her hair, which she had worn up that day, was a mass of grey, frizzy, curls.

'I've been home to see to Tammy but I wanted to talk to you.'

'You must have wanted that an awful lot to come out in this weather. Let me give you something warm to drink. I'll use the gas. You look frozen. Why didn't you use the back door as usual?'

'I didn't want to give you a fright.'

Jerusha just laughed. 'You did give me a fright. I thought I had locked the front door.'

Holding their candles before them they went into the kitchen where Jerusha lit some more candles. 'Looks like we are holding a séance,' she said and busied herself boiling milk for hot chocolate.

'Wonder if my lights are out and how long it is going to go on?'

'You wanted to talk about the trial.'

'It's going on into tomorrow. So far it's a catastrophe. The prosecutor demolished Lorna. In the end she didn't know whether she was here or there, high or low.'

'I think she is going high, anyway. That will really set her off. Who were the others giving evidence?'

'Chris Rutherford. He came through it quite well.'

'Was Ena there?'

'No. Others in the witness box were Miss Ross, Claude and Jean. Jean was in tears most of the time. Didn't know whether to defend her father or her mother. A terrible tug of war. Poor soul.'

'They mentioned Hamish, then?'

'Of course they mentioned Hamish. He was one of the key players in the cover-up.' The usually even-tempered Sheena had had her emotions whipped up by the trial and the wind.

'Nothing has been proved yet,' said Jerusha stubbornly although she was alarmed by her friend's tone.

'You're right.' Sheena's annoyance quickly subsided. 'And Derek has not been questioned yet. He is pinning all his hopes on the jury deciding it was an accident. Because that's what it was, a desperately sad accident.'

'They must see that.'

Sheena pushed one arm across the kitchen table and leaned her head on it. One of the candles flickered and died. Jerusha carried a lit candle through to the dining room and found a replacement. She sat down heavily and she told Sheena about Rudy and how she was not looking forward to giving the news to Lorna.

17

CREATING A PLAN

Having been up with Lorna half the night Jerusha woke with a migraine, which was fortuitous only in that she could use it as an excuse for not going to the second day of the trial. Oswald and James were driving Lorna in again and Jerusha saw them off with concealed impatience. However, when it came to being alone in the house she was very edgy. She genuinely missed Rudy but Lorna's reaction to news of her dog's death was so extreme that Jerusha was battling to get it in proportion, to find a confident and mellow approach to death. Rudy had unleashed the spectre of death, as we all will come to know it. Jerusha liked to think of darling Rudy as having gone to a better place. She acted her way into a pleasant acceptance then found something to divert her attention. The winds may have died down but had they ravaged the saplings in the field? She grabbed her jacket and went outside, the migraine having in part abated. She walked through the garden and over to the field. She wandered down it touching the fragile trunklets of beech and sycamore, birch and oak in sheaths. They were intact. They had escaped the worst thrust of the gales.

She spent the rest of the day baking cakes and scones, for nobody in particular, although someone would eat them because she saw that as the best way of channelling her energy and distracting herself from thoughts of the trial. She was beginning to form another plan in her head, this time about how to redeem Hamish's memory. So far it was powdered yeast in her consciousness. But it started to rise like dough. It couldn't yet be shared with anyone.

When it became dark she took a bath with foaming bath salts then washed and dried her hair. She put on the Chinese tunic, opened a bottle of wine, and ate a meal by candlelight in the dining room; a meal that Hamish would have loved. She had created an atmosphere, a bubble, around her that defied criminal proceeding. She wandered through to the sitting room, ignoring the television. Who knew what would be considered national news? The case had been featured on BBC news before. She picked up a celebrity magazine and flipped through the pages. Having picked up one or two bits of gossip, she let the magazine drop in her lap. For some reason she started to think of Sonia and Callum. Was their's a perfect marriage? Could there be other perfect marriages apart from her's and Hamish's? She knew what an imperfect marriage could be. She'd had two of them. But Sonia and Callum had religion binding them as well as a very obvious love for each other. She had spoken to Sonia on the 'phone only last week. The young woman said they were fine. Instead of Sonia going to university as her father had suggested, Callum was at university studying architecture. Sonia was teaching at a church primary school. Saul had given them the money to put down the deposit on a flat. They were both loving the sunshine.

Jerusha occupied her mind with idle thoughts, to do with anything but the trial. She tuned into Classic FM and drifted on until the little shock of Oswald and James' arrival. They came in without knocking and slumped into armchairs. Jerusha tensed and became alert in anticipation of what they would have to say. 'I gather it went badly,' she said. 'Where is Lorna?'

'They've taken her to a secure mental institution,' said Oswald, as if this were a personal affront.

'She's to be there for two years,' said James. They were both extremely tired.

'The jury acquitted her of the charge of accessory to crime on the grounds of diminished responsibility but they found her guilty of arson. God knows what effect a mental institution will have on her. I've no idea what they do to people in places like that,' said Oswald.

'Can we visit her?' asked Jerusha.

'Don't know. All too new,' answered Oswald.

'And Derek. You'll want to know about Derek,' said James. 'He was given a sentence of seventeen years for second-degree murder. His argument that the whole thing was an accident didn't wash. But the court dropped the charge of breaking and entering because, with the owner's permission, he had a key to the front door. And then, of course, you didn't want to press charges for assault.'

'The defence is already preparing an appeal. We all know that he didn't plan to kill Françoise,' said Oswald.

'Well, he didn't. Sheena must be in the depths,' said Jerusha.

'She said to send her love. She's gone into hiding again. The press was pestering her. She came straight here to pick up Tammy and then she disappeared,' said James.

'Seventeen years is a long time to be in prison. Poor Derek. So there's not much to celebrate tonight.'

No one even suggested a drink.

When they went away she loaded up their arms with scones and cakes in tins.

18

A LOT MORE IS AT STAKE

It was cold under a pale sky. It had snowed the night before, leaving a sprinkling of white on the grass. Jean had organised her mother's funeral virtually single-handed. She had contacted as many people as possible with some connection to Françoise and had urged them to come. She chose to ignore the fact that they were burying bones, the remains of fourteen years of disintegration. She encouraged those who wanted to send flowers and these were heaped around the freshly-dug pit in the graveyard of the Church of Scotland church in the heart of the village. About eighty people were filing into the church building, among them, Jerusha.

'Please, you must come, Jerusha,' Jean had pleaded with her. She had to plead because Jerusha did not want to go. She felt Françoise was too controversial a figure to warrant such a conventional funeral. She felt angry with her for causing Hamish so much pain. How can anyone go to a funeral when they did not like the deceased? However, she must have guessed Jean would persuade her for she had made the black suit. She, like many, was of the opinion that mourners should wear black. She wore a small, pillbox hat with a veil, wide-netted so people could only make out her facial features if they looked hard enough. She wasn't to know that the hat made her look the shape of a stately pyramid. She thought she was looking gracious and respectful, solemn and noble, even sad. She was right. As she scanned the mourners through the black netting she had her act fine-tuned. She was someone who could care enough about the fate of her husband's first wife to attend her funeral, someone with the character to rise above scandal and bad press to take the time to say goodbye to her predecessor. This was, after all, the end of a sad tale; they were putting to rest a tragic moment in the village's history, in the family history. It was, in fact, going to be more difficult than it seemed on the day of Françoise's funeral.

It was Jean who, consulting Jerusha, decided that her mother would be buried in the village graveyard. Sir Ewan made a half-hearted attempt to have Françoise buried in the family graveyard, at a short distance from Hamish's headstone, but when Jean objected on the grounds of her parents' story, he backed down. So much so, that he was noticeably absent from the funeral.

Jerusha sat down carefully next to Jean and Claude at the front of the church but her act was threatened when she felt a sharp prick in her thigh. She stiffened and kept her composure. She had left a pin in the hem of her skirt. She felt around discreetly, if that were possible, until she found the stray pin but, in doing so, she missed the beginning of the service. When she could concentrate again. She began to listen to the minister, the same person who had married her and Hamish, who seemed to be talking a lot about sin and forgiveness, that Jesus Christ died for our sins so that we might be forgiven and have everlasting life. He was aware of the family's sins but in no way sought to outline them. He never strayed very far from the Bible.

It was Jean who was to shine throughout that mournful service. Soft-voiced, she gave a trembling address in praise of her mother:

'My mother lived life to the full. Before her tragic death she was one of the most lively, dynamic people anyone could hope to meet.'

Jean faltered here, trying to ward off tears. 'She gave Claude and me hugs and kisses and, what is more important, she gave us a role-model. If I know how to have fun it is because Françoise Burnett showed me the way. She showed me how to reach out to people and cajole them into seeing the funny side of life. Unfortunately, this afternoon is an exception. Her death and its consequences has been so sad, so unnecessary and so shrouded in mystery. I can't tell you the pain of not knowing where she was for fourteen years. Dead or alive? This afternoon may be sombre but it is also charmed because we can lay her to rest with the respect and friendship she deserved. And we can also remember things.'

'I remember how she used to read us children's stories with a sparkle and animation that was hers alone. Her Pooh Bear was unique. I still read Winnie the Pooh and feel close to her. I wasn't very old when she disappeared. I was nine. But I remember those early years and how vivacious she was. She was *not* always there for me as she was an outgoing person but, when she was there, she was with us one hundred percent.'

'And I recall the times when the four of us were together as a family. Mummy, Daddy, Claude and me. These memories are very precious to me.'

Jean started to cry but, after a lot of nose-blowing was able to continue. 'There are just two more things I want to say. First of all, don't believe everything you read in the newspapers. Life is more complex than a news story. The second thing is that we felt it inappropriate to have a wake after the burial. However, the publican at the Sheep and Goats assures me that all of you will be very welcome at his pub, with one free round per group.'

'Finally, please feel free to donate to research into cancer, the illness that killed my father. Collection plates are at the back of the church.'

Jean came back to sit between Jerusha and Claude, dry-eyed now and determined to go through with the rest of the service.

'Well done. You are very brave,' whispered Jerusha giving Jean's arm a squeeze.

The church was heated and moderately warm but outside the cold was bitter. It was almost too cold for snow. Not all the congregation went to the graveside but nonetheless there were a fair number of people solemnly standing around the grave decked in coats, scarves and gloves with bouquets of flowers scattered at their feet. They watched the coffin sink into the ground; hence Françoise's remains passed from grave to grave. Dust to dust. Ashes to ashes. The minister, in his pristine vestments, was blue with cold, his nose a puce, frozen thing.

Now the children had closure. They saw their mother, solemnly and gracefully, settled in the ground. Claude was stony-faced but Jean's tears it seemed would never stop. When Claude threw the first clod Jerusha felt a shudder pass through her whole body. It was as if all the tensions of the discovery of the remains, the confession, the trial had all come to a climax with one simple symbolic goodbye. For Jerusha, this was to prove just a fleeting feeling of release for, at the end of the service as she turned to leave the graveside, one arm around Jean's shoulders, she was confronted by a man and a woman in black coats.

'You've got a nerve coming here today,' said the man, stepping close up to confront Jerusha.

Jerusha pulled herself up to her full size and pierced him with her eyes through the veil. 'And who, might I ask, are you?'

'Your husband was an accessory to the murder of the woman we have just seen buried and you have come to the funeral.' He was short, stocky and bearded. His knuckles were white as he clenched his fists. His breath was hot in her face.

'If you'd like to tell me your name we might have this conversation on a more suitable occasion.'

'Barry Gilmore and this is Tina. Tiny Tina, we call her.' He patted the woman's arm. Jerusha looked at the fragile, petite female beside him. The woman smiled lavishly, as if she were used to being petted. Barry held out a business card and Jerusha took it. 'Pity he didn't live to stand trial. Guilty as sin, I say.'

'Mr Gilmore, this here is Jean Burnett. You perhaps didn't recognize her or you wouldn't speak this way. You're talking about her father, not to mention my husband. Could you please step back. We'll discuss this another day.'

'I will hold you to that.' Barry Gilmore moved back, slung an arm through Tina's and the couple walked away over the white-coated grass.

Jerusha shuddered. 'People like that make my blood boil.'

'Then why are you going to contact him, Jerusha?'

'Because I have a plan. I want to wipe clean his argument.' Over and over, she repeated Hamish's name.

'I don't know why you don't just leave things to fade in people's memories. I don't believe anything nasty I read about Daddy in the press, or anything I heard at the trial.

And, as for gossip . . . I have forgotten anything but good said about my father.'

'You are a dear.' Jerusha squeezed Jean's arm. 'I'm sorry to say, I tried that way of complete denial but now I can't ignore the words of recrimination that are flying around in my head. I have to try another way to clear Hamish's name.'

'Just don't get hurt by whatever it is you are going to do. Oh, look, here is Miss Ross. How nice of her to come.'

'I'm very sorry about your loss, Miss Jean.' Miss Ross came up shyly, wringing a handkerchief in her hands.

'Yes, it's incredible but I'm very glad she has been buried in the right way at last.'

'Well, I just wanted to pay my respects. You'll be glad the trial is over.'

'You are too right. Have you got a lift home?'

'Françoise's aunt brought me. She is still driving and she's over eighty. Here she is now.'

An elderly woman approached the threesome, using a stick to walk. Her voice was frail and her back bent. 'Jean dear.' She kissed Jean on both cheeks.

'Aunt Charlotte.'

'I must say, your eulogy was marvellous. Must have been very difficult not to succumb utterly to tears. It's so nice that this tragic saga has finally been laid to rest.'

'That's just what I was saying,' said Jean.

'Just shows you never know what goes on behind closed doors. Your father must have been tormented, all those years.'

'Daddy must have had his reasons.'

'You must be torn between the two.' Aunt Charlotte had a shrewd look in her eyes.

'Not really. I love them both and they loved each other.'

'If you say so. Come, Miss Ross, I think we should be getting along. So sorry, Jean.'

They walked back to Aunt Charlotte's ancient car and Jerusha and Jean made their way up to the house. Neither of them wanted the sociability of the pub. When they were nearly at the house they heard someone panting up behind. Vernon appeared alongside them. 'Hello, Jean. Sorry about this tragedy. Jerusha, can I have a word in private?'

Jean was silent. She was in a world of her own but she came out of it enough to register Vernon' request. She walked into the driveway, up the steps and through the front door as though it were only habit that told her what to do.

Vernon drew Jerusha towards him with a conspiratorial air. 'You've got problems with Claude,' he said.

'I always have problems with Claude. What has he done now?'

'He came to me with a request,' said Vernon.

'In your professional capacity?'

'Yes. He wants to prove that Hamish was of unsound mind when he buried his wife.'

'That is totally untrue. Hamish was always well-balanced. He did what he did out of a sense of duty to a friend. Mental illness might be in the family but he didn't inherit it.'

'There's more.'

'I tell you who is unbalanced. It's Claude. He has a warped mind.' She hesitated. 'What else?'

'He wants to prove that Hamish was of unsound mind when he wrote his will, leaving this property to you.'

'I might have thought there would be money behind this.'

'He wanted me to instigate proceedings.'

431

'And you refused, otherwise you would not be telling me now.'

'Precisely. But what I've said to you must remain completely confidential. I needed to warn you.'

'He has gone to another lawyer?'

'Nigel Stevenson. A lawyer with quite a reputation.'

'I've heard of him. I think I've even met him. Claude can't possibly have a case. It is five years since I inherited the bulk of the estate. I cannot give up Kirkfield now.' She was angry and on the verge of tears.

'Hold on a minute, Jerusha. I don't think he has a hope of pulling this one off. To begin with, as you've pointed out, it was a long time ago . . .'

'How could Claude denigrate his own father? He has always been self-seeking.'

'As I say, he has little chance, even if Nigel takes him on.'

'This Nigel Stevenson.' Jerusha was pulling herself together. 'This lawyer, have you got his contact details for me?'

'Not here, but I can email them to you. I have to go now but I'll keep in touch. Get in touch if there is anything I can do.' He walked off from where they had been standing by the gateless gate.

As Jerusha walked into the house she was feeling a mixture of emotions, the uppermost being indignation. 'Where is Claude?' she asked of Jean who was in the kitchen.

'Gone back to London.'

'What about you? I thought he was to give you a lift.'

'Rodger is coming for me. We're going up to see Ewan.'

'That's good.'

'Not if you believe the weather forecast. Apparently, we're in for a hard winter.'

'Did Claude say anything to you?' asked Jerusha.

'About what?'

'Anything legal?'

'He hardly said anything. He seemed in a great hurry. Said he was annoyed with the press there this afternoon. He kept out of the way of cameras. That might explain why he hung back?'

'Perhaps?'

'Jerusha, do you know something I don't know?'

'Maybe. I can't tell you.'

'All right, then. I won't pry. Tell me when you're ready. I do hope it's not any more scandal. That would give the newspapers something else to shout about. And I don't think I could take any more revelations.'

'It's nothing, darling. Don't worry.'

'I'm glad we've given mother a decent burial.'

Jerusha did not know what to say. Should she say that the funeral had been a success? Are funerals ever successful, as if the deceased were some kind of performer? Jerusha could have said she was glad along with Jean, but somehow the girl seemed to have ownership of feeling glad just because it was her mother she was talking about. Then Jerusha thought, funerals are a celebration. They celebrate the stark fact that those mourned have crossed to the other side—painful, like the process of being born. So, she didn't say anything. Instead, she gave Jean a big hug.

⟋ᴍᴍᴍ⟍

A week later, Jerusha was in the village post office buying a stamp for a letter to Sonia when a newspaper caught her eye. The local weekly had come up with week-old news. Despite her stone-walling of the media, this edition grabbed her attention. On the front page was a picture of herself and a tearful Jean at the funeral. She picked it up and followed its instructions to see the centre-page spread. There were more pictures and the text read: "The scandal that has rocked the village of Kirkfield was laid to rest with the funeral of Françoise Burnett in a local church last week.

Villagers have been thrown into turmoil ever since the remains of Françoise were found in a makeshift grave at Kirkfield House, ending a fourteen-year-old belief that she had simply disappeared.

'For all that time, her husband, Hamish Burnett, and his sister, Lorna, kept the secret of her death, protecting Derek McPherson, a well-known village resident.

Recently Derek was found guilty of second-degree murder and sentenced to seventeen years in prison. The court found that he caused Françoise to fall backwards down the long flight of stairs in Kirkfield House by attacking her with a ceremonial dagger. In the fall, she broke her neck, lying dead at the bottom of the stairs.'

'Hamish Burnett's culpability remains a mystery as he died of cancer five years ago, leaving his estate to his second wife, Jerusha. The second Mrs Burnett has a habit of avoiding the press but she has been heard to deny any knowledge of the cover-up by Hamish, Lorna and Derek that fateful night because she hardly knew her husband at the time of Midsummer's Night 1996.'

'The cover-up was an elaborate ruse that led sleuths to believe Françoise had walked into the sea never to return. Meanwhile . . .'

Jerusha, standing in the post office with the paper before her on its shelf, had read enough. She felt exposed and annoyed that the newspapers would never let Hamish rest in peace. She felt not just annoyance, but anguish. If people didn't think ill of Hamish already, they would after reading that. The problem was that there had been no trial of Hamish, no chance to prove his innocence. She was determined to do that for him.

She walked out of the post office, refusing to buy the newspaper. When she got home, James and Oswald were there. They still had a key and were sitting in the kitchen over cups of tea when she got in.

'You look browned-off,' said James as soon as she appeared in the doorway.

'I am.' She hardly noticed the fact that the two men were in suits and ties, with carnations in their buttonholes. She did not take in the jubilant expression on Oswald's face. Nor did she see the basket of fruit, the champagne and the chocolates on the table. All she could make out was an image of herself, with an arm around Jean, published for all to see. And the words of the article leapt out with their damning indictment of Hamish.

'Tell us, Jerusha. We can help,' said James.

'You can't help. The damage has been done.'

'It's the newspaper article, isn't it?' asked Oswald.

'Yes,' she said flatly.

'Newspapers are ephemeral,' said James. 'Today's news is gone tomorrow.'

'I thought you looked rather nice, in the picture,' said Oswald, wanting her to forget the newspaper and join in their celebrations.

'Humph,' said Jerusha. 'Anyway, what's with the suits and ties and all these goodies on the table?' She stood, still in the doorway, looking expectant. Perhaps there was some good news?

'We've become civil partners.'

'Speak up. I didn't hear you.'

They repeated the words in unison. 'We've become civil partners.'

'Good grief. Why didn't you tell me? I could have been there . . .'

'We wanted a very private ceremony,' said Oswald. 'But you are the first one we've told and we've come straight here to celebrate.'

'You sly devils. Congratulations!' She ran over and hugged and kissed them both on the cheeks. 'Open the champagne. We're not going to let anything spoil this celebration.' She was pink with pleasure.

They tucked into the champers and toasted each other many times. It was almost like the old days when James and Oswald were living at Kirkfield. In fact, they were planning a temporary comeback. 'Very severe weather is forecast,' said James, 'and we don't want to get snowed in. Could you put us up for a few days, or weeks. I don't mean right now. As soon as the snow starts falling.'

'What a great idea. I don't want to get snowed in all on my own. Your bed is made up. You won't want to drive after you have been drinking. Stay tonight. Good. That's settled. I'm now going to match your champagne with a bottle of my own. You need some spoiling now that you've tied the knot.'

'I'm not saying no to more champagne but the civil partnership does not make any difference to how we feel about each other. You must not treat us as if we're changed all of a sudden. Legally, we're on a different footing but, otherwise, I'm just your James. Oswald is just your Oswald.'

'That's okay,' said Jerusha, not really understanding. 'Who needs an excuse for a party, anyway?' She popped the cork and filled up their glasses. 'Darlings. At least take off those ties and we can get down to some fun and games.'

'Before that,' said James, 'I want to drink a toast to my sister. May she regain her health and get out of that ghastly place.'

James and Oswald had been to visit Lorna in the Secure Mental Institution in Edinburgh. What struck them was how dark and spare it was, not an environment conducive to mental well-being. The walls were green and grey in broad bands of paint, the curtains patterned in green and black, someone's bleak idea of colour coordination. They had to go through several locked doors to where Lorna was sitting in a hard chair pointed towards a blaring television.

'She wasn't watching the television. She was crying. She hardly recognised us,' said James.

'The main thing making her unhappy was that the staff would not let her wear her wig and they would not let her have any scissors to cut her hair. She said she felt naked and lost,' said Oswald. 'We had a word with the nurses on duty and they said that wearing the wig would not help Lorna face up to her true self, that it was a crutch, a disguise she had to learn to do without.'

'Who were we to argue?' asked James. 'I must say that most of the other patients seemed heavily drugged. To straight-jacket them with medication couldn't be the best way of helping them to find themselves.'

Jerusha gulped. She could not bear the thought of Lorna in an institution. As yet, she couldn't contemplate visiting her in that place. She raised her glass. 'To Lorna.' She now drank to escape this vision of her sister-in-law and of the ghastly newspaper article. This sadness aired, they all returned to the celebration of the day. James and Oswald loosened their ties and they began to play the game that Claude thought was the most boring of country entertainments—charades. They laughed hysterically at each others' efforts at mime. One turn had Jerusha on all fours pretending to be a tiger. There was a sense of carelessness in the way she played the game. They all dived into the present, unafraid of making idiots of themselves. They trusted each other to forget when it came to the morning after.

The following morning came with headaches all round. So too, came the first fall of snow that was set to last until Christmas. Oswald and James moved back into Kirkfield House. When they had gathered around a fire in the sitting room Jerusha confided in them that while they had been away she'd been so alone that she had taken to seeing visions of Françoise. The dead woman was not exactly a ghost but an imaginary person who screamed as she fell backwards down the stairs. Then she lay dead at the bottom. Jerusha said she could smell blood. 'That won't happen while you're here,' she said.

'We won't be here forever,' said Oswald.

As it turned out, they were there a lot longer than expected. The Borders, along with the rest of the country, was in for a Siberian winter with snowfalls of up to ten inches at Kirkfield.

It was an interlude, all silent snow, white skies, little sunshine, and inside the house it felt to Jerusha as if they were high on central heating and stillness, only broken when they spoke or played the fool. And they did the latter all the time, each gale of laughter going some way towards dismantling the snow trap. At least they had electricity and could see to prance, dance or fall about. They had a meeting each late morning to decide what they were to do that day. It would go like this—snow fight, sledging, baking cakes, Scrabble, Rumikub. Jerusha refused to go tobogganing with the men because it reminded her too much of Hamish and their first kiss, but James and Oswald went and came back exhilarated. Part of the day's programme was a trip to the village shop through thick snow and slushy tyre marks. A few people were getting out in their cars. For the most part cars had been parked in the same place for days, their roofs under a thick blanket of snow, their wheels buried in mounds of the white stuff. After a week of home entertainment the three were getting bored and frustrated, even although their lifestyle had only changed marginally. They disliked not being able to use their cars and James was missing his new house. Meanwhile, airports had been shut, cars overturned on icy roads, people struggled in to work, the elderly balked at the cost of heating, farmers struggled to feed livestock, food lorries had difficulty getting through to the shops. The village shop did a manful job because the whole village, instead of driving to a supermarket, was relying on it for basic supplies.

By the eighth day of the Big Freeze, as the media called it, desperate measures were called for. They had a meeting earlier than usual and unanimously decided they had to burst out of there. Fed up with the claustrophobia of feeling snowed in, they decided to lay their hands on some of the spades that had been used for the tree planting and clear the drive. Latimer helped and Jerusha did her bit although her shovelling was more act than effort. By midday they had cleared a path from under the wheels of the four-wheel drive to the gateway and then on to the road. The road had been used and the tracks were not yet icy. They wore wellies, scarves and hats and, most important, waterproof gloves to keep their hands from freezing. James and Oswald were quite solemn in their work, unlike when they dug the grave for the unknown dummy. It was back-breaking but they all wanted to get out. Anywhere. Just out. They were shattered by the effort of clearing a foot of snow from an expansive area; all except Latimer who had stripped down to his T-shirt, muscles rippling. When they had finished, he slipped away to his cottage and the three stamped on the newly-cleared steps to rid themselves of blobs of icy white. It had started snowing again. They were very tempted to reward themselves with a tot of brandy but none of them was prepared to get into a car in these treacherous conditions with even a sip of alcohol inside them.

They changed into warm, dry clothing and clambered into the car, Oswald driving. They were off to find a cash machine and after that to do a café crawl in Galashiels. The roads were slippery but passable, and they found a parking place in the centre of town that was designated for a maximum two-hour stay. One didn't pay much attention to such details in this weather. The pavements were slushy with brown downtrodden snow but the lights of the shops were bright and hopeful. Jerusha was very glad of her boots that she had bought in town at a shop they passed on their way to a new café-cum-restaurant called Popinjay where they would start the crawl. Oswald skidded along the dodgy pavement well ahead of them.

'When is he going to grow up?' asked Jerusha, skidding along herself.

'I like him the way he is,' said James, taking timid steps behind her. Then, even although he was being so careful, his front foot went for a slide and he was down on his back in the slush made by multiple footsteps, and onto the hard pavement beneath.

Jerusha shouted at Oswald to come back and she rushed over to where James was lying like a beetle on its back, in a temporary state of shock. She and Oswald felt around the beleaguered James to see whether he had broken any arms or legs. Jerusha concentrated on his wrists. 'Can you move this?' she asked.

'Yes. Yes. I'm all right.I just feel a fool.' James pushed her away and got up, unravelling, from the bent posture of an old man to the straightened back of a middle-aged man. It appeared that he was all right, as he had said.

They walked into Popinjay, James wet from his fall, looking forward to hot chocolate and a good meal. The morning's work had created a healthy appetite. They swung open the glass door, Jerusha going first, oozing the impression that she had *arrived*. The restaurant offered straight-backed chairs and some more comfortable, lower lounging chairs. There were several people, mainly women, ranged around the room. Jerusha claimed a chair and stood behind it. As she was about to sit down she realized there was a complete silence in the restaurant. The room was silent as the new-driven snow, so silent that a whisper could be heard across the room. 'It's that woman in the paper,' a woman nudged her neighbour.

Jerusha's reaction was swift and spontaneous. 'It is I,' she said and opened her jacket to reveal her buxom chest ensconced in an orange sweater. She wiggled her frontage, took off her jacket and sat down. Oswald and James followed suit. They were sitting in the middle of the room.

'I didn't mean . . .' the woman was embarrassed.

'I think we should leave Mrs Burnett to her meal. It's a free country,' said a voice, strident and high. Jerusha realized she knew that voice and looked over to where it had come from. Tilda was sitting in one corner with a friend. The newly-converted Tilda, changed by the tree planting. She smiled and waved and Tilda lifted one hand ever so slightly from the table. Conversation among the customers resumed and the tactless whisperer left with her friend. Jerusha, James and Oswald were free to scour the menu.

A waitress appeared from the back. 'Can I take your order?' She showed no signs of recognizing Jerusha's notoriety and they were free to order baked potatoes and coronation chicken, lasagne, roast beef and mustard paninis, hot chocolate with whipped cream, coffee. It was the feast they had been looking for. They would have the dessert at the next café.

Moondogs, a café dedicated to art and eating, was just around the corner. Oswald and James made their way there at a leisurely pace while Jerusha crossed the road to a cash machine. She preferred to pay cash, although the café took plastic cards. They had cleaned poor old Oswald out when he paid for the first round. Moondogs was lively, strewn with leather bean bags as well as upright chairs, decorated with antiques and lined with glass cases containing artwork in felt and beading. James favoured the bean bags but Oswald bluntly said, in her absence, that Jerusha would never get out of one if she sat down on it. So the slatted chairs it was and Jerusha soon joined them. This time there was no controversy resulting from her arrival and the staff gave them a warm welcome. However, Jerusha was distraught. Coming back from the hole in the wall she had been approached by a middle-aged woman who spat in her face as she said, 'I think it is despicable what your husband did' and then walked on before Jerusha could reply.

Jerusha longed to have Hamish by her side to comfort her. Oswald and James consoled her and the cakes were comforting but it just wasn't the same. They left the café before it got dark and slid their way home. At that point it was getting dark at about four in the afternoon. They were so deep in winter that Jerusha hadn't been able to get her plan going.

The incidents in Galashiels spurred her on to make renewed attempts to contact Claude, who had not been answering his 'phone since the funeral. She tried again that night but got no reply, not even an answer phone. She had psyched herself up for the call, remembering she wasn't supposed to know about his plot. She was relaxed but suspicious when he 'phoned her that weekend.

'Claude here. I'm sure you have been trying to 'phone me, Jerusha. I've been very busy.'

'Busy doing what?'

'Didn't I tell you, I'm planning to set up my own IT company. All being well, provided no one gets in the way, we'll have lift-off in the spring.'

'When you say we, who do you mean?'

'The royal we at present, depending on funding.'

'And where are you going to get your funding?'

'Och. That would be telling. But I can hear you're not particularly interested. Information technology is not your forté, is it, Jerusha? You prefer magic and tricks. Anyway, the point is, the reason I 'phoned is to warn you that you'll be hearing from my solicitor shortly, Nigel Stevenson.'

Jerusha decided to play the daft lassie. 'I thought Vernon Brown was your solicitor.'

'We had a falling out. No. Don't get me wrong. Vernon simply couldn't see my side of the story.'

'What story?' She tried to lead him on.

'Events. Now, I really must be going. I've got a million and one things to do.' He put down the 'phone.

It was still cold but not snowing, although there were snow clouds in the sky. Jerusha, Oswald and James were again thrown together in retreat from the winter weather. As their supply of booze was running low, Oswald set off in the four-wheel drive to stock up on whisky, wine, and champagne. James and Jerusha made a fire and huddled over it with blankets on their knees. The central heating was working but they had it down low. It was a large house to heat. The fire warmed James' spirits but Jerusha was worried. If Claude had his way, she might have to leave all this. Kirkfield estate had become a part of her heart. She had done so much living here, so much cooking, so much cleaning, with Hamish and without Hamish. She loved the very walls of Kirkfield House. Even the lethal stairs could not change that.

'I love this place,' she blurted out.

'You are not the only one,' said James.

'I would hate to lose it.'

'What are you worrying about? You're not going to lose it.'

'I could, if Claude has his way.'

'What do you mean?'

Jerusha had waded in so deep now that she had to tell him.

After she had told him what Vernon had said, he paused and said, 'Remember I was an executor of Hamish's will. Everything appeared to be in order. Hamish was physically ill but he was mentally alert.'

'He always was, even when he covered up Françoise's death.' There, she had said it. She had acknowledged that Hamish had had a part in burying his first wife. She had admitted Hamish's guilt because she couldn't bear him to be thought of as insane. And, if he were guilty, others were more so. What she intended to do, her plan, was to make certain people show their cards. When she had her way in this, Hamish would be shown in a good light. In the first instance, she had to prove Claude wrong and destroy his claim on her property, her stocks and shares and her capital.

'Claude has always been a negative influence on the family,' she said.

'Just so,' said James, staring into the fire. 'As a child he was always sulky and insensitive.'

'I suppose he has had to come to terms with the whole tragedy.'

'Doesn't mean he has to take it out on other people.'

'He has to try and sympathise with both his father and his mother.'

'Jerusha, do you realize the enormity of what he is attempting to do? You would lose this property and your income if he wins. There was an earlier will which, I believe, left everything to the children. Hamish showed it to me, at some point, long ago.'

I couldn't bear it, James. I gave up my job to be with Hamish. It was an act of faith, of trust. I would have done anything for him. For him, and not for his money.'

'Did Hamish ever have counselling?'

'No. Never a day's mental ill health.'

'Claude is going to have a tough time proving his theory. I think the whole thing is a scam to get you to cough up money to finance his new business. I think you should just go along with his game. You're a winner, Jerusha.'

'I am. I just don't like being at odds with Hamish's flesh and blood.'

'Whose flesh and blood?' Oswald had come into the room, holding a bottle of whisky, and had heard the tail end of the conversation.

'Never mind,' said James. 'I'll tell you in good time.'

Oswald poured generous helpings of whisky into their glasses and made a place for himself by the fire. 'Some of the shelves in the supermarket are empty but there was still plenty of alcohol. I propose a toast to the long-distance lorry drivers. And, we'd better do a food shop tomorrow before the place is cleaned out.'

❧

The snow was receding but very slowly and the roads and pavements were very icy. Jerusha and James had become used to being confined indoors, but with Oswald it was a different story. Without jogging and cycling he was a deprived person. He was restless and frustrated. It did not help that James had persuaded him to sit for a full-length painting. James didn't normally paint people. He wanted to experiment with his partner. The walls of the new home were beginning to fill up with paintings by James, mainly landscapes, and he thought a picture of Oswald would do well in the dining room. So the sitter sat, grumbling and fidgeting. James had tried to insist he wear a suit, never mind the tie, but had to compromise by letting him wear his jogging tracksuit. He had arranged Oswald in an armchair with legs crossed, hands resting loosely on the arms of the chair, looking like a dressed-down lord of the manor. James carefully combed his balding hair. The trouble was that Oswald kept getting up and pacing, then sitting down again; he would forget which leg to cross over. And then there was Jerusha's contribution. To make him smile, she pulled a face at him from behind James' back. This had the opposite effect from the one she intended. He scowled.

'Jerusha, you are not helping,' said James. 'What we want is a serene expression of Oswald at peace with the world. He needn't smile.'

'But you don't want him scowling,' she replied.

'Well, then don't distract him.'

'Excuse me. I'm here. You don't need to discuss me as though I'm some sort of dummy. This whole idea is silly, anyway,' said Oswald.

'Silly. My painting is not silly.' James had assumed an artistic temperament. 'Could I not have a little cooperation, Oswald. Think peaceful thoughts. Jerusha, go and do whatever it is that you do.'

'I'm culling my filing cabinet. I just came through for a break. But, if you are going to be like that, I'll go and get on with it. She walked off leaving James and Oswald stifling their laughter.

⚬⚭⚬

Jerusha was sorting through her filing cabinet but there was one letter, lying separately on the desk, that she kept going back to. It was from Nigel Stevenson WS and it called for a joint consultation regarding the validity of Hamish Burnett's will, scheduled for the week before Christmas. Although she had known it was coming, when she first read it a thrill of fear went through her. Would she be disinherited by Christmas, thrown out, alone in the snow? Anger with Claude followed. He was an unkind, money-grubbing, little jerk who would attack his father's character to get what he wanted. However, after all, look what his mother was like. This was the worst thing she could think about Claude. He was Françoise's son. That said it all.

◯◯◯

It turned out that James had also been summoned to the consultation, as the only living available executor of the deathbed will. Derek had also been an executor and, as they all knew, he was otherwise occupied. The letter to James did not reach him because no post was getting through to his snow-bound road and, obviously, he was not there to collect any post. It was only through a 'phone call from Vernon, who was to preside with Nigel, that James heard of his involvement. He was not pleased, calling the whole thing a cheap trick. However, he agreed to attend.

The consultation was being held in Nigel's practice in the High Street in Galashiels. Jerusha, James and Vernon met at Kirkfield and travelled in one car and entered the door of Stevenson and Clark WS, to be greeted by a receptionist. It was a recently-refurbished set of offices on the ground floor with blinds shielding long windows. Jerusha took a peek into Nigel's office as he was coming out of it. The walls were covered with shelves supporting books and documents.

'That's all right, Miss Dawson. I'll see them into the meeting room. This way please.'

They followed him into a bland room, clearly designed for concentration and focus on the issue at hand. It was centrally heated and warm. Miss Dawson had taken their coats. Nigel enquired after their health, obviously making every effort to allow them to feel comfortable. He was a rosy-faced gentleman, probably public school educated, well-spoken, cosy, a bit like Hamish, if ever anyone could be like Hamish, but younger. Today he wore a tartan waistcoat He was confident, polite and seemed very at ease. He was going to keep control of this meeting. Having enquired after the health of each one of them he offered them tea or coffee, then got Miss Dawson to organise the drinks.

'I must, first of all, explain to you that Mr Claude Burnett has been delayed. You might be aware that he is flying from London to Edinburgh and getting a bus to be here. Of course, the Borders still hasn't a railway network. As it is, he 'phoned from the bus station in Edinburgh to say he had missed his bus and would catch the next one.

'Will he be flying back tonight?' asked Jerusha. Claude as an opponent wasn't going to use Kirkfield for an overnight stay.

'I believe so,' said Nigel.

Vernon, who had been quiet up until now, spoke up. 'You might have warned us, Nigel. We could have come later,'

'He only let us know in the last half an hour. You would have been on your way when I 'phoned. Claude does have the furthest to come.'

'Let us at least start proceedings,' answered Vernon.

'No. My client must be present at all proceedings.'

Claude kept them waiting another hour during which Nigel organised some food for them. 'Lunch is on me,' he said. It was the dependable Miss Dawson who actually went to fetch the baguettes and paninis, forgetting in her fervour to get anything for herself. Vernon spent most of the time on the 'phone to his secretary. Fortunately, a client had cancelled her early afternoon appointment so he had some leeway. Nigel ate lunch with them but then got caught up with 'phone calls in his office.

'You don't suspect Claude is doing this deliberately?' Jerusha asked James.

'I wouldn't put it past him. Keeping people waiting means power,' said James.

When Claude did arrive, he looked immaculate and in control. He accepted a cup of tea from Miss Dawson as if there were no hurry. He did not apologise for being late or try to explain it away. He simply did not mention it. He sat down at the opposite side of the room from Jerusha, James and Vernon, a large expanse of table between them. Nigel, who had been sitting at the head of the table cosying up to them, now took a seat beside his client. The tone of the meeting became one of assertion and aggression. Nigel, being on home territory, was setting out to dominate. He started by explaining: 'For a joint consultation we usually meet in the law courts. Each party is in a separate room and the lawyers liaise. As you realize, in this case we have decided, partly because of adverse weather conditions, to make this a more informal meeting, hopefully a friendlier one. My client's case, which I put before you, concerns Hamish Burnett's deathbed will in which he left his assets and capital to his second wife, Jerusha Burnett, née . . .'

'Forget the née,' said Jerusha abruptly.

'The estate of Hamish Burnett was left to Jerusha Burnett and thereafter to Claude and Jean Burnett. However, there was an earlier will that left everything to the deceased's children. This is important and I have a copy. It was dated . . . now let me see.' He looked down at his papers. 'Aah yes, the eighteenth of March, nineteen ninety four.'

'You haven't explained the importance of an out-of-date will,' Vernon interrupted.

Jerusha looked around the room at each person and all had their arms crossed, except for Nigel who was shuffling papers.

'That brings me to the thrust of my client's argument. Can we be sure that my client's father was of sound mind when he made the will leaving everything to Mrs Burnett in 2005?'

'He dictated that will to me and I was perfectly satisfied that his mind was alert. His body was frail but there was nothing wrong with his mind,' said Vernon.

Nigel ignored this. He was clearly more interested in Claude's argument. 'Some facts emerged in the recent court case which have led my client to suspect that his father was not always altogether stable. That is, his father covered up his first wife's death in a bizarre way.'

'There was nothing bizarre about it. He did it for a friend.' Jerusha was angry. James put a hand on her arm.

'A dubious way then,' Nigel corrected himself.

Could Claude have been smiling slightly out of embarrassment?

Nigel continued. 'Hamish's sister suffers from bipolar disorder, which is commonly thought to be genetic.'

'No. No. Brother and sister were different.' Jerusha banged a fist on the table.

Vernon intervened, seeing that Jerusha was becoming overwhelmed. 'Let's get back to the point. If, as you are suggesting, and I doubt this, if Hamish was mentally unstable when he wrote the legitimate will, could he not have been unfit to write the 1994 will leaving everything to his children?'

'We are suggesting that it was Françoise Burnette's death that caused his instability.'

'And how are you going to prove that? You simply haven't got a case. I would have thought Jerusha Burnett was the one to testify,' said Vernon.

'Yes. I will testify to his sanity.'

'You did not know Dad before Mummy was killed.' Claude was drawn in and his words were faintly childlike. It was clear that he felt aggrieved, done out of his inheritance by his stepmother. He, however, recovered from this lapse and assumed his usual patronising air. 'I would have thought I was the best one to testify as I have known him all my life. And Jean will testify.'

'She will do no such thing,' Jerusha shouted. 'She would never do that to your father.'

'Do what to my father? Let's face it, Jerusha, the one you're thinking about is you. Wasn't it convenient that you received so much money on the death of a man you hardly knew, a man you persuaded to marry you on his deathbed.'

'The one thing you don't do is belittle my relationship with Hamish. We loved each other, not money. It's only your cynicism talking. Not everyone is like you. And please leave Jean out of this. She's barely coping with her grief.'

'We all know your sense of drama, Jerusha. You should have been an actress, not a barmaid.'

'I think it's time we took a short break,' Nigel said, ushering Claude into his office.

'I could kill him. He doesn't believe in good in anybody. He's so . . . so . . . cutting and negative.' Jerusha got up. 'And these chairs are very hard.' Jerusha was in the thrall of her emotions—anger verging on fury, frustration, temporary hate. 'Do we have to continue with this?' she implored, looking directly at Vernon.

James spoke up for the first time during the consultation. 'By getting emotional you are giving him what he wants, Jerusha. Can't you see, they are on very shaky ground. If you react like this you are validating what they are trying to do.'

'Of course, I don't want to lose all I've got but it's the attack on his father I can't bear.'

'You can put a stop to this, Jerusha,' said Vernon.

'How?'

'Offer him a deal. That's what he is angling for. Think about it and think quickly, before they come back. Remember, we did speak about the possibility.'

'A hundred thousand pounds to set up his new business.' She was relieved to think there might be a way out. She came and sat down.

'Offer him half, to start with.' Vernon spoke with a life-time of experience behind him.

'I don't think my nephew deserves anything,' said James.

'I'm prepared to pay him if he will stop blackening Hamish's name.'

'But, will it? Will it stop him slandering Hamish?' asked James.

'That is a chance you have to take, Jerusha,' said Vernon.

'I'll do anything to shut him up.' Jerusha tore out a piece of paper from her notebook and screwed it into a ball, which she threw under the table.

'I will throw the idea into the arena,' said Vernon.

'It's blackmail, pure and simple,' muttered James.

The second part of the consultation was masterminded by the two lawyers. Both were aware that it was difficult to contest a will once it had been executed. Nigel had almost turned Claude away, as Vernon had done, but he saw this case as a challenge. Professionally, he saw a chance of bringing about a deal which he estimated that Jerusha could afford to make. Neither party would be insuperably damaged and he would have done his job.

'I'd like to consult with my client on her own,' said Vernon, and the three others left the room. 'Jerusha, it's the best deal we can make under the circumstances.' He was sitting close to her and that was the first time she'd noticed what a fine pair of eyes he had. At that moment, she was mesmerised by them and what he was saying. She was frozen on the verge of panic. Vernon continued, 'You give Claude one hundred thousand pounds and he agrees not to pursue his case. It's a case which, whether or not it succeeds, will attract publicity and do further damage to Hamish's name.'

The threat to Hamish's name brought her to her senses. 'But, will it put a stop to the slander and blackmail if I give him the money?'

'We'll see to it in any contract we draw up.'

'Will anyone else make such cruel accusations?'

'That, I can't tell. Do you want to give Claude one hundred thousand pounds in return for his silence?'

'Of course I don't want to part with that amount of money. But if he wanted to set up his IT business why didn't he just ask me for the money in the first place? He is Hamish's son. He didn't need to go through this charade. It's strange to think that charades is the game he detests the most.'

'Focus, Jerusha. Think what is at stake.'

'I'll do it.'

'We'll see that he withdraws his claim. And you will keep Kirkfield.'

19

GROUNDWORK FOR THE PLAN

Something solidified inside Jerusha as a result of the clash with Claude and, consequently, her act hardened. She even calculated that by asking Claude for Christmas she would be there to oversee what he said about his father. Claude, however, was going to be busy and scarcely had time for Christmas. Jean, also, was busy but not at office work. She had made promises to her boyfriend, Rodger. 'I'm sorry, Jerusha, Rodger's mum is expecting us on Christmas Day.'

'Darling, don't worry. As long as you have a good time, that's what I want.'

'Rodger's mother is a lover of tradition so we'll be doing the usual thing, turkey and tree etcetera.'

'Have a good time.'

'Jerusha, Claude appreciated you asking him to Christmas.'

'You mean, he took it as a point scored.'

'Now you are beginning to sound like him.'

'That's as maybe.'

So, it was to be a small Christmas at Kirkfield. Herself, Oswald, James and Sheena. Sheena had come back to live in the village, judging that the press had lost interest in Derek's case. She and Tammy had come to see Jerusha the first day they were back. The big question was how was Derek getting along in prison and Jerusha, after she had enquired after Sheena's health, asked about it. 'He's still in a cell with a man convicted of premeditated murder. This man murdered his father-in-law and he swears the father deserved it. 'It was either him or me,' says this murderer. And Derek says you should see the look on his face when he says it. Pure evil.'

'Is Derek afraid of him?'

'I think so. Yes. But what can he do? At least the cellmate admits his guilt. Most of the others say they are innocent. The cynicism that arises from that makes it so difficult for Derek, who is innocent. Derek is afraid he will be refused leave to appeal.'

'If the worst comes to the worst, he will get time off for good behaviour.'

'This will turn him into an old man. The prisoners get some exercise but not enough for Derek's liking. And the food is ghastly.'

'Talking of food, I've got here a catalogue you might like to see. I thought we could send Lorna a hamper for Christmas.' Jerusha tried to change the subject.

'It's a bit late now and the postal service has been disrupted by the snow.'

Jerusha could see that Sheena was in a negative mood. How unlike her, she mused.'She'll appreciate it whenever she gets it. What do you say?'

Sheena perked up a little. Now she was more like the old Sheena. 'You're on.'

Christmas and New Year came and went and, as far as Jerusha was concerned, it was another perfect Christmas and another perfect New Year. They knew how to celebrate at Kirkfield House and her guests were all darlings. In March she set about executing her plan, the plan that had been simmering, bubbling in and out of her subconscious. It would take time and effort but she was more and more devoted to it. The first thing she did was to go and visit Chris and Ena in their new house on the outskirts of Galashiels. They lived on an upmarket housing estate built by Len. As she drove in, Jerusha couldn't help admiring the way Len's architect had used the hillscape. The roads were curved and the gardens cultivated to fall in line with that.The Rutherford's front door was covered with clematis. Inside Chris led her up some stairs to the sitting room. Ena looked ill at ease, as if she thought her house was too grand for her. Her hair had greyed noticeably and she was wearing spectacles. Chris had been grey for years and age had made him more handsome. He hustled his wife downstairs to the kitchen to make some tea then bounded back up to sit beside Jerusha. He had always bounded upstairs and would do so until the last possible moment in his life. Jerusha remarked to herself that men are just as keen to ward off old age as women. He was now looking at her quizzically although he would never be so rude as to ask her why she had come. She opened with some concerned questions. How was the house? How was retirement? He seemed to think that both of these things were fine. So she probed a little further. Was he missing the post office? That touched a chord.

'I'm in there every second day. Rashid must be sick of me, although he is too polite to say so. The thing about a rural post office is that it's not just a place where people buy stamps and post letters. It's a meeting place.'

'And a hub of gossip,' added Jerusha.

'It's friendly, like.'

'And Rashid has kept that going?'

'You bet. He has an air about him, as if he knows something we don't.'

'People tell him things,' remarked Jerusha.

'They spoke to me, the same.'

'Oh, I wasn't saying that they did not.' She back-tracked quickly.

Ena came shyly into the room with some tea on a tray. She had been baking in the morning and offered Jerusha a melting moment or some gingerbread, giving her a side plate and a paper napkin. During these proceedings she kept her head bowed and moved very slowly.

'You'll want to know why I'm here,' said Jerusha between mouthfuls, to Chris.

You don't have to have a reason,' he said with a false smile.

She, in turn, led him on a false trail. 'You are something of an expert when it comes to wildlife. What I want to find out is how to attract wildlife to the new wood. You were a tree planter. You know the score. I'm imagining squirrels, birds, hedgehogs, foxes.'

'As the trees grow and when they have seen it's a safe place, they'll come. If you're lucky you might even get badgers.'

'I mean, do we put out food for them?'

'No. It's best if they don't rely on people to feed them. They need to be resilient and it's best to let nature run its own course. You've done your bit with the planting and now it's a question of waiting.'

'We were lucky most of the saplings survived the winter. One or two did not.'

'I think it's a very good idea,' piped up Ena and then she blushed.

'You have Sheena to thank for that,' said Jerusha.

'Aye, Sheena. How is she doing? I hardly ever see her. She must be lonely in that hoose by herself,' said Chris.

'Sheena still comes to see me but not as often as she used to. With Derek . . . er . . . away, she is alone a lot. She says it gets so that when she opens her mouth no voice comes out.'

'She doesn't seem to want to talk, when I've bumped into her,' said Chris.

'It's early days yet,' said Jerusha. 'Now, I must be running along. Thank you for the tea, Ena.'

Jerusha's motive for visiting Chris was not really to discuss wildlife or Sheena. She wanted to cultivate him because he would play a part in her plan. She was intent on gathering together a selection of Françoise's lovers and contriving to make them admit guilt and to declare that Hamish had been wronged.

⌒ⱮⱮⱮↄ

Because of his death, Hamish had not been tried in a court of law but the implications of his reported actions hung like a mist over his grave. Jerusha was no longer denying

466

he had anything to do with his wife's burial. Instead, she wanted, as a quasi judge, to prove that he had just cause and that his motives in aiding his friend, Derek, were sincere and even noble.

The next person she approached was Nigel Stevenson, the very same, the lawyer who had presided with Vernon over the battle with Claude. She couldn't think of an excuse to 'phone him directly so she engineered a meeting. For that, she would enlist James and Oswald. But first she had a word with Vernon.

'Nigel. What have I got to say about him? He's a damned fine lawyer, as you saw the other day. I think the only reason he took Claude on as a client is that he was fond of Claude's mother. He was one of Françoise's conquests. Of course, in those days he didn't have a receding hairline. But what do you want with Nigel, Jerusha?'

'He interests me.' Jerusha was deliberately vague. 'I mean, what makes him tick?'

'Aah, that's easy. Women and golf.'

'Does he have a wife?'

'Divorced. They quarrelled over Françoise's intrusion into their marriage, to all accounts.'

'And he still has fond memories of Françoise?'

'She was a magnetic woman. In a way, it's a good thing she didn't live to grow old, although some women never give in to grey hair and wrinkles.'

'And the other interest is golf, you say? Where does he play?'

'Over near Selkirk, at the Owl Club. There's a nice restaurant there too.'

'Is there now?'

She established that Nigel played golf every Wednesday afternoon and would often be seen having a drink in the restaurant afterwards. She mobilized Oswald and James and talked them into going for tea at The Owl the following Wednesday. For this, she donned her deepest red dress, which had the lowest cut bodice in her wardrobe. She put on lashings of mascara and sprayed herself liberally with Cerruti 1881 perfume. She ordered Oswald out of his tracksuit and into something smart casual. 'You're always fairly presentable,' she told James.

'But why do we have to be presentable, as you describe it, to go and have a cup of tea?' Oswald asked.

They were soon to discover that this was not just tea. It was afternoon tea *par excellence*. It was so good that Jerusha almost forgot why she had come there. They sat at a table by the window, which wasn't saying much because the restaurant was pure glass from ceiling to floor where it overlooked the golf course. A three-tiered cake stand arrived, with savoury snacks on the bottom tier, scones and jam with clotted cream in the middle and *petits fours* on the top.

'You have some ulterior motive for being here,' said Oswald, his mouth moustached with clotted cream. 'I can tell by the way you're acting. Well, not acting precisely because you always act. Behaving. That's the word.'

'And how am I behaving?'

'Full of anticipation. Like a little girl in a sweetie shop, on the one hand, and like a woman full of allure, on the other. It can't be just the cakes, of which you have had more than your fair share.'

Jerusha didn't deny this. 'We can always order more,' she said, supremely calm and in control. Out of the corner of her eye she saw Nigel coming off the course with a stranger, a man, both wheeling their golf clubs on trolleys. He looked vibrant and exhilarated, and he walked with a relaxed stride.

'Are we to order more cakes?' asked James who had scarcely been able to keep up with the appetites of the other two and was feeling a bit hard done by.

'Yes, darling. In a minute.' Nigel had left his golfing companion and was coming into the restaurant. Instead of calling over a waitress, Jerusha eased herself out of her chair, gracefully and with a pelvic tilt, and went over to the bar to order more cakes. She made quite sure there were no crumbs on her lips. Nigel was coming her way. 'Nigel. What a surprise!'

'Jerusha. We meet again. I take it from your most charming attire that you're not here to play golf,' said Nigel, a little suspicious of this sudden encounter.

She leaned on the bar, making her breasts plump up. She saw his suspicion and her response was to keep talking. 'Just here for one of The Owl's scrumptious teas. My friends here, Oswald and James, but of course, you have met James, were just admiring the delightful view of the course. Do you play here often? How did the game go?'

'I'll answer your questions one at a time. I play here every week, on a Wednesday. And I play tournaments. You'll have seen the cups in the display cabinet. As for your second question, I didn't perform particularly well today. I was soundly beaten.'

'Do you play to win?'

'Not entirely. I enjoy being out on the course, away from legal issues.'

'Don't worry. I'm not going to bother you with legal issues, as you call them. But, I'm forgetting my manners. Come over and meet Oswald, James' partner. Do come and have tea and cakes with us. Say you will.' She touched his arm lightly and he let her.

'I was going to have something stronger but my friend has had to go home. So, I'm good for tea with you.'

They went over to the table by the window and she introduced him to Oswald. As happens, Nigel and Oswald found a mutual interest in rugby. Usually this is happily done but it was not part of Jerusha's game plan. She had nothing to say on the subject of rugby and instead resorted to little flirtatious gestures. She crossed and re'crossed her legs, letting the red dress mould to her shape and drape suggestively. At intervals she reached across the table, leaning over it so that her revealed cleavage deepened. She reached out with painted fingernails for a *petit four* and popped it sexily into her lipstick-traced mouth. She sighed lustily.

Although he was in conversation with Oswald, Nigel noticed this performance going on opposite him and he was not displeased. He leaned back with his hands behind his head, armpits aired and he, too, sighed.

James was watching the two of them with a puzzled look. After all this was the lawyer who had just helped Claude fleece her of £100,000. Now, here she was openly flirting with him. He had seen her do it before. He knew her ways. It was quite funny really, how obvious she was being. 'Jerusha, if you've got a moment, can you pass me a scone?'

'Darling, for you I have all the time in the world.' She took his plate, daintily placed a scone on it, spread some butter then jam on it. 'Clotted cream?' He nodded. This was the *coup de théâtre*. She spooned up a generous helping of cream then dropped it expertly on the jam scone. 'There you are, sweetheart. Enjoy. Does anyone else want a scone while I'm about it?' Nigel and Oswald both wanted scones and she drew them away from rugby and into the tea party.

'I hope you don't think me rude, Jerusha. What with the World Cup coming up, rugby is an essential topic of conversation. By the way, I've been noticing what a lovely dress you're wearing. Designer label?'

'My own label. I made it myself from an adapted pattern. I sew, you see.'

'I've got a whole pile of mending that nobody is going to do.'

'I understand your wife if she doesn't want to do it,' said Jerusha, pretending she did not know Nigel was divorced. She wanted him to say it.

'Oh, no. I'm divorced. Have been for some time. That's when the mending began to pile up.'

Jerusha had no intention of taking in mending but she said, 'I'll have a look at it some time. But I have a better idea. I'm having a dinner party on April the first. Why don't you come?'

He looked in his diary, saw that he was free and agreed to come. The arrangements for an *exposée* were beginning to take shape. She invited both Chris and Ena and, as was to be expected, only Chris accepted. Now she had to think of a way to get Barry to come. That would be a good—if small—selection of Françoise's lovers. Barry had challenged her at Françoise's funeral. How dared she come to the funeral? He had asked this in a passionate way as if he were genuinely upset by her presence. She asked around about Dr Gilmore and built up a picture of him as a man of strong feelings who was devoted to his practice as a GP in Galashiels. He also drove a fast car and had a relationship with hair-brained Tina who was young enough to be his daughter. It was all very well sleuthing, but she calculated that a direct approach would appeal to him. She 'phoned him up one evening and got Tina. She explained who she was and said she would like to speak to Barry.

'Who do you say you are?' asked Tina. 'I don't think I know you.' Her voice was high and shrill, with some accent that Jerusha couldn't place.'

'Jerusha. Jerusha Burnett.'

'I take it you're not the Burnett who was buried the other day.' Tina giggled.

'I'm the second Mrs Hamish Burnett.'

'Oh. He had two wives. Lucky him.'

'You could put it that way.'

'Well, Barry . . . Doctor Gilmore . . .' she said this lovingly, '. . . he's working late as usual. I'll get him to ring you. What's your number?'

'No. I'll 'phone later.' Jerusha did not want to risk Barry forgetting to 'phone.

'Whatever you think best. After nine would be a safe bet.' Tina sighed as if to say she was used to playing second fiddle to his job.

Sheena was around that night, looking thin and haunted. To fill the time while Derek was in prison she had taken up charity work. She was a shop assistant in a cancer research shop in Galashiels two days a week and she drove for the WRVS on demand. She was knitting socks for another charity and cooked for a lunch club once a month. She was wearing herself out trying to pay back a debt to a woman she could have hated. She and Jerusha got together for a Stitch and Bitch once a week. Jerusha was knitting a scarf for Derek.

'Do you think he will be allowed to wear it? Do you think it's long enough? Do you think he will like the colour?'

'Navy has always been a favourite colour of his. Just imagine, Jerusha, how many winters he has got in that place. When he comes out, he'll be an old man. And I don't know whether I'll get my husband back, or some stranger.'

'He'll be a little older, a little wiser.'

'Wiser? What is he going to learn in that place where there are real murderers, real rapists? God, I've dropped a stitch.'

'What you've got to do is keep yourself well. You're tearing around like some sort of saint and you are not eating properly.'

'I'm only trying to give something to society.'

'Until there is nothing more to give?'

They sat in a silence broken only by the click of needles until Jerusha excused herself, saying that she had to make a 'phone call. She shut the door as she went out of the room.

〇ᗰᗰᗰᑎ

Barry Gilmore was very suspicious when he heard it was Jerusha on the other end of the line. She had expected that and she had decided to just keep talking until he accepted her invitation. 'At the funeral you wanted to know why I had the cheek to be there. I'll tell you why. Because my stepdaughter, Jean, begged me to go. You can imagine how ghastly this whole thing has been for the children.'

'Your husband's part in the whole thing raises some questions, especially as he has never been put on trial'

'He is being tried by the media and by gossip. He did not deserve this.'

'How could he do that to his children? All those years of not knowing whether their mother was alive or dead. And you? He deceived you.'

'He wanted to spare me pain. You've got to believe me, he was a fine man.'

'You need to prove this to me, my dear. I can hear that you are sincere.' There was genuine maturity in his voice.

'That's the thing. I'm having a little get-together on April first. I wonder if you and Tina would like to come along?'

'I've heard that you are unconventional . . .'

'Who told you that?'

'Just the same sources who will have told you I have a fiery temper . . .'

'I *have* heard that.'

'There you go. I'm looking in my diary to see if we have anything on. Just a moment. I'll ask Tina . . . Yes, we can do that. What time?'

'Eight o'clock.'

She was trembling slightly when she put down the phone. Arrangements were falling neatly into place and now the onus was on her. She went through to ask Sheena if she were free on April first.

'Is this an April Fools' trick?' asked her friend.

'You'll have a laugh but I mean serious business.'

'Expect the unexpected,' said Sheena.

'That's right.'

20

THE PLAN EXECUTED

The cars swept into the driveway—long, large, cream, green and red—driving around the circular centrepiece, the periphery of which Jerusha had lit with candles at regular intervals. The guests in formal evening wear climbed up the steps to the front door, Tina in sequined blue. Her dress was slit up one side revealing a thigh, both legs settled in black tights and supporting spectacularly high heels. Sheena looked as if she had made an effort but what an effort that had been, particularly as there had been no Derek to encourage her. She was behind Tina going into the light of Kirkfield and she envied her stylishness. Tina was mincing as best she could in the daring heels with one arm around Barry's neck. She wore a glittering stole draped around her own neck. She had actually needed Barry to prop her up after he had parked outside by the road, as if he wanted a quick getaway, and she had had to walk over the gravel in heels that slipped and slid.

Jerusha was at the door to meet Barry, Tina and Sheena. She wore a deep purple, plunging, Grecian-style long gown and she had brought some jewellery out of the bank. Her diamond necklace traced a pattern of teardrops around her neck and leafy diamond earrings hung from her earlobes. She wore her wedding rings. 'How nice of you to come, Darlings. Do come in.' She kissed the air around their cheeks then ushered them through to the sitting room from whence came the hum and throb of conversation. She weaved her way through the guests as if there were a roomful, leaving Barry, Tina and Sheena to follow her trail, until she reached the drinks table where she offered them cocktails. That having been done, hands on hips in momentarily inelegant pose, she appraised the guests. Eight here, one to come. 'Dear Vernon. I wonder where he can have got to?'

She scoured the room to see who was talking to whom. Sheena had gone over to Chris who was on his own. Her knee-length green dress, that looked as if it had come from her charity shop, was creased at the back. Nice embroidery on the bodice, though. She shifted from one foot to the other in flat, golden sandals, sipping her cocktail in a controlled fashion, as if she were using her lips and not her throat. She had a look of intense concentration on what Chris was saying. He seemed ill at ease and kept fiddling with his black bow tie as if he were unused to formal wear and not quite sure why he had been invited to this party. His grey hair, clean and tactile, crowned his head in stiff bristles. He had escaped balding for the time being. Could he have been more handsome when he was younger and Françoise was alive?

Poor Oswald. His hair was thinning rapidly. He was talking to Nigel. Oswald was a harsh critic but she loved him dearly. He also looked ill at ease in black tie. Perhaps she should have made the occasion less formal? No. This was how she wanted it. She wanted people to respect the proceedings she had in store for them. Poor darlings. They could not have anticipated the plan she was going to execute after dinner. But why should she feel sorry for them? Most were guilty of something or other. Take Nigel. He deserved his divorce. He would respond to any flirtation. When he arrived he had taken her hand and kissed it, brushing his lips over her wedding rings. He had put an arm proprietorially around her waist as they walked through the hall. 'Impressive jewels,' he had said. No doubt he and Oswald were discussing sport. He was a force to be reckoned with. Everything in his bearing said he was in control. Used to defending; used to prosecuting. But, this evening she was to be the judge. James, Oswald, Sheena and Vernon would be the jury.

However, her thoughts of what was to come were interrupted when Barry and Tina came over to her and Tina started revealing information in an open and ingenuous way, still hanging on to the firebrand Barry.

'Most people know that Barry, the doctor, picked me up off the street,' she said, speaking in her habitually high voice. 'I was as low as you can go and I thought there was no other way. I was as good as dead to my family.'

'To look at her now you would think she was exaggerating but it was as she says. I found her wandering the streets, cold, hungry and confused. And that made me angry. I had to do something,' said Barry.

'You must not think,' said Tina, 'that I was walking the streets, looking for men. Oh no, I was too weary for rumpy pumpy. I went to the Salvation Army and they gave me clothes and food and somewhere warm to stay for a while. This was in Edinburgh. Then I went back to my favourite spot under a bridge in the city and slept there.'

'Sleeping rough must be a nightmare,' said Jerusha. 'But one wonders what brings people to that. What had happened to you? I mean, before you became homeless?'

'I'll tell you if you promise to keep it confidential.' She let go of Barry for a few moments while she wiped perspiration from her hands on her glittering dress.

'I promise.'

'I was on drugs. Heroin, crack cocaine, you name it. Of course, I had a very unhappy childhood.'

'The only drugs she has now are legal. You've put all that behind you, haven't you, my cherub?' Barry seemed worried that the conversation had wandered off small talk and was taking a downward turn. Jerusha couldn't help but think of Jocky and how he had ended up. This young woman standing in front of her was almost two persons: the pampered pet of a thriving doctor and a woman with a torrid past.

'I'm sorry to bring this up now,' said Tina, looking at Barry with languid eyes.

Jerusha almost felt an admiration for Barry but she quelled it. After all, this was one of the men who had wronged her husband. 'Don't worry, Tina,' she said, 'I could tell you a thing or two about my past. I'm quite proud of it actually. Nothing is as it seems, my dear. Now, you must excuse me. I have to see to the food.'

When she got to the kitchen James was there. 'The bird is all but ready,' he said.

'Good. Then we'll get the guests through and serve up the starters. And James, let's make sure Tina gets an extra big helping. I don't know what we're going to do about Vernon. He'll just have to notch into whatever course we're on.'

'Have you tried 'phoning him?'

'No. You try. I'll get on with starters. I want them in place when the guests come through.'

She arranged the starters on place mats, carefully adjusting the cards with place names on them. Nigel, Barry, Tina etc., all had a special place. She left the table ends free. Hamish used to sit at the head of the table; she, at the other end. Now she put herself in the middle at one side with five seats. The other side had four seats. That was, from left facing the table, Nigel, Chris, Tina and Barry. The three men she was going to put on the stand, the three who had had affairs with Françoise. She, the judge, would sit in between Vernon and Sheena with Oswald and James at either end. It was to be a little bit of theatre. The guests had no idea what she was plotting and were still cautiously testing cocktails and attempting to chat in the sitting room. She wouldn't tell them at all what she was going to do. She would just do it. Meanwhile, she had an April Fools' trick to carry out. She encouraged them to come through to the dining room.

'The starter is hot, so don't delay. You'll find your names by your place settings.' For the time being she was any hostess at any dinner party, fussing around her guests to make sure they were comfortable and knew where to sit. The starter was tasty and the time spent eating it, uneventful. Oswald brought out the wine; each place had two wine glasses, one for the main course and one for dessert. They swapped stories about the hard winter Britain had had—the ice and accidents, the frozen pipes, the coming together in adversity. However in the cool but wet spring evening there was just so much they could remember about a world of snow and frost. The conversation ground to a halt and there was a short, uneasy silence. Tina broke it by saying, just as Jerusha had intended, 'That's a lovely vase.' She pointed at the tall, curvaceous, empty vase standing in the middle of the table. 'Where did you get that?'

'That was one of Hamish's gifts to me. Has been in the family for years. Priceless.'

'I'll say priceless,' said Barry. 'It's a Zoling vase.'

The vase stood admired by nine pairs of eyes, a voluptuous shape, coloured pink and blue on a white background with gilt edging.

'I don't know what it's doing on the table. Must be the S.S. She's our cleaning lady. 'I'll take it away.' She leaned across to the middle of the table and picked it up, cupping its sides, held it up like a trophy for all to see and then seemed to falter as she turned. The vase slid out of her hands and smashed into fractured pieces on the floor.

There was now a deeply troubled silence as the guests took in the shock of seeing a shattered, priceless object. The vase was in smithereens and Jerusha bent over it to pick up fragments. Barry, as if this were an emergency case, rushed around the table to where Jerusha was bowed down. Her shoulders were heaving and she was shaking. 'Be careful you don't cut yourself, Jerusha,' he said.

'I expect you're insured, Jerusha,' said Nigel.

'How can you worry about insurance at a time like this,' said Tina. 'Her husband gave it to her.'

'You can get a restorer to put it together again,' said Sheena, wanting to console Jerusha who was still bent over, shoulders heaving.

Oswald got up to see if he could help, then saw as he came closer to the scene of the accident that Jerusha was not crying. She was laughing. 'I know what this is. It's an April Fools' joke,' he said.

Jerusha burst up from her crouching position, holding shards of broken china. 'April Fools'! It's a cheap replica. The real one is locked up. You don't really think I would leave a Zoling vase lying about the house. Gotcha!'

Tina began the relieved laughter and it rippled around the table. 'You've still got to clean up the mess,' said Oswald in a flat tone. 'You've surpassed yourself tonight.'

'You haven't seen anything yet,' she retorted.

Oswald and Barry got a dustpan and picked up the pieces of what was a very nice vase, if inexpensive. As they were doing this and conversation was back in circulation, the doorbell rang.

'I'm so sorry, my babysitter was late.' Vernon's hair looked as if he had been raking his fingers through it although the rest of him was neat and presentable.

'You haven't missed much. Just the star turn. And the starter,' said Oswald.

'I'll just slot in then, shall I?' Vernon sat down in his designated chair.

'Is the babysitter all right?' asked Sheena.

'Yes. Yes. Fine. Missed her bus—that's all. I shouldn't call her a babysitter really. Child minder is a better description. The boy is going on ten.'

'And it doesn't worry you to leave him?' asked Sheena.

'Since his mother died I've had to get used to leaving him to his own devices.'

'A very self-reliant young man,' said Jerusha.

As there was a paucity of parenthood among the group, not even Chris was about to become a grandad, the conversation turned to the old faithful of dinner parties, the safe subject of food. Foraging for wild food was a topic that kept them going for a full half hour, the conversation traversing the long table until most of the diners had had a say, the Zoling vase breakage and the April Fool element quite forgotten. Barry did try to bring up politics but nobody took him up on it. Tina gave him a squeeze, which distracted him from any more challenging forays.

The glasses sparkled and Oswald replenished them, although nobody was drinking to excess. There had been an element of suspicion all evening. Why had Jerusha brought them here? What was her agenda? She seemed inscrutable. Nigel was the only one who nursed the belief that she fancied him and that satisfied his more sensible queries. Chris felt left out by the others. He had not dined at the most famous restaurants nor did he have an allotment. He didn't even know how to cook. That was Ena's preserve. She guarded her kitchen jealously. It was Ena's food he appreciated. Barry was eating to stay sober. He was waiting for an opportunity to address a few questions to Jerusha. He wished Tina would stop draping herself over him. It was weakening his resolve. She, on the other hand, had felt him bristling all night and she was trying to soften him into being her own Barry, forceful but susceptible to her touch. She didn't try to enter the exchange about food. She, like Oswald, had known what it was like to be hungry.

The main course, the biscuits and cheese, the dessert, all had been eaten; the cocktails, the main-course wine, the dessert wine had been drunk; the dishes had been cleared away. Jerusha announced the arrival of liquors and coffee, which were brought in by James and Oswald. Barry was the only one to put his hand over his glass so that all, bar one, were still happily indulging when Jerusha picked up a clear wine glass. Standing up, she tapped it with a teaspoon. 'Ladies and gents,' she said in an assertive way. 'We've come to the end of our dinner and I sincerely hope you have enjoyed it. We've also come to the end of the small talk because I want to get on to something far more serious. I want to speak about love.'

'Did you consider the possibility that your guests don't want to talk about love? It comes near to politics on the scale of controversy,' grumbled Barry.

'There are no party politics in love,' replied Jerusha.

'Are you kidding? One man's love is another man's tragedy.'

'I'm referring to Love with a capital 'L' *and* love with a small 'l',' said Jerusha.

'Will you sit down? You're acting like a schoolteacher.' Barry was becoming irritated.

'That's no act. That the absence of an act,' cut in Oswald He knew Jerusha better than most.

Jerusha sat down, not defeated but excited.

I want to say something,' piped up Tina. 'I think love means never having to say you are sorry. I heard that somewhere and it's very true.' She clasped her bejewelled hands together, for once not having to lean on Barry. 'Like when I burned your silk dressing gown with the iron. You just put the beautiful blackened gown in the bin, then bought a new silk gown and a steam iron. You didn't want to hear the word 'sorry' because you love me, don't you sweetheart?' She was breathless, as if she had won the race to give away secrets.

Barry leaned heavily on the table, silenced by his ingenuous partner's lack of cynicism. Jerusha wanted to help the group impetus. 'What about you Chris?' She pointed her teaspoon at him.

He cleared his throat. 'Love and marriage go together.' He faltered. 'My wife, Ena, and I have been married for forty years. That's a long time.' He chuckled. 'In the beginning we had to get used to each other but we were in love. That was the honeymoon period and, while that was going on, a deeper love developed and grew. I'm not saying I've never looked at another woman, but there is a strong bond between us that no one and nothing can break.'

There was a short pause and everyone looked at Nigel who, being on the left of Chris, was the next to speak. However, he was musing and was slow to get going.

'Come on lad. This is a chance to have your say,' Vernon urged.

'Yes. Your turn,' said Tina and clapped her hands so that Barry seized one and forced it against his thigh.

'Don't be shy,' said Sheena, pulling at the straps of her dress in a prim kind of way, an eager look on her face.

'All right then. This is it.' He stretched his neck and placed his hands, palms down, on either side of his place mat, his cheeks burning. 'Ever since we met . . . by chance as it were, at the golf club, Jerusha has been flirting outrageously and obviously with me. She's doing it now. Fluttering her eyelashes, intent on every word I say. Showing her bare flesh and magnificent cleavage. Women do this to me. I wonder what they want. Do they want a fling? Do they want to make love? Do they want me to attend a dinner party where the rules are set by the hostess and the purpose of which defeats me. When my marriage was over, broken by Françoise Burnett, I used to give in to these female sirens but now I have created a womanless peace that no one can destroy. I'm talking about lovelessness but I'm also talking about lack of complications. Without love, I am at peace. With love, I am in the wilderness.'

'Poor Nigel,' said Tina.

'I don't have to worry about women any more,' said Oswald. 'My love is James.'

'I love Oswald,' said James. 'And, in a different kind of way, I love Jerusha. Like a friend. She is warm, compassionate and good company.'

'Thank you, James. Incidentally, Nigel, I've been flirting with you for fun and to get you to come tonight. As far as I'm concerned it goes no further. Shame on me. And now we get to Sheena, another good friend of mine.'

Sheena hung on to her white, starched napkin as if it were giving her the words. 'I would not be so foolish,' she paused, 'as to describe my love for my wronged, suffering husband. My love for him is private and constant. I would point out, however, that in Greek, and particularly in ancient Greece, there are three types of love. There is Eros, which is passionate love such as that expressed by the deluded Françoise. Then there is Philia, which means friendship in modern Greek.'

'It is this loving friendship that existed between Hamish and Derek,' interrupted Jerusha.

'Yes.' She was starting to cry. 'You finish,' she said to Jerusha.

'And then there is the Christian love, Agape, found for instance, in the 'love chapter' in the Bible—1 Corinthians 13. It begins like this:' "If I speak in the tongues of men and of angels, but have not love, I am only a resounding gong or a clanging symbol." Jerusha paused.' Bear with me. It ends like this:' " . . . now these three remain: faith, hope and love. But the greatest of these is love." 'Sonia and Callum have both Eros and Agape in their relationship. That's why their commitment looks solid.' Jerusha was in earnest.

Oswald was beginning to think Jerusha should have been a preacher.

'Who are Sonia and Callum?' asked Nigel.

'My niece and her husband,' replied Jerusha.

'And while we are personalizing love, we seem not to have mentioned the one person everyone wants to talk about: Françoise. In my opinion, her death is why we have been asked to this unconventional dinner party,' said Nigel. 'It's my guess that half the guests knew her in a biblical sense or, to put it another way, had an affair with her. Do you want to exact some sort of revenge, Jerusha?'

'That's it. We're going.' Barry hauled Tina to her feet.

'You can't go,' said Jerusha. 'The doors are locked.'

'Then I'll call the police. Where's my mobile?' Barry was fuming.

'You left it in the car, sweetie.' Tina leaned towards him and gave him a hug. 'Anyway, let's not go yet, honey. The conversation is just beginning to get interesting.'

'That's because you don't understand half of it.' He plumped himself back in his chair.

Tina followed suit but, pulling herself up straight in her seat, she said, 'It's my opinion, my humble opinion, and I'll have some more Baileys please, that love is a drug. They say there are chemical changes in the brain when you fall in love. I've experienced this. I wonder if any of you have also?' Silence. 'What's more, I'm interested in poor Françoise.' A longer silence.

Oswald poured her some more liquor, grateful for something to do. He refreshed any glasses that needed refreshing.

'You haven't really locked the doors, Jerusha? I don't believe you would do that,' said Chris, shifting in his chair. 'I've got to get back to Ena.'

'Ena will understand, as she always does.' Jerusha's statement was loaded with innuendo. If Ena knew of Chris's affair with Françoise, she would have forgiven him. Briefly, she felt a little empathy for the loyal wife, but it was the business of the keys they were asking about. The locked doors. She wasn't going to let this issue side-track the conversation, the debate which she was commandeering. She bent down and picked up a large, silver ring from which keys hung like fronds from a palm leaf. She flung it into the middle of the table. 'Can't be too careful these days,' she said. 'The doors are locked but the keys are all here. You just have to take your pick. Front door, back door, garden door . . . if you go now we'll believe that you have something to hide.'

'I've got something to hide but I'm not going to. My wife still doesn't know about my affair with Françoise. It was so short, you see, so foolish . . . fifteen years ago . . . it still haunts me.' Chris was serious and ashamed.

'Haunting is not the word,' Barry practically shouted. 'She was beautiful, quick-witted and betrayed.' He slammed a fist on the table.

'She was alluring but dangerous.' This was Nigel, sounding sentimental and bitter at the same time.

This was the way Jerusha wanted the conversation to go. It was flowing, open and focused. As she listened to Nigel tell how his marriage had broken up because of his affair with Françoise, she clung to every word against her archenemy, the woman in red who had fallen to her death in this house. Hamish's abiding enemy. Even in death, Françoise threatened Hamish's stature, his morality, his whole reputation. She was the gong that sounded every time Jerusha walked up or down the fatal stairs. She was the amoral being who blocked Hamish's peace. Now, she was being exposed by a one-time lover. Jerusha was triumphant. But her goal was not yet achieved. She had to get these lovers to exonerate Hamish. That, ultimately, was what she was after.

When Nigel had finished, it was Barry who spoke up. 'It takes two to tango, my friend. It is hardly ever the fault of only one party. It's like those keys sitting there on the table where Jerusha put them. No one has picked them up. No one has taken on the challenge. She locked the doors. We could have unlocked them. That isn't to say I am dancing to Jerusha's tune but I am now too intrigued to want to end this party. Let's continue in the vein that is Jerusha's life blood. Amongst those who have been ominously silent there is one who is not showing his cards.'

Jerusha felt a rising panic. This was not part of her game plan. She did a quick reckoning. Barry, Chris, Nigel. The others couldn't have had a relationship with Françoise unless the dead woman had been undiscriminating about gender or sexual preference. Her summary accounted for everyone, except for Vernon. She turned a hard stare towards him.

'You can't expect me to disclose matters concerning my private life when I have a client present. I have to do business with Jerusha. She relies on me as a confidante and lawyer. Don't let Françoise destroy another positive relationship.' He turned to Jerusha, whose facial expression had softened. 'My dear woman, end this round of recrimination.'

Jerusha took a deep breath. This was her moment. 'It may not look like it but I have not brought you here to dwell on Françoise's wrongdoings but to salute Hamish. It's certainly true that by looking at Françoise's character and deeds you will learn to understand Hamish's behaviour.'

'Yes. Faking her suicide and sending her to a cold, unmarked grave. Not to speak of his lies to his children,' said Barry.

Jerusha continued. 'You are right, Barry. It took me a long time to accept the truth. But he did that having endured pain, the long years of pain delivered by his wife. Probably, most of you do not know that Hamish was considering divorce. He had had enough. It was in this light that Hamish turned his love towards a friend, Derek, who stood to lose his job, his wife, his reputation due to a bizarre chain of events.'

Sheena, now dry-eyed, spoke. 'He gave Derek a reprieve. As Jerusha loves Hamish, I love Derek—never, ever breaking my marriage vows—and the two of them were very good friends at the time of the *accident*.' She was flushed with emotion.

'So it all boils down to love, really. Love and perspective,' Jerusha continued. 'There is a verse in the Bible, in Proverbs. It goes like this, 'Hatred stirs up dissention but love covers over all wrongs.' You may . . .'

'As you keep mentioning the Bible, what about the beam in your own eye? You've had three marriages. Do you love all your husbands?' asked Oswald.

'Hamish is my brother.' James spoke the words as if that said it all.

'No. Go on. Answer Oswald,' said Barry.

'It's no secret that I've been married three times, no secret that I've been divorced twice and widowed once. And it should be no secret that I committed adultery during my second marriage. Perhaps people don't know I was unhappy in that marriage and I actually loved my lover. This was Eros. This was passionate love and it did not stand the test of time. I wouldn't want to have gone through life without these experiences. They enable me to measure the strength of my love for Hamish. I love him as a husband, brother, son, friend. If you can see your way to sharing this love you will go away having found him not guilty.' She looked around at her guests. 'That's all I can hope for. The keys are there on the table. You, Oswald and James, usher our friends out.'

As she was leaving, Tina finally succumbed to the height of her heels. She tripped, tumbled and fell down the front steps of Kirkfield, landing in a crumpled, sequined, kicking mass on the gravel. Her gown was hitched up for all to see her svelte, gorgeous legs clad in black tights leading to the hump of her dainty bottom. Face-down, she trembled and cried. Jerusha and Barry went to rescue her, although her dignity had departed. She had a few cuts and would have some bruising. That was all. No broken wrist or ankle. This time, at Kirkfield, a fall had not led to a broken neck.

After the other guests had gone, Oswald and James stood with Jerusha in the driveway beside James' car, James ready with the ignition key.

'Darlings, I'm quite sure that now everyone has forgiven Hamish. They understand. They see that he is not guilty.'

'Quite right,' said James

Oswald screwed up his face.

'What does that look mean, Ossie? Do you not think so?' She gripped his arm.

'I'm not so sure,' muttered Oswald, gently removing her hand and giving her a hug. After more hugs, the two men

495

climbed into their seats and left for home. Jerusha stood looking at the turreted façade of Kirkfield for some time, standing completely still in her purple gown, not unlike the figure of a bride on a wedding cake. 'Love covers over all wrongs . . .' she said to herself as she slowly walked up the steps to the front door and went inside.

She was destined to spend long, luxurious hours cleaning up after the guests she fondly believed she had converted to her way of thinking.

You can reach the author on www.patmosel.co.uk

Author's Biography

As a writer, all Pat Mosel needs is a notebook and pen (and a good man, and children, and a pet and friends, and the memory of having climbed Mount Kilimanjaro) and she is happy.

Geographically speaking, she was born in 'Southern Rhodesia', now Zimbabwe. She was called 'Tish' by her sister and is now called either Pat or Patricia. Mosel is her maiden surname and is pronounced the French way – as Moselle – although it is thought to come from the German, Von Mosel.

She describes her childhood as "idyllic, if you find it possible to disregard the racism and war. Big skies and clambering over rocks in bare feet…"

She emigrated to Britain via two universities and three major English language daily newspapers in South Africa, a beautiful country but, then, under the grip of an extremely cruel political system. She arrived in England by ferry from Holland in May 1976. "Since then, it has been like a 'Life of Pi', that is, like being shipwrecked with a zoo!"

Jerusha's Tricks is her first novel to be published. The second – entitled 'Ruth' – is also about human relationships but this time about loss and, also, the virtually real.

5170352R00296

Printed in Great Britain
by Amazon.co.uk, Ltd.,
Marston Gate.